PENNY
JORDAN

Frenchman ...
than 200 ...
100 ... ies!

Penny Jordan's novels are read and loved by
millions of readers all around the word in many
different languages. This beautiful collection of six
volumes offers a chance to recapture the pleasure
of a special selection of her fabulous stories.

As an extra treat, each volume also includes an
introductory letter by a different author. Some of
the most popular names in romantic fiction share
their personal thoughts and memories, which
we hope you will enjoy.

Passionate
nights

Every page of these three classic, sizzling,
seductive novels is red-hot reading!
A treat to warm up winter!

Mills & Boon® proudly presents
a very special tribute

PENNY
JORDAN
COLLECTION

PENNY JORDAN
COLLECTION

Passionate
nights

MILLS &
BOON

Published in Great Britain 2012
Mills & Boon, an imprint of Harlequin (UK) Limited,
Eton House, 18-24 Paradise Road, Richmond, Surrey TW9 1SR

PASSIONATE NIGHTS © Harlequin Enterprises II B.V./S.à.r.l. 2012

The Mistress Assignment © Penny Jordan 1999
Mistress of Convenience © Penny Jordan 2004
Mistress to Her Husband © Penny Jordan 2004

ISBN: 978 0 263 90229 7

028-1212

Harlequin (UK) policy is to use papers that are natural, renewable and recyclable products and made from wood grown in sustainable forests. The logging and manufacturing processes conform to the legal environmental regulations of the country of origin.

Printed and bound
by CPI Group (UK) Ltd, Croydon, CR0 4YY

Dear Reader,

It was a standing joke between Penny Jordan and myself that we'd become a couple of Mills & Boon's 'oldest inhabitants.'

My writing career with the company began in 1975—the Golden Age—when the authors were free to go wherever our imaginations took us, except inside the bedroom, of course. The door to that was barely ajar in those days. Romance has always been a tremendously personal genre—a shared fantasy between author and audience, so whatever happened when the door shut was all in the mind rather than on the page, and possibly none the worse for that.

The dark, dangerous hero with a touch of cruelty about him was what the readers wanted then, and titles containing words like 'Lucifer', 'Satan' and 'Devil' added an extra, anticipatory thrill, as vulnerable but spirited girls were pitched against men who rarely took 'no' for an answer.

When Penny began writing for Mills & Boon in the early eighties, she was one of the leaders in demolishing the lingering sexual taboos. Her books, with their powerful alpha male heroes, immediately touched a chord with millions of women worldwide and she was a phenomenal success.

Penny was also immensely hard-working and prolific, partly because, as a shrewd North-country lass, she didn't altogether trust her success, about which she was unfailingly modest. In addition, she was always generous and helpful to beginning writers, who came to regard her as a friend as well as mentor.

She will be sorely missed, so it's good to have these tribute editions, if only to remind us all how marvellous she really was.

Goodbye, Penny love, and God bless.

Sara Craven

Penny Jordan is one of Mills & Boon's most popular authors. Sadly Penny died from cancer on 31st December 2011, aged sixty-five. She leaves an outstanding legacy, having sold over a hundred million books around the world. She wrote a total of a hundred and eighty-seven novels for Mills & Boon, including the phenomenally successful *A Perfect Family, To Love, Honour & Betray, The Perfect Sinner* and *Power Play*, which hit the *Sunday Times* and *New York Times* bestseller lists. Loved for her distinctive voice, her success was in part because she continually broke boundaries and evolved her writing to keep up with readers' changing tastes. *Publishers Weekly* said about Jordan: 'Women everywhere will find pieces of themselves in Jordan's characters' and this perhaps explains her enduring appeal.

Although Penny was born in Preston, Lancashire, and spent her childhood there, she moved to Cheshire as a teenager and continued to live there for the rest of her life. Following the death of her husband she moved to the small traditional Cheshire market town on which she based her much-loved Crighton books.

Penny was a member and supporter of the Romantic Novelists' Association and the Romance Writers of America—two organisations dedicated to providing support for both published and yet-to-be published authors. Her significant contribution to women's fiction was recognised in 2011, when the Romantic Novelists' Association presented Penny with a Lifetime Achievement Award.

The Mistress Assignment

PENNY JORDAN

CHAPTER ONE

'WELL, here's to Beth; let's hope that this trip to Prague is a success and that it helps her to get over that rat Julian,' Kelly Harris announced, picking up her glass of wine.

'Well, she certainly deserves *some* good luck after all that's happened,' Anna Trewayne, Beth's godmother, sighed, following suit and pausing before drinking her wine to add worriedly, 'I must admit that I feel partly to blame. If I hadn't persuaded the two of you to open your shop here in Rye-on-Averton, Beth would never have met Julian Cox in the first place.'

'There's only *one* person to blame for Beth's unhappiness,' the third member of the trio, Dee Lawson, Beth and Kelly's landlady, announced starkly, 'and that's Julian Cox. The man is a complete and utter...'

She stopped speaking momentarily, lifting her glass to her lips, her eyes darkening painfully as she quickly hid her expression from the others.

'We *all* know what he's done to Beth, how much he's hurt and humiliated her, telling her that he wanted to get engaged, encouraging her to make all those plans for their engagement party and then telling her the night before that he'd met someone else, making out that she'd misunderstood him and imagined that he'd proposed. Personally, I think that instead of bemoaning what's happened what we should be doing is thinking of some way we can punish Julian Cox for what he's done to her and make sure he can never do it again.'

'Punish him…?' Kelly enquired doubtfully. She and Beth had been friends from their first days together at university and Kelly had enthusiastically agreed to her friend's suggestion that they set up in business together.

'Rye-on-Averton is the kind of pretty rural English town that artists and tourists dream about, and my god-mother was only saying the last time I was there that the town lacked a shop selling good-quality crystal and chinaware.'

'Us…open a shop…?' Kelly had protested a little uncertainly.

'Why not?' Beth had pressed enthusiastically, 'You were saying only last week that you weren't particularly enjoying your job. If we found the right kind of property there's no reason why you shouldn't be able to make your own designs to sell in the shop. With my retail experience I could be responsible for the buying and we could share the work in the shop.'

'It *sounds* wonderful…' Kelly had admitted, adding wryly, '*Too* wonderful… We'd need to find the right kind of premises, and it would only be on the strict understanding that we share the finances of the business equally,' she had warned her friend, knowing that although Beth had no real money of her own her grandparents were rather wealthy and Beth was their adored and adoring only grandchild.

But Beth had swept aside all her objections, and in the end Kelly had been as enthusiastic about their shared project as Beth herself.

Over the last twelve months since the shop had first opened they had gone from strength to strength and then, just over eight months ago, Beth had met Julian Cox.

He had pursued her relentlessly whilst Kelly had stood helplessly to one side and watched as her friend became more and more emotionally dependent on a man whom Kelly had never liked right from the start.

'Don't you think you're letting him rush things a little bit?' she had suggested gently, just after Beth had announced that they were getting engaged. But Beth's face had clouded and they had had their first real quarrel when she had responded uncomfortably, 'Jules said you'd say something like that... He...he thinks that you're...that you're jealous of us, Kelly... I told him that just wasn't possible, of course...'

Jealous of them! With that comment Kelly had been forced to acknowledge that Julian Cox had very skilfully robbed her of the chance to pass on to her friend a piece of information she ought to have given her weeks before. But right now, under the influence of her second glass of the strong Italian wine the three of them had been drinking in the busy Italian wine bar where they had gone for a drink after they had seen Beth off on her buying trip to Prague, the idea of revealing Julian Cox as the unpleasant and untrustworthy character they knew him to be seemed to have taken on the air of something of a crusade, a moral crusade.

'Why should he be allowed to get away with what he's done, to walk away from his guilt in the same manner he walked away from Beth?' Dee had asked the others now.

'Walk away! What he did was even worse than that,' Kelly exploded. 'He practically forced Beth to publicly humiliate herself. I can't believe how many people seem to have fallen for the lies he's been spreading about her, implying that not only did she misunderstand his intentions but that she also actively pursued him, to the point where he was supposedly thinking of taking legal action to stop her. Bunkum! I *know* which one of them was doing the lying and it wasn't Beth. For goodness' sake, I even heard him telling her how much he loved her, how much he couldn't wait for them to be married.'

'That would have been around the time when Beth's grandfather was so seriously ill, I expect?' Dee said grimly.

Kelly looked at her in surprise, but it was Anna who answered her question first, exclaiming, 'Yes, that's right! It was when her grandfather was ill that Julian proposed.'

At thirty-seven Anna was the oldest member of the quartet. As Beth's mother's younger cousin she had just missed out on being a bridesmaid at the wedding through a serious bout of German measles. In compensation Beth's mother had asked her several years later to be one of her new baby's godparents. Only a teenager, Anna had been awed and thrilled to be considered grown-up enough for such a responsibility and it was one she had taken very seriously, her relationship with Beth even more precious to her since she and her husband had not had any children of their own.

'What's the connection between Beth's grandfather's illness and Julian's proposal of marriage?' Kelly asked Dee curiously.

'Can't you guess?' Dee responded. 'Think about it. The girl Julian dropped Beth for is known to have a substantial personal trust fund.'

Kelly made a small *moue* of distaste and looked shocked.

'You mean that Julian proposed to Beth because he thought…'

'That her grandfather would die and Beth would inherit a lot of money,' Dee finished for her. 'Yes. Once he realised that Beth's grandfather was going to recover he must have really panicked, but, of course, he met this other girl, whose inheritance is far more accessible...'

'It sounds like something out of a bad melodrama,' Kelly protested, her forehead puckering as she added, 'Besides, I thought that Julian was wealthy in his own right. He certainly gives that impression.'

'He certainly *likes* to give that impression,' Dee agreed. '*Needs* to, in fact. That's the way he draws the innocent and the naive into his web.'

Kelly's frown deepened as she listened to Dee.

At thirty, Dee was older than Kelly and Beth but younger than Anna, and the two girls had originally met her after their estate agent had suggested that they might want to look at a shop property Dee owned and wanted to let.

They had done so and had both been pleased and impressed with the swift and businesslike way in which Dee had handled the letting of her property to them. She was a woman who, although at first a little reserved and cool, and very choosy about her friends, on later acquaintance revealed a warmth and sense of humour that made her fun to be with.

Anna, who had lived in the town for the last fifteen years following the tragic death of her young husband in a sailing accident off the coast of Cornwall, had known Dee a little before Beth and Kelly had arrived on the scene. After the death of her father Dee had taken over his business affairs as well as his position on several local charities, and so was quite a well-known figure in the town.

Dee's father had been an extremely successful entrepreneur, and others in her family were members of the local farming community, and the more Kelly and Beth had come to know her, the more it had astonished them that such a stunningly attractive woman, and one whose company the male sex quite plainly enjoyed should not have a man in her life.

'Perhaps it's because she's so busy,' Beth had ventured when she and Kelly had discussed it. 'After all, neither of us have partners at the moment...'

This had been in her pre-Julian days, and Kelly had raised her eyebrows a little, reminding Beth wryly, 'We've only been in town a matter of weeks, and besides...I *saw* the look in Dee's eyes the other day when we all went out to dinner and that little girl came trotting up to talk to her-the one from the other table. Do you remember? She made an immediate beeline for Dee and it was as though the pair of them were communicating on some special wavelength that blocked out the rest of us...'

'Mmm... She *does* have a very definite rapport with children,' Beth had agreed, adding helpfully, 'Perhaps she's just not met the right man yet. She strikes me very much as a woman who would only commit herself to a relationship if she was a hundred and fifty per cent sure it was right for her.'

'Mmm...' Kelly had agreed reluctantly. 'Personally I think there must be rather more to it than that.'

'Well, maybe,' Beth had agreed. 'But I wouldn't like to be the one to pry into her past, would you?'

'No,' Kelly had agreed immediately.

Friendly though the four of them had become, and well though they all got on, there was a certain reserve about Dee, a certain sense of distance, an invisible line over which one knew instinctively one would not be encouraged to cross.

'*You* seem to know a lot more about Julian's background than the rest of us,' Kelly told Dee now.

Dee gave a dismissive shrug.

'He's...he grew up locally, and in my position one...learns things.'

Kelly's frown deepened.

'But surely if you knew his reputation was unsavoury you could have warned Beth?'

'I was away when she originally met him,' Dee reminded her, adding dryly, 'And anyway, I doubt she would have listened...'

'No, you're probably right,' Kelly agreed. 'I never liked him, but Beth was so loyal to him she wouldn't hear a word against him. It's all very well saying that we ought to do something to show him up for the rat he really is, but how can we? He's dumped poor Beth, humiliated her, and he's got clean away with it.

'I'd like to tell this new girlfriend of his just what he's like...' she continued darkly.

'It wouldn't work,' Dee warned her. 'She's as besotted with him as Beth was. No, if we're going to have any chance of getting any kind of restitution for Beth, any kind of public recognition of the way Julian lied about her as well as to her, we're going to have to use his own weakness, his own greed against him.'

'We are? But how...?' Kelly asked her curiously. Beth was such a loving, gentle, kind person, the last thing she had needed was the kind of pain and humiliation Julian had handed out to her, never mind the potential damage it could do to their own just burgeoning business. The whispering campaign Julian had so carefully and cleverly instigated when he had dropped Beth, insinuating that she had been the one pursuing him, obsessed by him, was bound to have its repercussions.

'I do hope that Beth will be all right on her own in Prague,' Anna put in anxiously, joining the conversation.

Fine-boned and very youthful-looking, Anna was, in many ways, so far as Kelly was concerned, the epitome of a slightly old-fashioned type of femininity and womanhood.

Married young and then tragically widowed, in a medieval century she would have been the type of woman who would no doubt have withdrawn to the protective security of a small convent, or perhaps in the Georgian or Victorian age she would have been the doting aunt to her siblings' large broods of noisy children.

As it was, she was apparently content with her single life, her pretty little house and her pets—a large fluffy cat and a smaller but just as fluffy dog. Her home had become for both Kelly and Beth a surrogate home from home since they had moved into the area and, whilst Kelly could never for a minute imagine Anna ever stepping into the role so vigorously occupied by her own energetic and feisty mother, there was still something very comforting and special about the gentle concern Anna showered on them both.

It was a pity she had never remarried, in Kelly's opinion, and she knew that Beth agreed with her.

'She adored Uncle Ralph; they were childhood sweethearts and they had only been married a few months when he died,' Beth had told her.

'Beth will have a wonderful time,' Dee responded robustly now. 'Prague is the most beautiful city.'

'I've heard that it's a very *romantic* city,' Anna agreed a little wistfully, or so it seemed to Kelly. 'I just hope it doesn't make her feel even worse. She's lost so much weight and looks so unhappy.'

'She'll be far too busy going round glass factories to think about anything other than business,' Dee predicted firmly.

'Mmm… It's a godsend that this trip came up when it did,' Kelly agreed. 'And that's all thanks to you, Dee. That was a brilliant idea of yours to suggest to her that we should think about buying some crystal from the Czech Republic. It's been so awful for her.

'You'd think that after what he's done to her and the way he's let her down Julian would at least have the decency to keep a low profile with his new girlfriend, but he actually seems to enjoy flaunting their relationship.'

'Like I said, the man needs teaching a lesson and being given a taste of his own medicine,' Dee reiterated. 'And if you want *my* opinion we're just the ones to do it.'

'Us…? But…' Anna started to protest uneasily.

'Why not?' Dee overruled her. 'After all, you are Beth's godmother, Kelly here is her best friend… If the three of *us* can't be relied upon to do the right thing by her…if she can't depend on *us*…then who can she depend on?' Dee said firmly.

'It sounds a good idea in theory,' Kelly allowed, moved by Dee's obvious emotion. 'But—'

'Have some more wine,' Dee interrupted her. 'There's still over half a bottle left.'

Deftly she refilled both Kelly's glass and Anna's.

'I—'Kelly started to protest but Dee cut her off.

'It's got to be finished and *I* can't have any more; I'm driving.'

It was true. It had been Dee who had taken charge when Beth had virtually collapsed after Julian had callously told her that he no longer wanted her, just as it had been Dee who had come up with the suggestion that Beth travel to Prague on a buying trip that would also hopefully take her mind off Julian and her unhappiness.

And it was Dee who had driven them all to the airport so that they could see Beth off on her journey, and now it seemed that Dee was still taking charge and making plans for them.

'So, now that we've agreed that Julian *has* to be punished and exposed for what he is, what we need to decide is *how* we're going to put our plans into action.'

She paused and then looked at Kelly before saying slowly, 'What I think would be best would be for us to punish him through his greed. You mentioned the other week, Kelly, that almost right from the first time you met him Julian was coming on to you, making overtures to you, trying to encourage you to date him behind Beth's back…'

'Yes. It's true, he was,' Kelly agreed. 'I didn't tell Beth at the time because I didn't want to hurt her and then, when it was too late, I wished I had…' She paused and then added uncertainly, 'Dee, it's all very well to *talk* about us punishing Julian for the way he's hurt her so badly, but realistically what can we do?'

Dee smiled grimly at her before turning to Anna.

'Anna, you've told us how Julian approached you for a loan, claiming that he wanted the money to use as a deposit on a house he was planning to buy for Beth and himself…'

'Yes…' Anna agreed. 'He called round out of the blue one afternoon. He said that all his cash was tied up in various investments, but that Beth had seen this house she was desperate for them to buy and he didn't want to disappoint her. He said he'd only need the money for a few months—'

'Yes, no doubt because he was expecting that by then Beth would have received her share of her grandfather's estate,' Kelly cut in angrily. 'How *could* anyone be so despicable?'

'We aren't talking about anyone,' Dee pointed out acidly. 'We're talking about Julian Cox, and Julian has a long record of very skilfully and deceitfully depriving the innocent and naive of their money—and not just their money,' Dee concluded quietly.

There was a look in her eyes that made Kelly check and study her a little woozily. The wine Kelly had drunk was beginning to make her feel distinctly light-headed, no doubt due to the fact that she hadn't had very much to eat, but she knew she was *not* imagining that unfamiliar combination of vulnerability and haunted pain in Dee's distinctive tortoiseshell-coloured eyes. Even so, there was something she still felt bound to pursue.

'If you knew just what kind of man Julian is, *why* didn't you say something to Beth?' she asked Dee for a second time.

'I told you why—because quite simply, when she first became involved with him, if you remember, I was in Northumberland nursing my aunt. By the time I'd come back and realised what was going on, how deeply she was involved with him, it was too late; she was on the verge of announcing their engagement.'

'Yes, I remember now,' Kelly acknowledged. It was true—Dee *had* been away for several months earlier in the year, looking after an elderly relative who had undergone a serious operation.

'It seems so unfair that Julian should get away with convincing everyone that poor Beth is some kind of compulsive liar as well as breaking her heart,' Anna put in quietly. 'I *know* her and I *know* she would never, could *never* behave in the way he's trying to imply.'

'He's very adept at maintaining a whiter than white

reputation for himself whilst destroying the reputations of those who are unfortunate enough to become innocently involved with him,' Dee informed them bitterly.

Kelly was feeling far too muzzy with wine to take Dee up on what she had said, but she sensed that there was some kind of past history between Julian Cox and Dee, even if she knew that Dee would not welcome any probing into it on her part.

'What we need to do,' Dee was telling them both firmly, 'is to use his own tactics against him and lure him into a position where his true nature can be exposed. It's no secret now to any of *us* that the reason he dropped Beth is because he realised that there wasn't going to be any financial benefit to him in marrying her.'

'Since we do know that, I can't help but agree with Kelly that we ought to do something to warn his new girlfriend and her family just what kind of man he is,' Anna suggested gently.

Dee shook her head. 'We know how blindly in love Beth was, and, although I hate to say this, we could all be done an untold amount of harm if Julian Cox started trying to tar us with the same brush he's used against Beth to such good effect. The *last* thing any of us needs is to be publicly branded as hysterical, over-emotional women, obsessed by some imaginary sense of injustice.'

She was right, Kelly had to acknowledge.

'Besides, if my plan works successfully, and it will, then he'll drop his current victim just as swiftly as he dropped Beth, and for very much the same reason.'

'Your *plan*? *What* plan?' Kelly asked her uneasily.

'This plan. Listen,' Dee commanded. 'We are going to mount a two-pronged attack against Julian where he's most vulnerable.

'I happen to know that one of Julian's clever little

ways of funding his expensive lifestyle is to persuade gullible people to invest in his apparently initially sound financial schemes. By the time they realise that they are anything but sound, it's too late and their money has gone.'

'But surely that's fraud?' Kelly protested. Dee shrugged her shoulders.

'Technically, yes, but Julian relies on the fact that his victims feel too embarrassed or are too timid to complain. For that reason he tends to prey on the elderly and the vulnerable, the innocently naive, too trusting and honest themselves to see what he really is until it's too late.'

'The man's a menace,' Kelly complained sharply.

'Yes, he is, and we're going to expose him as he fully deserves to be exposed,' Dee told her. 'You, Kelly, are suddenly going to become an extremely rich young woman. You have a great-uncle, previously unknown and now deceased, who has left you a considerable amount of money. This inheritance isn't something you yourself have made public, of course; in fact you refuse to talk about it—its existence is something you wish to keep a secret—but its existence has subtly filtered through the town's grapevine, at least as far as Julian's ears.

'We already know that he finds you attractive; you've told us both that he made advances to you whilst he was pretending to Beth that he loved her... All you have to do is let him believe that you're prepared to commit yourself, and, more importantly, your future to him. His own ego and greed will do the rest.'

'But I can't pretend that I've inherited money...I can't lie about something like that,' Kelly said. 'What will people think when they know?'

'Only *Julian* will ever know about your supposed inheritance,' Dee assured her. 'Just as only Julian will ever know that you are a wealthy widow and have money to spare for investment,' she told Anna.

Anna looked at her uncertainly.

'He has already tried to borrow money from me, Dee, it's true, as I've just told you both, but I'm certainly not a wealthy woman and...'

'Look, when it comes to convincing Julian that you both have financial assets that we all know simply don't exist, you can leave everything to me. I promise you that Julian is the only person who will be made aware of these imaginary fortunes.'

'But will he believe it? Surely he'll...'

'He'll believe it,' Dee assured Kelly. 'He'll believe it because he'll *want* to believe it. He needs to believe it,' she told them grimly. 'From what I've learned, his own financial position is so perilous at the moment that he'll grasp just about any straw he can to save himself.

'Once he switches his allegiance from his current girlfriend to you, Kelly, and once he tries to draw you, Anna, into one of his financial scams, we'll be able to publicly reveal him for the cheat and liar that he genuinely is...'

'It sounds plausible,' Kelly acknowledged. 'And it would certainly exonerate Beth if we could pull it off.'

'As well as preventing his current girlfriend from suffering a potential broken heart and losing *her* inheritance,' Anna supplied protectively.

'So it's agreed,' Dee slipped in quickly. 'We don't have any option but to go ahead and bring him to book.'

'No, I suppose we don't,' Kelly acknowledged.

She still wasn't totally convinced that she was going to be able to carry off the role Dee had apparently cast for her as a wealthy heiress, but her head felt too muzzy for her to protest properly.

There was one thing she had to say, though.

'How can you be so sure that Julian *will* drop his current girlfriend for me?'

'He wants you, we already know that,' Dee told her forthrightly, 'and besides, you're on your own, unprotected... It's *your* money...yours to do with as you please... His current girlfriend isn't; she's got a brother who stands between Julian and her inheritance. Julian is running out of credit and credibility. He won't be able to resist the bait you're dangling, Kelly. He can't afford to resist it.'

'The bait...' Kelly swallowed shakily. The bait Dee was referring to, as she knew only too well, wasn't just her imagined fortune, it was Kelly herself, and since she personally thought that Julian Cox was the most loathsome, obnoxious, revolting and undesirable man she had ever met...

'But if Kelly's going to pose as a wealthy heiress, then surely Julian won't be interested in my money as well,' Anna protested.

'Don't you believe it,' Dee corrected her. 'Julian is greedy and avaricious; he won't pass up any opportunity to get his hands on some extra cash.'

'But I've already refused to help him once,' Anna pointed out.

'You're a woman; you can change your mind,' Dee told her mock-sweetly. 'Look, you can both leave all the details of putting our plans into action to me. All I want from you is your agreement, your *commitment*, to help Beth, and I *know* I can rely on both of you completely for that... Can't I?'

Kelly and Anna exchanged uncertain looks.

'Beth is very dear to us,' Dee reminded them, looking first at Kelly and then at Anna.

'Yes. Of course…of course you can,' Anna agreed immediately.

'Yes. Of course you can,' Kelly agreed a little less confidently. Something warned her that, foolproof though Dee's plan sounded, things might not fall into place just as easily as she assumed, but her brain felt too clouded by the wine she had drunk for her to be able to formulate any determined assault on Dee's confident arguments and besides, Dee was right about one thing— she *did* feel that Julian deserved to be exposed for what he was…

For the next few minutes they continued their discussion, and as they did so Kelly's doubts as to the feasibility of Dee's plan resurfaced.

'I've got an early start in the morning, so if you don't mind we really ought to make a move,' Dee announced finally, checking her watch.

As she stood up Kelly realised dizzily just how strong the red wine she had been drinking actually was. To her relief Anna seemed equally affected by it. Of the three of them, Dee was the only one who seemed to have a properly clear head, which was just as well since she was the one doing the driving.

As she shepherded her two slightly inebriated charges out into the car park and to her car, Dee acknowledged ruefully that she would thoroughly deserve it if both of them blamed her in the morning for their thick heads— she, after all, had been the one who had kept on refilling their glasses—but she comforted herself with the knowledge that what she was doing was right; she owed it to—Her eyes closed. She must not think of the past, only the future—a future in which Julian Cox would meet the fate he so richly deserved!

She hadn't been able to believe it when she had discovered that Julian was up to his old tricks, but this time he wasn't going to get away with it. This time…this time he was going to discover to his cost just how strong and powerful a woman's desire for justice could be.

With an almost maternal concern she helped her two friends and fellow conspirators into her car. She intended to take very good care of them from now on, very good care… As they settled a little woozily into the rear seat Dee reflected that it was just as well that they couldn't read her mind and that they didn't know the truth. There had been one or two decidedly awkward moments back in the restaurant when Kelly had tried to question her, to dig a little deeper into the past, but fortunately she had managed to sidetrack her.

'Poor Beth…' Anna hiccuped mournfully as Dee started the car engine.

'Poor Beth,' Kelly agreed, blinking as she tried to clear her increasingly blurry vision.

'No, not *poor* Beth,' Dee corrected them sternly. '*Lucky* Beth. Just think how much more unhappy he could have made her if he'd waited until after they were engaged, or, even worse, until after they were married before betraying her,' Dee pointed out to them.

'It's going to be easier for her this way. If she had married him…'

Instinctively she glanced down at her own wedding ring finger. It was slightly thinner than its fellows as if once…? Then determinedly she looked away.

In the rear of the car her two fellow conspirators were succumbing to the effects of the extremely potent red wine she had deliberately fed them, their eyes closing.

She knew she ought to feel guilty about what she was doing—they were both so innocent and unaware, so unsuspicious…

CHAPTER TWO

KELLY woke up with an aching head and a dry mouth. Groaning, she rolled over and looked at the alarm clock on the bedside table.

Ten o'clock. She must have slept right through the alarm. Thank heavens it was Sunday and the shop didn't open until later than usual.

Swinging her legs out of bed, she winced as the ache in her head became a thunderous nausea-induced pounding.

It was all Dee's fault, insisting that they finish that bottle of red wine.

Dee...

Kelly froze in mid-step and then collapsed back onto the bed, groaning. What on earth had she done? She would have to telephone Dee straight away and tell her that she had changed her mind, that there was totally, absolutely, completely and utterly no way she could go through with the ludicrous plan she had agreed to last night.

Tottering towards the phone, still clasping her head, Kelly saw the answering machine light was flashing. Obediently she pressed the reply button.

'Kelly,' she heard. 'This is Dee. I'm just calling to confirm the plans we made last night. I've discovered that Julian and his new girlfriend will be attending a charity bash at Ulston House this evening. I've managed to get you a ticket and an escort—just as a bit of extra insurance. Julian is going to find you even more of an irresistible challenge if he thinks you're with someone else. Remember, all you have to do is egg him on whilst playing just that little bit hard to get. I know how close you and Beth are and I know that you wouldn't dream of reneging on our plan or letting her down.

'Harry, your escort, will call for you at seven-thirty. He's my cousin, by the way, and completely to be trusted, although, of course, he knows nothing of our special plan. He thinks you just need a date for the evening because you're attending the do for business reasons. That could be the truth, incidentally—an awful lot of influential local people will be attending the dinner and the ball afterwards. Bye for now...'

What on earth did Dee think she was doing? Kelly wondered as she stared at the phone like someone in shock. And how on earth had she managed to get two tickets for that ball at such short notice? Kelly knew all about it. Those tickets were like gold dust. Not that she intended for one minute to go. Dee was taking far too much for granted and Kelly intended to tell her so. Where on earth had they put her telephone number?

Kelly winced as pain throbbed through her head. Last night's red wine had an awful lot to answer for—oh, an awful, awful lot!

Dee's number had to be somewhere and she certainly had to speak with her. Ah, there it was; she had missed it the first time in the address book. Breathing out noisily in relief, Kelly punched in Dee's telephone number.

The tell-tale delay before the call was answered warned her what was going to happen even before she heard the familiar sound of Dee's voice on the answering machine message.

'I'm sorry, I shan't be able to take your call today. Please leave your number and I'll call you back tomorrow,' Dee was announcing. Thoroughly exasperated, Kelly hung up.

Perhaps she could drive over to Dee's and persuade her that they ought to change their minds and their plans. What had seemed a reasonable plan last night, this morning seemed more like a totally implausible, not to say highly dangerous thing to do. For one thing, it went totally against all her own principles and, for another, how on earth was she supposed to give Julian Cox the impression that she found him attractive and desirable enough to want to break up his relationship with someone else when the truth was that she found him loathsome, reptilian and repulsive?

Yes, physically he was an attractive enough looking man, if you went for his boyish brand of fair-haired good looks, but looks alone had never been enough to attract Kelly, and there had been something about him, something about his attitude not just towards Beth but towards *her* as well, which had set alarm bells ringing in Kelly's head virtually from the first moment she had seen him. She had made a point of keeping out of the way whenever he was around and when they had had to meet she had kept a very cool and formal distance from him.

So how on earth was she supposed to convince him now that she suddenly found him the epitome of male sexiness?

She couldn't. She wasn't going to try. She had been a fool even to *think* of agreeing to Dee's outrageous plan, but she *had* agreed and something warned her that it wasn't going to be easy to convince Dee that she wanted to change her mind.

And if *she* backed out and Anna didn't, how was it going to look? She was, after all, Beth's best friend and, indeed, perhaps the best way of convincing Dee that her plan wouldn't work would be for her, Kelly, to show her how impossible it was going to be, by going to tonight's ball. She would be safe enough. There was no way that Julian Cox was going to repeat his attempt to come on to her, not after the way she had put him down the first time. And once she had failed to re-attract his notice Dee would surely accept that she had done her best and allow the subject to drop.

Yes, far better to do things that way than to risk offending Dee, who was, after all, only acting out of kindness and affection for Beth.

Where on earth were those wretched headache tablets? She had pulled everything out of their small medicine cabinet without finding them, and she knew she had bought some. And then she remembered she had given them to Beth, after the terrible crying jags she had had after her break-up with Julian had left her with a splitting headache. Glumly Kelly made her way to their small kitchen and filled the kettle.

The flat above the shop was on two floors; on the upper storey were hers and Beth's bedrooms and their shared bathroom, and on the lower floor was their comfortably sized living room, a small dining room and an equally small kitchen.

Outside at the rear of the property was a pretty little garden, and at the bottom of it was the workshop which Kelly had made her own territory. That was where she worked on her new designs and painted the china she had accepted as private commissions. Painting pretty porcelain pieces and enamel boxes was her speciality.

Before joining forces with Beth, Kelly had worked as a freelance from her parents' home in Scotland, supplying her pretty hand-decorated enamel boxes to an exclusive London store.

At three o'clock, with the shop still busy with both browsers and buyers, Kelly acknowledged that she was not going to be able to make time to snatch so much as a quick sandwich lunch, never mind drive over to Dee's.

Ironically this Sunday had been one of their busiest since they had opened the shop, and she had not only sold several of her more expensive pieces, she had also taken orders for seven special commissions from a Japanese visitor who had particularly liked her enamel-ware boxes.

At four o'clock, when she was gently showing the last browser out of the shop so that she could lock up, she was beginning to panic, not just about the fact that it was becoming increasingly obvious that she was going to have to go through with Dee's plans for the evening but, femalely, because she knew that she simply did not have in her wardrobe a dress suitable for such an occasion. She and Beth had ploughed every spare bit of cash they had into their business—both of them had been helped with additional loans from their bank, their parents and Beth's grandfather. Anna, too, had insisted on making them a cash gift, to, as she'd put it, 'cover any extras'. They were beginning to show a small profit, but they certainly weren't making anything like enough to warrant the purchase of expensive evening dresses.

Ordinarily, knowing she was attending such an occasion, Kelly would have done as she had done for her graduation ball and trawled the antiques shops and markets to find something she could adapt, but on this occasion there simply wasn't time, and the smartest thing she had in her wardrobe right now was the elegant dress and coat she had originally bought for her brother's wedding and which, though smart, was hardly the kind of outfit she could wear to a charity ball.

After she'd checked that she had securely locked the shop and that the alarm was switched on she made her way up to the flat. She was still finding it hard to understand what on earth had possessed her to agree to Dee's outrageous scheme last night. She was normally so careful and cautious, so in control of her life. Beth was the gentle, easily manipulated one of the two of them; *she* was far more stubborn and self-assured. Too stubborn, her brother often affectionately told her.

Certainly she knew her own mind; she was, after all, a woman of twenty-four, adult, mature, educated and motivated, a woman who, whilst she would ultimately want to have a loving partner and children, was certainly in no rush to commit herself to a relationship. The man with whom she eventually settled down would have to accept and understand that she would expect to be treated as an equal partner in their relationship, that she would expect in him the same qualities she looked for in a best friend: loyalty, honesty, a good sense of fun, someone who would share her interests and her enthusiasms, someone who would enhance her life and not, as she had seen so often happen in so many other relationships, make the kind of demands on her that would prevent her from living her life as she really wanted to live it.

'But what happens if you fall in love with someone who isn't like that?' Beth had once questioned when they had been discussing men and relationships.

'I won't,' Kelly had responded promptly.

Poor Beth. What was *she* doing right now? How was *she* feeling...? Kelly had never seen her looking so wretched or unhappy... Beth had really believed that Julian Cox loved her.

Since their break-up Kelly had heard rumours that

Beth wasn't the first woman he had treated badly. No, Beth was better off without him, Kelly decided as she went into their kitchen and filled the kettle. She gave a small shudder as she remembered the night she had returned early from a weekend visit to her parents to discover Beth almost unconscious on her bed. Taking too many sleeping tablets had been an accident, an oversight, Beth had assured her, and had pleaded with her not to tell anyone else what she had done as Kelly sat beside her hospital bed. Unwillingly, Kelly had agreed. Luckily she had found Beth in time...luckily...

Remembering that incident, Kelly slowly sipped her hot coffee. Was Dee really asking so much of her? No. She didn't relish the role she was being called upon to play—what modern woman would?—but it was only a means to an entirely justifiable and worthwhile end.

But that still didn't solve the problem of what she was going to wear. She and Beth were approximately the same size although Beth was fair-skinned and blonde, with soft, pretty grey eyes, whereas she was brunette, her skin tone much warmer, her eyes a dark purplish brown, damson—the colour of lilac wine, one besotted admirer had once called them.

The ball had been the subject of a great deal of excitement and speculation in town. It was to be the highlight of the town's social year. The de Varsey family, who owned the elegant Georgian mansion where the event was to be held, had been local landowners for the last three hundred years and, despite their cost, tickets had been snapped up and the event sold out within a week of them going on sale, which made it even more extraordinary that Dee should have been able to produce a pair at such short notice.

Kelly could remember how thrilled and excited Beth

had been when Julian had told her that he had bought tickets for the event.

'I'll have to hire something really special. This isn't just a social event for Julian, it's a very important business opportunity as well,' she had told Kelly breathlessly.

Kelly had never properly discovered just exactly what line of business it was that Julian was in. He had talked very grandly about his own financial acumen and the hugely profitable deals he had pulled off, and he certainly had spent a lot of time talking into the mobile phone he took everywhere with him. He drove a very large and very fast BMW, but lived in a surprisingly small service flat in a new and not particularly attractive apartment block on the outskirts of town.

Kelly hadn't been at all pleased when she had learned that he had suggested to Beth that she allow him to have some of his business mail addressed to their flat, but she had refrained from making too much fuss, not wanting to upset her friend.

Beth had been thrilled at the prospect of attending such a prestigious social event with him as his fiancée; now another woman would be going there with him in Beth's place.

'Remember she could be just as much a victim of his ruthlessness as Beth was,' Dee had reminded her and Anna last night when Kelly had commented that she didn't know how any woman could date a man who she knew was supposedly committed to someone else.

If that was the case, Julian Cox deserved to be revealed as the unpleasant and untrustworthy creep that he was, for her sake as much as Beth's, Kelly acknowledged, frowning as she heard her doorbell ring.

She wasn't expecting any visitors. Although she and

Beth had made several new acquaintances since moving to the town, as yet they hadn't progressed to the stage of many close friendships. Getting up, she went down-stairs to open the door that faced onto the main street.

A man was standing outside, a large box at his feet, a delivery van parked on the roadside behind him.

'Kelly Harris?' he asked her, producing a form for her to sign. 'Just sign here, please...'

'What is it?' Kelly asked him uncertainly, automati-cally signing the form, but he was already picking up the box and handing it over to her.

Fortunately, despite its awkward shape, the box was very light. Mystified, Kelly carried it up to the flat and then, placing it on the sitting-room floor, sat down beside it to open it.

The outer layer of strong brown paper, once removed, revealed an elegant, glossy white box. There was a letter attached to it. Opening it, Kelly quickly read it.

Dear Kelly, you'll need this to wear this evening. Good hunting! Dee.

Intrigued, Kelly opened the box and then folded back the tissue paper inside it to reveal a dress that made her catch her breath in delight.

Two layers of material, one in conker-brown, the other a toning deep, dark damson, in the sheerest silk chiffon, floated through her fingers. Picking up the dress, she hurried into the bedroom and held it against herself, studying her reflection in the full-length mirror.

In both colour and design it might have been made with her in mind, the toning shades of chiffon so perfect with her colouring that they immediately drew attention to her eyes and made them look even more dramatically pansy-dark than usual. And as for the style the current vogue for Jane Austen-type high-waisted, floating, revealing evening dresses was one that could, in the wrong hands, look insipid and totally unflattering to anyone over the age of seventeen, but Kelly knew instinctively that this dress was far from insipid, and that its deceptively sensuous cut could never be worn by a woman who was anything less than totally at ease with herself and her sexuality. In other words, Dee couldn't have chosen a dress which would suit her more, and Kelly had no need to look at the immediately recognisable designer label attached to it to know that it must have been horrendously expensive.

Wonderingly she touched the fine chiffon. Although the dress was fully lined, the flesh colour of the lining meant that in a dimly lit room it could easily look as though she was wearing a dress that was virtually transparent.

Dee had even managed to get the size exactly right, Kelly acknowledged ruefully. Placing the dress reverently on her bed, she went back to the sitting room.

Inside the box beneath another layer of tissue paper lay a pretty matching chiffon stole and a pair of high-heeled satin sandals with a matching satin evening bag.

Dee had thought of everything, she admitted as she sat back on her heels.

Fortunately she already had some flesh-coloured underwear she could wear underneath the dress a birthday present from her sister-in-law and the pearls which had originally been her grandmother's and which her parents had given her on her twenty-first birthday would be perfect.

It was a dream of a dress, she acknowledged ten minutes later as she carefully hung it on a padded hanger. A dream of a dress for what could well turn out to be a nightmare of an evening.

There was no way that Julian Cox wasn't going to notice her wearing it. Although it was far too elegant and well designed ever to be described as sexy, Kelly knew even before she put it on that those soft layers of chiffon would have instant male appeal and be about as irresistible as home-made apple pie-although to a very different male appetite.

She glanced at her watch. If Dee's cousin was going to pick her up at seven-thirty she ought to think about starting to get ready. Her hair would need washing and styling if she was going to do full justice to that dress. Fortunately its length meant that it was very adaptable and easy to put up. Equally fortunately it possessed enough curl to mean that she could attempt a very similar if somewhat simpler style to that adopted by Jane Austen's heroines.

On the other side of town, someone else was also getting ready for the ball. Like Kelly, Brough Frobisher was attending it under protest. His sister had persuaded him to go, reluctantly wringing his agreement from him.

'Julian especially wants you to be there,' she had pleaded with him anxiously when he had started to refuse, adding slightly breathlessly, 'I think…that is, he's said…there's something he wants to ask you…'

Brough's heart had sunk as he'd listened to her. Initially when she had begged him to go with them to the ball he had assumed it was because her new boyfriend was looking for a backer for the new business venture he had already insisted on discussing with Brough; that had been bad enough, but now that Eve was dropping hints about Julian Cox proposing to her Brough was beginning to feel seriously alarmed.

At twenty-one Eve certainly didn't need either his approval or his authorization to get married, and at thirty-four he was mature enough to recognise that any man who married the sister whom he had been so close to since the death of their parents nearly fifteen years ago was bound, in the initial stage of their relationship, to arouse in him a certain amount of suspicion and resentment. Since their parents' death he had virtually been a surrogate father to Eve, and fathers were notoriously bad at giving up their claims to their little girls' affection in favour of another man; but, given all of that, there was still something about Julian Cox that Brough just didn't like.

The man was too sure of himself, too adroit... too...too smooth and slippery.

Eve had, after all, only known the man a matter of weeks, having initially met him quite soon after they had moved into the town.

Brough had decided that he had had enough of city life, and had sold out of the pensions management partnership he had founded, downsizing both his business and his equally hectic city social life by setting up a much smaller version of the partnership here in Rye-on-Averton.

Being a workaholic, city life—these were both fine at a certain stage in one's life. But lately Brough had begun to reflect almost enviously on the differences between his lifestyle and that enjoyed by those of his peers who had married in their late twenties and who now had wives and families.

'It's a woman who's supposed to feel her biological clock ticking away, not a man,' Eve had teased him, adding more seriously, 'I suppose it's because you virtually brought me up with Nan's help that you miss having someone to take care of.'

Perhaps she was right. Brough couldn't say; all he could say was that the prospect of living in a pretty market town which had its roots firmly secured in history had suddenly been an extremely comforting and alluring one.

As for wanting a wife and family, well, over the years he had certainly had more than his fair share of opportunities to acquire those. He was a formidably attractive man, taller than average, with a physique to match—he had played rugby for his school throughout his time at university and it showed. His close-cropped, thick, dark hair was just beginning to show a sexy hint of grey at his temples, and his almost stern expression was enlivened by the dimple indented into his chin and the laughter that illuminated the direct gaze of his dark blue eyes.

'It's not fair,' Eve had once protested. 'You got *all* our inherited share of charisma... Look at the way women are always running after you.'

'That isn't charisma,' Brough had corrected her dryly. 'That's money...'

In addition to the money both Brough and Eve had inherited from their parents, Brough's own business acumen and foresight now meant that if he had chosen to do so he could quite easily have retired and lived extremely well off his existing financial assets.

Perhaps it was his fault that Eve was as naive and unworldly as she was, he reflected a little grimly. As her brother, stand-in father and protector, he had perhaps shielded her too much from life's realities. Every instinct he possessed told him that Julian Cox simply wasn't to be trusted, but Eve wouldn't hear a word against the man.

'You don't know him like I do,' she had declared passionately when Brough had tried gently to enlighten her. 'Julian is so kind, even when people don't deserve it. When I first met him he was being stalked by this awful woman. It had gone on for months. She kept telling everyone that she was going out with him, calling round at his flat, ringing him up, following him everywhere. She even tried to arrange a fake engagement party, claiming that he'd asked her to marry him...

'But despite all the problems she'd caused him Julian told me that he just couldn't bring himself to report her to the police and that he'd tried to talk to her himself...to reason with her... He'd even taken her out to dinner a couple of times because he felt so sorry for her. But he said that he simply couldn't get through to her or make her understand that he just wasn't interested in her. In the end he said the only way to get her to accept the truth was for her to see him with me. Luckily that seems to have worked.'

When he'd heard the passionate intensity in his sister's voice Brough had known that it wouldn't be a good idea to give her his own opinion of Julian Cox. Certainly the man seemed to be very attractive to the female sex, if the number of women's names he peppered his conversation with were anything to go by.

No, he wasn't looking forward to this evening one little bit, Brough acknowledged grimly and he owed Nan a visit as well.

Nan, their maternal grandmother, was coming up for eighty but was still fit and active and very much a part of the small Cotswold community where she lived, and thinking of her reminded Brough of something he had to do.

His grandmother had in her glass-fronted corner cabinet a delicate hand painted porcelain teapot, together with all that was left of the original service which went with it. It had been a wedding present passed on to her and Gramps by her own grandparents, and Brough knew that it was one of her long-held wishes that somehow the teaset might be completed. Brough had tried his best over the years, but it was not one of the famous or well-known makes and it had proved impossible to track down any of the missing pieces. The only avenue left to him, according to the famous china manufacturers Hartwell, whom he had visited in Staffordshire, was for him to buy new pieces of a similar style and have them hand-painted to match the antique set.

'The original manufacturers we amalgamated with produce a small range of antique china in the same style, but unfortunately we do not produce either that colour nor the intricate detail of the landscapes painted into the borders,' the sympathetic Hartwell director had told him. 'And whilst we could supply you with the correct shape of china I'm afraid that you would have to find someone else to paint it for you. Our people here have the skill but not, I'm afraid, the time, and I have to tell you that your grandmother's set would be extremely time consuming to reproduce. From what you've shown me I suspect that each of the tea plates probably carried a different allegorical figure from Greek mythology in its borders, so your painter would have to be extremely innovative as well as extremely skilled. Your best bet might be someone who already works on commission— paints and enamels and that kind of thing.'

And he had suggested to Brough that he get in touch

with a particularly gifted student they had had working with them during her university days. No one had been more surprised than Brough when he had tracked down the young woman in question only to find she lived and worked in Rye-on-Averton.

The telephone number and the young woman's name were written down on a piece of paper on his desk. First thing in the morning he intended to get in touch with her. Time was running out; his grandmother's eightieth birthday was not very far away and he desperately wanted to be able to present her with the missing items from the teaset as a surprise gift.

Although his grandmother hadn't been able to take on Eve full time after their parents' death—her husband had been very ill with Parkinson's disease at the time—she had nevertheless always been there for them, always ready to offer a wise heart and all her love whenever Brough had needed someone to turn to for advice. She had a shrewd business brain too, and she had been the one to encourage Brough to set up his first business, backing him not just emotionally but financially as well.

She still took a strong interest in current affairs, and Brough suspected she would be as dismayed by Eve's choice of suitor as he was himself.

And tonight Eve was expecting him to put aside his real feelings and to pretend that he was enjoying Julian Cox's company, and no doubt, for her sake, he would do exactly that.

Eve might be a quiet, shy young woman, but she had a very strong, stubborn streak and an equally strong sense of loyalty, especially to someone who she considered was being treated badly or unfairly. The last thing that Brough wanted to do was to arouse that stubborn female protectiveness on Julian Cox's behalf when what he was hoping was that sooner or later Eve's own intelligence would show her just what kind of man he really was.

He looked at his watch. Eve was already upstairs getting ready. First thing tomorrow he would ring this Miss Harris and make an appointment with her to discuss his grandmother's china. For now, reluctantly he acknowledged that if they weren't going to be late it was time for him to get ready.

Seven miles away from town, in the kitchen of an old house overlooking the valley below and the patchwork of fields that surrounded it, Dee Lawson turned to her cousin Harry and demanded sternly, 'You know exactly what you have to do, don't you, Harry?'

Sighing faintly, he nodded and repeated, 'To drive into town and pick Kelly up at seven-thirty and then escort her to the charity ball. If Julian Cox makes any kind of play for her I'm to act jealous but hold off from doing anything to deter him.'

'Not if, but *when*,' Dee corrected him firmly, and then added, 'And don't forget, no matter what happens or how hard Julian pushes, you must make sure you escort Kelly safely back to the flat.'

'You really ought to do something about those maternal instincts of yours,' Harry told her, and then stopped abruptly, flushing self-consciously as he apologised awkwardly, 'Sorry, Dee, I forgot; I didn't mean…'

'It's all right,' she responded coolly, her face obscured by her long honey-blonde hair.

Seven years his senior, Dee had always been someone Harry was just a little bit in awe of.

Dee's father and his had been brothers, and Dee had been a regular visitor to the family farm when Harry had been growing up. It had surprised him a little that she had chosen to continue her career in such a small, sleepy place as Rye-on-Averton after her father's death. But then Dee had never been predictable or particularly easy to understand. She was a woman who kept her own counsel and was strong-willed and highly intelligent, with the kind of business brain and aptitude for making money that Harry often wished he shared.

There had only been one occasion that Harry could recall when Dee had found herself in a situation over which she did not have full control, a situation where her emotions had overruled her brain, but any kind of reference—no matter how slight—to that particular subject was completely taboo, and Harry would certainly not have dared to refer to it. As well as being in awe of his older cousin, it had to be said that there were times when he was almost, if not afraid of her, then certainly extremely unwilling to arouse her ire.

'Kelly will be expecting you. You'll like her,' Dee informed him, adding almost inconsequentially, 'She'd fit in very well here, and your mother...'

'My mother wants me to marry and produce a clutch of grandchildren—yes, I know,' Harry agreed wryly, before daring to point out, 'You're older than me, Dee, and you still haven't married. Perhaps we're a family who don't...'

'It's hardly the same thing,' Dee reproved him. 'You have the farm to think of. It's been passed down in the family for over four hundred years. Of course you'll marry.'

Of course he would, but when he was ready and, please God, to someone he chose for himself. Although he tried desperately to hide it, considering that such idealism was not proper for a modern farmer, Harry was a romantic, a man who wanted desperately to fall deeply and completely in love. So far, though, he had not met anyone who stirred such deep and intense emotions within him.

CHAPTER THREE

VERY gently Kelly fingered the soft silk of her gown. Once on it suited her even more perfectly than she had expected, the colour of the chiffon doing impossibly glamorous things for her colouring.

As she looked up she saw that Dee's cousin Harry was watching her rather anxiously. She smiled reassuringly at him as they waited in the receiving line to be greeted by their host and hostess. She had known from the moment he arrived to pick her up that she was going to like Harry. He was that kind of man—solid, dependable, reassuring, as comfortable as a familiar solid armchair, with the kind of down-to-earth, healthy good looks that typified a certain type of very English male. Just having him standing there beside her made her feel not merely remarkably better about the scheme which Dee had dreamt up but somehow extraordinarily feminine and protected. It was rather a novel sensation for Kelly, who had never been the type of woman to feel that she needed a man to lean on in any shape or form.

'That colour really suits you,' Harry told her earnestly as he arched his neck a little uncomfortably, as though he longed to be free of the restriction of his formal dinner suit.

'Dee chose it,' Kelly informed him, adding truthfully, 'I feel rather like Cinderella being equipped for the ball by her fairy godmother... Although...' She paused and then stopped. There was no point in discussing with Harry her doubts about what she was doing.

41

They had reached the line-up of dignitaries now. Kelly smiled mischievously as she caught the discreetly admiring second look the Lord Lieutenant of the county gave her before he shook her hand.

It's all right, it's not me, it's the dress, she wanted to reassure his rather austere-looking wife, but then, remembering her new role as a *femme fatale*, instead she gave him a demure little smile plus a wickedly sultry look from beneath lowered lashes. It worked... His Lordship might be close on sixty, but there was no doubt that he was still a very virile man at least if the look he was giving her was anything to go by.

Perhaps the evening wasn't going to be so much of a challenge to her thespian talents as she had originally believed, Kelly mused as they passed down the line and then turned to accept a glass of champagne from one of the hovering waiters.

As Kelly already knew, the tickets for the ball had been unbelievably expensive, with only a relatively small number available, but, as she glanced appreciatively at her surroundings, she could well understand why.

Instead of more conventionally attaching a large marquee to the house to accommodate the event, guests were allowed to wander at will through the elegant antique-furnished reception rooms. Her own Regency-inspired dress couldn't have been more felicitously in keeping with the decor, Kelly recognised, her attention caught by a pretty inlaid Chinese lacquered cabinet in one corner of the room, its shelves filled with what she suspected were Sèvres figurines.

Touching Harry's arm, she pointed it out to him.

'I'd like to go over and have a closer look,' she told him. Nodding, Harry gallantly forged ahead to make a pathway through the throng of people now filling the hallway.

Kelly had almost reached her destination when abruptly she stopped dead. There, not a dozen feet away from her, stood Julian Cox. He hadn't seen her as yet. He was busy talking with a pretty fair-haired young woman standing with him. In looks she was very similar to Beth, Kelly recognised, and she looked somehow as though she too possessed the same gentleness of nature that so characterised her best friend.

She doubted very much that that same description could be applied to the man standing on the opposite side of her. Tall, with incredibly powerful shoulders and frowning heavily, he looked extremely formidable and extremely masculine, Kelly recognised as her heart gave a sudden unsteady lurch against her ribs and her breathing quickened idiotically.

As though impossibly, surely he was somehow aware of her attention, he turned his head, seemingly focusing fiercely on her.

Kelly's heart gave another and even sharper lurch. He had the most intensely dark blue eyes, and such a penetrating gaze that she felt almost as though he could see right into her soul.

Now she *was* being ridiculous, she told herself stoutly, firmly assuring herself that there was no way that either he or anyone else could have guessed what was going through her mind as she looked at him. And anyway, she reminded herself as she determinedly looked away from him, she was not here to start fantasising about the admittedly very interesting sensual allure of an unknown man; she was here for a very specific purpose, and that did *not* include allowing herself to be side-tracked by anyone or anything—not even her own still very disturbed heartbeat.

Even so, she managed to sneak a second brief glance at him, and she wished she had not done so as she saw the tender and protective way in which he was bending towards the soft-featured blonde girl who was standing close to Julian. Was she, as Kelly had first assumed, the new woman in Julian's life, or was the other man her partner? Had those magnetic blue eyes that had focused on her so directly and so immediately been giving a stern warning that he was *not* available to any other woman, rather than conveying a virile, masculine awareness of her female curiosity?

Well, no doubt before the evening was over she was going to find out, she reminded herself. Julian had not seen her yet, but... She took a deep breath and started to move discreetly into his line of vision.

'Are you okay?' she heard Harry asking her in concern. 'You look a bit flushed. It's pretty crowded in here and hot...'

Rather guiltily Kelly gave him a reassuring smile. Any heat flushing her face had rather more to do with her emotional and physical reaction to the sexily masculine good looks of the man standing with Julian Cox than with the heat of the room.

Irritatingly, Julian had now turned away to talk to someone so that she was out of his line of vision. Boldly she deliberately changed direction, plunging through the crowd in order to bring herself back into it and, in the process, losing Harry, who became separated from her by the busy throng.

Julian might not be aware of her presence, she recognised after a discreet glance in the trio's direction, but *he*, whoever *he* was, most certainly was. Slightly breathlessly she instinctively curled her toes, and a delicious thrill of feminine reaction ran through her as she realised just how intently she was being studied. Sternly she reminded herself of just why she was here and the role she had to play. The temptation to abandon it and to revert to her normal self beckoned treacherously. She had never been a flirt, never been the kind of woman to go all out deliberately to attract a man's attention she had never needed to and she had certainly never wanted to!

But, almost as though it was fate, just as she was wavering, a direct pathway opened up between her and Julian. Sternly she made herself take it.

'Julian... How lovely to see you...'

Had she got the note of flirtatious invitation in her voice pitched correctly? Anxiously she held her breath as Julian turned his head to look at her, wariness giving way to a look of lustful male appreciation as she continued to smile at him.

'Kelly! What a surprise...'

'A pleasant one, I hope.' Kelly pouted, deliberately stepping closer to him, angling her body so that she was placing herself with her back to the blonde girl standing silently at Julian's side and thereby excluding her from their conversation.

'I thought for a moment that you'd forgotten me...'

'Impossible,' Julian assured her with heavy flirtatiousness, his glance deliberately and meaningfully lingering on her body.

Really, he was a total creep, Kelly decided.

'Here on your own?' Julian quizzed her.

Throwing back her head, Kelly gave a small, sexy laugh.

'Of course not,' she chided him, her voice and the

look she gave him emphasising that *she* was the type of woman who would *never* be without a male escort.

'You're looking very well,' she praised him, adding purringly, 'Very well…'

'Then that makes two of us,' Julian told her smoothly.

'Julian, I think it's time we started to make our way to the table.'

The cool, authoritative male voice intruding on their conversation caused Kelly to turn her head to look at its owner.

Close up he was even more sizzlingly sensual than she had first imagined. It must be the new persona she had assumed that was making her aware of him in such a very intimate and sexual way, she decided dizzily as her glance slid helplessly from the dark watchfulness of his eyes to his very sensual mouth. Certainly she could never remember an occasion previously when she had been so immediately and so shockingly physically aware of a man's sexuality.

'Oh, must you go so soon?' She pouted again, a little disconcerted to recognise how easily both the pout and the teasing but deliberately flirtatious glance she had given Julian's companion came to her. 'We haven't even been introduced…'

She could sense Julian's surprise at the way she was behaving, and managed to hide her own reservation at her unfamiliar behaviour. Kelly could sense Julian's reluctance to comply with her request, but his companion was already saying with a steely, not to say with a grim note in his voice, 'Yes, Julian, *do* introduce us to your friend…'

'Er… Eve, Brough, may I introduce you to an old friend Kelly? Kelly, please meet Eve and her brother, Brough Frobisher.'

While Kelly waited for him to expand a little more on the relationship between the other couple and himself she could see from the look in Brough Frobisher's eyes that he was decidedly unimpressed by her flirtatious manner.

At least she had had one of her questions answered, she acknowledged as Harry finally arrived at her side just as Brough was determinedly turning away from her.

Eve and her *brother*, Julian had said.

Ridiculous to feel that dizzying surge of excitement and relief just because Brough Frobisher appeared to be unattached.

'We're on table twelve,' Harry was informing her as he manfully forged a pathway for them both through the press of people making their way towards the banqueting room.

Table twelve was well positioned, with a good view of the top table and close enough to the long row of French windows which opened out onto the terrace to offer the comfort of a cool walk along it should one wish to avail oneself of such a facility.

Curiously, though, as they approached the table a small altercation appeared to be taking place there between a harassed-looking couple, the man red-faced and plainly angry whilst his wife looked flushed and embarrassed.

'*You* told me we were on table twelve,' he was saying to her as Harry and Kelly approached.

'And so we were… At least, that was what Sophie said…' his wife was responding, adding helplessly, 'She must have got it wrong. You'll have to go back and check the table plan.'

As she watched the hapless couple making their way back to the entrance to the room, Kelly couldn't help feeling a little bit guilty. *Was* she being overly suspicious in suspecting Dee's magical sleight of hand might somehow be responsible for their missing seats, especially when she could quite plainly see from where she stood that the place cards the couple had been studying with such bewilderment bore hers and Harry's name?

A middle-aged couple and their daughter, the Fortescues, Kelly realised, were taking their places at the table, and another couple were taking their seats opposite Harry's and Kelly's own, which left three spare seats to Kelly's left. Discreetly she leaned across to study the place cards, her heart thumping just a little bit too fast as she read, 'Mr Julian Cox, Miss Eve Frobisher, Mr Brough Frobisher.' She had no idea just how Dee had managed to get them seated next to Julian, nor did she wish to be enlightened. Dee was turning out to be a master tactician, an expert in the art of gamesmanship and subterfuge.

'Kelly, you're on our table! What a coincidence!' Julian was exclaiming with very evident pleasure as he walked up.

Demurely Kelly said nothing, instead simply smiling at him from beneath down-swept lashes.

Half an hour later, when they had all been served with their main courses, Kelly acknowledged that Julian was even less likeable than she had previously guessed. Ignoring his girlfriend to flirt with her, he had progressed from blatantly sexually motivated compliments to the kind of sensual innuendo which Kelly found teeth-grittingly unwelcome.

Her conscience overcoming her sense of duty, she leaned across the table to ask Eve gently how long she had been living in the town and if she liked it.

'It's very pretty,' was her slightly hesitant response, and Kelly didn't miss the way she looked first at her brother before replying to her, as though seeking either his support or his approval.

Kelly felt distinctly sorry for her. She was no match for a man of Julian's unwholesome calibre, that much was more than evident to her, and Kelly hadn't missed the way she had bitten her lip once or twice when Julian's compliments to herself had pointedly underlined just how sexually attractive he found her.

'What do you do?' Kelly asked her, trying to draw her out a little, but it seemed she had asked the wrong question because immediately the younger woman flushed and looked helplessly at her brother before replying.

'Oh, nothing... I'm afraid my art degree isn't... doesn't...'

Her voice trailed away and Julian cut in boastfully, 'Eve doesn't need to work, do you, my sweet? She has her own income...a trust fund...'

As he spoke he reached for her hand and squeezed it, lifting it to his lips to kiss her fingers in what Kelly considered to be an excessively exaggerated and insincere manner, but to judge from the pretty pink blush that coloured Eve's pale skin she didn't seem to find anything wrong with his manner towards her.

What would she say, Kelly wondered grimly, if she knew that whilst he was kissing her fingers his other hand was resting meaningfully on Kelly's chiffon-clad knee, and she had in fact just had to edge determinedly away from him to stop him from rubbing his leg potentially even more intimately against hers?

He really was totally repulsive, Kelly acknowledged with repugnance as she started to turn towards Harry, stopping when unexpectedly Brough Frobisher entered the conversation, telling her coolly, 'As a matter of fact, Eve works for me. What about you? What do you do?'

Before Kelly could answer him, the Master of Ceremonies called on them for silence whilst their host made a speech.

Gratefully Kelly got to her feet, glad to have the opportunity to shake off Julian's wandering hand. Her dislike of him was growing by the minute—and not just on her own behalf. The minute Julian had mentioned Eve's trust fund Kelly had immediately been aware from his avaricious expression just where the other girl's attraction for him lay. Poor thing, like Beth before her she was obviously too unworldly and naive to see through him, but surely her brother *must* be able to recognise just what Julian was like.

Although he had listened in silence to Julian's conversation throughout the meal, more of an observer than a participator, Kelly had been keenly aware of the intensity of his silent scrutiny of them all. *Was* she being over-sensitive in thinking that he had been particularly watchful where *she* was concerned? At one point, just before the Master of Ceremonies had provided his welcome diversion, Kelly had actually felt as though Brough Frobisher's gaze was somehow burning a laser-like beam right through the table to where Julian's hand was resting on her leg. Not that she had wanted it to be there. She gave a small shudder. He repulsed her now even more than he had done before.

'I can't encourage him. I don't like him. He's loathsome,' she had protested despairingly to Dee last night.

'All you have to do is let him *think* that you're interested in him,' Dee had soothed her. 'All we need is for him to show himself in his true colours so that we can…'

'So that we can *what*?' Kelly had pounced, but Dee had simply given her a mysterious smile.

The speeches were almost over; the Master of Ceremonies had announced that there would be dancing in the ballroom. Hopefully then she would be able to escape Julian's unwelcome attentions, since he would be duty-bound to dance with Eve.

'Your lipstick's all gone and your hair needs brushing,' she heard Julian saying critically to Eve as the speaker sat down.

'I'm afraid Eve doesn't really have much idea about how to dress properly. She isn't into designer clothes. I dare say you didn't have much change out of a thousand pounds when you bought yours?' he questioned, and Kelly knew from the look in his eyes that the news of her supposed inheritance had already reached him via that mysterious 'grapevine' Dee seemed to know so much about. As he spoke Julian's glance slid from Kelly's eyes to her mouth, and he murmured in a much lower voice, 'Mind you, one has to admit the poor darling doesn't exactly have the right kind of raw material…unlike you… Has anyone ever told you that you have the most amazingly sexy eyes…and mouth…?'

Kelly had to fight to suppress the dark tide of colour threatening to betray her feelings. It wasn't embarrassment that was driving the hot blood up under her skin, but anger. How dared he behave so insultingly towards his girlfriend? No wonder she was looking so unhappy. But that was no reason for her brother to give her, Kelly, such a contemptuously angry look. *She* wasn't the one who was responsible for Eve's humiliation.

'I was just going to go to the Ladies to tidy up myself,' she fibbed, smiling warmly at Eve. 'Do you want to come with me?'

'Oh, yes...'

Smiling with relief, Eve got up to accompany her.

'Have you known Julian long?' she asked Kelly shyly as they stood side by side in the elegantly decorated cloakroom, studying their reflections in the mirrors in front of them.

'Mmm...quite a while,' Kelly responded.

'He's a very special person, isn't he?' Eve enthused, her eyes shining with emotion, her expression betraying just how deeply involved with him she was.

Kelly's tender heart ached for her, and she only just managed to resist the impulse to tell her exactly what she thought of Julian Cox and why. Instead she asked, 'What about you? Have *you* known him long?'

'Er, no...not really... That is...' She paused and then said in a breathless rush, 'He's asked me to marry him. Everything's happened so quickly between us that I still can't quite... It's quite a frightening feeling when you fall in love, isn't it?' she asked Kelly with a small, poignant smile. 'This is the first time that I... Brough thinks it's too soon... Julian gets quite cross with me sometimes because he thinks I rely too much on Brough, but he's taken care of me ever since our parents died and...

'I haven't met many of Julian's friends yet,' she confided, changing the subject slightly. 'Julian says that he wants to keep me...us...to himself for a little while...' She smiled and blushed. 'He's so very romantic and loving.'

Oh, yes, Kelly wanted to agree sarcastically. So very romantic and loving that he broke my best friend's heart, just the same way he is probably going to break yours. But caution made her hold her tongue.

How much did Eve know about Julian's relationship with Beth?

Along with the revulsion and dislike Julian had aroused within her was a growing sense of anger and an unexpected surge of desire to protect Eve from suffering the same fate as Beth. Perhaps she herself was a rather stronger and more determined character than she had previously realised, Kelly acknowledged. With every word that Eve spoke she could feel an increasing awareness of how right Dee was to want to have Julian exposed in his true colours, and an increasing desire to help achieve that goal, even if it meant putting herself in an unpleasant, but thankfully temporary, position. Much as it went against the grain with her to subtly encourage Julian's amorous advances, much as she disliked the role she was being called upon to play, there was a real purpose to it.

Checking her own freshly applied lipstick, she gave Eve a warm smile.

'Don't let Julian bully you,' she advised her.

The younger girl's face went scarlet.

'Oh, he doesn't. He isn't... It's just that he's used to women who are so very much more glamorous than me and of course he wants...expects...'

'If he loves you then he must love you just the way you are,' Kelly pointed out, but she could see from Eve's expression that she did not want to hear what Kelly was trying to say.

Perhaps when she saw exactly what kind of man Julian really was she'd realise just how unworthy of her love he was. Kelly certainly hoped so.

Brough frowned thoughtfully as he watched his sister and Kelly weaving their way back through the crowd to their table. Kelly puzzled him and, yes, if he was honest, intrigued him as well.

Having watched the way she behaved towards Julian, subtly encouraging his advances, it would be easy to assume that she was an extremely sophisticated and worldly young woman who was used to using her undeniable feminine sensuality and attractiveness to get whatever she wanted from life—*whoever* she wanted from life, regardless of whether or not the man in question was attached to someone else. But Brough had also observed the way she behaved towards her escort, Harry, and to his own sister, and there was no denying that with them she displayed a warmth, a consideration, an awareness and respect for their feelings that couldn't possibly be anything other than genuine.

One woman, two diametrically opposite types of behaviour. Which of them revealed the real Kelly, and why should it be so important to him to find out? Not, surely, just because the man she was making a play for was the same man her sister claimed to be in love with? After all, there was nothing he wanted more than for something, someone, to make his sister see just how unworthy of her Julian Cox actually was.

Discreetly he studied Kelly. Her dress was expensive, and fitted her as though it had been made for her, but something, some experienced male instinct, told him that she was not quite so comfortable and at home in it as she wanted others to believe. Every now and again she gave a betraying glance down at herself, rather in the manner of a little girl uncertain of the wisdom of wearing her mother's borrowed clothes. As Julian had so admiringly pointed out, she was immaculately groomed, but personally Brough would have rather liked to see her dressed casually in jeans, her skin free of make-up, her wonderful hair soft and tousled and her even more wonderful eyes and mouth...

His eyebrows snapped grimly together as he recognised the direction his thoughts were taking. It was a long time since a woman had attracted him as powerfully or as immediately as Kelly—or as dangerously. On two counts. If she *was* the type of woman she was portraying to attract Julian Cox's attention, then she was most decidedly not *his* type. And if she wasn't...if that unexpected and alluringly enticing chink of vulnerability and uncertainty he had so briefly glimpsed beneath the sophisticated image she was trying to portray was the real Kelly...then that would make it even more imperative that he didn't involve himself in any way with her. His life was already complicated enough as it was, with Eve. One day he would marry, settle down, with a nice, calm, sensible girl—a woman who did not pretend to be something she wasn't.

Of course, there was one way he could probably find out just what sort of woman Kelly really was. The way a woman responded, reacted, to a man's first kiss could say an awful lot about just what kind of person she was, Brough mused.

His frown deepened. What on earth was he thinking? There was no way he could justify that kind of behaviour—or those kinds of thoughts.

His last serious relationship had been when he was in his very early twenties. He had thought himself in love— had thought that she loved him. They had met at university and then she had taken a year out to travel while Brough had stayed at home to be near Eve. When they had met up again both of them had been forced to acknowledge that whatever they'd had had gone.

Since then he had dated...there had been women...but

by the time he had reached thirty he had decided that he must be the kind of man in whom logic and responsibility always won out over passion and impetuosity. And so he was...wasn't he?

'I want to dance with you.' Kelly's heart sank as she saw from the loaded, explicitly sexual way that Julian was regarding her as he spoke to her just how successful Dee's plan had been. There was no doubt just what was on Julian's mind, even without the heavy, lingering glance he gave her breasts.

He was being too obvious, too potentially hurtful to Eve and insulting towards her, Kelly decided as she shook her head and reminded him, 'You haven't danced with Eve yet...'

'I don't want to dance with *her*; I want to dance with *you*,' Julian insisted as he reached out to raise her from her seat.

Unhappily Kelly fought her conscience. This was too much, and inexcusable. Just how much wine had Julian had to drink? she wondered uneasily, wishing that Harry hadn't chosen just that moment to disappear.

'Kelly has already promised this dance to me.'

The interruption from Brough Frobisher was just as unexpected as his coolly uttered, authoritative fib.

Without allowing Julian the opportunity either to protest or argue, Brough came over to her, holding out his hand. Shakily Kelly stood up. She didn't particularly want to dance with him, but dancing with him was infinitely preferable to having to dance with Julian.

Good manners suggested that she ought to thank Brough Frobisher for rescuing her, but to do so would surely be to step out of the role Dee had cast for her and, perhaps even worse, to give him the opportunity to point out that she herself had been actively encouraging Julian to believe that she was interested in him.

'Your sister is very sweet,' she commented awkwardly as Brough led her onto the floor.

'Sweet?' His dark eyebrows lifted as he gave her an appraising look. 'An excess of sweetness can be unpleasantly cloying. I don't consider her to be sweet, rather a little too naive and vulnerable. How long have you known Cox?'

His abrupt question caught her off guard.

'Er...a while... He...we're old friends,' she stammered, boldly remembering her role.

'Old *friends*,' he repeated, stressing the word as he looked hard at her. 'I see.'

Kelly hoped devoutly that he did no such thing.

As they reached the dance floor he touched her lightly on the arm, turning her expertly towards him. The band was playing a slow, intimate dance number, and immediately she felt his arm go round her Kelly tensed.

It wasn't that she wasn't used to dancing in close proximity to a man, it was just that somehow it was unnerving with *this* man—

'Enlighten me,' he was saying to her. 'What exactly is it about Cox that quite patently makes him so attractive to your sex?'

Kelly glanced warily up at him. He was immaculately dressed and she could just catch the scent of the very masculine cologne he was wearing, she noted approvingly. Julian's apparent addiction to very strong and no doubt trendy aftershave was not to her personal taste at all. But despite Brough's elegant grooming she suspected that without the shave he must have had before coming out this evening his very thick and very dark hair must mean that most evenings his jaw must be shadowed and slightly rough to the touch, adding a delicious extra frisson of sensuality to being kissed by him, especially if you were a woman who, like her, possessed slightly sensitive skin.

Appalled by the direction of her own unruly thoughts, Kelly realised that she had still not answered his question.

'Er…Julian likes women,' she told him lamely.

Immediately his eyebrows rose.

'He certainly does,' he agreed silkily. 'Doesn't that bother you? In my experience, most women prize loyalty and exclusivity in a relationship…'

'Julian is simply a friend,' Kelly reminded him sharply.

'A very intimate friend?' Brough pressed.

He was digging too deep, questioning her too closely, Kelly recognised, and in order to answer him she was either going to have to commit herself to more lies or risk betraying the fiction she was creating.

'It's hot in here,' she complained, pulling free of him. 'I need some fresh air.'

It wasn't entirely untrue; she *was* hot and the terrace she could see beyond the ballroom's open French windows did offer a much needed escape from the cause of that heat—which was not so much the air in the ballroom as the presence of the man beside her and her own feelings of trepidation and guilt.

As she headed for the terrace, it didn't occur to Kelly that he would follow her. She could guess from the way he had been questioning her just what he thought of her, and she knew that in refusing to answer him she had equally plainly confirmed those suspicions.

It was a relief to reach the cool shadows of the terrace, and, avoiding the other couples strolling its length, Kelly turned instead to descend the flight of stone steps that led into the garden.

She was almost at the bottom when a sharp stone underfoot caused her to stumble, but instead of experiencing the ignominy of falling to her knees on the gravel pathway she was scooped up in a pair of hard male arms and she heard Brough's voice against her ear telling her calmly, 'It's all right, I've got you...'

He certainly had, and it seemed he had no intention of letting her go, either. Against her body she could feel the heavy thud of his heartbeat as he helped her to her feet but still continued to hold onto her. Disconcertingly her own heart suddenly started to race, and she discovered that she was finding it hard to breathe.

'Did you twist your ankle? Can you put your weight on it?'

'My ankle...' Dizzily Kelly looked up into his eyes, and then at his mouth, and then foolishly she did exactly the same thing again. The effect on her nervous system was like a shock wave of mega-force, a subterranean uprising of such intensity that it blew every fuse on her internal alarm system—and then some.

Unwisely she licked her inexplicably dry lips. What had he said about her ankle? What ankle? Helplessly her gaze clung to his. Surely no man should have such ridiculously long lashes, such darkly intense eyes. She felt as though...as though...

'Kelly. Kelly...'

'Yes,' she whispered in tacit acknowledgement of what she knew was going to happen.

A kiss was simply a kiss...wasn't it? How could she be so foolish, so unaware...so naive as to think *that*? *This* was certainly no mere kiss, this meeting, caressing of her mouth by and with his. But even as she tried to analyse what was happening, to hold onto some protective shred of sanity, the thread holding her, it snapped beneath the weight of what she was feeling. Blissfully she gave herself up to sensation—to the smooth, rough, hot, sweet feel of his mouth against hers, to the swift ascent from careful, hesitant exploration to the dizzying heights of a complete and passionate explosion of need she could feel shaking her body.

'Kelly!' As he whispered her name Brough's hand reached out to touch her face, to stroke tenderly along her jaw, to support her head as his tongue-tip parted her sensuously swollen lips.

'Brough!'

Was that really her whispering his name in a sigh that was all soft yearning and longing, exposing dangerously the tender, vulnerable heart of herself which she normally kept so carefully guarded?

Unable to stop herself, Kelly reached out and touched his jaw with her fingertips. His skin felt cool and strong. Hard, masculine. Shivering in pleasure, she stood still beneath his kiss. His arms tightened around her almost as though he wanted to guard and protect her.

Shyly Kelly opened her eyes, unable to resist the temptation to look at him whilst he was caressing her mouth with the most unbelievably erotic brush of his lips against hers, but to her shock his own eyes were open and he was looking right back at her.

The sensation of looking so deeply into his eyes whilst he kissed her felt like the most intimate experience she had ever had. Her earlier shivers had become deep tremors of intense emotion, and when he stopped kissing her and raised his mouth from hers to look searchingly at her Kelly made a small sound of distress, her fingertips touching his lips in a gesture of silent longing.

This time it was *his* turn to shudder, racked by a surge of male desire so strong and so open that Kelly felt her own body start to respond to it—to it and to him.

This time, when they kissed, she couldn't remain passive beneath his mouth, but returned each caress, mirroring every touch, every sound as they kissed and broke apart, only to kiss again.

'Kelly, are you out there?'

The sound of Harry's worried voice from the terrace above them brought Kelly back to reality. Hot-faced, she stepped back from Brough, not sure whether to be pleased or insulted that he had released her immediately.

His own face was turned away from her as he looked up towards the terrace, and so she couldn't see his expression nor guess what he was thinking until he said coldly to her, 'You're a very popular woman. First Julian and now Harry—but you'll forgive me, I know, if I decline to join the queue; enticing though what you have to offer undoubtedly is, I'm afraid my tastes run to a woman less practised and more genuine...'

Before Kelly could answer him he had gone, plunging past her into the darkness of the garden.

Shakily she turned towards the steps.

'Thank goodness I've found you,' Harry told her as he saw her. 'Dee would have had my guts for garters if I'd let anything happen to you. I'm under strict instructions to take care of you...' He started to frown, and then told her a little uncomfortably, 'It's none of my business, I know, and Dee's not told me what's going on, but Cox isn't a man I'd want any sister of mine to get involved with, and...'

'You're right,' Kelly agreed in gentle warning. 'It *isn't* any of your business, Harry.'

When they returned to their table they were just in

time to see Brough leaving; giving Harry and Kelly a curt nod, he ignored Eve's protests that it was too early for him to leave.

'I've got a meeting at nine in the morning,' Kelly heard him telling his sister.

'Oh, but you haven't forgotten that you promised to talk with Julian? He has something special to ask you, and there's his new venture, too,' Eve reminded her brother anxiously.

Immediately Kelly's ears pricked up. If Julian was looking for someone to finance a new business venture then Dee would certainly want to know about it. But as though he had somehow sensed her curiosity Brough touched his sister lightly on the arm and told her, 'I'm sure that Harry and Kelly aren't interested in our private family affairs. Cox...' He nodded briefly in Julian's direction before telling him, 'I'll arrange for a taxi to collect Eve—if I were you I'd leave your car behind and organise one for yourself.'

Was she imagining it or had he actually emphasised the word 'private', underlining its significance by giving her a cool, distancing look as he did so?

Whatever the case, Kelly could feel her face starting to burn slightly.

There was no point in her trying to deceive herself. From his demeanour towards his sister, she suspected that he was normally a man who regarded her sex with respect and genuine appreciation, even if at times he did allow his natural male instinct to protect anyone whom he might consider to be vulnerable to surface through his otherwise very politically correct manners. But where she was concerned he had displayed the kind of behaviour that was very far from treating her with respect. That kiss they had exchanged, which for her had been an act of heart-shakingly emotional and physical sensual significance, a complete one-off in her life and totally different from anything she had done or experienced before, had for him simply been an endorsement of the fact that her deliberately flirtatious behaviour with Julian meant that she was open to all manner of unpleasant male behaviour.

The kiss, which had seemed so deeply meaningful and intimate to her, had quite obviously for him merely been a reinforcement of his contempt for her, an emotionally barren male reaction to what he must have seen as some kind of casual, careless open invitation from her.

This kind of situation was so alien to her that Kelly had no knowledge of how to deal with it, and her instinctive desire to confront him and challenge his attitude towards her was further complicated and hampered by the role she was having to play.

Anyway, she decided firmly half an hour later as Harry was driving her home, why was she bothering wasting so much time worrying about what Brough Frobisher may or may not think about her? Why indeed! Julian, though, certainly seemed to have taken the bait, as Dee had planned he would. Kelly gave a small shudder of disgust the heel.

She grimaced a little, remembering the open interest Julian had shown in the pearl earrings and solitaire ring she had been wearing an inspired addition to her outfit on her own part; unlike her couture gown and earrings, the ring was anything but genuine, but Julian had certainly been taken in by it just as his unworldly naive victims had been taken in by him. Dee was right it was time someone turned the tables on him but, much as she wanted to help her friend, Kelly had to admit to wishing there might be some other way she could do so.

'You, Kelly are suddenly going to become an extremely rich young woman,' Dee had told her. 'All you have to do is let him believe that you're prepared to commit yourself and, more importantly, your future to him. His own ego and his greed will do the rest.'

Kelly hoped that she was right, because there was certainly no way she was going to be able to give Julian any physical, sexual confirmation of her supposed desire for him. No way at all!

CHAPTER FOUR

KELLY looked up as she heard the shop doorbell go. She was expecting Dee. They had spoken on the phone earlier when Dee had announced that she intended to come round to collect the ballgown accessories which had, in fact, been hired from an exclusive dress shop and to discuss what had happened at the ball.

Kelly had had a pleasingly busy morning with several customers. She hoped that Beth *was* going to be able to source a supplier of high-quality glass in the Czech Republic as this morning alone she had promised three potentially interested customers that they were hopefully going to be able to provide them with the sets of stemware they wanted.

'Something different...something pretty...something not too expensive...' had been the heartfelt pleas of their potential customers. Fingers crossed that if Beth's quest was successful they would be able to meet all three requirements.

'Right,' Dee commanded briskly as she walked up to the counter. 'How did the ball go? Tell me everything...'

'Julian was there with his new girlfriend,' Kelly began, pausing before she added quietly, 'I felt so sorry for her, Dee. She's plainly very much in love with him and so young and naive... I hate the thought of doing anything that might hurt her...'

'She'll be hurt much, much more if Julian succeeds in persuading her to marry him, which he's going to go all out to do. His finances are in a complete mess and getting worse by the day. He's desperately in need of money. She's quite wealthy in her own right and then, when you add on the financial benefits which could accrue to him through her brother... But from what Harry has told me Julian was making a very definite play for you...'

'Yes, he was,' Kelly agreed, tracing an abstract design with the tip of her finger on the polished glass counter before saying hesitantly, 'Dee, I'm not sure if I can go on with what we planned. I don't like Julian, and, whilst I like even less what he's done to Beth and what he's doing to Eve Frobisher, I...'

'Would it help if I gave you my solemn promise that on no account and on no occasion would I *ever* allow a situation to arise where you would have to be on your own with him?' Dee asked her.

Kelly stared at her. How on earth had Dee guessed what was troubling her?

'You're quite right,' Dee told her, answering the question Kelly still had to ask. 'I wouldn't want to be on my own with him either, especially if I thought that there was any risk that he might guess what we're up to... Harry is quite aggrieved with me, you know,' she added with a chuckle. 'He not only feels that as your friend and landlady I ought to put you wise to Julian's real character, he also shares your concern on behalf of Eve Frobisher.

'In fact,' she told Kelly ruefully, 'I'm afraid he's rather taken me to task over the whole thing.'

'Does he now know what we're doing, then?' Kelly asked her in some surprise. Instinctively she had felt that Dee was a woman who exercised her own judgement, made her own decisions and played her cards very close to her chest.

'Not entirely,' Dee admitted, confirming Kelly's private thoughts. 'Harry is a sweetie, as solid and dependable as they come. He wouldn't recognise a lie if he met one walking down the street; subterfuge and everything that goes with it is very much alien territory to him, which does have its advantages, of course. He's wonderful potential husband and father material...' She cocked a thoughtful eye at Kelly. 'He's comfortably off, and I know for a fact that his mother is dying for him to settle down and produce children. If you were interested...'

'He's a honey,' Kelly told her hastily, 'but not, I'm afraid, my type.'

Nor, she suspected, was she his, but she rather thought she knew someone who might be. She hadn't missed the anxious and protective looks Harry had been giving Eve over dinner the previous night.

'Mmm... Pity... Look, I've got to dash,' Dee told her. 'When Julian rings you—which he will—I want to know about it...'

'Dee,' Kelly said, but it was too late; the other woman was already heading for the door, ignoring her half-panicky protests.

What was Dee saying? Julian wouldn't ring her. He wouldn't dare. Flirting with her last night was one thing, but...

In her heart of hearts Kelly knew that despite her desire to do the right thing by Beth and the rest of her sex she was secretly reluctant to have anything more to do with Julian. Not because she feared him. She didn't. No. Contempt, dislike, anger...those were the emotions he aroused within her.

Admit it, she told herself sternly ten minutes later as she locked the shop and disappeared into the small back room to have her lunch, 'you just hate the thought of anyone thinking you could possibly be attracted to him. *Anyone*…or a specific someone…a *very* specific someone.

Pushing aside her half-eaten sandwich, Kelly started to frown. Don't start that again, she warned herself. He's not much better than Julian… Look at the way he treated you. Kissing you like that.

Kissing her… Abruptly she sat down, her insides starting to melt and then ache.

Watch it, she warned herself, deriding herself fiercely. It isn't just your insides he's turning to mush, it's your brain as well.

Her frown deepened as she heard someone ringing the shop doorbell. Couldn't they read? They were closed. The ringing persisted. Irritably Kelly got up. There was no way she could finish her lunch with that row going on.

Opening the communicating door, she marched into the shop and then stopped abruptly as she saw Brough Frobisher standing on the other side of the plate-glass window.

Her hand went to her throat in an instinctive gesture of shock as she breathed in disbelief, 'You.'

Shakily she went to unlock the shop door. Brough was frowning as he stepped inside.

'I'm looking for Kay Harris,' he told her abruptly. The sense of shock that hit her was so strong that for a moment Kelly was unable to reply.

'She does work here, doesn't she?' Brough was demanding curtly, looking at her, Kelly realised, as though he doubted her ability to answer him competently.

'Yes. Yes, she does… I do… It's Kelly, not Kay,' Kelly corrected him shakily. 'K is just my initial.'

'You!'

Sensing his reluctance to believe her, Kelly drew herself up to her full height and told him in her most businesslike voice, 'My partner and I run this shop.'

'You paint china?' His disbelief was palpable and insulting.

Kelly could feel her temper starting to ignite. There were many things she was not, and she had her fair share of human faults and frailties, but there was one thing that she was sure of and that was that she was extremely good at her chosen work—and that wasn't merely her own opinion.

'Yes, I do. Perhaps you'd like to see my credentials?' she suggested bitingly.

'I thought I just did—last night.' The long, slow, arrogantly male look he gave her made her face burn and her temper heat to simmering point.

'What is it exactly that you want?' she demanded angrily, adding before she could stop herself, 'If it's simply because you're some sort of weirdo who gets off on insulting women, I should have thought your behaviour towards me last night would have more than satisfied you.'

Kelly knew that she had overstepped the mark. She could hardly believe what she had just heard herself say, but it was too late to withdraw her remarks. Retaliation couldn't be long in coming, she recognised, and she was right.

'If you're referring to the fact that I kissed you...' he began silkily, and then paused whilst he looked straight into her eyes. 'Allow me to say that you have a rather...unusual...way of expressing your...displeasure...'

He didn't say anything more—he didn't need to, Kelly

acknowledged; the expression in his eyes and the tone of his voice along with the masterly understatement of his silky words was more than enough to leave her covered in confusion and angry, self-inflicted humiliation.

'I... You... It was a mistake,' was all she could think of to say.

'Oh, yes,' he agreed dulcetly. 'It certainly was. Now, I'm afraid that I am rather short of time. I have a commission I would like to discuss with you.'

Kelly blinked. All that and he *still* wanted to talk business with her.

Her thoughts must have shown in her face because he explained gently, 'You're my last resort. You have, or so I am told, a very particular and rare skill. It will soon be my grandmother's eightieth birthday. She has a Rockingham-style teaset, a much cherished family heirloom, but some pieces are missing, broken many years ago. The set has no particular material value; its value to her is in the fact that it was a wedding gift from her grandparents. I have managed to find out that Hartwell China bought out the original manufacturers many, many years ago and, whilst they still produce china in the same shape, they no longer produce the same pattern.

'To have one of their own artists copy such an intricate floral design would, they say, prove far too costly— the work would have to be done by one of the top workers, which would mean taking him or her off work they already have in hand. They recommended that I got in touch with you. Apparently there is no one else they would allow, never mind recommend, to do such work.'

'I...I worked for them whilst I was at university,' Kelly explained huskily. 'That was when I discovered that I had some talent for...for china-painting. I would have to see the design... It wouldn't be easy...or cheap...' she warned him.

Against her will she had been touched by the story he had told her, but *she* knew, even if he didn't, just how intricate and time-consuming the kind of work he was describing could be.

'I've managed to cadge one of the tea plates from Nan, and Hartwell have very kindly said that I can use their archive records.'

'Do you have the plate with you?' Kelly asked him.

He shook his head, unexpectedly looking oddly boyish as he admitted, 'I'm terrified of breaking it. I've got it at home. I was wondering if it would be possible for you to call there to see it.'

Kelly wanted to refuse, but her professional pride and curiosity proved too strong for her.

'I could,' she agreed cautiously, 'but it would have to be when the shop is closed. My partner, Beth, is away at the moment.'

'Could you manage this evening?'

'I...'

'I don't have very much time left. Nan's birthday isn't very far away,' he told her.

Kelly sighed. There was no reason why she shouldn't look at the plate this evening.

'I suppose so,' she agreed reluctantly. 'Where do you live? I—' She broke off as the phone began to ring, automatically going to answer it, saying, 'Excuse me a moment...' as she picked up the receiver.

'Hi, Kelly, it's Julian. How are you, you delicious, hot, sexy thing...?'

Kelly almost dropped the receiver as Julian's loud voice seemed to fill the shop. Her face burning with embarrassment, she turned her back on Brough even though she knew that he could well have heard what Julian had said.

'Julian. I…I'm busy…' she protested. 'I…'

'I understand, babe. What you and I have to say to one another needs to be said in private, right?' Julian responded. 'God, but you turned me on last night, doll… I can't wait for us to get together…'

'Julian.' Kelly closed her eyes, as revolted by Julian's conversation as she was by his person. 'Julian, please—' she began. But he wouldn't let her finish, interrupting her to say thickly, 'I'll ring you later at the flat. I've still got the number…'

He had hung up before Kelly could object or protest, leaving her pink cheeked both with anger and chagrin— anger because of Julian's assumption that she, or any other woman for that matter, would be willing to see him when he was supposedly already involved with someone else, and chagrin because Brough could have overheard some of the conversation.

It was to be expected, of course, that he wouldn't let the matter go without comment, especially when the girl whom Julian was supposed to be on the point of becoming engaged to was his own sister.

'I appreciate that custom has it that there's supposedly safety in numbers, but don't you think you could be interpreting its validity just a little too generously?' he asked her smoothly.

'Julian is an old friend,' Kelly reminded him.

The look he gave her could have stopped Linford Christie in his tracks, Kelly felt sure.

'Really? Then I feel extremely sorry for you, not only in your unfortunate choice of *friends* but your misplaced and, no doubt, regularly abused loyalty.'

'Julian is dating your sister,' Kelly felt compelled to remind him defensively.

He had turned to walk towards the door, but now, abruptly, he stopped and turned back to Kelly, and said quietly but with grim force, 'Yes, he is, isn't he?' And then, almost without pausing, he added coolly, 'Shall we say eight tonight? This is the address...'

Kelly was still looking bemusedly at the business card he had placed down on the counter as he closed the shop door behind him.

Why on earth hadn't she said something, objected to his high-handed assumption that she would not merely be free this evening but that, additionally, she would fall in with his plans, agree to his request, especially in view of the way he had spoken to her?

Reluctantly she picked up the card. Kelly had a vague idea where the house was since it was on the same road as a customer who had ordered a special commission from her.

Ten minutes before she was due to re-open the shop, the phone rang again. This time the caller was Beth, ringing from Prague.

'Hi. How are things going?' Kelly asked her eagerly.

'Not too bad, in fact really quite promisingly. I've been given several contact numbers, and I'm due to drive out of the city tomorrow to visit a crystal factory.'

'And you're managing okay, despite the language barrier?' Kelly asked her. This had been one of Beth's main concerns about her trip and Kelly was anxious to know how her friend was coping.

'Oh, I've got an interpreter,' Beth told her.

Kelly frowned. The offhand tone of Beth's voice was both unfamiliar and slightly worrying.

'And she's helping you, visiting factories with you...?'

'*She* is a he,' Beth told her shortly. 'And as for *helping* me...' There was a small pause. 'Honestly, Kelly, men. I'm totally off all of them. Just because a person has a fancy degree and a whole string of letters after his name, that does *not* give him the right to try to tell *me* what to do. And as for trying to force me to visit factories that *he's* chosen, with tales of theft and gypsies—'

'Beth.' Kelly interrupted her in bewilderment. 'I'm sorry, but I don't understand.'

'Oh, it's all right, I'm just letting off steam. It's Alex, the interpreter. He's half-English, as it turns out, and his grandparents left Prague for political asylum in the west when his mother was a child. Alex returned after the revolution to search for his family and he's stayed on here.'

'Sounds like he's been confiding rather a lot of personal history to you for someone you don't get on with,' Kelly told her wryly.

'Oh, he tells me what he wants me to know. He's insisting that I visit a glass factory run by his cousins, but I'm not inclined to go. He obviously has a vested interest in anything I might buy. I've managed to track down somewhere that produces this most wonderful design I've seen, and he's acting all high and mighty and trying to tell me that it's all a con and that the stallholder saw me coming a mile off. He says there *isn't* any factory where they've told me to go and the glass I wanted to buy couldn't have been genuine. He says it's a well-known ploy to get hold of foreign currency that is often worked against naive people like me...

'Oh, but Kelly, you should have seen this glass. It was wonderful, pure Venetian baroque, you know the kind of thing, and it would lend itself beautifully to being gilded for the Christmas market. I even thought that if the price was reasonable enough we could commission some special sets, hand-painted and gilded for special celebrations—weddings, anniversarie s...you know the kind of thing...'

Kelly laughed as she listened to her friend's excited enthusiasm. It was wonderful to hear that note back in Beth's voice again, and even more wonderful that she hadn't even asked once about Julian Cox.

'Anyway,' Beth was continuing determinedly, 'somehow I'm going out to this factory by myself. I'm planning to give my guide, and for that you can read jailer, the slip. It's obvious what he's up to,' she told Kelly scornfully. 'He just wants to secure our business for his cousins. He claims that their factory could probably reproduce the glass if they had a copy of it...'

'Mmm... Well, if that's the case, it might be worthwhile sketching the glass and seeing if they *can* reproduce it.'

'Never,' Beth asserted fiercely. 'There's no way I'm going to have Alex dictating to me... No. I've seen the glass I want and I know where to get it, and I'm determined to get an exclusive supply of it and at the right price. After all, if we did commission Alex's cousins, what's to stop them selling our design elsewhere, putting up the price to us because they know we want it? Look, I must go; Alex is picking me up in half an hour. He's insisting on making me walk over the Charles Bridge, and since it's raining today he says it should be relatively free of other tourists.'

'Sounds fun,' Kelly teased her, smiling as she said goodbye and hung up. The others would be so pleased to hear that Beth seemed to be getting over Julian Cox.

CHAPTER FIVE

As HE let himself into the hallway of their rented house and blinked at the teeth-jarring hard yellow paint of the room, Brough reflected that he would be glad when they could finally move into the large Georgian farmhouse he had bought several miles outside the town and which was presently undergoing some much needed renovation work. It had been empty for three years before Brough had managed to persuade the trustees of the estate of the late owner that there was no way anyone was ever going to pay the exorbitant price they were asking for it.

'If they don't sell it soon, they'll be lucky to have anything there worth selling,' he had told the agent crisply. 'It's already been empty and unheated for three winters, and if the government gives the go-ahead for the new bypass the area will be swarming with protestors just looking for an empty house to take over and make themselves comfortable in.'

Buying the house, though, had simply been the beginning of a whole spate of difficult negotiations. The property was listed, and every detail of his planning applications had to be scanned by what had felt like a never-ending chain of committees, but now at last the approved builder had started work on the property, and, with any luck, he should be able to move into it within the year, the builder had assured him cheerfully on his last site inspection.

For now, he would have to live with the last owner

of his present house's headache-inducing choice of colours.

'Brough, is that you?'

He grimaced wryly as Eve came rushing into the hallway, her face pink with excitement as she told him breathlessly, 'Guess what? Julian rang; he's going to be free this evening after all, so he's taking me out to dinner. Oh, Brough, I was so afraid he was going to be angry with me when you insisted that you couldn't help him with his new venture.'

As he listened to her Brough could feel himself starting to grind his teeth. There was no point in wishing that his sister had a more worldly and less naive outlook, nor in blaming his grandmother and the old-fashioned girls' school she had insisted he send her to for the part they had played in her upbringing. He might just as well blame their parents for dying—and himself for not being able to take on the full responsibility for bringing her up without his grandmother's help.

He knew how upset his grandmother would be if she knew how ill-prepared the select, protective girls' school she had chosen so carefully for her had left Eve for the modern world, and some day in the not too distant future Brough was afraid that his sister was going to have her eyes opened to reality in a way that was going to hurt her very badly.

As he'd thought a number of times before, there was no point in him trying to warn Eve about Julian Cox. She had a surprisingly strong, stubborn streak to her make-up, and was very sensitive about both her own independence and her judgement. To imply that Julian was deceiving her, that she was totally and completely wrong about him in every single way, was almost guaranteed to send her running into his arms, and not away from them, which would have been bad enough if what she stood to lose from such an event was her emotional and physical innocence—more than bad enough. But Eve stood to inherit a very sizeable sum of money from their parents' estate when she reached her twenty-fifth birthday, and Brough was convinced that Julian Cox would have no compunction whatsoever about marrying her simply for that reason alone.

Brough had had Julian's financial affairs thoroughly investigated. To describe them as in total disarray and bordering on the legally fraudulent was no exaggeration, nor was his emotional history any less murky. But, of course, Eve wouldn't hear a word against him. She considered herself to be in love.

'Oh, I'm so pleased. He was awfully upset this morning after you told him you really couldn't help him... That was mean of you,' she reproached Brough.

'On the contrary, it was simply good business sense,' Brough told her dryly. 'I know how you feel about him, Eve but...'

'Oh, Brough, please don't start lecturing me,' she begged him. 'Just because you don't want to fall in love...because you don't have someone to share your life with...someone special...that doesn't mean... I love him, Brough,' she said simply.

Brough sighed as she went upstairs. He wished he could find some way to protect her from the ultimate inevitability of having her heart broken, but he suspected that even if he were to confront her with incontrovertible evidence of Cox's real nature she would simply close her eyes to it.

Women! There was no way of understanding how their minds and, even more, their emotions worked. Look at Kelly. A bright, intelligent, beautiful young woman who was apparently as oblivious to Cox's faults as his own sister. Not that he thought that Kelly's other choice of male was any better—but for very different reasons. Harry was quite obviously an extremely estimable young man, the kind of man whom he would have been only too pleased to see dating his *sister*, but, as a partner for a woman of Kelly's obviously feisty and quicksilver personality, surely a totally wrong choice. She needed a man who could match the quickness of her brain...who could appreciate the intelligence and artistry of her work...who could share the passion that he could sense ran so strongly through her at the very deepest level of her personality... A man who...

Abruptly he caught himself up.

Nothing he had experienced in his admittedly brief contact with Kelly had indicated that she had the kind of insecure, needy personality that would make her a natural victim for a man like Cox.

Eve, on the other hand, if he was honest, desperately needed to feel loved and secure, to have a partner who would incorporate into their adult relationship the kind of protective, emotional padding she had missed from the loss of their father and experienced in a different way at school. Eve needed a man who would treat her gently, a man with whom she could have the kind of relationship which he privately would find too unequal. The woman he loved would have to be his equal, his true partner in every aspect of their lives. There would have to be complete and total honesty and commitment between them, a deep, inner knowledge that they would be there for one another through their whole lives—he too had suffered from their parents' death, he acknowledged wryly.

And Eve was wrong about him not wanting to fall in

love…to marry. At the end of his present decade lay the watershed birthday of forty, comfortably in the distance as yet, but still there on the horizon. When he thought of himself as forty, it was not particularly pleasant to visualise himself still alone, uncommitted…childless… But the woman he married, the woman he loved…

Unbidden, the memory of how Kelly's lips had felt beneath his flooded his body, sharply reminding him that if a male's sexual responses were at their fastest and peak in his teens, then they could still react with a pretty forceful and demanding potent speed in his thirties— disconcertingly so.

The dichotomy he had sensed within Kelly at the ball which had so intrigued him had turned to a more personal sense of irritation this afternoon. Did she really think he was so lacking in intelligence…in awareness…that he couldn't see how alien to her personality her relationship with Julian was? What the hell was it about the man that led a woman like her to…? It was almost as though he held some kind of compulsive attraction for her or had some kind of hold over her.

In another age it might almost have been said that he had cast some kind of spell over her as she was beginning to do over him?

Kelly paused in the act of picking up her keys. In the close confines of the flat's small entrance hall she could smell the scent of her own perfume. Defensively she told herself that wearing it was simply second nature to her and meant nothing, had no dark, deep, psychological significance, that the fact that she was wearing it to, and for, a meeting with Brough Frobisher meant absolutely nothing at all.

She wasn't a woman who was overly fond of striking

make-up, nor strictly styled hair, but she did like the femininity of wearing her own special signature scent, even if normally she wore it in conjunction with jeans and a casual top.

Tonight, though, those jeans had been exchanged for a well-cut trouser suit—not for any other reason than the fact that wearing it automatically made her feel more businesslike. And that was, after all, exactly what this evening's meeting was all about—business. And as for that small spurt of sweet, sharp excitement she could feel dancing over her vulnerable nerve-endings, well, that was nothing more than the arousal of her professional curiosity.

Hartwell china always evoked special memories for her. It had been the Hartwell china she had seen on a visit to a stately home as a girl which had first awoken her interest in the design and manufacture of porcelain, and it had been the Hartwell factory where she had first had her actual hands-on experience of working on the physical aspect of copying the designer's artistry onto the china itself. And so it was only natural that she should feel this surge of excitement at the thought of seeing a piece which sounded as though it was extremely rare.

It didn't take her very long to drive to the address Brough had given her. Rye-on-Averton was only a relatively small and compact town, virtually untouched by any effects of the Industrial Revolution and still surrounded by the farmland which had surrounded it way, way back in the Middle Ages.

Parking her own car and getting out, Kelly carefully skirted the expensive gleaming Mercedes saloon car parked in the drive and climbed the three steps which led to the front door. Brough opened it for her virtually as soon as she rang the bell.

Unlike her, he was unexpectedly casually dressed in jeans and a soft cotton checked shirt.

The jeans, Kelly noticed as she responded to his non-verbal invitation to come into the house, somehow or other emphasised the lean length of his legs and the powerful strength of his thigh muscles.

As a part of her studies at university she had, for a term, attended a series of lectures and drawing classes on the human body, and whilst there had been required to sketch nudes, both male and female, but that experience was still no protection against either the images which inexplicably filled her thoughts or the guilty burn of colour which accompanied them.

What on earth was she doing, mentally envisaging Brough posing, modelling for a classical Greek statue? That kind of behaviour, those kinds of thoughts, simply were not her.

'It's this way,' Brough informed her, the cool, clipped sound of his voice breaking into the dangerous heat of her thoughts as he indicated one of the doorways off the hall.

The yellow paint in which the hallway was decorated made Kelly do a slight double-take, a fact which Brough obviously noticed because he commented dryly, 'Bilious, isn't it? Unfortunately its shock effect doesn't lessen with time.'

'You could always redecorate,' Kelly pointed out austerely, refusing to allow herself to feel any sympathy with him, even in the unfortunate colour of his walls.

'Not really. This house is only rented. I'm only living here until the one I've bought has been renovated.'

'Oh, so you've moved into the area permanently, then?'

Kelly berated herself furiously as the question slipped out, her curiosity getting the better of her, but to her relief Brough made totally the wrong connection between her question and its motivation as he responded even more dryly, 'Yes, we have, so I'm afraid you can't look to our removal from town as an easy way of removing my sister from your lover's life.'

'It isn't necessary for me to do any such thing,' Kelly denied furiously through gritted teeth, momentarily forgetting her allotted role.

'Eve believes he intends to marry her. How do you feel about that?' he challenged her.

'How do you feel about it?' Kelly sidetracked.

'He's a liar and a cheat and most probably guilty of financial fraud as well,' Brough told her bitingly. 'How the hell do you think I feel about it?'

'She's *your* sister.'

'Strange,' he continued softly, 'you don't look particularly surprised or shocked. Perhaps you *like* the idea of having a married lover, especially one whose wife is both extremely rich and extremely in love.'

'No. That's not...'

Immediately she realised what she was saying, Kelly stopped.

'That's not what?' Brough goaded her. 'Not what you want? He's *your* lover...'

'And Eve is *your* sister,' Kelly pointed out again quickly. 'My relationship with Julian is no one's business other than our own. If you dislike him so much, *disapprove* of him so much, why haven't you told Eve so?'

'She's too much in love to listen to me or to anyone

else. What *is* it you see in him? What possible attraction can he have for any woman when he...?'

'Why don't you ask Eve?' Kelly suggested.

Ridiculously, dangerously, she was actually starting to feel sorry for him. It was plain how worried he was about his sister, and with good reason, and it was equally plain that he felt helpless to do anything to alter the situation. Even so, she couldn't resist punishing him just a little, both for what he thought about her and what he had said...and done...

'It's obviously hard for a man to see just what it is about Julian that appeals to our sex. Perhaps you feel jealous of him.'

'Jealous...? Look, just because last night I *kissed* you, that doesn't mean—'

'I mean jealous because Eve loves him,' Kelly interrupted him shakily.

'You wanted me to look at this plate,' she reminded him, anxious to return their conversation to a much more businesslike footing.

'Yes. It's in here,' he told her, ushering her into a large, high-ceilinged room which was painted a particularly unpleasant shade of dull green.

'Hideous, isn't it?' he agreed, correctly interpreting her thoughts. 'The owner must be colour blind or worse. You should see the bedrooms; the one I'm occupying is painted a particularly repulsive shade of puce.'

'Puce...? I don't believe you,' Kelly protested. 'No one would paint a bedroom that colour.'

'If you want to see for yourself I'll show you afterwards...' Brough started to say, and then stopped to study Kelly's bright pink face with interest.

'Now there's an interesting conundrum,' he mused

sardonically. 'Why should a woman who openly admits that she is sleeping with another woman's boyfriend blush at the mere mention of a completely altruistic visit to another man's bedroom? It *was* my bedroom I was suggesting you view,' he added gently, 'not my bed...'

'I was *not* blushing,' Kelly protested. 'It's just...it's just...it's very warm in here...'

'Is it?' Brough asked, adding, 'Then what, may I ask, are these?'

Before she could stop him he was running a hard fingertip down the full length of her bare arm, right over the rash of goose bumps which had lifted beneath her skin when they'd entered the room's unheated atmosphere. And what made it worse was that the brief and totally sexless stroke of his finger had made the goose bumps even more prominent—and not just her goose bumps, she acknowledged, mortified by the unwanted discovery that her nipples were inexplicably pressing very hard, tightly aroused, against the constraining fabric of her bra.

Instinctively she turned away from him, lifting her arm in what she hoped was a natural and subtle gesture which he wouldn't guess was designed to conceal the evidence of her body's extraordinary behaviour from him.

He had seen it, though, seen it and been both disgusted and angered by it, she recognised, if the look she could see in his eyes was anything to go by.

My God, but she had got it badly if even the mere fact of talking about Cox could arouse her body like that, Brough fumed as Kelly turned her flushed face and aroused breasts out of his eye-line.

It had been bad enough when he had simply wanted to protect and rescue his sister from the man, but now...

'The plate's over here,' he told Kelly curtly.

Silently she followed him, keeping her distance from him as he unlocked the small corner cupboard and removed the plate, but as he walked over to her and she saw it she couldn't resist giving a small cry of pleasure, closing the distance between them so that she could take the plate from him and study it more closely.

'Oh, it's beautiful,' she enthused as she traced the design lovingly with her fingertip. 'Almost Sèvres in style and execution...'

'Yes, that's what they said at the factory. They suspect that the whole set might have been a showpiece set made by a particularly gifted apprentice. Apparently, when they finished their time in apprenticeship the artists were often given the opportunity to do something to act as a showcase for their skills.'

'Yes, I know,' Kelly agreed absently, barely able to take her glance off the plate. 'Oh, it's lovely—so detailed and intricate.'

She stopped and shook her head.

'What's wrong? Don't you think you can copy it?' Brough asked her.

Kelly paused.

'I don't know,' she admitted. 'It's very complex, and the gold leaf work alone would be so expensive in materials... I... Can't Hartwell recommend anyone else to do it for you, someone more experienced?'

Brough gave her a level look.

'According to them there *isn't* anyone more experienced,' he told her quietly.

To her annoyance Kelly knew that she was blushing again.

'I... I... It's very kind of them to say so, but...'

'They also told me that you turned down a very lucrative and secure contract with them to go into business by yourself.'

'I...I like being my own boss,' Kelly told him quietly.

'Even though it doesn't pay you anything like as well as working for them would have done...?'

'Money isn't that important to me,' Kelly admitted after a small pause. There followed a very stiff, very pregnant silence during which Kelly recognised that she had said something wrong, but was not sure what.

'I suppose you don't agree with that kind of outlook at all,' she challenged him when the silence had made her skin start to prickle. 'I expect *you* feel that when a person doesn't exploit their...talents to the best possible financial advantage, then—'

'On the contrary,' Brough interrupted her firmly. '*I* feel extremely sorry for anyone who feels obliged to accept a way of life, a means of living, that doesn't make them happy.'

'But you can't believe that earning money isn't of prime importance to me,' Kelly insisted.

'What I can't believe is that a woman holding the views you've just expressed would in any way consider a man like Julian Cox to be a good partner for her,' Brough corrected her.

'I...I didn't come here to discuss my relationship with Julian,' Kelly told him tautly, handing the plate back to him as she did so, giving it a last lingering look of regret. There was nothing she would have loved more than to copy the design and replace the missing pieces of the teaset, especially under the circumstances Brough had outlined to her. But she couldn't do anything that would bring her into closer contact with him. There was too much risk involved in far too many different ways.

But before she could vocalise her decision, Brough

himself was speaking, telling her coolly, 'We don't have much time left before my grandmother's birthday, so I've arranged for us to visit the factory on Wednesday. They told me when I was there that you'd need to collect the unpainted china from them and get supplies of paint.'

'Wednesday? But it's Monday today; I can't possibly…' Kelly began.

But he was already overruling her, telling her, 'I know what you're going to say and I've asked Eve if she will stand in at the shop for you for the day. She's agreed. And before you say anything you needn't worry-she did a stint at Harvey Nicks during her last year at school.'

'Harvey Nicks?' Kelly exploded, adding pointedly, 'This isn't Knightsbridge…'

'No, it isn't,' he agreed. 'We'll need to get a pretty early start, so if I pick you up at, say, eight I can drop Eve off at the same time.'

'Just a minute,' Kelly objected. 'I haven't agreed that I'm going—'

'What's wrong? Are you afraid that Cox might object to you spending the day with me?'

'This has *nothing* to do with Julian,' Kelly told him angrily.

'Good. So I'll pick you up at eight on Wednesday, then,' Brough repeated cordially as he walked over to the door and held it open for her.

There was no way she was going to be able to make him understand that she wasn't going to Staffordshire with him, Kelly recognised, irritably marching straight past him and heading for the front door, where he caught up with her and commented dulcetly, 'I take it you've decided to accept my word about the colour of my bedroom walls…'

Kelly shot him a fulminating look. 'The colour of your bedroom walls, be they puce, chartreuse or vermilion, is totally and absolutely of no interest to me,' she told him.

'Vermilion,' Brough mused. 'The colour of passion. Interesting that you should suggest it…'

'*Suggest* it? I did no such thing.' Kelly seethed. 'What do you think you're *doing*?' she demanded as, instead of opening the front door, he very gently and totally unexpectedly placed his hands on her upper arms and turned her round.

'I'm going to make you a cup of cocoa before you go home,' he told her, adding suavely, 'It warms the blood and soothes the passions. The Aztecs used to believe it had aphrodisiac powers, as did the Regency bucks. There's no point in you rushing back. Julian is out with Eve.'

'What's that got to do with me? I've got a deskful of paperwork needing attention, and anyway, I *loathe* cocoa,' she told him pettishly.

'A glass of wine perhaps, then,' he suggested.

Kelly started to shake her head, and then for some reason found that she was nodding it slowly instead.

'This way,' he told her, directing her further down the hallway and into another room, which was a cross between an office and a study, comfortably furnished with a couple of deep armchairs and a huge desk which dominated the space in front of the window.

'For Christmas the year before last, Eve rented for me a row of vines in France. The idea is that you get the wine from your own vines and you can, if you wish, take part in some of the preparation of the wine. Surprisingly, it's rather good…'

'So you'll what?' Kelly asked him. 'Buy the vine-yard?'

An unexpected smile tugged at the corners of his mouth.

'Not this particular one,' he admitted. 'But it's certainly an idea. I wouldn't have an objection to a life of viticulture and semi-retirement... Tuscany, perhaps, close to one of those unbelievably visually breathtaking medieval towns...'

'It sounds idyllic,' Kelly responded enviously, without thinking, and then bit her lip, telling him curtly, 'Look, I really can't stay. Paperwork isn't really my strong suit and...'

'I understand,' Brough accepted. His face was in the shadows but there was no mistaking the stiffness in his voice. Quite patently he was angry with her again, Kelly decided, suppressing a soft sigh. So why should she care either what he thought or what he felt? This time, as she headed for the front door, he made no attempt to persuade her to stay, simply opening it for her and formally thanking her for her time.

As he watched her until she was safely inside the car, Brough wondered what on earth had possessed him to reveal that long-held dream of his to her. What possible interest could it be to her, and, more disturbingly, why should he want it to be?

She was an enigma, a puzzle of unfathomable proportions, and he was a fool for even beginning to think what he was thinking about her.

As he went upstairs and switched on the light in his puce-walled bedroom, his glance rested on the neat white line of his bed. He had been lying when he had told her that it was his bedroom he had been inviting her to see and not his bed. Already, with remarkably little effort at all, he could picture her lying there in it, tucked securely beneath its protective sheets as they outlined the warm curves of her body, holding out an invitation which she mirrored as she held out her arms to welcome him.

Eve hadn't had a good night. She and Julian had had an argument, a small altercation which had blown up out of virtually nothing, simply her innocent comment that Kelly was a very attractive and vivacious woman and that she and Julian were obviously very good friends. But Julian had reacted as though she had accused him of some crime, exploding into a rage so intense that he had actually frightened her.

Shocked and in tears, she had run from his flat, ignoring his demands to her to come back as she'd fired the engine of her car, and here she was now, her car parked in the town centre as she walked unhappily along the riverbank, desperately trying to avoid looking at the entwined pairs of lovers enjoying a romantic stroll along the river path.

'Eve... Eve...'

Instinctively, she stopped as she heard the male voice calling her name, her breath catching in her throat as she recognised Harry hurrying towards her.

'I saw you as I walked over the bridge,' Harry told her with a warm beam as he indicated the bridge she had just passed, his smile fading as he saw her miserable expression. 'What is it? What's wrong?'

'Nothing,' Eve fibbed, but his concern, his sympathy and most of all his sturdy male warmth and reassurance were too much for her already shaky composure, and as she spoke she gave a small hiccuping sob and a tear ran betrayingly down her face.

'It's Cox, isn't it?' Harry guessed, revealing an intuition which would have surprised his relatives, who considered him to be good hearted enough but a trifle lacking in anything requiring mental agility and speed.

'We've had a row,' Eve admitted, immediately adding protectively, 'It was my fault. I...I mentioned Kelly and that made him angry... I shouldn't have brought up the subject. Of course he's entitled to his past and to...'

She stopped as Harry gave a fierce snort of disapproval.

'Of course you're upset,' he comforted her. 'You've every right to be, especially after the way...'

'He was flirting a little with Kelly at the ball,' Eve agreed, guessing what he was going to say. 'But I know that they're old friends and Julian is such an attractive man...'

Harry gave another snort.

'Oh, I know that you probably don't like him. After all, Kelly is your girlfriend.'

'No, she isn't,' Harry told her promptly. 'I don't have a girlfriend...haven't ever really wanted one until... I escorted Kelly because my cousin asked me to...'

'Oh, I see. So you aren't actually going out with Kelly, then?' Eve asked him ingenuously.

Harry shook his head. 'Nice girl but not my type,' he told her.

Inexplicably, as they walked, Eve discovered that she had moved so close to Harry that when they had to pass another couple it seemed the most natural thing in the world for him to shield her protectively by placing his arm around her.

It was very pleasant to be treated as though she was so fragile, so vulnerable and valuable, Eve acknowledged. It made her feel very safe and very protected...

It made her feel happy. Nothing like as happy as she was with Julian, of course, she decided loyally as Harry gently drew her into the protection of a small grove of trees just off the river path.

'Now look,' he told her firmly, 'you mustn't let Cox upset you. He's damn lucky to have a lovely girl like you...damn lucky...'

'Oh, Harry, *I'm* the one who's lucky,' Eve corrected him. 'I'm just plain and ordinary, but Julian...'

'You're no such thing' Harry contradicted her immediately. 'You're beautiful, Eve,' he told her huskily as he looked at her mouth. 'Thought so the moment I saw you...'

An odd quiver of sensation ran right through her body as she recognised the way Harry was looking at her mouth. She might be naive, as she was constantly being told, but she wasn't *that* naive. She was woman enough to know when a man wanted her all right...and when one didn't.

Julian hadn't wanted her tonight. He had pushed her away when she had tried to snuggle into his arms.

'Harry,' she whispered huskily.

'Don't look at me like that, Eve,' he groaned, adding gruffly, 'I want to kiss you so damn much... In fact, I'm *going* to kiss you,' he announced boldly.

Going into Harry's arms was like going home, Eve decided blissfully, all warm and cosy and safe. Happily she turned her face up to his and waited.

She didn't have to wait very long.

His kiss was everything she had known it would be— gentle, reverential, asking, not taking; and it was something more as well, something entirely unexpected and exciting, she recognised as the tiny quivers darting through her body began to grow and gather strength.

'I shouldn't have done that,' Harry told her harshly as he suddenly pushed her away. 'In fact...'

Without saying anything more he turned his back on her and started to walk very quickly away from her.

Feeling as though she had been completely abandoned, Eve stared after him. *Why* had he left her like that? Had he lied to her about not being involved with Kelly? She knew instinctively that Julian had done so when he had told her that Kelly meant absolutely nothing to him. She wasn't completely blind. She had seen the way Julian had been watching Kelly at the ball, but she loved Julian so much...far too much to give him up... Far, far too much to enjoy kissing another man... Hot-cheeked, she pressed her hands to her face. What on earth had she been doing? And why?

It was no wonder, really, that Julian had been so out of sorts and cross, she decided compassionately as she made her way back to her car. It had been a big disappointment for him, poor darling, when Brough had refused to finance his new venture.

She had tried to tell him tonight that she had absolutely no influence at all over Brough's decision, and then he had started to ask her about her own inheritance and she had had to tell him that she couldn't touch a penny of it until she was twenty-five.

'That's four years away,' he had exploded irritably. 'What happens if we get married and you need some money to buy a house?'

If they got married...

'I don't know,' she had confessed, adding brightly, 'Maybe the bank would lend me some money against it... I'd have to check with Brough...'

'No! No, don't do that,' Julian had told her hastily.

'Yes, because when we get married I shall move in

here with you, won't I?' she had agreed, blissfully trying to snuggle up against him.

'Yeah...' he had said so unenthusiastically that she had started to frown.

It was then that she had made her first mistake, asking him uncertainly, 'You *do* want to marry me, don't you, Julian? Only I couldn't help noticing at the ball that you seemed awfully interested in Kelly...'

'Kelly's an old friend,' he had told her angrily. 'Not that it's any business of yours...'

Poor darling, of course he was irritable and on edge with all the money worries he was having. It really was too bad of Brough to refuse to help him. Eve's brow creased. She knew, of course, that her brother didn't really like or approve of Julian, but he didn't *know* him the way she did.

CHAPTER SIX

'HI, KELLY, it's Dee.'

Kelly smiled as she recognised their landlady's voice. It was eleven o'clock in the morning and Kelly had just served her third customer and put on the kettle to make herself a cup of coffee.

'Anything to report?' Dee asked her. 'Has Julian been in touch?'

'He rang yesterday,' Kelly told her, 'but I couldn't really talk to him; I had someone here in the shop. You know that Julian is hoping to persuade his girlfriend's brother to finance some new venture he's getting started?'

'*Was* hoping,' Dee corrected her wryly. 'Brough has turned him down.'

How did Dee know that? Kelly wondered curiously.

'Look, we could do with having a meeting,' Dee told her. 'How about lunch tomorrow?'

'Tomorrow? No, I'm afraid I can't,' Kelly told her. 'I'm going to Staffordshire.'

'Staffordshire?' Dee queried sharply. 'On a buying trip? But I thought...'

'No, not that. Actually I'm going with Brough; he's asked me to undertake a private commission for him.'

'And you've agreed?' Dee asked her. 'Be very careful, Kelly. Don't forget his sister is dating Julian and hopes to marry him and he's bound to be extremely suspicious of your role in Julian's life. You haven't told him the truth, have you?' Dee demanded.

'No, of course I haven't,' Kelly reassured her immediately.

'Well, you mustn't. It would ruin everything.'

'I'm not a complete fool, you know, Dee,' Kelly informed her a little irritably. She liked Dee, but sometimes her autocratic attitude irritated her a bit. She wasn't like Beth, who accepted Dee's slight bossiness with placid gentleness even whilst she accepted that the older girl's heart was in the right place and her motives good.

'No, not a complete fool,' Dee agreed dryly, 'but certainly foolish enough to agree to go to Staffordshire with Brough. I understand he's a very attractive man,' she added slyly.

'Not so far as I'm concerned,' Kelly responded immediately, 'but the china he wants me to copy certainly is and, not only that, it's extremely rare and may even be unique. It's a wonderful opportunity, Dee,' she added, warming to her theme, her enthusiasm for the project colouring her voice. 'An almost once-in-a-lifetime chance to work on something very different and very special.

'Oh, Beth rang, by the way,' Kelly informed Dee. 'She's having problems with her interpreter, apparently, but she never said a word about Julian, thank goodness.'

'That *is* good news,' Dee agreed.

'I do feel worried for Eve Frobisher,' Kelly told her.

'You must concentrate on the business in hand,' Dee advised her. 'Eve Frobisher has her brother to protect her interests. Has he said anything about Julian to you, by the way?'

'He's certainly made it plain that he doesn't approve of my relationship with him,' Kelly informed her.

'Mmm... You know, I've been thinking... It could

work to our advantage if you let him think that he might be able to persuade you to have second thoughts about Julian. Men love that feeling that they're taking charge, doling out advice to some poor, helpless little female. It feeds their egos, and it wouldn't do any harm to get Brough Frobisher on our side.'

'He isn't going to fall for any "helpless little me' act from me, Dee,' Kelly informed her.

'You don't know until you try it,' Dee told her persuasively. 'There's no saying what helpful information we could pick up about Julian's business affairs via him if he—'

'I *don't* know, because there's no way I am going to try it.' Kelly cut across her comment swiftly. 'Tricking Julian into believing I find him attractive is one thing, lying to Brough is quite another...'

'It is? Why?' Dee asked her interestedly.

'Because I don't like lying to anyone,' Kelly told her sharply. 'The only reason I've agreed to deceive Julian is because of what he did to Beth and to stop him from doing it to anyone else. Persuading Brough to believe that I'm some kind of helpless little creature who needs protecting and rescuing from her own emotions, who can't take responsibility for her own life or her own actions, is just so gross that there's no way I would even contemplate it. Besides, he wouldn't believe me. He'd see through what I was trying to do immediately.'

'He knows you that well after spending...how long...a few hours or so with you, does he?' Dee mused. 'Amazing...'

'He believes that I'm intent on trying to take Julian away from his sister. Let's just leave it at that whilst we're ahead of the game, shall we?' Kelly told her curtly, ignoring her gentle jibe.

'Okay,' Dee soothed her, adding, 'Look, I need to have a word with Anna about her making contact with Julian to offer to lend him the money he needs for this new venture. Now that Brough has turned him down he's going to be too urgently in need of financial backing to question Anna's motivation too deeply, which suits us very nicely. Brough has unwittingly done us a very big favour in turning Julian down.'

'I'm sure he'd be delighted to hear that,' Kelly told her *sotto voce.*

'Oh, by the way, Harry sends his best love,' Dee told her teasingly. Kelly grimaced into the receiver.

'He does?' she questioned, unable to resist the temptation to tell Dee dryly, 'That's odd; he seemed far more interested in Eve at the ball than he was in me. Now there's a match. The pair of them are so well suited they might have been made for one another.'

'Eve loves Julian,' Dee pointed out to her.

'No, what she loves is the man she believes that Julian is,' Kelly corrected her soberly. 'Poor girl, he's going to break her heart.'

'Well, if you're right, Harry will be more than willing to help her to mend it,' Dee told her practically. 'Remember, Kelly, you've got to convince Julian that you want him; that way when you drop him as publicly as he dropped Beth he'll never even guess what's going to happen until it does and…'

'I'm not sure that he'll leave Eve for me,' Kelly warned her. 'Eve believes that he's going to marry her…'

'So did Beth and look what happened to her,' Dee pointed out. 'He's going to be furious when he finds out how we've tricked him, furious and totally and completely humiliated,' she said cheerfully. 'And it couldn't happen to a more deserving man.'

'You really hate him, don't you?' Kelly recognised.

'Yes. I really hate him,' Dee agreed, and she put the receiver down. Kelly thought she heard her saying, But nowhere near as much as I hate myself, but she couldn't be sure, and anyway it was too late to question Dee any further since she had hung up.

Wednesday morning came round too soon. Kelly was awake early—too early, she decided as she watched the sun rise.

It still wasn't too late to refuse to go to Staffordshire but what excuse could she realistically give?

Impossible to tell Brough the truth—that she was afraid of going with him, afraid of what she might say, of what he might guess...of what she might feel... But if she didn't go...

Julian had rung her again last night. Reluctantly she had agreed to meet him for a drink at a local wine bar this evening.

'Julian, you're dating someone else,' she had reminded him coldly, 'and so am I...'

'Harry,' he had scoffed. 'He's no match, no man for a woman like you, Kelly.'

'And I suppose that you are,' she had taunted him, holding her breath at the recklessness of what she was doing.

'Try me,' he had told her, sniggering suggestively. 'I promise you, you won't be disappointed.'

Kelly had been glad that the telephone meant he couldn't see the shudder of revulsion she gave.

'You and I are two of a kind, Kelly,' he had told her thickly. 'We take what we want from life. We're both adventurers, exciting…passionate… I knew that the first time I saw you. I knew then how good we'd be together…'

'When you were dating Beth, you mean,' Kelly had reminded him coldly.

'Beth is history,' he'd told her dismissively. 'But you and I…you and I are *now*, Kelly…'

'You and I are *nothing*,' she had told him.

'Tomorrow night,' Julian had countered. 'Be there, Kelly… You know you want me and I sure as hell want you…'

Want him? Completely revolted both by his conversation and his tone of voice, Kelly had replaced the receiver.

She could just imagine what Brough would have to say.

Brough.

Now why on earth was she thinking about him? she asked herself pointedly as her alarm started to ring. He was almost as bad as Julian Cox, although in a completely different way, of course. He had, after all, misjudged her just as badly.

Eve smiled tentatively at Kelly as Kelly opened the door to her and Brough and they stepped into the shop.

'I'll just run through a few things with you before we leave,' Kelly told her reassuringly. 'Wednesday isn't normally a very busy day so you should be okay, but if you do have any problems—

'You've got my mobile number, haven't you, Eve?' Brough interrupted Kelly. 'Any problems and you can get in touch with Kelly on that.'

'Thank you, but I have my *own* mobile, Brough,' Kelly told him frostily.

'What I was going to say, Eve, is that I've left you the number of our landlady, Dee. She knows that you'll be working here and she may very well call in to check if everything's okay. She can be a bit daunting, but she's really very kind... She's Harry's cousin,' she added, and then stopped as Eve suddenly went bright red.

'I...I saw him Harry the other day when I was walking along the river,' Eve blurted out. 'I...I don't know if he mentioned it, but...'

'No. No, he didn't,' Kelly told her, before adding gently, 'But then, there's really no reason why he should...'

'No. No, of course not,' Eve told her quickly. 'I just meant... Well, I just thought...'

'We really ought to leave,' Brough informed Kelly, frowning slightly as he glanced at his watch. 'The motorway is bound to be busy.'

'I think it's wonderful what you're doing,' Eve told Kelly admiringly. 'I'd love to have that kind of talent,' she added wistfully.

'It's more of a learned skill than a natural talent,' Kelly told her wryly. 'I was just lucky enough to be in the right place to learn it at the right time, and besides, I haven't actually done anything yet.'

'No, but Brough says...' Eve stopped and glanced anxiously at her brother.

What had Brough said? Kelly wondered curiously ten minutes later as he opened the passenger door of his car for her and helped her inside.

She could always ask him, of course. Perhaps later on she would.

The Potteries where the factory was based wasn't too far up the motorway, but Kelly was still feeling extremely apprehensive about the journey. What if Brough used it as an opportunity to take her to task about her relationship with Julian? If he did, then she would just have to remind him ~~again~~ that it was none of his business, she told herself firmly as she leaned back in her seat and very deliberately closed her eyes, hoping that he would correctly interpret this as a sign that she didn't wish to talk.

Unfortunately, though, the subtleties of her body language appeared to be lost on him because almost immediately he asked her, 'Tired? I'm sorry we had to have such an early start. We should be able to stop for a short break and a cup of coffee before too long, though.'

He made it sound as though he was taking his ancient maiden aunt out for a Sunday drive, Kelly decided wrathfully, immediately sitting bolt upright in her seat and denying fiercely, 'No, I am not tired, and neither am I unable to travel a distance of less than a couple of hundred miles without the necessity of a comfort stop.'

She used the American phrase very deliberately and pointedly, underlining her comment by adding, 'I'm twenty-four, not seventy-four...'

'I, on the other hand, am thirty-four,' he told her gently, 'and *I* prefer to take life at a reasonably relaxed pace.'

Kelly gave him a surprised look. This was not the sort of comment she expected to hear from a man who had built up a business as successful as Brough's was.

'My parents died in their late thirties,' he told her tersely. 'They were killed in a plane crash. My father had been trying to get to Switzerland for an urgent business meeting and, being unable to get a scheduled flight in time, he'd hired a private plane. They got caught in a bad storm ~~and~~ that was that.

'Afterwards, I made a vow to myself, a promise that I'd never forget that there was far more to life than meetings, deadlines, and making money. I was nineteen when they were killed, just an adult. Eve was six.'

Only nineteen. Kelly swallowed hard on the large knot of compassion which had lodged in her throat.

'What about you? Do you have any family?' he asked her.

'A brother who lives in South Africa with his wife and their three children. My father took early retirement and my parents normally spend the winter months in South Africa with Jamie and his family and summer at home in Scotland.'

'You're not from Rye-on-Averton? What brought you there?'

'Beth, my partner. Her godmother lives in the town and she suggested to Beth that there was an excellent business opportunity for us there. She was quite right. The shop is beginning to pick up well, and I've had several commissions, but, best of all, the way we divide things between us leaves me enough time to work on my own designs and to accept freelance stuff as well.'

'All in all, a good partnership.'

'Yes, it is,' Kelly agreed tersely. She didn't want Brough to start asking her too many questions about Beth. She had no idea whether or not he knew that Julian had been on the point of getting engaged to Beth when Eve had come into his life, and she could well imagine just what kind of assumptions Brough would make.

Unnervingly, though, he seemed to follow the direction of her thoughts because he suddenly said, 'You've said that Cox is an old friend of yours, but I get the impression from what you've just told me that your business hasn't been established very long.'

'Our accountant told us when we first started that it took three years to establish whether or not a business was going to succeed,' Kelly responded cagily.

She hated having to behave like this, she admitted. According to her family, one of her faults was that she was, at times, almost painfully honest. Prevarication of any kind was anathema to her. So why on earth had she ever allowed Dee to persuade her to adopt a role which even one minute's reflection would have told her was going to be so alien to her that it would be almost impossible to sustain? Because Dee had caught her at a weak and emotional moment, that was why.

Dee, as Kelly was fast coming to appreciate, possessed the dual gift of a very shrewd insight into people's weak points plus an ability to turn them to her own advantage. Not that she could help liking the other woman. She was, intrinsically, a very nice person. Kelly was well aware of the fact that the rent they were being charged was far less than the going amount Dee could have asked for for such a prime site, and then there had been all those little extras she had thrown in. Her concern for them had been almost sisterly and protective in many ways, and Kelly knew that they would never have made the progress they had made without Dee's help, both overt and covert. She had lost count, for instance, of the number of people who had come into the shop commenting that Dee had recommended it to them.

But that still didn't absolve her from the fact that she had deliberately used a moment of weakness to persuade Kelly into a deceit which was becoming, hourly, more stressful to maintain.

Desperate to change the subject, she asked Brough, 'Do you manage to see much of your grandmother?'

'Not as much as I'd like,' Brough admitted. 'Either

Eve or I try to get down to see her at least once a month. As it happens, we're going down the weekend after next; if you'd care to come with us you'd be more than welcome. In fact, it might actually be a good idea; that way you could see the teaset *in situ*, so to speak.'

Go with them…on a family visit…to see his grandmother?

Kelly opened her mouth and then closed it again.

'Oh, I couldn't,' she protested finally. 'There's…'

'The shop; I know,' Brough responded for her.

Had she imagined it or had that really been a note of almost cynical irony in his voice as he shot her a brief sideways glance?

It was impossible… *Anna would always stand in for you…* Hurriedly she closed her mind to the tempting little voice that was reminding her that Anna had made a point of telling her that she was more than willing to take charge of the shop during Beth's absence should Kelly want some time off.

And Brough was right in saying that it would be helpful for her to see the whole of the teaset—when she would already have had the benefit of the archivist's records.

No. No. It was completely impossible, and besides, Brough was quite obviously relieved that she hadn't accepted his invitation, because he had made no attempt to press the matter or persuade her to re-think her decision.

'The last time I drove up here I found a decent pub in a village just off the motorway at the next turn-off. Unlike you, I'm afraid I do need the odd "comfort stop",' he informed her dryly as he swung the car over from the fast lane of the motorway.

Rural Warwickshire was a part of the country with

which Kelly was relatively unfamiliar, and she couldn't quite suppress a small gasp of pleasure as they left the motorway access roundabout and Brough took an exit onto a pretty country road. Farmland stretched to either side of them, and in the distance Kelly could see the gleam of water where a river made its way between tree-lined banks.

The village, which lay concealed just beyond the brow of the hill, was reached via a meandering road which wound down to a cluster of cottages, some of which were thatched, set around a tranquil duck pond.

'Good heavens,' Kelly marvelled as Brough drove in under an archway to the rear of a pub which could quite easily have featured in a film set for a Dickens novel. 'Why on earth isn't this place swamped with tourists? It's almost too perfect...'

'It's an estate village,' Brough explained. 'Originally all the houses, like the land, were owned by the same family, but apparently when the last Earl died the new one, his grandson, decided to sell off the houses, but only to tenants who had family connections with the village.'

The pub was as quaint inside as it looked outside, and there was even a large marmalade cat sitting on an arm-chair in front of the empty fire.

The coffee room was cosy and prettily furnished, with windows overlooking a paved patio area filled with tubs of flowers.

When the coffee came, it arrived in a large cafetière with, Kelly noted with approval, a choice of both milk and cream—proper milk and proper cream in jugs, not fiddly little plastic containers—and there were even crisp, deliciously scented cinnamon biscuits to go with it.

As she poured herself a cup, Kelly couldn't help but notice how pleasantly Brough spoke to the waitress who had brought in the coffee for them, his manner exactly right, and she was not surprised when the girl gave him a genuinely warm smile before she left.

Kelly had only eaten out with Julian once when, by accident, she had bumped into him and Beth at a local wine bar and he had insisted on her joining them. His attitude then towards the young boy serving them had made her cringe with embarrassment and anger, and she had been unable to look Beth in the eye as she'd wondered how on earth she managed to put up with Julian's arrogant, overbearing attitude.

Kelly might be a thoroughly modern woman, but she still believed that there was a place and a need in her modern world for good manners from both sexes, and she couldn't help feeling not just a warm sense of approval for Brough's behaviour but, far more alarmingly, an additional feeling of pleasure and female pride at being with him and guessing that the waitress thought she was fortunate to be accompanied by him.

'More coffee?' Brough asked her ten minutes later when she had finished her first cup. Regretfully, Kelly shook her head. From the window she could see the river and the pathway that lay enticingly alongside it and, as though he had guessed what she was thinking, Brough commented, 'I thought we could stop here on the way back, perhaps have a bite to eat and a walk round the village, if that appeals to you.'

What could Kelly say? After his earlier display of good manners, the last thing she wanted to do was to appear gauche and ill-mannered by refusing such a pleasantly phrased invitation. It surprised her a little to discover how much she was enjoying this unexpected state of harmony which had arisen between them. When he was not cross-questioning her about Julian Cox, Brough could be very relaxing to be with.

Relaxing...? Who on earth was she kidding? Kelly asked herself a little grimly five minutes later as she checked her appearance in the ladies' cloakroom and reapplied her lipstick. If she was so relaxed then what, pray, were those goose feathers, those distinctive flutters of sensation she could feel giddying around inside her? Those sharp little darts of sensation, of reaction and warning, which kept zipping along her nervous system. If this was relaxed then she would hate to know how it felt to be really on edge in the presence of the man, she derided herself mockingly.

Admit it, she cautioned herself as she replaced the top on her lipstick, he's one very sexy man! So what? She had met sexy men before.

Met them, yes, but reacted to them in the way she was reacting to Brough, no! This was crazy, she told herself sternly. She didn't even like him. Look at how angry he had made her... Look at the things he had said to her...done to her... That kiss for instance...

Hastily Kelly looked away from the mirror and the sudden unexpected pout of her freshly lipsticked mouth.

'Okay?' Brough asked her when she rejoined him in the coffee room. The smile he gave her did uncomfortable things to her heart, causing it to somersault upwards, forwards and then backwards, leaving her breathless and slightly flushed.

'Fine,' she told him crisply, adding in a voice that was designed to show him that so far as she was concerned this was simply a business exercise and that the only thing on her mind was business, 'How long will it take us to get there?'

'Not much longer now,' Brough answered her as they made their way back to the car.

Their destination was familiar to Kelly from the time she had worked there, and as the factory gates came in sight a small, slightly rueful half-tender smile curled her mouth as she reflected on the nervous excitement of the girl she had been when she had first walked through that entrance.

'Nothing ever quite approximates the feeling of earning one's first wage packet, does it?' Brough asked her softly as they drove through the gates. 'I can remember just exactly how it felt to hold *my* first paper-round money in my hand...'

As they shared a look of mutually amused laughter his expression suddenly changed, sobering and clouding slightly.

'It concerns and grieves me that so many of our young people today will never experience the sense of self-esteem earning one's own money brings. We're in danger of creating a society of "haves" and "have nots", not merely in the material sense but in the sense of *owning* one's self-respect and self-worth which, so far as I am concerned, is almost as basic a human need as our need for air to breathe and food to eat. Like love, a strong sense of self cannot be quantified, analysed or bought, but without it our lives are empty and unfulfilled.'

His thoughts, so in tune with her own, made Kelly shiver a little as his words touched a chord within her.

It left her feeling dizzy, disorientated, as though she had somehow strayed off her normal familiar terrain, the feeling both exhilarating and frightening. The thought of what might have been had things been different trembled through her mind. That kind of bond was so rare, so precious, so...so unthinkable and impossible, she warned herself as Brough parked the car and told her mundanely, 'We're here.'

CHAPTER SEVEN

'YOU'RE very quiet. Not having second thoughts, I hope.'

They were on their way back to Rye-on-Averton, the original late-morning meeting with the archivist having turned into a full tour of the factory in addition to an inspection of its archive records, followed by an early dinner as the archivist, delighted to find a fellow enthusiast, had insisted on showing them both some examples of some of the company's rarest pieces as well as advising Kelly on just how she might best mix and colour her paints to achieve an authentic antique tone.

'Not second thoughts about wanting to do the work, just worrying about getting the paint right,' Kelly told him ruefully.

'Mmm…I must admit I hadn't realised that modern paint colours wouldn't be suitable,' Brough acknowledged. 'It's certainly a fascinating and complex business.'

'Yes,' Kelly agreed. 'I thought I knew most of what there was to know about the history of British porcelain, but listening to Frank today I realise just how wrong I was and how little I do know.'

'Mmm…I could see how thrilled he was to be able to talk with you.'

'Well, he certainly couldn't have been more helpful. But, as he says, there really isn't any substitute for seeing the rest of the teaset at first hand for ensuring that I get the colour matches right.'

'It isn't too late to change your mind about coming with us on our next visit,' Brough said.

'I...I'll have to think about it...' Kelly told him.

The evening was already turning to dusk. They had left Staffordshire just before eight o'clock. Frank Bowers had insisted on taking them out to dinner and Brough had taken her to one side after Frank had delivered his half-hesitant invitation, to say quietly to her, 'If it doesn't conflict with any other plans you may have made, I think we should accept. He's plainly enjoyed the opportunity to talk about his work-and I know we did talk about stopping off at the Lion and Swan for a meal and a walk along the river on the way back, but I should hate to disappoint Frank...'

'I agree,' Kelly had responded instantly, and they'd both returned to where Frank was putting away the company records.

'Yes, I understand you'll need to think about the weekend visit,' Brough was telling her cordially now as he swung the car out into the fast lane of the motorway. 'I should hate to interfere with any private plans you might have.'

It was the emphasis on the word 'private' that made Kelly glance warily at him. Was he trying to insinuate that he suspected her of hesitating in accepting the invitation to visit his grandmother because she was either planning to see Julian Cox or hoping to see him? It seemed that, with their return to Rye-on-Averton imminent, the cessation of hostilities between them was over.

Very well, if that was the way he wanted things, she decided hardly, suppressing the unwanted quiver of disappointment that sharpened almost to an actual pang of pain.

'I'm not sure just what you're trying to suggest,' she told him frostily, 'but the *main* reason I can't give you a yes or a no at this stage is because I need to find someone to take charge of the shop for me. *You* may be able to walk away from your business commitments for a whole weekend—I'm afraid that I can't.'

'I'm sorry,' Brough returned equally formally and coolly. 'Forgive me, but I had assumed that since this commission *was* business...'

Immediately hot colour burned a mortified flush up her throat and over her face.

'I realise that,' she retorted stiffly, and of course she did, even if very briefly earlier in the day she had momentarily forgotten.

But, in truth, hadn't there been a few brief but oh, so telling occasions during the day when the sharp line that in the past had always divided her professional life from her personal one had become dangerously blurred—when she had looked at Brough, compelled to do so by something he had said, only to find that it was not the client she was seeing but the man?

And what a man!

Kelly groaned in dismay, lashed by a delicate shiver of sexual awareness. This wasn't what she wanted, what she needed in her life right now.

Her reaction to Brough would have unnerved her even without the added complication of the situation with Julian Cox. When she added to that the already highly combustible mixture of anger and attraction she felt towards Brough, the dangerous extra ingredient of emotional awareness and longing she was confronted with became a potentially lethal cocktail which she knew could destroy her if she wasn't careful. After all, put together all those ingredients and the result was as dangerous as some magical, mystical sorcerer's potion, because the result was quite simply love. And Brough was the last person she could ever allow herself to love. He didn't like her now, so what on earth was he going to feel about her when he discovered~~as~~ discover he surely must~~that~~ that she was deliberately trying to take Julian away from his sister?

She could try telling him, of course, that her motives were truly altruistic, but somehow she doubted that he would believe her, that he would even want to believe her.

'Tired?'

The unexpected concern in his voice brought a small, anguished lump to her throat. Unable to reply without betraying her emotion, she shook her head.

'It's been a long day,' Brough told her, adding ruefully, 'I must admit I had no idea of the complexity of the task I was asking you to take on when I first approached you.'

'It will be a challenge,' Kelly admitted, relieved to be back on a safer subject. 'But I am looking forward to it. My biggest worry is that your grandmother is going to be disappointed. The teaset must mean so much to her... When Frank showed us those jugs this afternoon, which had been in the same family for six generations, and he told us how much each generation had to reinsure them at, it really brought it home to me that it isn't the material value that means so much but the fact that they represent a part of a family no longer there in person, a piece of very personal history…memories…'

'Yes,' Brough agreed soberly. 'I can see from the look in Nan's eyes when she touches her teaset that it's Gramps she's thinking about.'

A little enviously Kelly wondered what it must be like

to have experienced such love, and to still be able to warm oneself by its embers.

What was Brough's grandmother like? What had his grandfather been like? Brough? Her heart gave a small, uneven thump. In thirty years from now Brough could be a grandfather himself. Her heart gave another, even more uneven thud, and then a series of short, frantic, accelerating mini-beats as she contemplated her own future. In thirty years from now how would she feel when she looked back on today? Would the sharp ache of newly discovered love for Brough she had recognised today have dulled to nothing more than a dim memory, or would she be looking back in sadness and regret for what had never been?

They were almost home now, the lights of the town shining in the valley ahead of them as Brough turned off the motorway. Kelly sat in silence beside him as he drove through the quiet streets towards the shop. Rye-on-Averton was a genteel town, its residents either middle-aged or retired in the main. Its wine bars and restaurants, though, were well patronised, as were the shows put on by the excellent local amateur dramatic and operatic societies.

'I'll come up with you,' Kelly heard Brough saying as he parked his car outside the shop.

Immediately she shook her head, but Brough was already climbing out of the car.

'It really isn't necessary,' she said as he opened her car door for her.

The flat had its own entrance, and she had already removed the keys in readiness from her bag and was holding them in her hand, but to her chagrin Brough quietly removed them from her grasp.

'I know this is a relatively crime-free and safe area,

but I'm afraid my grandmother's influence means that I would feel I had failed in my male duty if I didn't see you safely inside.'

So he was only acting out of duty. What had she imagined? she derided herself as she walked silently towards the rear entrance of the flat. That he was insisting on seeing her inside because he wanted to delay the moment when he parted from her for as long as he could? How utterly ridiculous. He probably couldn't wait to see the back of her.

'It's this way,' she told him unnecessarily, indicating the rear ground-floor door.

Stepping past her, Brough inserted the key in the lock and then opened the door for her.

'Thank you…' Kelly started to say as she stepped past him, but it seemed he still did not consider his duty to be fully done, because he shook his head and stepped into the small hallway with her, glancing towards the stairs as he did so.

'Would you like me to come up with you and look around?' he asked her politely.

Immediately, Kelly shook her head.

In the hallway on a small console table was one of the first pieces of china she had painted. She saw Brough looking at it.

'One of your pieces?' he asked her.

'Yes,' she told him. 'The inspiration for it came to me when I was on holiday in South Africa with my family.'

The piece, all greens and blues and surf-whites, always made her think of the magnificence of the Cape's beaches. Such a dramatically beautiful country with such a horrifically cruel history. She touched the curving contours of the piece of china with gentle fingers. It held many happy memories-days when she had played with her brother's children, running in and out of the surf with them, evenings when she had strolled along the beach with her parents and her brother and his wife. Very happy memories. She shuddered a little to imagine what they would think of her current involvement with Julian Cox.

'Are you cold?' Brough asked her, frowning slightly and taking a step towards her just as Kelly, too, stepped forward, away from the table.

Automatically, she put her hand out to prevent them bumping into one another as she shook her head in response to his question, but unwisely, as she did so, her gaze was drawn to his face and then his mouth.

The shape of it had been tantalising her all day-the sharp masculine cut of it, the sensual fullness of his lower lip, the dangerous and somehow illicit knowledge she had of just how it felt to have it moving on her own.

Now, just when she knew she needed to be at her coolest and most in control, her breathing had become erratic, her pulses racing, her pupils betraying the surge of feminine longing that was overpowering her.

Her brain begged her body to behave sensibly, her eyes to break contact, her breathing to slow down and become properly measured, but her senses had become flagrantly disobedient.

Very slowly Kelly lifted her gaze from Brough's mouth to his eyes. It was like gazing into deep waters, so cool that they made her body tremble as though she had touched ice, and yet so hot that her bones felt as though they were going to melt. Every sense she possessed, every centimetre of flesh covering her body, suddenly seemed to have become a thousand times more sensitive than normal, a thousand times more receptive.

She could hear Brough breathing, feel the heat of each breath he drew against her skin, sensing even the tension that coiled like fine wire through his body, feeling just what was burning through him as she gave herself up to the dark blaze of passion she could see in his eyes.

Her body swayed towards him, seeking his strength and offering in return the promise of her own pliant responsiveness, the instinctive age-old body language of woman to man, yielding and promising, whilst at the same time demanding that he show that he had the strength, the manhood, to take up the challenge she was offering and to protect her weakness.

'Brough.' She whispered his name, her eyes heavy-lidded, mysterious, luminous with passion as she turned her face up to his, an enchantress, powerful and strong. Irresistible.

And yet she still placed her hands flat against his chest, as though to deny the promise in her eyes and the desire running through her body, heavy and hot as molten gold.

She could feel his arms wrapping around her, enfolding her, as he drew her close, so close that her hand could feel the wild, fierce, heady drumming of his heartbeat, fast and furious as a cheetah during the chase. Boldly Kelly kept her eyes open. His were hot, dark, deep, glittering with male arousal.

Once again she looked at his mouth, a wild thrill of elation gripping her body. Now she was the hunter, her body tight, coiled, waiting…hungry.

Their mouths met, hers wanton, responsive, and yet at the same time soft and waiting. Brough was kissing her, sliding his hands up over her back, caressing her over and over again, his body hard and powerful against hers. Her own body felt molten and plain, reminding her of glass before it was shaped and blown, liquid running free, waiting to be formed and shaped, a wild natural element that could be coaxed but never forced.

Brough's hands were on her shoulders, gripping them hard as his tongue searched her lips for an opening. Eagerly she gave it to him, her own nails digging into the long muscles of his back.

She was experiencing a wildness within herself, a sensuality she had never encountered before, and it both exhilarated and terrified her. Beneath her clothes her breasts ached and peaked. No need for Brough to even lightly caress them to arouse her need for him, but when he did—!

Was that really her making that low, hungry, almost semi-tortured sound deep down in her throat? Was that Brough growling in fierce exultation beneath his own breath as his thumb-pad returned demandingly to caress and probe the taut peak of her nipple?

She wanted him. Wanted him…wanted him so badly. Wanted to feel his body, his skin, next to hers, his touch, his love…

Kelly made an urgent keening noise deep in her throat, her body arching against Brough's in a sexual mixture of longing and pleasure.

Somehow all the barriers there had been between them, all her doubts and fears, her refusal to believe that it was possible for her to feel like this, for her to love like this, so immediately, so intensely, so unexpectedly were banished, vaporised by the sheer force of her feelings.

Now, here in his arms, she was all feeling, yearning, loving woman, her natural female instincts overturning the conditioning of modern society and its demands. As boldly as some long-ago ancestor might have done, she was recognising and claiming for her own her man and her right to love him.

'Brough.' She whispered his name throatily, a husky purr of aroused pleasure, heavy with sensuous promise shot through with love.

'You feel so good. I want you so much…' Was that *her* saying that, or was it Brough? Was *she* the one reaching for him or was he the initiator of their increasingly passionate caresses? The shadowy confines of the hallway, normally surely the last place she would have ever thought of as romantic, now seemed as private and protected as the most secret of sanctuaries. And it was a dizzying, tantalising thought to know that not so very far beyond its closed door lay her bedroom—her bed.

Her whole body shuddered as it wantonly followed where her thoughts were leading, where she already ached for Brough to lead her. A feeling of the most incandescent joy filled her; a sense of throwing off the past and turning to welcome the future and their love made her feel as though suddenly something unacknowledged deep within her had sprung to life, as though the person she had been before the wonderful, miraculous discovery that she loved Brough had been someone who was only half alive, someone who had been deprived of the true pleasures and meaning of life.

'I don't want you to go…'

As she murmured the words against Brough's mouth she could feel him start to tense; his mouth left her throat, which he had been kissing and nibbling, sending a cascade of tiny erotic shivers all the way from the top of her head to her toes.

'I don't want to either,' he whispered back as his thumb caressed her throat and then her jaw, slowly moving towards her mouth. 'But I must. I'm expecting a call from Hong Kong—I had some business dealings there, which I've sold out of, but there are still some legal ends I need to tie up. And tomorrow I have to go to London to see my accountants. But when I come back…'

As he turned away he paused and then turned back, taking hold of her hand and urging her gently towards him.

'Thank you…' he told her softly.

'For what?' she managed to ask him in a shaky voice.

'For today…and this…and you…' he told her throatily as he bent to place a soft kiss on her half-parted lips.

For *her*… For a moment Kelly felt close to tears. There was so much more about her that he still didn't know. So much that she still had to tell him—especially… But now, when he was on the point of leaving, wasn't the time to start explaining about Julian and Beth.

'I know you're only being like this because you're worried about how much I'm going to charge you for the teaset,' she told him teasingly and a little chokily.

'Aha…so you've seen through my dastardly plot, then,' Brough responded in the same vein.

Suddenly anxious, she clung to him and whispered, 'Oh, Brough, it's all so new, so unexpected. I don't…'

'It's perfect…*you're* perfect,' Brough assured her as he tightened his arms around her and cradled her head against his shoulder. '*We* are going to be perfect…together… Right now, there's nothing I want more than to stay here with you.'

He looked betrayingly towards the inner doorway to the flat and, guessing what he was thinking, Kelly quickly reassured him. 'I know and I understand. You've got your responsibilities, and anyway, perhaps… Everything's happened so quickly, so…'

'I'll call you the moment I get back from London,' Brough promised her huskily.

'There's so much I haven't told you,' Kelly protested as he started to release her.

'Such as?' Brough grinned. 'I've already discovered for myself all that I need to know, and what I have discovered, what I do know...I love...'

'Oh, Brough...'

It was impossible not to throw herself back into his arms and share another passionate kiss with him, and then he was gone, leaving her to touch her fingertips to a mouth that still tingled from the passion of his kiss and to acknowledge with a small, cold shiver that he was wrong, that there were things that he still had to learn.

Would it change what he thought, what he felt, when he learned of her deceit, or would he understand and accept that her deliberate pursuit of Julian had been prompted by loyalty to Beth?

CHAPTER EIGHT

'SO YOU do understand, Dee, don't you?' Kelly asked the older woman anxiously as they sat opposite one another in Kelly's flat.

Kelly had telephoned Dee as soon as Brough had left, despite the fact that it was late evening. The disquiet she had experienced over the role she was playing *vis-à-vis* Julian had coalesced following Brough's departure into a sharp and intense need to free herself from the restrictions that her commitment to Dee's plans were placing on her. There was no way she wanted to deceive Brough, and there was certainly no way she could even pretend now to be anything other than totally revolted by Julian Cox.

'I think so,' Dee confirmed dryly. 'You're telling me that you've fallen in love with Brough Frobisher and that because of that you don't want to carry out your part of our scheme.'

'It isn't that I don't *want* to,' Kelly corrected her quietly, 'it's that I *can't*; and even before I realised how I felt about Brough... I'm not trying to be dramatic, Dee, but there's something about Julian I just don't trust.'

'Join the club,' Dee told her sardonically. 'I don't want to cast a shadow over love's sweet dream, Kelly, and you're certainly old enough and I believe mature enough to be the best judge of your own feelings, but Brough is Eve's brother, and he *does* have a vested interest in monitoring your relationship with Julian therefore.'

Kelly looked at her for several seconds before asking her sternly, 'What are you trying to say? That Brough is deliberately and callously pretending to…to care about me because he wants to leave his sister with a clear field to Julian Cox?'

'No. What I'm *trying* to say is that you would be well advised and wise to be aware that things are not perhaps as straightforward as they could be, that people do have hidden motives and personal agendas for what they do. After all, on the face of it, so far as Brough is concerned, he has a potential rival for your love in Julian, hasn't he?'

'I wanted to explain to him but I just didn't have the chance, and then I decided that I owed it to you to let you know what I intended to do first,' Kelly told her quickly.

She had found it extremely unsettling and disturbing listening to what Dee had to say. Dee was wrong, of course; Brough would never do anything like that… Would he?

'I know you must feel that I'm letting you down,' Kelly told Dee quietly.

'I'm disappointed, yes,' Dee acknowledged, 'but I *do* understand. I have been in love myself, you know, and I do—' She broke off, and to Kelly's surprise she saw that the older girl's face was slightly flushed.

Why?

Dee was only thirty, and what could be more natural, after all, than that she should have experienced falling in love?

'I can't pretend that I don't wish you'd change your mind,' Dee continued honestly, 'but at least Julian seems to be biting on the bait so far as Anna is concerned. Anna was able to ''accidentally' bump into him at yesterday's mayoral function, and vaguely mentioned that she had recently received rather a large sum of money from an insurance policy which had matured and that she was looking for somewhere to invest it with a view to making the maximum amount of profit.'

'You do realise, don't you,' Kelly said a little uncomfortably, 'that I'm going to have to say *something* to Brough about our…about what we planned?'

Dee's eyebrows rose.

'Dear me, it *is* love, isn't it?' she acknowledged dryly. 'I appreciate what you're saying, Kelly,' she responded firmly, 'but I would at least ask you to keep my part in our plans to a discreet minimum. I'm sure your Brough isn't one to tittle-tattle or gossip, but I *do* have a certain position within our local community and I wouldn't want our plans bruited about.

'I personally believe that Julian Cox deserves all that we planned for him and more, that what we intended to do doesn't come to even one tenth of the punishment he deserves, but I have to be honest and admit that there *are* people who might take a very different view, and I certainly don't want to be judged as some sort of melodramatic woman, bent on exacting revenge for some imagined slight…'

'Oh, I'm sure Brough would never think that,' Kelly assured her, so quick to defend her beloved.

'Maybe,' Dee acknowledged, 'but others might.'

'Well, if you prefer it, I could simply say that we'd all agreed that Julian needed to be taught a lesson,' Kelly offered.

'I thought that was what we *had* all agreed,' Dee commented wryly as she stood up.

'One thing that does still worry me,' Kelly told her

as she followed her to the flat door, 'and that's Eve, Brough's sister. She's desperately in love with Julian...'

'And he, by all accounts, is still desperate to secure her—if he can't get you,' Dee concluded. 'I certainly don't envy you *that* relationship, Kelly...Julian Cox as your brother-in-law by marriage.'

'Oh, no, don't say that,' Kelly pleaded with her. 'He'd make Eve so dreadfully unhappy. Maybe I should try to talk to her, warn her...tell her what he did to Beth.'

'Do you think she would listen?' Dee asked her doubtfully. 'Julian's told so many lies, it might be hard to convince her.'

'I've only met her a couple of times,' Kelly said, 'but she strikes me as someone who would think deeply about the situation if we put it to her.'

'Mmm... You and Harry both. He's been singing her praises to me ever since the night of the ball. When are you seeing Brough again, by the way?'

'I don't know. He's going to London on business in the morning, but he said he'd get in touch just as soon as he could.'

'Goodnight, then,' Dee told her as she opened the flat door and stepped out into the fresh air.

Dee had parked her car quite close to the shop, but instead of going directly to it she chose, instead, to walk in the opposite direction through the town and down towards the river.

The walk along the river path had been one of her favourites as a girl. It had been her route home from school and, later on when she had gone to university, it had been one of the first places she had headed for on her return home.

Her family had lived in the area for many generations;

her mother had died shortly after Dee's birth and her father, older than her mother by some eighteen years, had died just before Dee was about to take her degree.

She had returned home to sort out his affairs and to discover that she was an extremely wealthy young woman.

One of the first things she had done with her money had been to make a large, interest-free loan to her uncle in order to enable him to modernise the family farm and buy more land.

Her own father, his brother, had sold his share of the family farmland as a young man, preferring to deal and speculate in the commodities market rather than follow the custom of his forebears, and it had seemed to Dee to be a good memorial to him that she should help her uncle to buy back the land he had sold away from the family. The two brothers had never quarrelled over his decision, and had always got on amicably for two such very, very different people, but Dee, who had inherited her father's intelligence, knew that it was becoming increasingly difficult for small farmers to make a decent living and she had seen that there could come a time when her uncle, for financial reasons, would either have to sell up or rent out his lands.

With the rest of the money she had made several donations to local charities, and then amused herself by finding out if she had inherited her father's gift for making the right investment.

It had turned out that she had.

But, at twenty-one, a girl wanted far more from life than a healthy bank balance, and Dee had had all the normal urges and needs of her sex and age—a man to love and love her, the prospect of a relationship that would last a lifetime and one which included commitment, children...love...

And, for all too brief a space of time, while she had been at university, she had thought she had that relationship...that love...*had* thought...but had thought wrongly. Had made the worst, the most disastrous decision of her life, had prejudiced everything she had, everything she was, because of someone who had proved to be so false, so cruelly betraying that even now she still bore the scars.

She stopped walking, shoving her hands deep into the pockets of her lightweight jacket, and stared angrily up towards the stars.

She had waited a long time for this opportunity to turn the tables on Julian Cox, to get him in a position where he was vulnerable and unable to protect himself...as she had once been. Oh, yes, she had been vulnerable...

Fiercely she bit down hard on her bottom lip. She wasn't being vindictive, she was simply exercising her right to have justice, avenging the wrong which had been done to her, and neither were her motives totally selfish. She *had* been concerned for Beth's pain and heartbreak and, despite what Kelly seemed to think, she was aware of the difficult position she had potentially put her in, and of the heartache that Eve could suffer if no one warned her what Julian was.

She had, of course, assumed that Eve would immediately refuse to have anything further to do with Julian once his involvement with Kelly became public knowledge; Brough would have surely insisted on that for his sister's own sake and, from what she knew of him, Brough was certainly a strong enough character to be able to achieve that end.

It was a pity that Kelly had changed her mind, but the

game wasn't over yet, not by a long chalk. One way or another, Dee was determined that Julian Cox was going to make full recompense for the debt he owed her. *Full* recompense...with interest, the interest at the punitively high rate caused by the sheer extent and weight of the emotional anguish and despair she had suffered.

There was no despair like that of suffering a broken heart, destroyed dreams, the complete desolation of a once promising future.

Determinedly, Dee started to head back towards the town centre. It was time for her to go home. Yes, Kelly's decision was going to cause her a problem, but no problem was insurmountable unless you allowed it to be and she, Dee, was certainly not going to do that.

Where was Brough now? Kelly wondered dreamily as she said goodbye to the customer she had just served. In another five minutes she was going to close the shop for the day and then she was going to go upstairs and indulge in the delicious pleasure of curling up in a chair whilst she relived every second of yesterday, and most especially what had happened after Brough had insisted on seeing her safely inside the flat.

Even now she felt as though it couldn't be real, as though she had to keep mentally pinching herself to make sure she wasn't imagining everything.

She *had* felt guilty telling Dee that she couldn't go on with their plans, but wisely Kelly knew that even without the discovery of her love for Brough she would have found it extremely difficult to continue to practise the deceit her role had called for.

Where was Brough? Still in London? On his way back? When would she hear from him...see him... hold him?

She caught her breath as she heard the shop doorbell ring behind her, and out of the corner of her eye she caught the male outline of the person walking in.

'Brough!'

She turned round eagerly, his name on her lips, only to be swept by a surge of disappointment as she recognised that her visitor wasn't Brough but Julian.

'What happened to you last night?' Julian demanded without preamble. 'We had a date...at the wine bar...remember?'

Guiltily Kelly frowned. She had completely forgotten about that, but even if she hadn't... The last person she really wanted to see was Julian Cox, but since he was here she could at least make it abundantly clear to him just where she stood, and, turning away from him so that he couldn't see her face, she managed a dismissive shrug.

'I changed my mind,' she told him carelessly. 'In fact...'

Summoning all her courage, she turned round and announced crisply, 'In fact, Julian, I think it would be best if you didn't try to get in touch with me any more.'

'What are you trying to say?' Julian demanded furiously, his mouth tightening as he stepped in front of her, blocking her exit. She couldn't do this to him. He had got it all planned—Kelly, with her substantial fortune, unfettered by any access restrictions, was a much better proposition than Eve with her trust fund and her brother, and besides, he wanted Kelly. She excited him in a way that the Beths and Eves of this world could never do.

'I'm trying to say that I think we've both made a mistake,' Kelly informed him as diplomatically as she could. 'You are dating someone else...'

'So?' Julian demanded. '*You* didn't seem to consider

that much of a problem the other night at the ball, nor when I rang you up...'

'Maybe not,' Kelly allowed. 'But since then I've had time to think things through... Eve loves you, Julian,' she told him directly.

To her disbelief, instead of looking embarrassed, he smiled triumphantly.

'You're jealous, aren't you?' he challenged her. 'Well, you needn't be. Eve's a child, Kelly, but you're a woman... The things you and I could do...' he promised her thickly. 'You know what I mean. You want them too. I've seen it in your eyes... Eve is a mistake. It's you I want, Kelly.'

Thoroughly revolted, Kelly tried to step back from him, but the hard edge of the counter was behind her, jarring her back. She looked anxiously towards the door, wishing a customer would walk in and put an end to their unwanted privacy. Unwanted on her part, that was. Julian, far from accepting what she had told him, seemed to be trying to be deliberately obtuse, Kelly recognised. Was he really so vain that he didn't realise how much she loathed him? If so, she would simply have to take a stronger line with him.

'Julian, I meant what I said,' she told him firmly. 'I don't want to see you. If I gave you the wrong idea—'

'If?' he broke in, his face changing as he understood the forcefulness of her determination. No way could he afford to let her go, he acknowledged inwardly. When he had first met Eve he had not realised just how much control her brother had over her financial affairs. There was no love lost between him and Brough at all.

'You were giving me the green light, Kelly, all the way to your bedroom door. I want you, Kelly, and I intend to have you.'

'No!' Kelly protested, shocked.

'Oh, come on,' he overrode her. 'You want me too; I can see it in your eyes...your mouth...' As he spoke he reached out and pressed his thumb hard against her bottom lip. 'There's no way I'm going to let you go.'

Taken off guard, Kelly immediately tried to push him away, making a sharp sound of distress.

He actually made her feel physically sick, and not just sick but afraid as well, she recognised as she saw the ugly look in his eyes.

'I want you to leave, Julian,' she told him shakily. 'Now...'

'Oh, you do, do you?' he responded aggressively. 'And what if I choose not to? What if *I* choose to make *you* come good on all those sexy promises you've been giving me, Kelly? What are you going to do about it? How are you going to stop me?'

'What you're talking about is sexual harassment,' Kelly told him bravely. 'If you don't stop threatening me and leave straight away, Julian, I shall report you to the police.'

To her dismay, instead of responding as she'd hoped, he threw back his head and laughed.

'Do you think they'd believe you...after the way you've been coming on to me? Get real, Kelly. You're just being hysterical.'

Hysterical—wasn't that what he had accused Beth of being?

Outrage and panic paralysed Kelly, rooting her feet to the floor as she stood trapped in the maniacal beam of his almost colourless, cold eyes.

Julian was a desperate man, she recognised numbly. He was also *enjoying* her fear, feeding off it, not just emotionally, she sensed with increasing, horrified disgust and fear, but physically as well. Oh, please God, let someone come into the shop and save her, she prayed mentally as she fought not to succumb to the awful, fearful heaviness filling her body. To say that she was afraid in no way came even close to describing what she felt. Her whole body had gone icy cold. She knew, she just *knew*, that Julian meant every word he said, that nothing, nothing she could do or say would persuade him to leave. Now, when it was almost too late, she recognised how much she had underestimated how dangerous he really was.

Brough had been delayed in London longer than he had planned. There had been a couple of time-consuming delays in the finalisation of the transaction with Hong Kong. He had been tempted to ring Kelly just as he left the city, but he had wanted to clear his mind of everything to do with his work before he spoke to her again. And besides, when he told her he loved her he wanted to see the look in her eyes, to hear that wonderful female adorable catch in her breath as she looked at him, to know that she felt the same way that he did.

Impossible now to think that he had imagined that first time he had held her in his arms that he was immune to the risk of falling in love-and besides,   *what* risk? Loving her was *heaven...paradise*...the fulfilment of his every previously unacknowledged dream.

He would go home, shower and then drive round and see her...surprise her...

So why, having made that decision, did he suddenly, when he was within a hundred yards of his own driveway, suddenly succumb to an almost overpowering sense of urgency, so strong a need, so immediate and intense, that he drove through a set of traffic lights on

amber and broke the speed limit just to get to her. He
drew up several yards away from the flat and got out,
forgetting to lock his car as he strode quickly towards
the shop.

As he approached the door he could see two people
inside. Kelly was standing with her back half turned towards him so that he could only partially see her face,
her head submissively bent towards the man who was
wrapping his arms around her. To anyone else their pose
might have seemed to be that of lovers, but Brough knew
immediately and incontrovertibly that it wasn't love that
was keeping Kelly immobile in Julian Cox's embrace,
but fear. Just *how* he knew it he didn't stop to question
as he pushed open the door and rushed to Kelly's side,
forcibly thrusting Julian away from her. As he did so he
could see not just the relief and shock in her eyes, but
also an anguished pain that cut right to his heart. His
love, his darling, felt shamed by the fact that she was
being attacked by…

He could quite happily have slowly roasted Julian Cox
over a very, very hot fire, just for that act of violation
alone—he, a man of peace and logic. Brough could see
the fury and the fear in the other man's eyes, and the
urge to punish him, hurt and frighten him, as well as
release his own fury against him, was so strong that for
a second Brough was almost tempted to give in to it.

But over Julian's shoulder he could see where Kelly
was standing, white-faced, her eyes blank with shock,
and instead he released Julian and told him in disgust,
'Get out of here before I give in to the temptation to
forget that non-violence is the making of a truly intelligent man.'

'You've got it all wrong…' Julian started to whine as
he backed towards the door. 'She's the one who's to

blame, not me. She's the one who's been leading me on, coming on to me,' he started to protest, but Brough had heard enough. Grabbing hold of his collar, he virtually marched him to the door and opened it, pushing him through it.

'If I find out you've so much as even tried to speak to her again, I promise you you're going to regret it,' he told Julian in a steely voice.

As Brough locked the door he turned towards Kelly. She was still standing motionless, her face grey-white, her eyes huge and unfocused. *She* was his prime concern now. He could talk to her later, find out later just what had been going on and why Cox had been terrorising her.

At the back of his mind as he walked towards Kelly lay the knowledge that he was now going to have to take very firm action over Julian's relationship with his sister, but right now Kelly was his only priority.

'Kelly... It's all right, my darling, he's gone, you're safe...'

As she heard Brough's familiar, warm voice, Kelly turned her head and looked towards him, towards him but not at him. How could she? How could she *ever* come to terms with the pain, the humiliation, the defilement of what she had just experienced? Julian's verbal attack on her, his threatened assault on her, had left her feeling totally physically shocked and degraded. The thought passed through her mind that if this was how *she* felt how on earth did rape victims feel? How did *they* cope? Julian's abuse of her had come nowhere close to anything like that...

'Come on...I'm taking you upstairs...' she heard Brough telling her. Desperately she struggled to get back to normality, her always keen sense of responsibility reminding her of her duties.

'I can't—the shop,' she began to protest, but Brough overruled her.

'The shop is closed,' he told her firmly, adding more gently, 'You're in shock, my love; there's no way you can work. You need...' He paused and started to frown. 'Who is your GP? I think perhaps that...'

Immediately Kelly shook her head.

'No, no, I'm fine...' Her bottom lip started to tremble. 'Honestly, Brough, I will be fine,' she told him in a thready voice. 'I don't need... I don't want... It was my own fault,' she told him huskily, dropping her head so that he couldn't look into her eyes and see the truth she felt must be clear there. 'I shouldn't have—'

'You shouldn't have what?' Brough interrupted her immediately and fiercely. 'You shouldn't have let him in? No way was it your fault, Kelly. I *saw* what was going on... There was *no way* you were inviting or enjoying what was going to happen.'

The sureness in his voice, the conviction, the trust and the love were too much for Kelly's fragile composure. Hot tears filled her eyes and started to roll down her face as she shook her head.

'Oh, no, please, my love, don't cry,' Brough begged her with a small groan. 'I shouldn't have let him walk away from this... The police...'

'No...no, please. I don't want anything like that,' Kelly protested sharply. 'I just want to forget about it, Brough... I just want...'

She started to tremble violently, reaction setting in as the realisation of what had happened swamped her.

'Come on, I'm taking you up to your flat,' Brough

told her masterfully, holding her gently by the arm and leading her towards the door.

Five minutes later she was standing in her own small kitchen drinking the fortifying mug of coffee Brough had just made her, liberally laced with brandy. She could feel the strong spirit going straight to her head, relaxing her both physically and emotionally, releasing her from the rigid self control she had been exercising ever since Julian Cox had walked into the shop.

'Brough, Julian wanted…' she began huskily, suddenly desperately anxious to tell him everything, to explain to him what she had been doing and why, but before she could finish what she had been about to say she suddenly became very dizzy.

Immediately Brough reached for her, rescuing the half-empty mug she had been about to drop, gathering her in his arms as he told her gruffly, 'I know *exactly* what Cox wanted… He's gone, Kelly. You're safe— forget about him…'

'No, you don't understand,' Kelly protested, but it was impossible to keep on trying to form rational thoughts and make difficult and painful explanations when Brough was holding her so tightly, one hand stroking her hair whilst the other tilted up her chin so that he could look down into her eyes.

'I should *never* have gone home and left you last night,' he whispered rawly to her. 'I certainly didn't want to…'

'*I* didn't want you to either,' Kelly admitted bravely, adding tremulously, 'Oh, Brough, I wanted you to stay so much, but…I still can't quite believe all this is happening…that you and I… It frightens me a little,' she admitted, her tongue as well as her self-control loosened by the potent mixture of shock and alcohol. 'I've never been in love before, never wanted... Loving someone means risking that they might hurt you and—'

'I could *never* hurt you, Kelly,' Brough interrupted her to tell her passionately. 'And I know that you would never hurt me.'

'How *can* you know that?' Kelly protested nervously. 'Brough, there's so much about me that you don't know...'

'Mmm...so much about you that I still have to discover...' Brough agreed softly as his lips started to caress her willing mouth.

'Brough...' Kelly whispered, but it was only a token protest. There was nothing she wanted more than to be held like this by him, kissed like this by him, unless it was to lie naked in bed with him, his body her only covering, his hands caressing her, leaving hers free to explore him...

'Mmm...well, if you're sure that's what you want, I'm certainly not going to argue with you,' she heard Brough saying hoarsely as he gently stepped back from her and turned her to face the kitchen door, and it was only then that Kelly realised that what she had thought were her most private and unspoken thoughts she had in fact spoken out loud to him.

'Oh, Brough...'

Her face pink, she looked helplessly at him, but far from being shocked by the desires and wishes she had expressed he was looking at her as though...as though... Kelly felt her heartbeat start to pick up. Suddenly she was finding it extraordinarily difficult to breathe properly; suddenly her mind was full of the most extraordinarily detailed and sensual images of them both together; suddenly she couldn't wait to make those private wanton thoughts a reality.

It took them almost ten minutes to reach the bedroom, primarily because Brough insisted on stopping virtually every foot of the way to hold her and kiss her and tell her that she was the most wonderful, the most wanted thing that had ever happened to him.

'I never imagined you could be like this,' Kelly breathed in ecstatic pleasure as the look in his eyes confirmed that he meant every romantic word he was saying to her. 'When we first met, you seemed so disapproving…so…'

'So desperately afraid of revealing to you just how totally and completely I'd fallen for you,' Brough admitted softly as he cupped her face and very slowly started to kiss her.

Dizzily Kelly clung to him. They were in her bedroom now, and Brough was very carefully, but *very* thoroughly and determinedly, starting to remove her clothing whilst continuing to kiss her with a passion which caused her heartbeat to slow to a sensuously heavy thud and her body to melt into eager compliance and longing.

This was not how it was meant to be for a modern nineties woman. *She* was supposed to take her own initiative, remove her *own* clothes and expect her lover to remove his with equally mature independence, and when a modern woman did make love it was an open-eyed, clear-minded 'I know what I'm doing and why' thing. Wasn't it?

So *why* was she, who considered herself to be such a thoroughly modern woman, simply standing there, not merely allowing Brough to dictate the pace of their lovemaking but positively *yearning* for him to do so? *Why* was she experiencing this unfamiliar, heady sense of pleasure and excitement, of anticipation and, yes, just a tiny thread of nervousness as well, at the thought of what lay ahead? Why, much as she wanted him, ached for him, *loved* him, did she actually want *him* to be the one, initially at least, to show her how much he loved and wanted her?

Because she loved him enough to do so! Because she trusted him enough! Because there was, after all, something inalienably sweet and precious about admitting, *allowing* herself to be so vulnerably female in his presence, in being able, for the first time since childhood, to acknowledge a need for another person, for their love…their touch…

'Brough…'

She shivered in delicious pleasure as he slid her top away from her body and then gently unclipped her bra, freeing her breasts to his gaze and the softness of the air against them. As she felt and saw her nipples peak into hard, excited, aroused nubs of flesh, Kelly knew immediately what was responsible for their arousal—or rather who. It wasn't cold in her bedroom and, anyway, she undressed in here every night without her body reacting like this.

'Beautiful…beautiful…' Brough murmured thickly as he reached out and gently traced the curve of one breast, brushing its softness with his finger, the lightest of light touches, and yet it was enough to send a sensuous shudder of sensation curling through her entire body.

'Beautiful,' Brough repeated as he bent his head and, cupping her breast very carefully, kissed one erect nipple and then the other, and then repeated the whole process again and then again, and each time his mouth returned to graze and suckle on one swollen point the other ached jealously for the loss of the delicious pressure of his mouth against it.

'Brough…'

Heavy-eyed, Kelly bent her head towards him, leaning its weight on his downbent shoulder. Beneath her cheek she could feel the fabric of his shirt. Quickly she started to pull it free of his waistband, making a little frustrated sound of protest deep in her throat, a small feline growl of longing as she realised that unless and until she unfastened the buttons of his shirt and physically removed it from his body she was going to be denied the sensation of his skin against her own which she craved so much. But if she did that he might have to stop kissing and caressing her breasts in that delicious way.

But somehow Brough seemed to have divined her thoughts, because he gently eased her slightly away from him, kissing her deeply on the mouth as he lifted her hands to the front of his shirt and then, whilst he was still kissing her, placed his own hands over her breasts, gently teasing her erect nipples with his thumbs and fingertips. Already sensitised by the erotic attention of his mouth, they reacted to this extra stimulation by causing such a curling, coiling, tightening feeling to gather deep inside her body that Kelly cried out in soft protest against the intensity of what she was feeling.

Her fingers stilled over the task of unfastening his shirt and then, as the sensation within her body refused to be controlled, her actions quickened, becoming urgent and demanding, her lips pressing tiny hungry kisses against Brough's jaw, his throat, and then lower, following the reckless speed of her fingers as she tugged and wrenched at the recalcitrant buttons, the progress of both her hands and her mouth only halted when she suddenly realised that she had reached the barrier of his belt.

Now it was Brough who was losing control, groaning rawly as he took her hands and guided them over his body. The feel of him even through the fabric of his clothes, hard, hot and aroused, filled her own insides with a heaviness, a dull, unfamiliar ache, and an instinctive knowledge that there was only one way, one way it was going to be eased...satisfied...

Kelly needed no encouragement nor coaxing to remove the rest of his clothes. Now she *was* an all nineties woman, wanting her man and not ashamed for him to know it, proud of her own body, her own sexuality as he stripped the rest of her clothes from it with a fierce eagerness that matched and fed her own longing.

When they were both completely naked she looked at him and then told him breathlessly and meant it, 'Brough, you are *so* beautiful. So perfect...' Hot-faced with female appreciation, she ran a delicate but oh, so possessive fingertip down the length of him, teasingly avoiding the thick dark shaft of aroused manhood that was almost awesomely powerful to her as a woman in some ways an almost primitive visual reminder of the human race's sexuality and its genetically encoded gift and goal of ensuring its own continuity and yet still somehow a reminder of how very vulnerable a man could be, how very much in need of a woman's love and even of her protection of his maleness, of her appreciation of it and of him.

Very, very gently and carefully, caringly, Kelly reached out and ran her fingertip the entire length of the engorged shaft, lovingly circling its tip, smiling a mysterious, sultry, female smile of power and love as she caught Brough's audibly indrawn breath and saw the fierce leap of passion darkening his eyes before he closed them on a helpless moan of aching male pleasure.

'Oh, God, that feels so good,' he told her throatily, and then, opening his eyes, he admitted, 'Too good, Kelly; if you do it again I don't know...'

'You don't know what?' Kelly teased, obliging him with an opportunity to find out as she delicately ran her fingertip back up the way it had just come.

'I don't know whether to kiss you…or…'

Far too quickly for Kelly to stop him, he grabbed hold of her, rolling her down onto the bed and very gently keeping her there as he carefully parted her thighs, kissing the inner flesh of each one before looking up at her uncertain face and smiling tenderly at her.

'No,' Kelly protested, guessing what he was going to do and knowing instinctively that once she felt his lips, his mouth against that most vulnerable and sensuously responsive part of her body there was no way she was going to be able to hold back the response that had been building up inside her ever since their first kiss.

But of course she knew that Brough wasn't going to listen to her denial, and she knew as well that there was no way she really wanted him to do so.

The gentle brush of his lips against the soft mound of her sex was the most blissful, the most sensual, the most erotic and achingly beautiful sensation she had ever experienced, she told herself dizzily. And then, for good measure, she told Brough as well, interspersing the words with soft, husky, imploring pleas for him to stop before…because… Her voice finally trailed away into a soft sob of delirious pleasure as the dragging ache inside her changed shape and texture and form and became a living, pulsing, fiery sensation that exploded sharply inside her in a cataclysmic surge of pleasure which to her surprise left her not drained and empty but somehow feeling as though she was just on the edge of some previously unguessed and undreamed-of new universe of delight, heralded by the tiny but unmistakable little excited pulse that still throbbed inside her body.

Very gently, but very determinedly, she urged Brough towards her.

'I want you,' she told him shakily. 'I want you now, Brough…'

'Now,' he repeated, but he was already responding to her, answering her, his body starting to move within hers slowly and then with gathering pace, gathering force, so that with each thrust he lifted her and carried her a little further, a little closer towards the goal her body now so desperately craved.

'Yes, now,' she whispered back. 'Now, Brough… now…now… Oh, Brough… Brough… Brough…'

She could feel the world exploding around her, the whole universe filling with light and love and Brough.

Brough… Brough whom she loved so much, whom she would always love so much…who loved her…

Satisfied, satiated, Kelly snuggled down into his arms. Sleepily she remembered that there was something she had to tell him, something she had to say…something…

Her eyes were already closed, her breathing slowing…

Tenderly Brough curled her into the warmth of his own relaxed body.

There had been a moment, a heartbeat, just then, when, just before the end, he had felt his eyes start to burn with emotional tears. Strange how, until he had met her, he had never even known how much he had wanted to find her, how desperately he must secretly have been searching for her… How good and right she would feel and how complete she would make his life.

He must remember to tell Eve that when he was trying to explain to her why Julian Cox wasn't the man for her.

Kelly!

God, but he loved her…had loved her, he now recognised, the moment he saw her, even though she had been behaving in a way which he now knew was way, way out of character. He started to frown. There were still things they needed to discuss. She had originally claimed Cox as an old friend, but the way he had been behaving towards her earlier had been anything but friendly.

His frown deepened as he heard a familiar sound from the landing where he had left his jacket. Gently easing his body away from Kelly's, so as not to disturb her, he padded towards it, flicking the receiving switch on his mobile phone. An unfamiliar voice on the other end of the line announced that he was Brough's grandmother's GP.

'She's had a fall-a-neighbour found her. We've admitted her to hospital, but unfortunately she's developed pneumonia. It can happen with elderly patients…'

'I'm on my way,' Brough told him grimly.

Back in the bedroom, he quickly dressed. Kelly stirred in her sleep and opened her eyes, frowning as she saw what he was doing.

Still half asleep, she questioned anxiously, 'Brough…?'

'It's all right,' he told her. 'Go back to sleep. I've got to go… I'll explain later…'

Her eyes were already closing again. She was exhausted, he recognised, the shock of Cox's attack on her no doubt now taking its toll along with the brandy he had given her and the intensity and passion of their love-making.

His mind raced ahead. He would have to tell Eve about their grandmother. But he didn't want the additional delay of driving home. He would call her on his mobile. Dear God, but he hoped Nan was going to be all right. She was a fighter, he knew that, but a serious fall at her age, followed by the complication of pneumonia... No wonder the doctor had sounded so grave.

Quietly Brough let himself out of Kelly's flat and headed for his car.

CHAPTER NINE

'AND you're sure that Nan's going to be all right?'

'Yes, Eve, the doctors say she's over the worst now, and although they want to keep her in hospital for observation they're confident that she's on the mend,' Brough assured his sister gently as he heard the concern in her voice.

He had arrived at the hospital just as his grandmother's pneumonia entered its most critical stage and had sat with her, willing her to draw strength from him and pull through, holding her hand tightly in his, even though the doctor had told him kindly that she was probably not aware of his presence. At one point she had turned her head, opening her eyes as she looked at him, and Brough had felt his eyes smart with tears as she'd called him by his grandfather's, her late husband's, name.

It was now ten o'clock at night, three hours and ten minutes since he had left Kelly. He was longing to speak with her, and longing even more to be with her, but first he had an important brotherly duty to perform.

'Eve, I appreciate that this might not be a good time to tell you this. You know that I've never been exactly happy about your relationship with Julian Cox, but I've no—'

'Brough, before you go any further, there's something I have to tell you,' Eve interrupted him nervously.

Brough felt his heart sink. He knew how loyal she was, and how trusting, how stubborn as well, but surely if he told her that he had actually found Julian attacking Kelly…

'Eve—' he began.

But she overruled him, begging shakily, 'Brough, please let me speak. I'm so nervous about telling you this, but I'm legally an adult now, and we've both talked the whole thing through, and even if you, as my trustee, withhold the allowance from my trust fund from me it wouldn't stop us. We love each other, Brough, and we want to be together. We *have* to be together. Oh, Brough, I love him so much,' she told him, the emotion in her voice so strong that Brough almost felt the air around him humming with it. 'If you'd ever been in love yourself, you'd understand… I don't want you to hate me for what I'm doing, but even if you do…'

Brough closed his eyes and took a deep breath. He hated having to do what he was going to have to do…hated having to destroy her dreams…her love, but what option did he have when he knew what Cox really was?

'Eve,' he said gently. 'I'm sorry, I understand everything you're saying, and you're wrong—I do understand what it means to be in love, to love someone; but you can't marry Julian Cox.'

The silence that followed his announcement was so complete and so intense that for a moment Brough thought she had actually hung up, and then he heard her saying shakily, 'Brough, I'm sorry; I haven't…I didn't… It isn't Julian I'm in love with…'

Now it was Brough's turn to be silent.

Not Cox. Then who? What…?

'It's Harry,' Eve blurted out.

'Harry!' Brough repeated in bemusement. 'Harry—'

'Harry Lawson,' Eve explained, adding ernestly, 'You remember he was at the ball we went to...'

'You mean the Harry who was escorting Kelly?' Brough questioned her sharply.

'Yes. But there's nothing between *them*. He was simply escorting her because his cousin had asked him to,' Eve told him defensively, before adding eagerly, 'Oh, Brough, I love him so much and so, I know, will you.'

'Yes... Yes...I'm sure I shall,' Brough agreed obediently, mentally reviewing what little he knew of Harry. A pleasant, solid-looking young man, phlegmatic in the extreme, Brough would have guessed, reliable, solid, trustworthy, an excellent foil for his sister's far more vulnerable and fragile personality.

A sense of relief began to fill him as he digested what he had just learned.

'Tell me again that Nan is going to be all right,' Eve implored, adding, 'I want to come down and see her, Brough, and I want to bring Harry with me.'

'Leave it a few days, until she's back at home,' Brough suggested. 'She'll feel more like company then, and you know she's going to want to give your Harry a thorough interrogation...'

Laughter bubbled along the line.

'Yes. I've warned him about that already. Brough, we don't want a big wedding...just a quiet family ceremony. Harry says Christmas would be best for him because it fits in best with the farming calendar...'

'We'll talk about it when I get back,' Brough promised her, pausing before asking, 'What about Cox, Eve? Have you told *him* that—?'

'No, not yet,' Eve responded quickly. 'I know I'm going to have to but...' She paused. 'I...*we* wanted to tell you about us first...'

'Well, whatever you do, Eve,' Brough cautioned her, 'make sure you aren't on your own with him when you do tell him or better still let me tell him for you.'

'No, Brough,' Eve told him gently. 'It's all right. Harry and I will handle this together.'

After he had terminated his call to his sister Brough took a deep breath and walked the length of the hospital car park whilst he assembled his thoughts. What he had just learned seemed nothing short of a small miracle, even if her Harry was rather an unexpected magician. He certainly seemed to have performed some very special magic in his sister's life, Brough recognised ruefully.

Although, technically, as Eve had just reminded him, she was legally an adult, he had always taken his brotherly responsibility towards her very seriously, and now, with one stroke, he was being freed, not just from that responsibility but also from the necessity of worrying about her emotional and financial future security, which meant...

Eagerly Brough reached for his mobile phone and punched in the number of Kelly's flat. Odd how easy it was to memorise certain vital numbers, how they seemed instinctively to lodge themselves in one's memory, he reflected wryly as he waited for Kelly to answer his call.

Five...ten minutes and three attempts later, he was forced to acknowledge that she must have gone out. He glanced at his watch. He wanted to have a further talk with the ward sister before she went off duty. He intended to spend the night in his grandmother's house just in case he should be needed urgently at her bedside. By the time he got there it would be too late to ring Kelly she would no doubt be in bed and sound asleep but first thing in the mornin g...

* * *

After she had replaced the telephone receiver following Brough's call, Eve turned to Harry, her eyes shining with love and relief.

'See, I *told* you he would understand,' Harry chided her lovingly.

'Yes, I know, but he was so…so stern and disapproving over Julian that I thought he'd be bound to think I couldn't possibly know my own mind when I told him I'd realised that I didn't love Julian at all and that you…'

She made a small happy sound beneath her breath as Harry put an end to her speech by kissing her very firmly and very determinedly. That was what she liked…*loved* about her Harry… He understood her so well…*knew* just how she felt…just what she wanted…knew that she was not like the majority of her peers in that she positively *wanted* someone to take control of her life and herself, that she adored having someone to stand beside her and protect her, to guide her masterfully.

But that someone had to be kind and gentle as well… He had to have the intuition and the love to know that the guiding hand she liked on the reins of her life had to be so delicately light that it could never chafe nor hurt her. Julian hadn't been like that. Julian had sometimes been very cruel to her, saying the most cutting and hurtful things…making her cry… Harry would never do that.

'You still have to tell Cox,' Harry reminded her quietly.

'I know,' Eve responded, 'but he frightens me a little, Harry… He keeps on telling me that he wants us to get engaged and he gets very angry when I tell him that Brough won't agree. He says it doesn't matter whether Brough agrees or not… I think he's more interested in my money than me,' Eve admitted in a small voice.

Privately, Harry thought so as well, and Cox was a

fool, in his opinion. He always had been, and not just a fool either, Harry reflected, his forehead creasing as he recalled certain things...certain old items of gossip he had picked up at home. But Harry was not the kind of person to pry into another person's personal life, and if Dee, his cousin, chose to place an embargo on certain events in her life, then he, for one, was quite happy to abide by it.

'Would you like *me* to tell him for you?' Harry suggested.

Immediately Eve's face lit up.

'Oh, Harry, would you...?'

Standing on tiptoe, she kissed him happily and then gave a small feminine gasp as he drew her closer and kissed her back, but much more deeply.

They were going to be so happy together, she and her Harry... She couldn't wait for the babies they were going to have, filling the old farmhouse with their presence and the love they would all share. All houses needed love and she certainly had plenty to give. She had already briefly met Harry's family, not officially as his intended bride because although she and Harry knew how strongly they felt about each other it had only been a *very* short time since they had first met, but she had seen from the looks his parents had exchanged that they had guessed how they felt about one another, and she had known straight away that she would get on well with them. Harry's mother was, in many ways, a younger version of her own grandmother, a plump, motherly woman who would draw her daughter-in-law safely beneath her maternal wing and keep her secure there.

'I'll go and see Cox first thing in the morning,' Harry promised her as he reluctantly released her.

'You could stay here tonight if you want,' Eve suggested daringly. 'Brough won't be coming back and...'

She stopped as she saw the stern look Harry was giving her.

'We agreed that we'd wait until we're married,' he reminded her.

Eve pouted and smiled.

'I know, but I love you so much and... Don't you want me, Harry...?'

The passion in the kiss he gave her was the only answer she needed.

'If I stay now, I'll have to make love to you, and if I do that... The Lawsons have a family tradition that the first child is born nine months virtually to the day of the wedding...I don't want our child to arrive ahead of that day,' he told her simply.

He had such pride, such moral fibre, such strength, Eve decided adoringly as she snuggled closer to him and whispered blissfully, 'Yes, Harry...'

Kelly came out of the darkness of a very deep sleep so abruptly that for a few seconds she was totally disorientated. Why was she alone in bed? Why...?

Frantically she sat up, searching the darkness of the room, and then the dim memory of Brough saying something to her about having to go came filtering back, clouded and fuzzy from the combined effects of the shock- and brandy-induced depth of her sleep.

Shakily she went to get herself a drink of water. Her throat felt dry and her eyes were scratchy and sore. In the cold pre-dawn chill of the kitchen she shivered a little as she stared into the darkness.

Had she and Brough really made love so intensely, so passionately, so poignantly? Had they really exchanged

vows of love and commitment, told each other of the
depth of their love for one another, or was it all simply
a self-created fantasy...a dream? But no, she could feel
the difference in her body, and knew that the words re-
verberating through her mind and her heart had been
said...exchanged... Oh, Brough... A little weepily she
started to tremble. Where on earth had he gone and why?
If only she knew. Why *hadn't* he woken her up properly
and spoken to her? Had he really meant what he had
said to her, or...?

There was still so much they didn't really know about
one another, despite the intimacy they had shared. So
much he didn't know about *her*. She had tried to tell
him about Julian...to explain...but her explanations had
been swept away by the passion of the moment. What
had he thought when he had walked in and discovered
Julian with her like that?

Her thoughts began to chase one another around inside her head until she felt sick and dizzy with the
weight of them, clasping her head in her hands as she
protested aloud, 'No... No... Stop...'

It was too early for her to get up, and yet she knew
if she went back to bed she wouldn't be able to sleep.
After walking around her bedroom, touching the pillow
where Brough's head had lain and then lifting it to her
face to breathe in the scent of him and press the comfort
of it close to her hot face, she reminded herself that she
was a mature adult woman and that this type of fevered,
frantic behaviour belonged more properly to early ado-
lescence. Wearily she walked back into the sitting room,
and then frowned as the things she had brought back
from the Hartwell factory caught her eye.

Half an hour later she was blessedly engrossed in the
records she was studying.

Now, the prospect of painting the new pieces for Brough's grandmother didn't just appeal to her artistically but emotionally as well. How typical of Brough, *her* Brough, that he should think of doing this, and typical too that he should search so assiduously to find someone, the *right* someone, to do the work for him.

How fitting…romantic even…that it should have been his quest to replace the missing pieces of a teaset which had originally been a wedding present for his grandmother that had brought them together, Kelly decided dreamily, determinedly ignoring the small, unwanted voice that insisted on reminding her that they had first met because of Julian Cox. That might have been their first meeting, but their *first mutual* realisation of their feelings for one another had been brought about by the Hartwell china, and when she told their grandchildren about it it would be that day together she would tell them about.

Their grandchildren.

A tiny shiver struck her. *Was* she taking too much for granted, reading too much into what Brough had said, the way he had held her…touched her…? When he had spoken of love had he merely been speaking of an emotion, a desire of the moment, and not meant it as she had done that his feelings were so profound and deep that they were a commitment for life?

Suddenly her small doubts, tiny minnows nibbling at the sure structure of her belief in his love for her, had become a swarming shoal of destructive piranha eating greedily into and devouring her confidence.

Where was Brough? Why had he gone like that? She had a vague memory of him bending over her and speaking to her, but now, when it was crucially important to do so, she just couldn't remember what exactly it was he had said. Something about having to go...but why? Because once the immediate passion of the moment had been spent he had had second thoughts about loving her? Or had, perhaps, her declaration of love for him come too soon and, even worse, been unwanted? *Had* she assumed too much...*loved* too much?

Outside dawn was lightening the sky. Sternly she told herself that there was no point in allowing herself to think so destructively. Only Brough knew the answers to her questions. Only Brough could assuage her doubts. But where was he? She had his home telephone number; she could always ring him.

She looked at the telephone, her fingers itching to pick up the receiver and dial his number, but it was still only six o'clock in the morning. What if her worst fears were correct? What if he *had* regretted the intimacy they had shared? How would he react when he heard her voice, an unwanted intrusion into his privacy, and an even more unwanted reminder of something he might prefer to forget? And how would *she* feel, knowing that he didn't want to speak to her?

Give it time...give *him* time, she urged herself.

Six o'clock. Brough stretched and grimaced as he turned over in the small bed in his grandmother's spare bedroom. It was far too early to ring Kelly and too soon to leave for home. He wanted to check with the specialist that his grandmother was truly on the way to recovery before he did that, and they had told him at the hospital last night that he couldn't see the specialist until ten o'clock in the morning.

He would ring Kelly before he left the hospital to come home, he comforted himself. God, but he missed her...wanted her. He frowned as he remembered the look of fear and revulsion on her face as Julian Cox held her. There was something that just didn't jell, that just didn't ring true to her character about her whole relationship with Cox—something he could sense without being able to analyse properly. It was obvious that she loathed him, but at the ball she had been actively flirting with him.

Brough frowned.

'We're old friends,' she had told him dismissively when he had challenged her, her whole attitude towards him almost aggressive. In a way that an animal was aggressive when it tried to cover up its fear?

Brough knew with a gut-deep instinct that there was no way Kelly, *his* Kelly, could *ever* have done anything so directly opposed to her open, straightforward nature as to be deceitful. It simply wasn't her. And neither would he have thought it would have been her ever to be even remotely attracted to a man like Julian Cox. It wasn't his own male ego or vanity that made him think that. He simply knew that she was too sensitive, too aware, too intelligent to be attracted by a man who held her sex in such obvious contempt.

But maybe, just maybe, it *was* possible that a much younger and more impressionable and vulnerable Kelly might have been unable to see through the façade that Cox was so adept at throwing around himself. His own sister, after all, had fallen for it, but that didn't explain why Kelly had been flirting so heavily with Cox on the night of the ball.

Wide awake now, Brough closed his eyes and tried to collect his thoughts. What was he doing? Whatever may or may not have happened in Kelly's past, it *was* her past. She had no need to make any explanations or apologies for it to him. He loved her as she was and for what she was, and if she *had* made an error of judgement...

An error of judgement? By allowing Cox to be her lover? The vicious kick of emotion he could feel in his stomach was an all-male gut reaction, but just as immediate and even more powerful was an instinctive awareness that there was no way Kelly would ever have shared that kind of intimacy with Julian Cox. Brough had no idea how he knew that...he just knew it. And, knowing it, he owed it to her and to their love to allow her privacy over the whole issue of just what role Julian Cox had played in her life prior to their meeting.

Whatever it may or may not have been, there was one thing Brough was one hundred per cent sure of: it most certainly didn't give Cox the right to behave towards her in the way he had been doing, half frightening the life out of her, bullying her.

Suddenly Brough was even more anxious to get back to her. Half past six... He was sorely tempted to ring her, but the things he wanted to say to her were so intensely personal that they simply could not be said over the phone.

Eve had told him that she and Harry wanted a Christmas wedding. Well, they could most certainly have it, but his own marriage to Kelly was going to take place first. Well, so far as he was concerned it was. Kelly, he suspected, might take a bit of persuading. She took her responsibilities to her partner, Beth, very seriously; that much was obvious.

Six forty-five. Brough groaned, quickly calculating how long it was going to be before he could get back to Rye-on-Averton and to Kelly.

'Are you awake?' Eve whispered softly to Harry.

Sternly he sat up in bed and looked at her. She might

have been able to persuade him that he should stay over-
night with her, but he had been very firmly determined
that they would sleep in separate rooms, and they had.
Eve was so sweetly naive that she had no idea of just
what she was doing to his self-control, curling up at the
bottom of his bed like that in her soft white nightdress,
her long hair flowing down her back.

'What are you doing in here?' he demanded.

'I came to talk to you…I couldn't sleep,' she answered, whispering excitedly, 'Oh, Harry, I'm so
happy…' Her face suddenly clouded. 'When are you
going to see Julian?'

'Nine o'clock,' Harry responded promptly, 'and then
you and I are going out to celebrate.'

As she looked down at her bare left hand he followed
her line of thought and told her gruffly, 'I've got my
grandmother's ring… I'd like you to have it, but if you
don't like it…'

'Oh, I'm sure I shall,' Eve breathed, pink-cheeked.
'Oh, Harry,' she repeated, flinging herself into his arms,
'I'm so excited. I still can't quite believe what's hap-
pening…'

Seven o'clock. Dee pushed back the duvet and padded
over to her bedroom window. Beyond it she could see
the soft rolling countryside, the fertile acres which had
been tended by her ancestors for so many generations.

Once, those ancestors had been as fertile as the fields
they tilled, but she and Harry were the only descendants
in their generation, a poor crop yield indeed. Harry
would marry, of course, and hopefully would produce
sons and daughters to continue the family tradition. She
would never marry nor have children since through her

own experience as a motherless girl she had formed very strong views on the need of a child to have the loving support of both its parents. An old-fashioned view in this day and age, perhaps, but it was hers and she had the right to have it just as she had the right to choose whether or not to yield to the demand of her own fast-ticking biological clock.

Yes, the future of their family was solely dependent on Harry. It needn't have been that way. There had once been a time when... But what was the point in dwelling on that now? Unbidden she had a sharp mental image of Julian Cox. Her whole body stiffened as a surge of pain gripped her.

She had waited for such a long time for the chance to punish Julian Cox for what he had done...to punish him in a way which would ensure that he suffered just as she had suffered...but once again it seemed that he was evading that justice, escaping it. There was no point in her being angry with Kelly. Love was a powerfully potent force. No one knew that better than she, but it wasn't over yet; there was still Anna's role to be played. Julian still needed money and he needed it desperately now. Brough had already refused to invest any money with him, thus closing down that avenue of escape to him. But Julian could still marry Eve and thereby gain access to her money.

But Brough was his sister's trustee, and once Kelly told him what Julian had done to Beth it was Dee's guess that Brough would never allow Julian to marry his sister. Julian was in debt up to his neck and sinking fast...very fast...

So maybe everything wasn't lost after all. Julian might have been clever enough technically not to break the law, but he had certainly come very close to doing so.

Through the people she had hired, Dee had discovered a vast hidden tangle of false names and hideaway companies, all of which could be linked to him if, like her, you used a little creative thinking. He might deceive others but he couldn't deceive her. There were the aliases with the same initials as his, the clever use of his mother's maiden name and the names of people now dead.

No, legally he might be able to laugh in the faces of his victims as he challenged them to claim restitution from him, but morally—But what did Julian know of morals? What did he care about the good name of others, about their pride in it, their shame at losing it? Nothing.

A bitter smile curled her mouth as her eyes closed on a wave of sharp pain.

Her father had been such a proud man. Distant and old-fashioned towards her in many ways, perhaps, but always, always scrupulously honest in everything he did...*everything*. But he was dead now, and it was pointless to dwell on how much closer they might have become once they had been able to meet as adults. That chance was gone, destroyed...like her option to marry and have children; stolen from her...

Stop it, you're getting maudlin, she warned herself sharply. It was time for her to get up. She had work to do. The markets in Hong Kong would soon be closing. She had investments there she needed to check on.

Julian enjoyed gambling on the futures market. Or at least he had done until recently, when he had begun to sustain such heavy losses, outsmarted and outbid, outbought and outsold by a shadowy rival who seemed to second-guess his every thought. Poor Julian!

When he woke up this morning it would be to find

that his investments had sunk without trace, that the profit he had been so in need of making had become a loss.

Suddenly Dee began to feel better.

CHAPTER TEN

WHITE-FACED, Julian stared at the screen of his computer, a sick feeling of shock and disbelief coagulating his blood.

He had woken up two hours ago, his tongue thick with yesterday's alcohol and his head throbbing. That bitch Kelly thought she was so clever; leading him on and then dropping him, but he'd get even with her. But first that hot tip he had picked up yesterday from his informer had sounded such a sure thing. He had bought heavily into it, using all his last reserves, but this morning when he had gone to check the market he had hardly been able to believe his eyes. The stock was gone, wiped out, finished, and with it everything he owned. *Everything.*

He pushed the computer screen off his desk with such violence that it hit the floor. He picked up the keyboard and flung it against the wall of his office in an attempt to relieve his panic and fury. What the hell was he going to do? He *had* to have money by the end of this month. He *had* to. And it wasn't just a matter of the banks calling in his loans and stopping him trading.

A long time ago Julian had hit on and discovered how easy it was to persuade gullible and often naively managed small private charities to accept his offer of free investment advice. Eagerly they had accepted, co-opting him onto their boards, offering him access to their monies, only too glad to have him remove from their shoulders the burden of managing their investments. Just so long as he provided them with an income which in-

164

creased from year to year they were happy and didn't enquire about their capital...

And that was exactly what he had done...until now... Never mind the fact that their capital was long since gone, used to fund his own lavish lifestyle, used to make investments so perilously on the outside of mere risky that no one else would touch them; just the excitement he had got from backing these outsiders had given him more of a buzz than sex and even drugs ever had.

Of course, the empty coffers of some of those early and rather clumsy siphoning-offs of funds had quickly come to light, but luckily he had been able to place the blame elsewhere and convince people that *he* was not the one responsible for the foolish investment and subsequent loss of their money, and he had even had the signatures of his co-investors to prove it. He had always been rather good at forging other people's signatures. The first time he had put his skill to a financial advantage had been when he had stolen a 'friend's' cheque book.

Those had been good days; fortune had favoured him and his investments and it had been no problem to move money from one place to another as and when it was needed. But now things were different. The markets were running against him and he had made heavy losses...too heavy... He needed money and he needed it urgently. It was all Kelly's fault. He had gambled heavily on being able to persuade her to allow him to advise her, on how best to 'invest' her inheritance. But now she had dropped him made a fool of him and no woman did that.

It was a pity that Eve didn't have access to her capital, and Brough certainly wasn't going to be easy to persuade to allow her to have full control over it; but still, it was better than nothing.

The sweat of fear that had soaked his skin was beginning to disappear and, with it, his earlier panic. He was worrying too much and too soon. What he needed was something to calm him down, help him relax...a drink...

He went to find the bottle of gin he had discarded in the kitchen the previous evening and then stopped as he heard his doorbell ring.

It was just gone nine o'clock.

It had been well gone ten o'clock when Brough had seen the specialist, who had declared very reassuringly that his grandmother would make a full recovery, and then Brough had gone from his office to his grandmother's bed to spend his allocated fifteen minutes with her. Kelly would be in the shop by now. Hurrying outside the hospital, he reached for his mobile phone.

Kelly had just opened the post when she heard the phone ring. As she reached for the receiver her heart started to beat very fast, her face flushing a soft pink, but to her disappointment her caller wasn't Brough but Beth.

'Hi... How are you?' her friend and partner asked her.

'I'm fine; how are you?' Kelly returned automatically.

'Not so good,' Beth responded. 'I'm still trying to fix up a visit to that factory I told you about.'

As Kelly listened to her friend's enthusiastic voice she suddenly heard the sound that warned her that a second caller was trying to get through on her line. Was it Brough? Even if it was, she could hardly cut Beth off in mid-sentence, she acknowledged frustratedly as her friend paused for a brief breath before continuing, 'Look, the reason I'm ringing is that I've decided I'm going to stay on in Prague for some more time. It could take me a while to track down this factory, and I'm determined to do it, Kelly, even if I have to learn the language to make myself understood,' she told her friend with unusual fierceness. 'I don't care how much Alex tries to put me off... I *want* that glass. Look, I'm intending to move into a cheaper hotel for the rest of my stay, but I don't know which one yet. I'll give you a ring once I've sorted something out.'

'Oh, Beth, you will take care, won't you?' Kelly begged her. 'If your interpreter doesn't think it's wise—'

'He's just being awkward and difficult,' Beth assured her firmly. 'I'm an adult, Kelly, not a child,' she added with un-Beth-like grittiness, saying before Kelly could raise any further objections, 'Look, I have to go; I'll be in touch. Bye...'

Frowning a little, Kelly replaced the receiver. Beth was obviously determined to track down this elusive factory, but her determination seemed so at odds with her normal gentle, almost passive behaviour that Kelly was a little puzzled by it. She certainly seemed to thoroughly dislike her interpreter, who, from what she had said, seemed to be doing his best to be extraordinarily obstructive.

Nervously Kelly dialled the numbers that would allow her to check her answering service.

Her heart started to thump as the recorded voice announced that she had one message.

'Hear message?' the tinny voice asked.

'Yes,' Kelly whispered, her throat suddenly constricted.

'Kelly, it's me, Brough. I need to talk to you...see you... I should be home around eleven-thirty; could you possibly call round? I'd come to the shop, but what I want to say I'd prefer to say in private... Bye now.'

'Repeat?' the tinny recording was demanding rather bossily. 'Repeat?'

'No. No...' Kelly responded automatically.

What did Brough mean? What *was* it he wanted to

say to her? Her mouth had gone dry and her heart was thudding heavily in a drumbeat of doom.

He *had* changed his mind, made a mistake... That was what he wanted to say to her and *that* was why he wanted privacy in order to do so. He *didn't* really love her at all.

Kelly started to shiver, causing the customer who had just walked into the shop to exclaim sympathetically, 'Oh, my, you do look poorly! It's not this virus that's been going round, is it? I should go straight to bed if I were you.'

If only the cause of her pain *were* merely a virus, Kelly reflected after her customer had gone. What time was it now? Eleven-thirty, Brough had said, his voice sounding remote and grave. He wouldn't have asked her to go round...

She would have to close the shop; it was too late to get someone in to take over from her. It would be the earliest lunch hour in history, she decided miserably. There was no point in trying to deceive herself or give herself false hope. Brough was only confirming what she herself had been thinking. He had had second thoughts, realised that her feelings were much, much stronger than his, and now he wanted to make the situation completely clear to her. That was the way he was. He wasn't the kind of man simply to walk away without any explanation.

He was sorry, he would tell her. He didn't want to hurt her. What they had had had been good...very good...but for him it had simply been a one-off and not, as she had obviously believed, the basis, the foundation, for a lasting relationship or a permanent commitment.

Five past eleven... She would leave at eleven-fifteen... Plenty of time for her to drive to where Brough was living. She reached mechanically for a cloth so that she could pass the time in polishing some of the items they had on display, but her hands were shaking so much she put it down again. In her present state of agitation she was likely to do more harm than good.

Julian stared drunkenly at the screen of his computer which he had picked up off the floor. His system had crashed...just like the whole of his life. The last thing he had expected when he'd opened the door to his caller two hours ago had been to discover Harry standing on his doorstep. The other man had asked him quietly if he could come in. Automatically, Julian had agreed.

'There's something I have to tell you,' Harry began calmly as Julian led him into his untidy, dusty sitting room, shaking his head when Julian offered him a drink, saying mildly, 'Rather too early for me...'

'It's never too early...' Julian responded boastfully as he poured himself another gin.

He had no idea what Harry wanted. He only knew the other man vaguely and totally despised him. Harry represented everything that he himself loathed.

'Eve has asked me to come and see you,' Harry began quietly. 'She and I are getting married...'

Julian stared at him in disbelief. Was he trying to play some kind of joke on him? He searched the other man's face, a slow sensation of sick realisation creeping like death along his veins. This was no joke.

'What the hell are you saying? She's marrying *me*,' Julian told him furiously.

Harry said nothing but just continued to look steadily at him.

'No! No! I don't believe it,' Julian insisted, starting to shake his head, trying to dispel the clouds of panic swamping him. 'I want to see her...talk to her...'

'I'm sorry, but I don't think that would be a good idea,' Harry told him politely.

'*You* don't think…?' Julian gave him an ugly look. 'Eve is *my* girlfriend. We're all but engaged, dammit, and—'

'She *was* your girlfriend,' Harry agreed quietly, 'although…' He stopped and gave Julian a steady look. 'It seems to me that you rather took her for granted. Perhaps if you'd valued her a little more…as she deserves to be valued…'

'Oh, my God, now I've heard it all—*you* telling *me* how to treat a woman…' Julian gave him a contemptuous look and tossed back the last of his drink. 'What the hell do *you* know about women? Nothing…' he jeered. 'She loves *me*; she told me so… She's besotted with me…' he boasted.

Harry said nothing, refusing to retaliate, simply watching him with a look in his eyes that goaded Julian into walking unsteadily across the floor and pouring himself another drink.

'You can't do this to me…and don't think I don't know who's behind it. It's that precious brother of hers; he never wanted—'

'This has nothing to do with Brough,' Harry corrected him. 'Eve and I are in love…'

'Eve in love…with you? Don't make me laugh. She loves *me*.'

She did love him. She had told him so in a soft, nervous little voice, her eyes big with wonder and excitement. It had been so easy to trick her into believing he had fallen for her. She was so trusting… She hadn't even questioned the fact that he hadn't taken her to bed.

'I respect you too much,' he had told her untruthfully.

The truth was that his drinking and the intense pressure of his lifestyle meant that sex was the last thing on his mind, the last desire he had. It took a woman like Kelly to arouse *that* need in him, not a babyish innocent like Eve.

Julian *knew* that it was her brother who was behind her decision to drop him. Brough had guessed that Julian was after her money, of course. Julian gave a small mental shrug. So what? He didn't give a damn what Brough had or hadn't guessed, and as for preferring Harry to him… That was ridiculous…impossible…

'I don't believe you… I'm going to see Eve-talk to her,' he announced, walking unsteadily towards the door, but oddly, when he got there, Harry was standing in front of it, barring his way.

'No, I'm sorry, but you're not,' Harry told him calmly.

Julian looked drunkenly at him.

'What is this? You can't stop me…'

Harry stood solidly in front of the door, simply looking at him. A little to his own surprise Julian discovered that he was actually backing off. What the hell was he doing? He wasn't afraid of Harry.

'I think you'll find it would be best for everyone concerned if you simply accept the situation,' he heard Harry saying gently to him, to his utter amazement.

'People will soon forget. After all, it isn't as though you were actually engaged, and neither Eve nor I shall say anything. People will simply believe that the two of you drifted apart. It happens all the time.'

Julian swayed and focused vacantly on Harry's face. What the hell was he trying to suggest? That he, Julian Cox, was in danger of being humiliated by people thinking that Eve had dropped him? No way!

'Eve mentioned that you have business interests in Hong Kong. I've heard it is a fascinating part of the world, even more so these days… Have you ever been there? I haven't myself... Farming doesn't combine well with travelling...'

Julian continued to gape at him.

Was Harry actually daring subtly to suggest to him, to *warn* him, that he should leave town...? No, it was impossible. Harry simply wasn't like that. He didn't have the nerve...nor the subtlety. No, he was imagining it, Julian assured himself. The other man was too unworldly to know that there was no way Julian could visit Hong Kong right now, not with the money he owed out there, the enemies he had made.

'I'll let myself out,' he heard Harry saying mildly. When he reached the front door, Harry turned to him and commented quietly, 'I should keep off the drink for a while if I were you.' Then he turned round and opened the door to leave.

Now as he sat staring blindly at the screen in front of him, Julian couldn't believe it. His life was in chaos, *ruins*... He had been counting on Eve and her inheritance. By God, but she wasn't going to do this to him. No way... He could soon make her change her mind.

He needed a drink. He lurched over to the kitchen worktop, frowning impatiently when he saw the empty bottle. Well, he would just have to go out and buy some more, wouldn't he? He still had enough money for that...he could still afford to buy himself a *drink*...to get drunk... By God, yes, he could still afford to do that, and once he had...

As Julian opened his front door the brilliance of the bright morning hit his eyeballs in fiery darts of pain. Oblivious to the looks on the faces of other pedestrians, he started to stagger towards the centre of the town. His car was parked outside the house, but some vestige of self-preservation warned him that it would be extremely unwise for him to drive.

Kelly too had made the same decision, but for very different reasons. It wasn't drink that made her aware that her reactions were simply not good enough for her to drive anywhere safely. She was trembling from head to foot as she opened the shop door, dreading her coming interview with Brough, and yet knowing that she was too proud to ring him up and simply tell him that it wasn't necessary for him to say anything; that she had already guessed what he wanted to tell her and that she understood.

Pride, was it? Was she *sure* it wasn't more of a desperate, anguished yearning on the part of a woman far too deeply and vulnerably in love to deny herself the masochistic pleasure of spending some last precious minutes with the man she loved?

It seemed to be adding an even finer edge of cruelty to her unhappiness that it should be such a wonderful day, the sun shining, the air soft and fresh, people walking about dressed in light clothes, smiling...

As she turned the corner at the bottom of the street she could see across the town square to the river, glinting happily in the sunshine. Rye-on-Averton was such a pretty town that normally just to walk through it lifted her spirits, but not today-no, definitely not today.

Head down, fighting to hold back the tears threatening to overwhelm her, Kelly walked quickly to Brough's house.

She was less than five yards away from it when she suddenly heard someone calling her name. Lifting her head, she froze as she recognised Julian Cox staggering towards her from the opposite direction. He was quite obviously drunk and looked totally repulsive, she decided as she saw his stubbly jaw and creased clothes.

'Kelly... What are you doing here...or can I guess? Come crawling round after Brough, have you? What happened? Dropped you, has he?' he tormented her jeeringly. 'Well, what did you expect? Surely you aren't really stupid enough not to guess what he was up to? He wanted to draw you off me because of his sister. That was all… Didn't you guess? Surely you must have realised that a man like him would *never* look seriously at someone like you, someone who's been to bed with half the town… Not that he minded getting a taste of what you've got to offer himself… He told me that…said he might as well have full value for his money…'

Julian had gone straight from his house to the supermarket, where he had discovered, contrary to his belief, he did *not* have enough money on him to buy any alcohol. Infuriated, both by this and Harry's interview with him, he had, instead of going home, headed for Brough's house, intending to try to persuade Eve to see reason and change her mind. She would more than likely be on her own at this time of day and he was pretty sure he could persuade her to listen to him.

But just as he had reached the house he had seen Kelly approaching it from the opposite direction, and immediately he had remembered just how she had rejected him and how, because of that rejection, Brough Frobisher had humiliated him—and, no doubt, brought pressure to bear on Eve to end their relationship.

All the fury and vindictiveness caused by this suddenly found a target in Kelly. What better way of getting back at Brough than by destroying his relationship with Kelly? If he knew anything about women—and he did— she would never stay if he told her that Brough had discussed her sexually with someone else.

Now, looking at her face, he knew he had been right—God, he was enjoying hurting her, making her pay for rejecting him.

'Did you really think he wanted you?' he taunted her cruelly. 'How could he? He saw the way you were all over *me* at the ball... He's a proud man, our Brough...far too proud to want *my* leavings...'

Brough had not made as good time coming back as he had hoped. Some unexpected road works had held him up and then, to make matters worse, he hadn't been able to park his car outside his house but had had to leave it much further down the street.

It was already gone half past eleven. Quickening his stride, he turned the corner to see Kelly standing outside the house with her back to him, facing Julian Cox. What the hell was he doing...?

Immediately Brough started to run.

Julian, who was facing him, saw him first, smirking triumphantly at him as he reached them, taunting Brough drunkenly, 'How did it feel having my leavings?' He waved his arms towards Kelly. 'She's pretty good, I know, but just in case you're interested I can recommend someone even better... They say that an enthusiastic amateur is better than a professional any day, I know, but...'

Kelly made a small, tortured whimper of protest but both men seemed to be ignoring her.

'Well, you saw for yourself at the ball how it was,' Julian continued tauntingly. He was beginning to enjoy himself now. The effects of the drink he had consumed earlier were beginning to wear off, sharpening his instincts. Kelly looked white and sick. Oh, yes, he really was enjoying this.

'Of course, Kelly and I are old mates. She and I had a little thing going when I was dating her partner, Beth. Kelly's like that. She *prefers* a man who belongs to another woman, don't you, my pet? She says it adds to the enjoyment…gives it an extra kick of excitement for her…and she certainly likes her excitement, does our Kelly. Has she…?' He used a phrase which horrified Kelly and made her face burn with shame. She couldn't bring herself to look at Brough. How could she defend herself against Julian's charges without going into lengthy explanations? And besides, what was the point? She already knew that Brough didn't want her, didn't *love* her as she did him.

Not returning her love was one thing, she reminded herself in anguish, but having him receive this kind of information about her, knowing how it *must* affect his judgement of her and his future memories of her, was quite another.

'It's okay, though,' Julian continued laconically. 'I've put her in the picture about Eve and she knows that you were just using her to draw… All you really wanted was to get her out of my life… Is…she in, by the way? I promised her I'd take her out this morning to choose an engagement ring.'

As he spoke Julian stepped determinedly past Kelly, almost knocking her over.

'I agree with what you said about her,' he commented loudly to Brough. 'She's really just a good one-night lay.'

Suddenly, as Julian looked into Brough's eyes, the drunken fumes momentarily cleared from his brain. He had, he recognised sickly, made a bad mistake—a dangerous error of judgement. But it was too late for him to have second thoughts now, he realised as the contempt in Brough's eyes became a seething fury.

Kelly couldn't bear to hear any more. Without turning to look at Brough she started to walk and then to run desperately away, ignoring the concerned stares of pass-

ers-by as she ran, head down, along the street, back in
the direction she had come.

Brough watched her like someone turned to stone.

'I need to see Eve, Brough,' Julian started to plead
whiningly.

Cold-eyed, Brough turned to look at him. 'Eve is marrying Harry,' he told him. 'You're not wanted here, Cox,
and if I find you *anywhere* near my sister for *any* reason...'

'Are you threatening me?' Julian began to bluster as
he knew he had gone too far in venting his rage against
Kelly.

'No. I'm *telling* you,' Brough said softly. 'And, by
the way, you've wasted your time coming here. Eve isn't
here; she's gone to visit her in-laws-to-be. Now, if you'll
excuse me I—'

'I wouldn't waste your time going after Kelly,' Julian
interrupted him, grinning. 'Everything I said about her
was true. But you must have found out what she's like
for yourself by now. She doesn't make a man waste
time; I'll give her that. Pretty energetic in bed, isn't she?
Pity she's not been a bit more exclusive about how she
hands it out...'

Julian never saw the blow that hit him, he certainly
felt it, though, as he dropped to the floor, trying to stem
the blood pouring from his nose. He started to curse but
Brough had already gone.

Instinctively Kelly headed for the river path and its protective seclusion.

She *couldn't* go back to the shop, not just yet, and
there was nowhere else, no *one* else, she could go to—
not like this...

Oh, but it had hurt, hurt more than anything else in
her life, knowing what Brough must be thinking about

her. None of Julian's crude accusations were true, of course—at least not in the way *he* had said them.

Apart from a brief, immature adolescent relationship with the boy who had been her first lover, there had been no one else in her life other than Brough, and certainly no one else in her bed. But how on earth could she prove that to Brough?

He might not love her but at least he had liked her, *respected* her, and she couldn't bear to think of him now carrying an image of her that Julian had painted for him. But even if she could bring herself to face him and explain, why *should* he believe her?

The river path was empty of other walkers, and Kelly's fast pace had slowed as the thoughts started to tumble around in her head.

'Kelly!'

The shock of hearing Brough's voice behind her made her stumble, but immediately he was beside her, catching her up in his arms.

'*Why* did you run off like that?' he demanded as her body stiffened defensively in his hold.

Agitatedly Kelly shook her head. The shock of him suddenly appearing, never mind what being held so close to him was doing to her nervous system, was too much for her to cope with.

'Those things that Julian said—it wasn' t...I never... You have been the only one—' Kelly stopped, unable to go on.

She could feel Brough's tension, and when he lifted his hand to raise her chin so that she was forced to look into his eyes Kelly felt as though she would die from the pain of what she was expecting him to say, but to her shock what she saw in his eyes wasn't contempt and rejection, but love and tenderness and, along with it, anxiety.

'Kelly, I don't understand. You surely don't think I could *possibly* place any credence on what Cox was saying?'

Kelly stared at him.

'You didn't...you don't believe him?' she whispered.

'Of course not. How could I? What kind of man do you think I am?' he demanded, his expression changing, darkening. 'I certainly don't need a man like Cox to tell me *anything* about the woman I love. I can learn about her for myself, and what I have learned...'

The woman he *loved*. Kelly felt as though her heart was going to burst with joy.

'You *love* me?' she asked him huskily.

He was still frowning.

'Of course I do. You *know* that. I told you... Kelly... Kelly, darling, please don't cry,' he begged her as he drew her closer. 'Please, please don't cry, my love...'

'You *left* me,' Kelly wept, more out of relief and joy than unhappiness; after all, what possible reason was there for her to be unhappy *now*, with Brough's arms around her, Brough's words of love ringing so sweetly in her ears, Brough's lips so close to hers?

'I *had* to,' Brough told her. 'I'd had a phone call to say that my grandmother had been taken into hospital. You were so deeply asleep I couldn't bear to waken you...'

'Your *grandmother*,' Kelly repeated, instantly asking anxiously, 'Oh, Brough, what...? How...?'

'She's fine... She had a fall followed by pneumonia but she's well on the way to recovery now and very much looking forward to meeting you.'

'You've told her about me?' Kelly asked him shyly. 'Oh, what...?'

'I told her you were interested in seeing her teaset,'

Brough teased her, relenting when he saw the uncertainty still clouding her eyes.

'I told her I love you and that I want you to be my wife,' he told her huskily. 'She can't wait to meet you and I've promised that I'll do my best to persuade you to come with me when I drive down to see her tomorrow...'

'Oh, Brough...'

'You're crying again,' he chided her.

'It's because I'm so happy,' Kelly assured him. 'Say that again...'

'What, that you're crying?'

'No...what you said about loving me and wanting to marry me,' Kelly told him softly.

'I love you and I want you to marry me,' Brough repeated dutifully, but before Kelly could respond to him he was cupping her face and kissing her tenderly and slowly, and then not tenderly at all as her emotions caught fire and she clung passionately to him, returning the demanding pressure of his mouth, her whole body singing with joy as it recognised just how much he truly loved and wanted her.

'Brough, about Julian...' Kelly began slowly when she had finally managed to persuade him to stop kissing her.

'What about him? He means nothing to us; he has no place in our lives, our future,' Brough pointed out.

'No. But, yes, he does have a place...sort of...in *my* past,' Kelly told him carefully, adding hastily, 'Oh, no, it's not that we were ever lovers.' She gave a small shudder. 'I couldn't...he's loathsome...and I... Well, as a matter of fact, you've been the only...that is... There was a boy when... Brough, how can I explain about Julian if you keep on kissing me?' she protested shakily.

'You don't have to tell me anything about your past,' Brough told her quietly.

'You are the person you are, Kelly, and that includes everything and everyone in your past that has gone to make up that person, that Kelly—*my* Kelly. Without those experiences you wouldn't be the Kelly I love so much... You didn't really think I'd place any credence on those ridiculous lies that Cox was telling, did you?' he asked her, obviously pained that she might have done.

'I... I...I thought, after the way you left me, that you'd had second thoughts about...about us. And then, when I got your telephone message, I thought you wanted to see me to tell me that...that it was...that I was...that there wasn't any future for us...'

Kelly bit her lip as she heard the incredulous sound he made, but she was determined to finish what she had to say.

'I...' She raised her head and looked him firmly in the eye. 'When you and I met at that ball, I *was* flirting with Julian, and it was because of that that I thought you might think...'

'What I thought that night was that even though I knew nothing at all about you there was something odd about your behaviour, something that somehow didn't ring quite true, something alien and quite patently uncomfortable for you in your behaviour towards Cox.'

'You felt all that but...but you kissed me as though—' Kelly began, but Brough stopped her.

'That was an experiment,' he told her boldly. 'I was curious about you, about the...er...discrepancies in your behaviour and the person I sensed you were, and I was curious about... I felt that if I kissed you I would immediately be able to tell—'

'You're fibbing,' Kelly interrupted him. 'How could you tell anything from just one kiss?'

'I could tell that I was falling in love with you,' Brough told her wryly, silencing her before continuing, 'It did puzzle me that you should be acting in a way that was quite plainly out of character for you,' he admitted quietly. 'But I decided that whatever your reasons for doing so, they were *your* reasons. You are a woman, adult, mature, perfectly capable of making your own decisions and doing whatever you decide is right for you. I have no right nor reason to question those decisions, nor would I want to do so,' he told her gravely. 'As I've already told you, Kelly, I love the person you *are*, and whatever you choose to do or not to do…'

'I did it for Beth,' Kelly told him quickly. 'It was Dee's idea…'

Briefly she explained what they had planned to do.

'Beth… So that was the girl Cox was seeing before he met Eve. Cox told Eve that she was obsessed with him and that—'

'No way…' Kelly told him indignantly. '*He* was on the verge of getting engaged to Beth when he met Eve and then he told poor Beth that she had imagined everything…that he had never said he wanted to marry her. But Beth's not like that. She's gentle and sweet, a passive, loving…'

'Rather like my sister, in fact,' Brough concluded grimly.

'A little like that,' Kelly agreed. 'But of course Beth didn't have any money…' She sighed. 'I'm sorry if I sounded unkind…'

'No, you're only corroborating my own thoughts,' Brough told her. 'However, fortunately that's not a problem we need to worry about any more, since Eve has informed me that she is in love with Harry and that they intend to get married at Christmas. Christmas, apparently, is a perfect time for a marriage in the farming community...'

'Harry...? I knew he was attracted to her,' Kelly admitted. 'He's Dee's cousin. That was why he was escorting me at the ball.

'Brough, what are you doing?' she demanded as Brough turned her round and, tucking her into his side, proceeded to walk briskly back in the direction they had just come.

'I'm taking you home with me,' he told her firmly, and then added huskily, 'Do you realise it's almost twenty-four hours since I made love with you?'

'Brough,' Kelly protested as he took her back in his arms and proceeded to show her just how long a time he felt those hours had been.

'Kelly...' he teased her softly as he nibbled at her bottom lip and felt the sweet response of her body and herself to his caresses.

'I've got to go back and re-open the shop,' she told him.

'Why?' Brough demanded. 'There's no point; all its stock has just been sold.'

'What...what are you talking about?' Kelly demanded in bemusement. 'Who...? What...?'

'I'm talking about the fact that if the only way I can get you to myself is to buy every piece of stock in your precious shop, then that's exactly what I shall do,' Brough told her rawly.

'You can't do that,' Kelly protested. 'It will cost you a fortune...'

'Yes, I can. I'm a very rich man,' Brough assured her sweetly, adding huskily, 'The richest and happiest man in the world now I've got you, my love, my precious only one true love.

'My grandmother's already nagging me about a white wedding.'

'Cream...' Kelly murmured, nuzzling closer to the promising intoxication of his mouth. 'Cream suits me better...'

'Mmm... Well, there's no way I intend to wait until Eve gets married...'

Kelly's heart gave a funny little jump.

'It takes at least three weeks for the banns to be read, and my family will have to come back from South Africa...'

'Mmm... Well, that certainly won't take three weeks, but I hear what you're saying. How about we make it the same time as Nan's wedding anniversary, which is several weeks away? I know it would mean a lot to her if you and I chose the same wedding day...'

'It sounds perfect,' Kelly told him happily.

'It *is* perfect...like you...perfect in every way...and don't you ever forget it,' Brough told her huskily as he drew her even more deeply into his arms.

EPILOGUE

'TRY not to feel too bad that things didn't work out,' Anna tried to console Dee gently. 'We may not have been able to reveal Julian in his true colours, but at least Beth seems to be getting over him. She never mentioned him once the last time she rang me, and in fact she seemed far more concerned about the problems this interpreter's causing her than her broken engagement. And just think, if it hadn't been for *you*, Kelly and Brough might never have met...'

Dee gave her a rueful look.

They were sitting in the pretty conservatory at the back of Anna's house, Anna's cat purring loudly on her knee whilst her little dog begged hopefully for crumbs of the home-made biscuit Dee was eating.

'I wish I could be more like you, Anna,' Dee told her in a rare admission of self-criticism. 'You have such a peaceful acceptance of life...'

'Maybe now,' Anna agreed with her gentle smile, 'but not always. When I first lost Ralph, my husband...' She paused and shook her head. 'But that's all in the past now.' She looked thoughtfully at Dee before continuing quietly, 'Have you ever thought, Dee, that it might be time for *you* to put Julian and whatever...?' She stopped and bit her lip as she saw the storm clouds beginning to darken Dee's magnificent eyes.

'No. Never. There's no way I can put Julian in the past until—'

Abruptly Dee stopped. Close though she had become to both Kelly and Anna these last few weeks, there were still some things she just couldn't bring herself to discuss with them, some confidences she couldn't even make to gentle, understanding Anna.

'It isn't over yet,' she said fiercely instead, reminding Anna, 'At least he's taking the bait in *our* trap.'

Their trap? Wisely Anna said nothing. Something that went far, far deeper into Dee's past than her relatively recent friendship with her own goddaughter, Beth, was motivating Dee in her need to see Julian get his just deserts.

'Julian's already made overtures to you, hinting that he could put you in the way of a highly profitable investment opportunity, hasn't he?'

'Yes, he has,' Anna agreed.

'Excellent. We'll get him yet, and when we do…'

'When we do, what?' Anna pressed her gently.

Dee turned to her, her eyes bleak with an anguished pain that touched Anna's tender heart as she told her grimly, 'When we do, we'll expose him for the liar and the cheat that he is! The liar, the cheat and the murderer,' Dee emphasised.

The *murderer*? Anna was too shocked to say anything, and Dee was already getting up, pausing only to give the waiting dog the titbit she had saved for him before turning to hug Anna and tell her, 'I'll be in touch. There are a few arrangements I need to make to ensure that you'll have sufficient cash available to properly tempt Julian. I think probably that fifty thousand pounds should do it…'

'Fifty thousand pounds!' Anna gasped in protest. 'Oh, Dee, so much. But…'

'It's nothing,' Dee told her quietly. 'Nothing compared with the cost of a man's life.

'Don't worry,' she reassured Anna as she saw her anxious face. '*You* won't be in any danger.'

No, maybe *she* wouldn't, Anna acknowledged as she watched Dee drive away ten minutes later, but what about Dee? Ridiculous though she knew other people would find it, in view of Dee's uncompromisingly self-assured attitude, Anna actually felt very protective towards her. No one could look into those tortoiseshell-coloured eyes and see, as she, Anna, had so briefly seen, the pain and anger that sometimes lurked there, without doing so.

And Anna knew all about pain and anger and, yes, there was guilt too. Emotions these women shared, but both chose to hide their pain from those around them.

Mistress of Convenience

PENNY JORDAN

CHAPTER ONE

'Wow, will you look at that? His Royal Highness and the industrialist everyone swears is not up for a knighthood. And don't they look cosy together for two people who are supposed to be sworn enemies.'

As Suzy struggled to hear the voice of Jeff Walker, the photographer from the magazine they both worked for, over the noise of the busy launch party, she heard him saying excitedly, 'I've just got to get a shot of that. Come on.'

This was her first month on the magazine, and immediately she followed him.

She had taken a couple of steps when she heard him saying bitterly, 'Hell! He's got Colonel Lucas James Soames with him. Ex-Commando, Special Forces, hero, and hater of the press!' he explained impatiently when he saw Suzy's uncertain frown. 'Despite the fact that a female reporter with a certain British news team practically dribbled with lust every time she interviewed him during his last campaign.'

Suzy tried to look as though she was up to speed with what she was being told, but the plain truth was that she knew nothing of Colonel Soames. Already unnerved by the photographer's comments, she looked round discreetly, but was unable to spot anyone wearing any kind of military uniform.

She knew she ought to be grateful to her university

tutor for recommending her for this job. He had been so enthusiastic about it, telling her what a wonderful opportunity it would be for her, that she had felt she would be letting him down if she didn't accept the probationary position. But after nearly a month working on the political affairs desk of the cutting-edge City magazine Suzy was beginning to suspect that she had made a mistake.

Maybe it was the fact that she had been out of the swim of things for so long whilst she nursed her mother through the last two years of her life that made her so uncomfortable about the methods the magazine adopted in order to get its hot stories. She had certainly felt immeasurably older than her fellow students when she had returned to university to complete her degree.

'I'm sorry—' She began to apologise uncertainly to Jeff. 'I can't see the Colonel.'

But she could see a man several yards away, who stood head and shoulders above every other man in the room—or so it seemed to Suzy. She was transfixed, every female hormone in her body focusing on him with an eager interest. Her mouth had gone dry and her heart had started to pound unevenly. The fact that he was standing alone, somehow aloof from everyone else, only piqued her interest further.

She had the most unexpected and dangerous urge to go up to him and make him... Make him what, exactly? Acknowledge her presence? Talk to her? Tell her that he was experiencing the same heart-wrenching, sanity-undermining, wholly unfamiliar need to be with her that she was experiencing for him? Was she going crazy? Her legs had gone weak and her heart was racing. She didn't know whether it was shock that was running through her body with mercurial speed or excitement. Her? Excited by a man? A stranger? She was too sensible for such stuff. Too sensible and too wary!

Determinedly she started to look away, but he had turned his head, and her heartbeat went into overdrive whilst a surge of explicit and bewildering arousal and longing raced though her. Longing for a man she had only looked at? How could that happen?

And yet Suzy couldn't help watching him. He wasn't looking at her, but past her, she recognised. However, whilst he did so, Suzy was able to stare at him and greedily absorb every tiny physical detail. Tall, dark and handsome went nowhere near describing his full male magnificence. He was more than that. Much, much more! Suzy could feel her whole body responding to just about the sexiest man she had ever seen and was ever likely to see. Her heart gave another small nervous flurry of thuds when he turned his head again, as though he knew that she was now looking at him. He was now staring straight at her, imprisoning her almost, so that she felt unable to move!

She felt as though she was being X-rayed—and that there wasn't a single thing he didn't know about her! Pink-cheeked, she realised that his incisive gaze had finished sweeping her and was now fixed on her mouth. She felt her lips starting to part, as though they were longing for his kiss. Hurriedly she closed them, her face still burning.

His eyes were a shade of intense dark blue, his skin tanned, his hair so dark brown that it was almost black. His profile was that of a Greek god and, as though that wasn't enough, Suzy was forced to acknowledge that he had about him that indefinable air that whispered into the female ear *sex*. And not just any old kind of sex either, but dream-breaking, heart-stopping, mind-blowing wonderful sex! In fact the kind of sex...

Somehow she managed to get her wayward thoughts under control just in time to hear Jeff telling her curtly, 'You're going to have to distract the Colonel's attention whilst I get my picture.'

'What?' Suzy asked, anxiously scanning the crowd packed tightly around the Prince.

'Where...where is he...?'

'Over there—next to the Prince and the Secretary of State.'

Wildly Suzy looked from the photographer's face to the man he had just indicated. *The* man. *Her* man...

'But...but you said he was a colonel. He isn't in uniform.' She was stammering like an idiot—behaving like a woman who had fallen passionately in love! Now she *knew* that she was crazy.

'Uniform?' Jeff's voice was impatient, contemptuous of her ignorance. 'No, of course he isn't in uniform. He isn't in the Army any more. Where have you been? He works on his own, freelance, providing a bespoke protection service for those who need it. Not that he needs to work. He's independently wealthy and well connected; his father was the younger son of an old county family, and his mother was American. He's ex-Eton. Cut his teeth in Northern Ireland and got made up to Major, then was decorated for service above and beyond the call of duty in Bosnia—that's when he got his next promotion. Like I just said, he isn't in the

Army any more but he still does the dangerous stuff—
acting as a personal bodyguard. He's in great demand
on the "I'm an important person and I need a top-class
protection service" circuit. Visiting politicians and
heads of state, et cetera.'

All this had been relayed to Suzy in a grim whisper,
but now suddenly Jeff exclaimed excitedly, 'Look at
that! Get that picture and I won't ever need to work
again. Yes, you stay right there, baby,' he crooned to
himself, before commanding Suzy, 'Come on! You'll
have to distract the Colonel so that I can get this shot.'

'What? What am I supposed to do?' Suzy asked anxiously, and she looked to where the Colonel was standing casually in front of the two men, screening them
from interruption.

Jeff gave her an exasperated look. 'Why the hell did
they land me with you instead of someone who knows
the ropes? I've heard that Roy has only taken you on
as a favour, and because he likes your legs—he probably interviewed you imagining what they'd look like
wrapped around him.'

Suzy struggled not to let Jeff see how upset she was
by his comments. Her boss's openly sexual and often
crude remarks to her were just one of the reasons why
she was becoming increasingly unhappy about her job.

'You're a woman, aren't you? Go over there and do
what comes naturally!' Jeff grunted, before pushing his
way through the crowd, leaving Suzy to follow him.

Do what comes naturally! Oh, yes, she could quite
easily do what came naturally with Colonel Soames...
A thrill of dangerous emotion spiked through Suzy as
she looked into the face of the man who was now

standing right in front of her. He was, Suzy acknowledged, quite definitely the sexiest man she had ever seen. Those broad shoulders, that handsome face!

She was beginning to feel seriously alarmed by her reactions to him! Her friend Kate was always scolding her, telling her she didn't get out enough, and now Suzy thought she might be right. To be affected like this, to react like this simply at the sight of one specific man... She closed her eyes, willing herself to be sensible, and then opened them again.

What was it about a man in a dinner suit? What was it about *this* man in a dinner suit? Well, for one thing he was wearing his with an unselfconscious ease that said he was used to doing so, and for another it fitted him somehow as though it were a part of him. What had he looked like in his dress uniform? In combats? A tiny shudder ripped through her.

And as for that tan and those teeth...teeth that she was sure gleamed nearly as white as his shirtfront! And she was sure there were real muscles beneath all that tailoring as well.

Out of the corner of her eye she saw Jeff glowering at her. A little uncomfortably Suzy took a deep breath and stepped forward, a muddled plan of action forming inside her head. A smile of recognition at the Colonel then a brief apology for having mistaken him for someone else. A few seconds' work, but long enough, she hoped, for Jeff to get his picture.

Gritting her teeth against the knowledge that this kind of behaviour was quite definitely not her style, Suzy ignored the nervous churning of her stomach and stepped forward.

And then stopped! One step was all she had taken—so how come she now had her nose virtually against the Colonel's pristine white shirt? How had he moved without her being aware that he was doing so? When had he moved? Suzy wondered frantically. In less than a blink of the eye he had somehow gone from standing a couple of yards away to being right in front of her.

Suzy's sensitive nostrils started to quiver as she breathed in a discreet hint of cologne, underwritten by something very male and subtle that sent her self-control crashing into chaos.

He reached out and took hold of her arm, his grip firm and compelling. Suzy could feel her blood beating up around his encircling fingers as her body reacted to his hold.

Like someone lost in a trance she looked up at him. An instinct deeper than any thought or action seemed to have taken control of her, and she was powerless to do anything other than give in to it. The navy blue gaze fastened on her own. Her heart jerked against the wall of her chest, and the polite social apology she had been about to make died unspoken on her lips.

In a haze of dizzying desire Suzy felt her gaze slide like melting ice cream from the heat of his eyes to the curve of his mouth. Her whole body was galvanised by a series of tiny tremors and she exhaled on a small, soft, female sigh of wanton pleasure.

Without knowing what she was doing she lifted her free hand to trace the hard, firm line of his mouth—to see if the flesh there felt as erotic as it looked. But then her hand dropped to her side as another even more pleasurable way of conducting her survey struck her.

She had to reach up on her tiptoes in order to press her mouth to his, but the hand holding her arm seemed somehow to aid and balance her. The busy hum of conversation in the room faded as her lips made the discovery that just touching his mouth with her own was opening a door for her into a whole new world.

Blind and deaf to everything and everyone else around her, Suzy made a soft sound of pleasure deep in her throat. An aching whisper of female recognition.

Closing her eyes, she leaned into the male body, waiting hungrily for the Colonel to return the pressure of her lips, to part them with the swift, hard thrust of his tongue, to share with her the devouring intensity of need and longing that surged through her.

As she sighed her pleasure and hunger against his mouth she felt its pressure, his kiss heart-joltingly male. One of his hands slid firmly into the thick softness of her red-gold curls whilst the other pressed into the small of her back, urging her body closer to his own!

Suzy knew she was not very sexually experienced, and what was happening to her now was way out of her league! The way his mouth was moving on hers—firm, warm, knowing—the way his tongue-tip was lav-ing the eager softness of her lips, was rewriting the logbook of her sexual history and adding a whole new chapter to it!

Lost in the rapture of what was happening to her, Suzy pressed closer, caught up in a cloud of hormone-drenched fantasy.

This was it! This was him! Her dragon-slayer and protector, the magical lover she had dreamed of in her most vulnerable moments. The hero she had secretly longed for all her life in her most private dreams. Her soul mate.

Suzy ached to tell him how she felt, how filled with delirious joy she was that he was here, how...

She gave a small shocked gasp as suddenly she was being pushed away.

Confusion darkened her eyes as she looked up at him, at a loss to understand what was happening until she saw the way he was looking back at her.

Instantly her joy was replaced with pain and despair. Shock gripped hold of her with icy fingers as she recognised the anger and loathing in the navy blue gaze boring into her.

'No!' She heard herself whisper the agonised denial, but it was no use. There was no mercy or softening in the hard, contemptuous gaze. Her whole body felt as though it was being drenched in shame and humiliation. Her soul mate? He was looking at her as though she were his worst enemy!

Anger, contempt, hostility, Suzy could see them all glittering in his eyes, before they were hidden away from her with a blank look of steely professionalism.

What on earth had she done? Why had she done it? She had made a complete and total fool of herself! What stupidity had made her resurrect that idiotic old dream of a soul mate? She'd thought she had had the sense to recognise it had no place in reality! It was a dream she had clung to for far too long anyway, like a child reluctant to relinquish the security of a worn-out teddy bear.

Her face was burning painfully—and not just because of the way he had looked at her. The shaky, sickly feeling invading her was surely a form of shock, a physical reaction to an emotional trauma. And she *was* traumatised, she admitted unwillingly. And not just by the Colonel's contempt and dislike!

Her own feelings had left her even more shocked and distressed...

She could feel his concentration on her, but she refused to look back at him. Because she was afraid to? Somewhere inside her head she could still feel the unspoken words 'I love you' banging frantically against the walls of their cage, like a tiny wounded bird desperate to escape. But Suzy knew they could never be set free. They had to be kept imprisoned for ever now, to protect her own sanity and self-respect!

' "*Down and Dirty* magazine." ' She could hear him reading the name-badge she was wearing. 'I should have guessed. Your tactics are as cheap and tasteless as your articles.'

Savage pain followed by equally savage anger spiked into her heart. Illogically she felt as though somehow he had actively betrayed her by not recognising the person she really was, by misjudging her, not caring enough to recognise what had happened to her.

'I think your friend is waiting for you.'

The curt words were distinctly unfriendly, his voice clipped and incisive, and the look he gave her was coldly dismissive. But deep inside her Suzy could still feel the hard pressure of his mouth on hers.

Shaking, she turned to make her way towards the door, where Jeff was standing, an impassive bouncer holding his arm—and his camera.

Jeff's face, she saw with a sinking heart, was puce with temper.

'What the hell do you think you were doing?' he demanded once Suzy reached him. 'I told you to distract the guy, not eat him!'

Red-faced, Suzy couldn't think of anything to say to defend herself. 'Did you get your picture?'

'Yes! But if you hadn't been so busy playing kissy-face with the enemy you would have noticed that one of his gorillas was taking my camera off me! Good, was he? Yeah, I'll bet he was—after all, he's had plenty of experience. Like I said, during his last campaign a certain news reporter really had the hots for him. He's got quite a reputation with the female sex, has the Colonel. A killer instinct in bed and out of it.'

Suzy was beginning to feel nauseated, disgusted by what she was hearing. And even more so by her own idiotic gullibility. She couldn't understand her reaction—never mind her behaviour. She must be going crazy—and certainly her friend Kate would think so, if Suzy was ever foolish enough to tell her what had happened.

Kate and Suzy had been at university together, and Kate had kept in touch with Suzy when she had decided to drop out of her course and go home to nurse her mother through her final illness. Kate was married now, and with her husband ran a very successful small, independent travel agency.

Kate was constantly urging Suzy to enjoy life a little more, but Suzy still had debts to pay off—her student loan, for one thing, and the rent on the small flat she had shared with her widowed mother for another!

Thinking of her mother made Suzy's greeny-gold eyes darken. Her mother had been widowed before Suzy's birth, her father having been killed in a mountain-climbing accident. It was Suzy's belief that her mother had never got over the death of the man she loved, nor ceased blaming him for having died.

As she'd grown up Suzy had been the one who cared for her mother, rather than the other way around. Money had been tight, and Suzy had worked since her teens to help—first with a paper round and then at whatever unskilled work she could find.

Suzy remembered now that Kate often said she had an overdeveloped sense of responsibility and that she allowed others to put upon her. She couldn't imagine Colonel Lucas James Soames ever allowing anyone to put upon him, Suzy decided bitterly. If anyone were foolish enough to turn to him for help or compassion he would immediately reject them!

Suzy tensed, angry with herself for allowing the Colonel into her thoughts. And yet running beneath her anger, like a silent and dangerously racing river, she could still feel an unwanted ache of pain. Fear curled through her with soft, deadly tendrils. Why had she had such an extraordinary reaction to him? She wasn't that sort of person. Those emotions, that fierce rush of sexual longing, just weren't her! She gave a small shudder of distaste.

It was an experience she was better off forgetting—pretending had never happened, in fact!

And that was exactly what she intended to do!

Luke studied the schedules in front of him. Meticulously detailed plans for his upcoming work. The

Prince had hinted that he would like him on board for his permanent staff, but that kind of role wasn't one Luke wanted. Perhaps his American mother's blood was responsible for that! He had never been someone who enjoyed mundane routine. Even as a boy he had liked the challenge of pushing back boundaries and continually learning and growing.

His parents had died in an accident when he was eleven years old. The Army had sent him home to his grandmother and the comfortable country house where his father had grown up. His grandmother had done her best, but Luke had felt constricted at the boarding school she had sent him to. Even then he had known he would follow his father into the Army, and the happiest day of his life had been the day he had finally been free to follow that ambition.

The Army had been not just his career but his family as well. Until recently. Until he had woken up one morning and realised that he had had enough of witnessing other people's pain and death. That his ears had grown too sensitive to the screams of wounded children and his eyes too hurt by the sight of thin and starving bodies. He had seen it happen too many times before to other soldiers to hesitate. His emotions were getting in the way of his professionalism. It was time for him to move on!

The Army had tried to persuade him to change his mind. There had been talk of further promotion. But Luke had refused to be swayed. In his own mind he was no longer a totally effective soldier. Given the choice between destroying an enemy and protecting a child Luke knew he could no longer guarantee he would put the former first.

And working for His Royal Highness was definitely not for him! Too tame after the demands of Army life. Although there were some similarities between the two! He started to frown. Female reporters! He loathed and despised them! They were a hundred times worse than their male equivalent, in Luke's opinion. He had seen at first hand the damage they could wreak in their determination to get a story. A shadow of pain momentarily darkened his eyes, and the newly healed wound just below his hipbone seemed to pulse.

And as for the lengths such women were prepared to go!

His mouth hardened. So far as he was concerned Suzy Roberts and her ilk were as contemptible as the rags they worked for.

Reporter? Scavenger was a more appropriate word.

He turned his attention back to his paperwork, but, maddeningly, she would not be ejected from his thoughts.

What the hell was the matter with him that he should be wasting his time thinking about Suzy Roberts? That auburn hair and the way her gold-green gaze fastened on him must have addled his brain.

Had she really thought he was so idiotic that he would be deceived by that obviously fake look of longing she had given him? That equally fake tremor he had felt run right through her body when he had touched her? And as for that faint but unmistakable scent he could have sworn he could still smell...

Angrily he got up and strode across the room, pushing open a window, letting in an icy cold blast of air. Perhaps the unintentional celibacy of his life over these last few years had suddenly begun to affect him. But to such an extent that he wanted a woman like Suzy Roberts?

Like hell he did! But the sudden tension in his groin told a different story.

It was late, and he had a business appointment to keep. Finishing what he was doing, he made his way from the office to the privacy of his own apartment, automatically watching and checking as he did so. Once a commando always a commando—even when he could no longer…

Suppressing thoughts he did not want to have to deal with, Luke walked into his suite and headed for the shower.

Stripping off, he stepped into it, the hot needle-jets of water glistening on his body as he moved beneath the shower's spray. The light fell on old scars on his chest, and the newer one low down on his body.

Having finished showering, he stepped out onto the marble floor, padding naked into his bedroom to extract a pair of clean white boxer shorts from a drawer. The phrase 'going commando-style' might have a certain sexual edge to it when used to describe the choice not to wear any underwear, but from his own point of view weeks, sometimes months of living in the field, in one set of sweat and dirt-soaked combats had given him a very different take on the matter! To anyone who had experienced desert combat conditions the luxury of quantities of clean water was something to be truly appreciated.

CHAPTER TWO

Six months later

SUZY paused and studied the sleek yachts clustered in the harbour of the small Italian coastal resort. Two women walked past her, expensively groomed and wearing equally expensive designer clothes. Suzy had dressed as appropriately as she could for this luxurious resort, in white linen trousers and a brief sleeveless matching top, with sandals on her feet and the *de rigueur* sunglasses concealing her eyes, but no way was she in their league—and no way was she made for such an exclusive resort.

She had tried to tell Kate as much when her friend had announced that since she and her husband could not take up the week's holiday they had been offered via their business they wanted to give the treat to Suzy instead.

'Oh, no, Kate, I couldn't possibly accept your generosity,' Suzy had protested.

'It isn't generosity,' Kate had retorted. 'You need this break, Suzy. You've been through a lot these last few years—nursing your mother and then losing her, working every spare hour you had to finish your degree, and then that awful job you had!'

Suzy had sighed. 'I shouldn't have handed in my

notice, really. My tutor had been so kind, getting the intro for me, I feel so guilty.'

'You feel guilty?' Kate had exploded. 'Why on earth should you? You said yourself that you hated the way the magazine worked, its lack of morality with regard to how it got its stories and everything. And when I think of the way that slimy boss of yours tried to behave towards you! If anyone should be feeling guilty it's them, not you, Suzy! I'm surprised they're allowed to get away with treating you as they did. You know my opinion—you should have reported them for sexual harassment!'

Just listening to Kate's words had been enough to make Suzy shudder a little.

'It wasn't as easy as that, Kate,' Suzy had reminded her. 'For one thing I was the only female working there. No one would have backed me up.'

Hearing the strain in her friend's voice, Kate had shot her a quick look of concern before continuing, 'Suzy, I know how strong you are, and how independent, but please just for once put yourself first. You need this break. You need time to relax and reflect, to pick up the threads of your life and weave them into a new pattern. You need this breathing space! I want to do this for you and I shall be very hurt if you refuse.'

Put like that, how could she refuse? Suzy had acknowledged ruefully. And besides, there had been enough truth in what Kate had said to make her see that her friend was right.

She still shook with anxiety and nervous tension when she thought about the scene in the *Down and Dirty* office the day she had handed in her notice. The crude insults her boss had hurled at her still made her face burn with embarrassment and loathing.

'You aren't leaving—I'm sacking you,' he had told her furiously. 'No jumped-up little nothing is going to mess me about!'

He had then claimed publicly that he was sacking her because she had offered him sex in exchange for promotion—but privately told her he would rescind his claim if she agreed to go to bed with him.

Her flesh still crawled at the thought.

Roy Jarvis might be the magazine's editor-in-chief, but so far as Suzy was concerned he was the most morally corrupt man she had ever met. And her opinion was not just based on his attitude towards her, but on the way he ran the magazine and obtained its articles. Roy Jarvis's reporters were told to let nothing stop them in their pursuit of obtaining a story. She had been like a fish out of water in such an environment.

And Kate had been right, Suzy acknowledged unhappily now. She *did* need some time out to reassess her life. And her emotions.

Suzy closed her eyes and tried to swallow past the hard ball of pain and misery lodged in her throat. Panic prickled over her skin as she fought against allowing herself to think about the cause of her pain.

Instead she switched her mind to more easily dealt with issues. The difficulties of the past few years, then the misery of realising she was in a job she hated, and working with people whose morals she could never accept, never mind adopt, had all affected her. But she still needed to earn a living—somehow! And giving in to Kate and accepting this holiday was not, in her opinion, going to aid that.

No, but it might stop her from dreaming about a man she should have forgotten.

And this pretty Italian fishing village, perched precariously on the steep sides of a small bay, was surely a perfect spot in which to chill out and ground herself, to assess her own ambitions and think again about her original desire to become an archivist, perhaps. Her tutor had scorned her ambition, but Suzy had a deep longing for the cloistered quiet of such career.

Skirting the pretty harbour, with its chic and very expensive restaurants, Suzy headed for the steep path that led to the top of the cliff.

Half an hour later she had reached it, and she paused to study the magnificent view and to take a couple of photographs to show Kate.

Another hill rose up a short way along the path, and Suzy headed for it, wondering what lay beyond.

Its incline was steep, and she was a little out of breath when she finally made it to the top. She gasped, her eyes widening in delight as she looked down into the lush valley below her at the stunningly beautiful Palladan villa at its centre. She just had to get a photo of it to show Kate and her husband.

Rummaging in her bag, she found the small digital camera Kate had insisted on lending her.

'If you get any really good pictures we can put them on our Web site,' she had announced when Suzy had tried to protest.

The camera was obviously expensive, and Suzy had said as much, but Kate had dismissed her concern,

shrugging it aside as she reassured her, 'It's insured—
and if you do lose it—which I know you won't—then
we shall replace it.'

Dutifully Suzy had photographed everything she
thought might be of interest to her friend, and she knew
that Kate would love this wonderful villa in its beautiful setting. From her vantage point Suzy could see the
layout of its formal gardens within the high walls surrounding them, and the lake that lay beyond with its
picturesque grotto.

Carefully she focused on the villa, pausing for a moment, as sunlight glinted on the metal casing, to stare
in bemused awe at the sight of four imposingly large
men in military uniform heading for an even equally
imposing large black Mercedes, almost hidden from
view beyond the entrance to the villa. What an impressive sight! She had to get a photograph of it—and
of them! Who on earth were they?

On his way across the courtyard—having escorted the
private security officers who had arrived to check out
the villa without giving any warning, and against
Luke's strict instructions, to their huge Mercedes with
its blacked-out windows—Luke froze as he caught the
unmistakable glint of sunlight on metal. Automatically
he reached for his binoculars, training the powerful lens
on the steep hillside above the villa.

He had done everything he could to avoid having to
take on this commission, but pressure had been put on
him, via his old commanding officer and certain other
people, and reluctantly he had given in—although not

without first enquiring grimly why on earth MI5 operatives could not be used.

'Because it is so sensitive, old boy,' had been the wry answer he had received. 'And because we don't have anyone in the field of your calibre.'

Reluctantly Luke had bowed to the pressure he'd been under.

Making sure that the Foreign Secretary was able to conduct a very politically sensitive meeting with the President of a certain turbulent African state, without either arousing the curiosity of the press or certain factions within the African state required optimum vigilance. And why on earth anyone had ever thought it a good idea to conduct such an exercise so close to a popular Italian resort—visited by the rich and famous and followed there by the paparazzi—Luke had no way of knowing.

Of course he had tried to initiate a change of venue, but he had been overruled.

A smooth-talking suit from MI5 had announced that no one would suspect that the Foreign Secretary would be seeing anyone political whilst enjoying a holiday with his children.

Children? Luke had baulked furiously at that point. No matter how many reassurances or platitudes the MI5 suit might choose to utter, this was potentially a dangerous mission.

The African President was insisting on bringing his own private guards with him, and he was a man who was obsessed with a fear of betrayal—both at home and abroad. If things should go pear-shaped Luke did not want to have to worry about two young children as well as their father. He had said as much to Sir Peter Verey when they had been introduced, suggesting that his children might be better left with their mother.

'My dear chap,' had been Sir Peter's drawled response. 'I wish I could oblige, but you see my ex-wife is insistent that they come with me. Thinks I'm not doing my fatherly duty and that sort of thing.'

Luke knew all about Sir Peter Verey's ex-wife. She had left him for a billionaire industrialist who had little liking of his predecessor's offspring, with the result that she had placed both children at boarding school.

Luke frowned as he swept the hillside for whoever had been responsible for that telltale glint.

The resort less than a couple of miles away seethed with celebrities and minor continental royals, all of whom seemed to be followed by their own pack of predators, feeding off them as if they were carrion.

It didn't take Luke's trained eye long to find its quarry—in fact, he reflected in disgust, it did not need a trained eye to spot her at all. She was standing there openly photographing the villa. She? Luke frowned as he studied the familiar features. Suzy Roberts! It was as little effort for him to conjure up her name as it had been for him to recognise her face. Suzy Roberts, reporter for *Down and Dirty* magazine. Automatically he swept the area around her to see if she was on her own, before focusing on her once again.

She looked thinner, paler—and what the hell was she doing standing in the strong sunlight without the protection of a hat when any fool could see that she had the kind of delicate skin that would burn?

How on earth had she got wind of what was going

on? The editor of the magazine she worked for got his stories by trawling in the gutter for them.

Luke's mouth compressed. The gutter, maybe, but then Roy Jarvis did specialise in 'revealing' the failings and vices of those in power, as well as breaking some extraordinarily sensitive news stories. Someone was supplying him with his information, and Luke knew that if he had been in charge of finding out who it was the leak would have been stopped a long time ago.

Luke refused to believe that anyone could have got through his own rigorous security, but he was not the only person who knew what was happening. Somehow Roy Jarvis had been given a tip-off about the upcoming meeting, and he had obviously sent Suzy Roberts to find out what she could and confirm the story so that he could publish it. After all, a reporter like Suzy had the extra assistance of her sexuality to help her get her story—and she would have no qualms about using it!

Lucas had seen it happen over and over again in the theatre of war, and of course he had already discovered for himself that there were no lengths Suzy Roberts was not prepared to go!

Silently Luke slipped out of the villa grounds, moving quickly and stealthily towards his quarry.

Oblivious to the danger, Suzy pushed her hair back off her face. The villa really was a gem. She paused to admire it again before lifting the camera to take another shot.

Luke, who had circled up behind her, waited until she had raised the camera before making his move.

As Suzy focused the camera he reached for it...

Someone was trying to steal the camera!

Instinctively Suzy turned round, and then froze in shocked disbelief whilst Luke took it from her.

'What are you doing?' she demanded as soon as she could speak.

Lucas Soames—here! She could feel the colour leaving her face and then surging back into it. Her heart was thudding in panic, and she felt as though she was trembling from head to foot. Emotions she had assured herself she had totally destroyed were taking a frightening hold on her, threatening to swamp her.

Frantically she tried to ignore them, to focus instead on what she should be feeling. These emotions had no right to exist. Lucas Soames meant nothing to her, and one of the reasons she was here on holiday was to make sure she was fully recovered from whatever it was she had experienced six months ago.

Willing her physical reaction to him to subside, Suzy demanded sharply, 'Give me back my camera!'

Her eyes widened as she watched Lucas delete the pictures she had just taken.

'No!' she protested, trying to snatch back the camera, to stop him ruining her photographs.

Luke reacted immediately, fending her off with one deceptively easy movement that kept her at arm's length from him, his fingers locked around her wrist as he finished what he was doing.

Despairingly Suzy closed her eyes, trying to blot out the physical reality of him in an effort to protect herself. But almost immediately she realised her mistake. Deprived of sight, she felt all her sensory receptors focusing instead on the feel of Lucas Soames's hand around her wrist—the texture of his flesh, the powerful strength of his grip, the coolness of his skin against the heat of her own. Weakening thrills of sensation were running up her arm, and she could feel the frantic jump of her pulse.

Panic and desperation speared through her. 'What are you doing?' she demanded, the sound of her voice raw and frantic in her ears as she recognised her fear and the reason for it.

What was it about this man that made her feel like this?

Luke studied her silently, assessing her behaviour and her reactions. She looked convincingly both distraught and distressed, and he mentally applauded her acting talent whilst cynically wondering how many victims she had honed it on.

Ignoring her anxious question, he asked one of his own. 'Why were you photographing the villa?'

His response caught Suzy off guard.

There was something about the coldly intense way he was watching her that unnerved her, and Suzy felt a shudder of apprehension run through her body. Stubbornly she fought against giving in to it—and to him!

'Why shouldn't I?' she shot back. Antagonism towards him was a far safer emotion than that dangerous and overwhelming surge of longing she had experienced the last time she had seen him. Don't think about it, she warned herself frantically. Don't remember. Don't feel...

Seeing him then had been like having the clouds part to reveal a miraculous space of blue sky and a dizzying vision of heaven. But things were different now, she reassured herself fiercely. *She* was different now!

Taking a deep breath, Suzy gave a deliberately non-chalant shrug before saying, 'That's what people on holiday do—take photographs.'

Her body language was flawless, Luke acknowledged grudgingly. Not by so much as the flicker of one of those ridiculously long eyelashes of hers was she revealing the fact that she was lying. He could feel his temper starting to rise. Immediately he checked it, alarmed that somehow she had managed to pierce the shield of his professionalism.

'On holiday?' He gave Suzy a comprehensive and cynical look. 'Oh, come on—you can come up with something better than that, surely?'

Just looking at her now—anger sparking her eyes to brilliant gold, flushing her cheeks with heat—anyone other than him would have believed immediately that she was a woman righteously defending herself from an unwarranted attack. But he knew she had to be lying, given who she was, and sure enough, as he continued to watch her, she was unable to continue to return his gaze.

What was Lucas Soames trying to say? Suzy wondered frantically. Had he guessed how he had affected her? Did he think she was nursing some kind of desire for him and that she had followed him here?

Her face began to burn again. If he did then she was going to make sure...

'Nice camera.' Luke interrupted her thoughts, adding assessingly, 'Expensive too.' Still nervously on edge,

Suzy told him stiffly, 'It isn't mine...it belongs to a friend.'

Luke could see the discomfort and the guilt in her eyes—but, to his own irritated disbelief, the knowledge that he was right to be suspicious of her made him feel more angry than satisfied. Determined to stamp on such feelings and destroy them, he responded coldly, 'A friend? So, Roy Jarvis is a friend now, is he, as well as your employer?'

Her employer!

Suzy shook her head.

'I don't work for the magazine any more,' she told him quickly. 'I...I left.' Even saying the words was enough to bring back the unpleasant memories, and she had to swallow against the bile of her distress.

'Oh, come on. You don't really expect me to fall for that, do you?' Luke demanded unpleasantly.

'It's true,' Suzy insisted fiercely. 'I no longer work for the magazine. You can check if you don't believe me!'

Her eyes were more green than gold now, Luke recognised. Reflecting her passionate nature? He frowned, irritated with himself for allowing his attention to be distracted from the professional to the personal.

'Oh, I have no doubt that officially you might have left, but it isn't unheard of for your boss, your *friend,* to use underhand methods to get what he wants. He has sent you here to work undercover—which is, as we both know, why you are up here photographing the villa and spying!'

Now cynicism had joined the cold disdain icing his

voice, and Suzy decided that she had had enough. Not allowing him to finish, she interrupted him hotly.

'That's ridiculous! Why on earth would he send me to do that? It's the resort that is full of the glitterati, not this villa, and as for my agreeing to spy on any-one—I have my own moral code!' She gave him a bitingly scornful look, but her glare might have been directed at an invisible shield for all the effect it had on its intended victim.

'Very affecting.' Luke stopped her. 'But you are wasting your breath and my time with this unconvinc-ing show of innocence. I know exactly what you are, remember? I've witnessed your professional reporting methods—and your *moral code*—at first hand,' he re-minded her grimly.

A telltale crimson tide of guilt and misery flooded Suzy's face. Illogically she felt not just humiliated by his words but emotionally hurt as well.

How could he say something like that to her? Hadn't he been able to tell that she had kissed him because of her own overwhelming need to do so and not for any other reason?

Unable to stop herself, Suzy discovered that she was reliving the feelings she had had then. Anguish filled her. Did he really think she was the kind of woman who would do such a thing for any other reason than because she simply had not been able to stop herself?

The very thought of what he had implied disgusted and nauseated her, and she burst out defensively, 'That wasn't—I didn't—I did it because—'

Abruptly Luke stopped her again. 'You did it be-cause you thought it would be an excellent way of providing a firescreen for your companion—yes, I know that!' he told her grimly. 'Unfortunately for you it wasn't very effective.' He paused, and then added curtly, 'And neither was the kiss!'

What the hell was he thinking of? Luke asked himself savagely as his comment fell into the silence between them and he was forced to remember the kiss they had shared. A woman as experienced as this one must have felt his body's arousal, and gloated over his response to her. Any minute now she would be reminding him of it and challenging him to deny it. And there was no way Luke wanted to be dragged into that dangerous and unreliable ground.

Yes, he had responded to her. He could not deny that! Yes, he had for a split second in time experienced the most extraordinary physical longing for her, and the most extraordinary emotions. But that had been a momentary weakness, quickly controlled, and of no lasting or real importance whatsoever!

'What did Jarvis tell you to do—apart from take photographs?' he demanded sharply, steering his questions back in the right direction.

Still grappling with her own feelings, Suzy told him angrily, 'He didn't tell me to do anything!'

Her anger must somehow have heightened her senses, she decided, because suddenly she was aware of the musky male scent of Lucas Soames's body. She could see the sunlight glinting on the fine dark hair of his muscular forearms. Her heart somersaulted and then attempted a cartwheel, crashing into her chest wall as it did so. She willed herself to drag her gaze away from his body, but somehow it was impossible to do so. The white tee shirt he was wearing, although not tight-fitting, still revealed an impressive breadth of shoulder and chest. Something dangerous was happening to her, and she seemed powerless to stop it.

Suzy began to panic.

The back of her head was burning from the heat of the sun. It was making her feel slightly sick and dizzy—or was it the intensity of the navy blue gaze, the shock of her own emotions that was responsible for her malaise?

She couldn't give in to such feelings, Suzy warned herself frantically. She must not give in to them! She must think of something else! She must get away from here—get away from here and from Lucas Soames, and the sooner the better. If she didn't leave, if she was forced to stay, she was terrified that she might be trapped into saying something that would betray how she felt about him. How she *had* felt about him, she corrected herself. Taking a deep breath, she searched for the right words.

'I'm sorry if you feel you can't believe me,' she began politely. 'But I assure you that I am telling you the truth. I do not work for the magazine any more and no one from it is responsible for my being here! Like I just told you, I am here on holiday!'

She was picking her words too carefully for them to be genuine, Luke decided.

'On holiday? Alone?' he challenged her softly. One dark eyebrow rose tellingly, and Suzy was hotly conscious of his merciless and unkind gaze sweeping her face and then her body.

'I needed time on my own...to...to think...'

She had to get away from him!

'Time on your own? A woman like you?'

The razor-edge contempt in his voice made her face burn, but before she could say anything he continued silkily, 'So, if you aren't, as you claim, working for Roy Jarvis any more, then who are you working for?'

His question caught Suzy off guard, and she had to wrench her thoughts away from the pain his insult had caused her in order to answer it.

'I'm not working for anyone at the moment. I haven't got another job yet...at least...' She paused, her eyes darkening as his question reactivated her own anxiety about her future. After the contempt he had already shown her there was no way she was going to tell him that in order to make ends meet she had taken a job in a local supermarket.

Suddenly she had had enough.

'Why are you questioning me like this?' she demanded wearily. 'Just because you're here, guarding some government bigwig, that doesn't give you the right to...to treat me as some kind of...of criminal. What is it? Why are you looking at me like that?' she demanded nervously, fear trickling through her veins as she sensed that somehow something had changed, that the anger she had sensed in him before had been replaced by a steely determination.

'How do you know who is staying at the villa?' Luke questioned quietly.

For a moment Suzy was too bemused to answer him. Was it *that* that was responsible for the intimidating change in him?

'I heard someone talking about it,' she told him honestly. 'I thought he was supposed to be here on holiday, but of course now that I've seen you, and those men who were leaving, I realise...'

Her voice trailed away, when she saw his expression, and Luke prompted her softly.

'Yes? What is it exactly that you now realise? Something you know your boss Jarvis would be very interested in? Something that you just can't wait to report to him?'

Suzy stared at him aghast.

'No! No—nothing like that. He isn't my boss any-more,' she denied. 'I've already told you that.'

Something about the way he was watching her made her feel very afraid.

'So I was right.'

Suzy could feel her heart bumping heavily against her ribs as the deceptively soft words penetrated her awareness.

'You realise, of course, what this means?'

Suzy stared at him uncomprehendingly. He had lost her completely now, she acknowledged, and she fought to drag her unwilling mind away from her worry about the physical effect Lucas Soames was having on her emotions to what he was saying to her.

'What *what* means?' she asked.

Lucas's mouth thinned. He had no time for games, no matter how much Suzy Roberts might enjoy her play-acting. One minute the *ingénue*, another the *femme fatale*. A tiny muscle twitched in his jaw as he tensed his body against memories he didn't want to have. Memories of the feel of Suzy's body against his own, the taste of her mouth, the scent of her skin...

Savagely he turned away from her. This—she—was a complication he just did not need. It was bad enough that Jarvis had sent anyone here at all—but that it should be her!

Angrily, he examined the facts—and his options! Yes, they both knew why Suzy was here, but just how much did she know? How much information did she actually have?

He had destroyed the photographs she had taken of the African President's private guards, but he could not eradicate that information from her memory. And he certainly could not allow her to pass it on to anyone else—and most especially not to Roy Jarvis, to publish in his wretched magazine!

There was only one thing he could do now, little as he relished the prospect!

Luke had had his fill of reporters, both male and female! He had seen at first hand the damage, the devastation their single-minded determination could cause. He had seen fighting men's lives risked and innocent civilians' lives lost for the sake of a 'hot' story. And he had seen... His mouth twisted, his expression hardening even further.

He'd seen children under school age, half starved, fighting for water and food...whilst excited reporters tried to film their pitiable situation. And worse! Much, much worse! He moved, and the scar low on his belly pulled against the wound it covered.

He had learned over the years to mistrust the media at large.

And Ms Suzy Roberts was not going to be an exception to his rule that all media personnel were to be treated as guilty and kept under strict surveillance!

Luke's gaze narrowed.

Despite the fact that he was trained to keep his body still for hours on end, he suddenly felt he needed to move, step back a little from Suzy, and he grimly suppressed the unwanted knowledge that her proximity was affecting him.

'You realise, of course, that I can't let you tell anyone what you've seen?' Luke informed her.

A cold thrill of horror ran through her.

'But I'm not going to tell anyone,' she protested.

'I suppose the best and easiest thing to do would be for me to confiscate your passport and then have you thrown in jail,' Luke said calmly.

'What?' Suzy's face paled. 'No—you can't do that…' She could hardly believe what she was hearing, but one look at Lucas Soames's face assured her that he was deadly serious.

'Oh, I think you'll find that I can,' Luke assured her. 'But, knowing what you are capable of doing in order to get what you want, I think the best place for you right now is where I can make sure you aren't able to make any kind of contact with Roy Jarvis.'

'What—what are you going to do?' Suzy asked anxiously,

'I'm going to take you back to the villa with me— as my partner.'

CHAPTER THREE

'*WHAT?*'

Suzy was totally lost for words as she struggled to comprehend what he had said. His partner! But that meant... Fear and then longing shot through her like a firework showering her insides and touching every single nerve-ending she possessed. Partners...lovers... soul mates! No. She just wasn't strong enough to withstand this kind of torture!

'No—no! You can't do that. I won't!' she protested shakily.

He had already released her wrist, and as she spoke she was backing away from him, adrenalin pulsing through her veins. She had to get away! She had to!

As soon as she was out of his arm's reach she turned and started to run, driven by her instinct to flee, to protect herself, to hide herself from the danger she knew lay waiting for her!

Intent on her escape, she did not even think about sticking to the path which led back to the resort, instead plunging headlong straight down the steep hillside, sending up a shower of dry earth and small stones as she did so.

Luke watched her, knowing how easily he could catch her, his grim look turning to a frown as he saw the obstacle ahead of her—a large boulder, right in her path. He waited for her to change direction to avoid it, knowing that if she didn't—if she ran right into it—which she *was* going to do!

He caught her with a couple of yards to spare, knocking the breath out of her body as she fell towards the ground. But somehow, to Suzy's astonishment, before she hit the ground their positions were reversed, and it was Lucas Soames who was lying on the hard earth, with her held fast on top of him. His arms were fastened around her like iron bands, one gripping her body the other cradling her head.

Winded and frightened, Suzy tried to free herself—only to find that she could hardly move.

'Let go of me!' she demanded, struggling frantically.

'Stop that, you little fool, otherwise we'll both be—' Lucas began, and then stopped as one of Suzy's flailing hands caught the side of his mouth.

Against instinct, certainly against training, and surely against wanting, he opened his mouth and caught hold of the two offending fingers.

Heat and shock poured through Suzy's body.

Lucas Soames had her fingers in his mouth and he was…

She completely forgot what had been happening, and her own desperate attempt to break free of his imprisonment of her. Her body, her mind, her heart—all flooded with pure undistilled pleasure as his tongue slowly caressed her flesh.

The warm, wet slide of his tongue against her fingers caused images of shocking and unfamiliar sensuality to burst into her head. She wanted to replace her fingers with her mouth, her tongue. She wanted… Suzy could feel the dangerous familiarity of the ache inside her, in her breasts and low down in her body.

Desperate to protect herself, she wrenched her fingers away.

Deprived of the feel of her soft, sweet flesh against his tongue, Luke reacted immediately. The hand at the back of her head forced her towards him, and his mouth covered hers in devastatingly sensual punishment.

Suzy tried to resist but it was too late. Her lips were betraying her, softening beneath those of her captor!

And it was no wonder Lucas Soames was taking their reaction as an indication that she was inviting him to investigate their closed line, to torment it with the firm flick of his tongue. He probed the effectiveness of her defence and discovered that it was all too easily penetrated.

Held fast on top of him, his hands controlling her ability to move, there was nothing Suzy could do other than submit.

Submit? This was submission? This eager opening of her lips? This hungry greeting of his tongue with her own? This feeling that was spiking through her, impaling her on a rack of tormented feverish longing and need, whilst her hands gripped his shoulders and she forgot every single word of the promises she had made to herself. She was responding to him! Allowing herself to be deceived that the fierce, demanding pressure of his mouth on hers meant something! That the feeling possessing her was also possessing him. That they were...soul mates?

She gave a small gasp.

Luke wrenched his mouth from Suzy's, his fingers

biting into her soft flesh as he tried to find a logical explanation for what he had done.

And for what he was feeling!

He could feel his muscles straining as he willed his aroused body into submission. What the hell was happening to him? Physically he might be able to contain what he was feeling—the urgency of his arousal, the savage need he had to hold her and possess her—but it was what was going on inside his head, not his body, that was causing him the most concern. He had never mixed his professional life and his private life. And he had certainly never needed anyone with the intensity with which he had just been driven to possess Suzy Roberts's mouth!

Angrily he fought to ignore both the ache the loss of contact with Suzy's body was causing him and the inner voice that was urging him to continue, to possess the soft warmth of her breasts with his hands, to stroke and explore their feminine softness until he could feel the tight buds of her nipples rising to his touch...

Furious with himself, Luke checked his erotic thoughts.

'Let go of you?' he challenged Suzy, as if the kiss had never happened, angling their bodies so that she could see the rocks below them. 'Take a look! You were heading right for them, and if I hadn't stopped you right now you would be down there.'

Lifting her head cautiously, Suzy looked down the hillside, her stomach lurching as the saw the jagged rock less than a yard away from them.

'I wasn't anywhere near it,' she lied.

But she was shuddering, and for some reason she

was closing her eyes and turning her face into his shoulder.

Immediately Luke stopped her, his fingers digging into her arms as he held her away, a look of tightly reined anger compressing his mouth.

'If I'd any sense I should have let you go ahead,' she heard him muttering. 'It would have saved me a hell of a lot of trouble.'

He loathed and despised her that much?

'Then why didn't you? I can assure you that as far as I am concerned it would have been preferable to what I've just been subjected to!'

Luke had an almost violent need to take her back in his arms and prove to her that she was lying, but instead he derided, 'If that's your way of trying to persuade me you're someone who'd choose death before dishonour, you are wasting your time!'

It wasn't him who was causing her such pain, it was her own anger, Suzy told herself fiercely.

She couldn't bring herself to look down at those rocks again, and she couldn't escape from the knowledge that if he hadn't actually saved her life then he had certainly saved her from hurting herself very badly.

No, she couldn't escape from that knowledge, and it seemed that she couldn't escape from him either. Right now, whilst the solid protection of his hard body beneath her own and the equally hard feel of his arms around her body might be protecting her physically, emotionally this kind of intimacy with him was not doing her any favours at all.

Emotionally? What was she thinking? Suzy knew perfectly well what she was thinking, even if she did not want to acknowledge it. With just one searing kiss Lucas Soames had shown her that, far from being over what she had fought so hard to convince herself had been a moment of uncharacteristic silliness the first time she had seen him, she was if any thing even more vulnerable to him now.

But not for much longer, Suzy promised herself determinedly.

She made a small movement, impatient to be free of him, and then froze with disbelief at the speed with which her flesh reacted to her careless action.

Her face was burning with mortified embarrassment, and she prayed that Lucas Soames could not feel, as she could, the sudden sensual tensing and swelling of her breasts. Her nipples were tightening and thrusting against her top, as though eager for his attention, whilst her stomach clenched and a slow ache possessed the lower part of her body. The urge to put her hand over her sex to quell its silent demand was so strong that it was just as well that his hold of her prevented her from doing so.

Prevented her from doing that, yes, but it didn't prevent her from reacting to the intimate pressure of his body against hers, and the soft mound covering her sex began to swell wantonly, a totally unfamiliar desire to grind her hips against him pulsing through her with increasingly demanding intensity.

Engrossed in her own dismay, she heard Lucas saying harshly, 'Unfortunately for me, on this occasion at least, I prefer to protect human life rather than to destroy it.'

'Protect human life?' Suzy demanded scornfully, secretly relieved to be able to focus on something other than her unwanted reaction to him. 'You were a soldier! Soldiers don't protect lives,' she told him with hostility. 'They—'

She wasn't allowed to get any further. His hold on her tightened. She could see the anger darkening his eyes as he looked at her, and her heart jolted painfully against her ribs.

'I suppose I should have expected that kind of ill-informed and gratuitously offensive remark from someone like you,' he said with scathing contempt. 'In the modern Army our purpose is to do the job we have to do with as little loss of human life as possible!'

His reaction had been immediate and savage—and surely out of proportion to what she had said, Suzy reflected inwardly, refusing to allow herself to be intimidated by it. He might generally prefer to save lives, but in her case she suspected he would have been more than ready to make an exception, if instinct and training had not been so ingrained in him!

Women reporters! Lucas felt the sour taste of old bitterness clogging his throat. And yet despite everything he was still holding on to her. He was holding on to her because he wasn't going to risk so much as letting her move a foot from his side, Luke assured himself acidly.

Even so...

'Time to go,' he announced, moving so swiftly that Suzy could barely catch her breath.

One moment she was lying on top of him on the ground, the next somehow she was standing up on her own, with Lucas next to her.

'Go?' she questioned warily 'You're going to let me go?'

That surely wasn't disappointment that was dampening down her relief, was it?

'I give you my word that I won't say anything about the villa to anyone,' she began to assure him earnestly.

'Your word?' Lucas rapped out contemptuously. 'We both know that your word is as worthless and overused—as…as you are yourself!'

The pain was everywhere. Inside her head, inside her heart, inside her body. With every breath she took she was breathing in its poison, its rank bitterness contaminating her.

Worthless…overused… Immediately Suzy wanted to hit back at him, to hurt him as deeply as he had hurt her, to mark him in a way that would leave him wounded for life, as she knew she herself would be.

Some women might shrug it off and even laugh at such a branding, but she was not one of them.

Overused. That was what he thought of her. She felt sick inside with emotional agony.

Something had changed. Some subtle shifting had occurred that had wrongfooted him, Luke's instincts told him. But he couldn't fathom what it was.

Suzy was staring fixedly past him, her body immobile. Was it her silence that was triggering the sixth sense that told him he had overlooked something? Had he expected her to argue with him, try to win him round, convince him that he was wrong and that she was to be trusted?

Frowning, he looked away, and so didn't see the

single tear that welled in each of Suzy's eyes, to hang glistening on her eyelashes before rolling down her face.

His words had hurt more than if he had physically attacked her—more than if he had turned and walked away from her—more than if he had simply left her to die in a crushed heap of flesh and bones against the jagged rocks from which he had saved her. One day she would be grateful for them, she promised herself. One day she would look back on this and know that what he had said to her had destroyed every minute seed of feeling she might have had for him with the force of a nuclear attack.

One day. But not this day. This day she felt as though she wanted to crawl into a hole and hide herself away, somewhere private and dark, where she and the pain would be alone to confront one another.

CHAPTER FOUR

SUZY could feel her legs trembling as she took a step away from Lucas Soames, her gaze fixed on the path ahead.

Did she really think he was just going to let her walk away? Luke could not credit her woeful lack of reality. He had grabbed her before she had taken more than a few paces, jerking her back towards him.

Suzy only had time to recognise that despite his violent gesture he did not actually hurt her before she was clamped to his side.

'You'd better get one thing clear,' Luke told her curtly. 'From now on where I go, you go. And you can take your choice whether it is by my side, two steps ahead of me or two steps behind. But two steps is going to be as far away as I let you get.'

'You can't do that. You can't make me!' Suzy protested shakily, real fear in her eyes as she looked at him.

'I can and will do anything and everything I deem necessary in order to protect the interests I am here to protect,' Lucas told her uncompromisingly. 'Now,' he demanded, 'where are you staying?'

Mutinously Suzy refused to answer him, compressing her lips and looking away from him. Out of the corner of her eye she saw him shrug.

'Very well then, we'll go straight to the villa. If you

choose to spend the next few weeks with only the clothes you are now wearing, then you may do so!'

Unable to stop herself, Suzy turned towards him.

'The next few weeks?' she protested in despair. 'I can't—I...'

'The name of your hotel?' Luke repeated.

Her lips numb, Suzy told him. Luke watched her in silence.

'Right, we'll go there now and get your stuff.' He glanced at his watch. 'It will soon be dinner time, and that will be a perfect opportunity for me to introduce you. Which reminds me—you had better get used to calling me Luke.'

'Luke?' Suzy checked him, confused. 'But I thought your name was Lucas?'

'Officially, it is,' he agreed coolly. 'Lucas is an old family name, from my father's family, but my mother always called me Luke.' His expression shadowed a little, and against her will Suzy felt an emotional tug on her heartstrings. 'My friends call me Luke, and as my partner so must you.'

'As your partner...' Suzy began shakily. Her heart was thumping, and not solely because of the speed with which Luke was forcing her to walk down the hill alongside him.

'Partner as in living together. Partner as in lovers!' Luke answered calmly.

Lovers? Suzy heart jerked frantically. She couldn't. She wouldn't!

'I... Will I have my own room?' Suzy could hear the wobble in her voice.

Luke stood still and looked at her. What kind of

game was she trying to play now? The Little Miss Innocent nervous act certainly didn't fool him, and he was surprised that she should try it.

'Of course you will have your own room,' he said silkily.

Suzy began to exhale in a rush.

'However, it will also be my room,' Luke informed her grimly. 'And let me warn you right now that I am a very light sleeper, and trained to wake at the slightest sound. If there's one thing I hate it's having my sleep disturbed, so if you were rash enough to try to leave the room during the night I warn you that I am not likely to react with either charity or gentleness. Do I make myself understood?'

Suzy lingered mentally over a handful of biting retorts before reluctantly abandoning in favour of safety and silence.

'And whilst we are on the subject I might as well point out to you that there are guards posted at every exit from the villa and my men patrol the grounds.

Trying not to look afraid, Suzy demanded, 'Won't it look odd for me to suddenly turn up at the villa? I mean, you're here on business, and you don't strike me as the kind of man who would allow his partner to just appear and expect…'

He was watching her with a narrow-eyed intensity that unnerved her.

'We had a quarrel about how much time we have to spend apart before I left London,' Luke told her smoothly. 'You've realised how idiotic you were being and you've come here to apologise to me.'

'I was being idiotic?' Suzy stopped him wrathfully,

her fear forgotten as she leapt to the defence of her sex. 'And now I'm apologising…?'

'Since I'm here on holiday with an old friend and his children—' Luke ignored her outburst '—what could be more natural than that you should join us?'

'You're here on holiday?' Suzy shook her head challengingly. 'I saw with my own eyes those men and that car and—'

'*You* may have seen them,' Luke said with cold menace, 'but I intend to make sure you do not get the opportunity to say so—to anyone. And most especially not to Roy Jarvis!'

'Why won't you accept that I do not work for the magazine any more?' Suzy demanded in frustration. 'And as for the men I saw—' She gave a dismissive shrug. 'I just saw them, that's all.'

'You just saw them? I saw you photographing them,' Luke reminded her damningly.

'Because I thought it would make a good photograph to show my friends. They run a holiday company,' Suzie told him in frustration. 'Look, I can give you their name and phone number and you can ring them and—'

'Credit me with some intelligence.' Luke stopped her dryly. 'Of course Jarvis will have set up an alibi for you!'

'No. You can ring them now. Look, I've got my mobile,' Suzy insisted, putting her hand in her pocket to retrieve it.

Instantly Luke's hand clamped over her own. 'I'll take that, thank you,' he announced, removing her hand from her pocket and then sliding his own into it to remove the phone.

The sensation of his hand pressing against her hip-bone made her whole body burn. Warily, Suzy held her breath, exhaling with relief when Luke removed his hand, along with her phone.

But, to her shock, once he had transferred her mobile into his own possession he reached out and took hold of her hand as they approached the resort.

To anyone else they would look like a couple enjoying the warmth of the Italian sunshine, Suzy recognised. But of course they were no such thing. Experimentally she tried to remove her hand, wincing as she felt the crushing pressure of Luke's imprisoning response.

'Where is your hotel?' Luke asked.

He might be addressing her, but his gaze was measuring everything and everyone around them, Suzy saw as she glanced up at him. He was scanning the happy crowd of holidaymakers surrounding them.

Even in casual holiday clothes there was still an aura of command and authority about him. Suzy could see the way women's heads turned towards him, their glances lingering on him.

Had they really been a couple… A quiver of emotion ran through her.

'Where's your hotel?' Luke repeated, shooting her a cold, impatient look.

Suzy wondered wrathfully how she could allow herself to be vulnerable to a man like this. A man who could not recognise the truth when it and she were standing here beside him!

'It's here,' Suzy told him reluctantly, nodding in the direction of the drive which led up to the discreetly elegant boutique hotel where she was staying.

'You're staying here?'

She could see Luke frowning as though he was surprised.

'Where did you think I'd be staying?' Suzy taunted as they walked through the entrance, their progress noted by the sharp-eyed doorman who seemed instinctively to know who was resident at the hotel without having to check. 'Somewhere brash and flashy?'

'Well, that would certainly be more in keeping with your boss's tastes,' Luke agreed coolly.

They had reached the hotel now. Originally a private villa, it had only recently been converted and extended into its present form. A cool tiled hallway led into the reception area and the clerk on duty smiled at Suzy in recognition, reaching for her room key before she had to ask.

'I'll take that,' Luke announced, ignoring the clerk's uncertain look.

'Ms Roberts will be checking out as of now,' he informed him. 'Where's your passport?' he asked Suzy, turning to look at her.

If the clerk had thought originally that she was taking Luke back to her room so that they could make love, and Suzy suspected he must have done, he obviously did not think so now. Suzy saw his manner towards Luke change from uncertainty to respect.

But then there was quite definitely something about Luke that set him apart from other men, Suzy acknowledged grudgingly, angrily aware of his presence behind her as she walked to her room.

Her room—the room originally to have been provided for her friends—was elegant and extremely luxurious, with French doors which led out onto a private balcony large enough for her to have had a tea party on, had she so wished.

'Expensive,' was Luke's cynical comment as he followed her inside, and then locked the door and leaned against it, pocketing the old-fashioned key. If there had been an ounce of truth in her story that she was unemployed she could never have afforded to stay in a place like this, he acknowledged.

'But then I'm sure your boss has his own way of making sure he gets value for money.'

Angry heat burned Suzy's face as she started to open the wardrobe doors. Her whole body trembled in reaction to his taunt that she would have sex with a man she loathed! Unable to stop herself, she turned to confront Luke, pride and anger burning red flags in her small face.

'I know what you're trying to insinuate, but you couldn't be more wrong. You know nothing about me, and yet you think—'

'On the contrary. I know a good deal about you.' Luke stopped her smoothly. 'Everyone who attended the Prince's reception was vetted, including you.'

Vetted, yes, but he did not have an in-depth report on her, Luke acknowledged, and made a mental note to inform his staff in London that he required one—if only for formality's sake.

The intensity of her own emotions was exhausting

her, and she just did not have the energy to argue with him any more, Suzy decided wearily.

'How long do you intend to keep me here in Italy?' she demanded as she opened her case and started to fold her clothes neatly.

'For as long as it takes,' Luke answered her laconically, his eyes narrowing as he focused on the clothes she was packing.

Neat round-necked tee shirts, modest pairs of walking shorts, a couple of long dresses—simple, anonymous clothes of a type he would have expected a conventional, rather cautions young woman to favour, hardly in keeping with the woman he knew her to be.

She had planned for her current role quite well, he acknowledged reluctantly as he watched the way she folded every garment before packing it.

Warily Suzy gave a glance in Luke's direction. He was still leaning against the bedroom door, arms folded, eyelids dropping over his eyes so that she couldn't be sure whether he was watching her or not.

She had packed virtually everything now, except her underwear, and for some ridiculous reason she discovered that she was reluctant to do so with him watching her.

She stole another glance at Luke.

'Finished?'

'Er, no…'

'Perhaps I'd better help you, then.'

Suzy's mouth opened and closed again as he levered his shoulders off the door and came towards her. Automatically she fell back, putting a protective hand on the drawer which contained her underwear.

She was trying to hide something from him, Luke recognised, his gaze narrowing on the betraying movement of her hand. What was it she had in the drawer that she didn't want him to see? He intended to find out.

'Have you got anything in the bathroom?' he asked casually. 'Toilet bag? Make-up?'

Unwittingly Suzy took the bait he had offered her. 'Yes...'

'You'd better go and get them, then, hadn't you?' Luke told her impatiently, glancing at his watch and informing her, 'You've got two minutes. After that, anything you haven't packed will have to be left behind.'

Automatically Suzy hurried to the bathroom.

The minute she was out of sight, Luke pulled open the drawer she had been guarding.

Neat piles of clean white underwear greeted his searching gaze.

Quickly and expertly he searched through it, frowning as his senses unwantedly relayed to him the cool, soft feel of the white fabric and its innocent virginal message.

Innocent? Virginal? Suzy Roberts?

She had researched her role well, he reflected, his frown deepening as he recognised that a part of him was reacting to the intimacy of what he was doing in a way that was both unprofessional and totally unfamiliar.

In his hand he held the semi-sheer white lace-trimmed bra he had just removed to check that the underwiring was just that.

He remembered with what ease and lack of any kind
of sexual interest or arousal he had removed the TV
news reporter's openly sexual underwear from the
'washing line' she had managed to delude one of the
raw recruits into erecting for her. It seemed incompre-
hensible to him that he should be feeling such a fierce
surge of sexual reaction now!

The sensation of his body beginning to strain against
the constriction of his clothes had him ceasing his
search to question what on earth his body thought it
was doing.

Suzy, her toiletries packed, emerged from the bathroom and froze at the sight of Luke standing in front
of the chest, one of her bras in his hand.

'What are you doing? How dare you touch my...my
clothes?'

Like a small whirlwind, Suzy dropped her toiletries
bag on the bed and snatched her bra from Luke's grasp,
bundling it and as much of the other contents of the
drawer as she could manage into her open case.

He had sent her into the bathroom deliberately so
that he could go through her things! What in hell's
name was happening to him? Luke wondered in disbelief as her angry, almost anguished movements
caused an unexpected and fierce resurgence of the erection he thought he had tamed.

Furious with himself for his physical response to her,
he told her sharply, 'Forget the shocked virgin act—it
doesn't work. It stopped working for any woman over
eighteen years ago, and when it comes to a woman like
you...'

What would he do if she turned round now and told

him just how wrong he was? Suzy wondered bitterly as her hands trembled over her final packing. But of course she already knew, didn't she? He simply would not believe her. He would not accept that her experience was limited to one fumbling incident whilst at university, in which she and her partner had both lost their virginity. Their relationship had ended with no regrets on either part when she had decided to give up her studies to nurse her mother…

'Time's up,' Luke announced tersely.

Another minute in this room, with its huge bed and her scent lying on the warm afternoon air, and he was not sure…

He was not sure what? Luke questioned himself brutally.

His body gave him an answer his professionalism wanted to deny.

He wasn't sure he wouldn't be able to stop himself from spreading her on that bed and…

Ignoring the savage ache in his groin, Luke searched the room silently, checking every drawer and cupboard and even looking under the bed and on top of the wardrobe before reaching for Suzy's suitcase.

CHAPTER FIVE

'COME on—and remember I shall be watching your every step and your every word. One move out of line and you'll be in an Italian prison faster than you can take another breath,' Luke warned Suzy as they stood in the late-afternoon sunshine of the villa's impressive forecourt, with the villa itself behind them and Suzy's case at Luke's feet. Any chance she might have had of escaping disappeared, as their taxi drove away.

'You will never be able to get away with this,' Suzy warned him angrily. 'Someone is bound to suspect…'

'If by "someone" you mean Sir Peter Verey, then I'm afraid you're going to be disappointed. He's far too busy trying to cope with his children,' Luke told her grimly.

'What do you mean "cope with his children"?' Suzy demanded.

Luke's comment had all the hallmarks of the kind of old-fashioned attitude towards parenting which she personally deplored.

'Why shouldn't he look after them? If his wife—'

Luke looked at her, well aware of her antagonism.

'Their mother is actually his ex-wife. She left him for someone much richer! And as for looking after his children… They are probably more capable of looking after him than the other way around,' Luke announced dryly. 'Peter is the product of a typical upper-class upbringing and totally incapable of any kind of hands-on parenting.'

Luke's grim words evoked Suzy's immediate sympathy on behalf of the two children. She too had had a parent—her mother, in her case—who had not been able to provide her with strong and loving parenting.

Suzy's eyes darkened as she became lost in her thoughts. Her mother had never really got over being widowed, and even before her health had begun to fail Suzy had found herself as a very young girl taking on the role of 'mothering' her own mother.

Her sympathies aroused on behalf of the children, she demanded, 'Why are they here, then? Or can I guess?' she asked angrily. 'I suppose you organised it for some machiavellian reason of your own. Have you no feelings? Don't you realise how much harm it could do them, to be here under such circumstances? Doesn't their mother—'

Luke listened to her passionate outburst in silence. What would she say if he were to tell her that he himself had been orphaned at a young age? Would that fiercely passionate championship he could see in her eyes for Peter Verey's children be there for the child he had been?

'Children are so vulnerable,' Suzy railed furiously. 'Surely their mother…'

Children are so vulnerable. Luke looked away from her, momentarily forgetting who she was. There was a bitter taste in his mouth and his gaze was clouded by painful memories.

Some children—as he had good cause to know—were more vulnerable than others. Abruptly inside his head images he didn't want to relive were starting to form. He banished them. They belonged to the past, and right now he needed to concentrate on the present.

'Their mother is more interested in scoring points against their father than concerning herself about the children they created together. She has a new partner now, who has no intention of playing happy families with them, so the children have become both a means of remaining a thorn in her ex-husband's side, and a punishment, because she now sees them as a burden she is forced to bear. She's put them both into boarding school, and it seems that the summer holidays and the departure of the girl she employed to take charge of them means their presence is a nuisance. Hence her decision to send them to their father. Conveniently, the day she informed Sir Peter he had to take charge of them was also the day she left on an extended holiday with her second husband.'

As she saw the anger in Luke's eyes Suzy immediately jumped to the wrong conclusion. It was obvious that he too considered the poor children to be an unwanted nuisance, she decided angrily—an inconvenience to mar his plans, just like her!

'Of course you don't want them here any more than their father,' she accused him.

'I don't want them here,' Luke agreed grimly.

He didn't want any child ever again to be anywhere it might be in danger, no matter how small that risk might be.

If he closed his eyes now Luke knew he would see the most terrible images of carnage and destruction etched in fire and blood. Images he would never be able to forget.

The situation here was dangerously volatile. The African President had a reputation for seeing threats round every corner and reacting punishingly to them. Violence was a way of life to him, and to his followers.

A simple mission, MI5 had called it. But how could it possibly be simple with a woman like Suzy Roberts and two innocent children involved?

'Come on,' Luke commanded, picking up Suzy's case. 'And remember, take one step just one centimetre over the line and you'll be locked up in jail before you can take another.'

He meant it Suzy recognised apprehensively, and she fought not to back away from him and let him know how much he was intimidating her.

'We're lovers, remember?' Luke warned her, closing the gap between them.

Ignoring the lynx-eyed look he was giving her, Suzy took a deep breath. Lovers! Panic shot through her as she recognised that her instinctive response to the thought was not one of abhorrence and rejection. Why wasn't it? She wasn't still holding onto that idiotic thing about them being soul mates, was she?

Lovers! Inside her head images were forming. Dangerous, wanton and tormenting images that made her body ache and burn.

Beneath her thin top Suzy could feel her nipples stiffening and peaking. Her heart thudding erratically, she turned away from him to look up at the villa. It was awesomely elegant and magnificent.

'Built by an Italian prince for his favourite mistress

and the children she had by him,' Lucas informed her.
'The frescoes around the hall and staircase include images of both her and their sons. Come on.'

The visually gentle clasp of his hand around hers
was in reality anything but, Suzy recognised and she
flinched beneath his tight grip.

'My things—' she began, but Luke shook his head.

'I'll get someone to come out for them.'

The supposed butler who opened the door to them
exchanged a look with Luke which made her suspect
that the man was more than just a servant. One of
Luke's men? Suzy suspected so, but before she could
voice her suspicions one of the doors off the hallway
opened and a young boy of around six came running
out, hotly pursued by a pre-teenage girl who was protesting crossly,

'That's mine, Charlie, give it back to me now.'

'Children! Oh—Luke.'

This must be the children's father, Suzy guessed, and
she waited to be introduced to her unsuspecting host.

He was tall and good-looking, with crinkly blue eyes
and a nice smile, but Suzy still recognised that of the
two of them it was obvious that Luke was the one in
charge.

'Peter, I am delighted to tell you that you have an
additional guest,' Luke announced. 'My partner, Suzy
Roberts. Darling, this is Sir Peter Verey,'

'Luke, I applaud your taste.' Peter Verey smiled
warmly, his words for Luke but his admiring gaze fixed
very firmly on Suzy.

There was something almost endearing about Peter
Verey, Suzy decided as she tried rebelliously to move

away from Luke, but then tensed as his fingers closed around her wrist in steely warning.

'I'm going to take Suzy up to my room. It's almost dinnertime…'

Suzy opened her mouth to say something, but Luke took immediate action to forestall her by the simple expedient of silencing her protest with the pressure of his mouth on her own.

Caught like a rabbit in a car's headlights, she stared up into his eyes and saw the warning glinting there. But the warning certainly didn't match the soft, sensual pressure of his mouth as it moved on hers, Suzy recognised as her heart thumped painfully. He was holding her, kissing her as though…

A huge lump formed in her throat and she had to close her eyes against the sharp pain that speared her heart. As she did so she felt him lifting his mouth from hers.

They were alone in the vast hallway, Sir Peter having discreetly disappeared.

'This way,' Luke announced curtly.

He had released her wrist and Suzy noticed that he made no attempt to re-imprison her. In fact as she walked numbly towards the stairs he seemed to deliberately hang back a little from her. The lump in her throat turned to icy panic as she realised how bereft her body felt at its lack of contact with him.

He was a monster. She ought to hate and loathe him. She *did* hate and loathe him. It was just her body that was vulnerable to him. That was all.

Stopping mid-step, she turned on the stair and looked at Luke. He was two stairs below her and their eyes were on the same level. As she looked into his her heart gave a funny little kick-beat before flinging itself at the wall of her chest.

'Do we really have to share a room?' she asked, anxiety thickening her voice to a husky whisper.

Something in the soft timbre of her voice was touching a nerve he didn't want to have touched, Luke recognised angrily—arousing a reaction he didn't want to have aroused. What the devil was the matter with him?

'Yes, because that will ensure that I can keep a very close eye on you, and it will reinforce the necessary fiction I've had to create that we are lovers,' Luke said to her prosaically, adding scathingly, 'I should have thought you could have worked that out for yourself. I assure you there's no other reason for it.'

Mutely Suzy looked at him, then turned away and began to climb the remaining stairs.

What was it about those eyes that made him want to take hold of her?

Infuriated by the effect Suzy was having on him, Luke followed her up the stairs.

'This way.' Tensing beneath Luke's brief touch on her bare arm, Suzy willed herself not to betray how emotionally vulnerable he was making her feel.

He had come to a halt outside a door which he unlocked and pushed open.

Warily Suzy stepped inside, her eyes widening as she took in the magnificence of her surroundings.

What she was standing in wasn't just a room but a suite. Almost an apartment, she decided, and she gazed around in awe, recognising wryly that her own small flat would have fitted easily into the elegant and spaciously proportioned sitting room in which she was now standing. Through the three tall windows she could see the grounds of the villa, but it wasn't the view from the windows that caught and held her attention. As she stared through the double doors which opened into what was obviously the bedroom Suzy felt her throat constrict.

Because she could see that the bedroom did in fact possess only one bed. A very large bed, admittedly, but still only one.

'I am not sleeping in that bed with you,' she announced flatly.

She looked and sounded shocked and outraged, Luke recognised. Pink flags of apparent distress were flying in her cheeks and her eyes were glittering with emotion. Even her body language, her tightly balled fists and tensely held body, was perfect for the part she had chosen to play.

She was good, he told himself angrily. She was very, very good. But he wasn't fooled!

'Well, you certainly won't be doing anything other than sleeping!' he told her emphatically. 'So you can disabuse yourself of any ideas you might be entertaining of favouring me with your sexual expertise. Because I'm not in the market for it.'

Somewhere inside her a small, sensible voice was trying to make itself heard, to tell her that she ought to be relieved by his words and the message of safety they held for her. But it was being drowned out by the outraged protests of her emotions, Suzy knew, and she recoiled from the rejection in Luke's words.

'I am not going to sleep with you!'

Could he hear the panic in her voice? Suzy no longer cared. All she cared about was saving herself from the humiliation of having to share a bed with a man she already knew had the most dangerous effect on her body—especially when he had made it so clear how he felt about her. She could not, *would* not share Luke's bed!

Was it because she was afraid that if she did she might somehow forget herself and...?

And what? Suzy derided herself mirthlessly. Seduce him? Her? Seduce a man like Luke?

'I'll sleep in the sitting room on one of the sofas,' she announced shakily.

'No!' Luke checked her immediately.

The cool word offered no hope of a compromise.

Uncertainly Suzy looked at him.

'Didn't you listen to what I told you?' he asked softly. 'I am not going to let you out of my sight! Night and day, wherever I go, you come with me. Besides, we are supposed to be lovers. I don't want the maids gossiping that we aren't sleeping together. Of course, if you prefer to spend the next few weeks in prison...' he offered cordially.

There was a cold look in his eyes that told her he wasn't joking. Wildly Suzy contemplated telling him that she *would* prefer the option of prison. Surely anything was better than having to share his bed! Than lying there beside him, terrified that she might somehow be overwhelmed by temptation and reach out to him and be rejected.

'The bathroom's through here,' she heard Luke informing her, quite obviously waiting for her to follow him.

A small spurt of rebellion surged through her. Suzy stayed where she was.

Luke paused and turned to look at her. 'Are you waiting for me to come and get you?' he asked softly.

Silently they looked at one another.

Something unseen and dangerous sizzled in the air between them. Suzy might not be able to see it, but she could certainly feel it. Inside she was trembling, teetering on a tightrope of hyped-up sexual excitement and overstretched emotions.

If she stayed here what would Luke do? Just the thought of his hands on her body in any kind of way sent a high-voltage shock of sensual longing jolting through her.

What was happening to her?

Gritting her teeth, she took a step towards him. Anything, even giving in to him now, was a million times better than putting herself in a position where she might humiliate herself by letting Luke see...

See what? What was there to see? she asked herself with angry defiance. But of course she knew!

How on earth could she be unlucky enough to have the kind of emotional and sexual feelings she did towards a man like Luke? And why, knowing what he thought of her, hadn't she been able to destroy them?

And, as if that wasn't enough for her to have to cope with, why had fate deemed it necessary to condemn her to this current situation, where she would be exposed day and night to Luke's proximity? Day and night!

Luke frowned as he watched the expressions chase one another over Suzy's face. That look of agonised despair he had just seen darken her eyes had surely been pure theatre!

Numbly Suzy followed Luke into the bathroom, then stopped dead to stare in disbelief and bemusement around the room.

'The current owner renovated the whole place, with particular attention to the bathrooms,' she heard Luke explaining calmly while she stood and stared, then turned and closed her eyes, and then opened them again.

The bathroom was like something out of a private fantasy!

The bath was huge, round and half-sunk into the floor. It was dark green marble with marble steps leading down to it and gold dolphin-head taps attached.

As though that were not enough five columns surrounded it, supporting a cupola-type canopy the centre of which was painted with…Suzy blinked, and then blinked again at the scenes of extremely explicit sensuality above her head. And not just above her head, she realised, but all along the wall frieze as well! Luscious-breasted women, each with her godlike Adonis entwined in a variety of intimate sexual embraces! Huge mirrors covered one of the walls, and on another she could see handbasins…

'I…' she began falteringly, shaking her head when her voice failed her and her gaze was drawn back to the frieze!

Hastily she refocused it on the bathtub, and then

wished she had not as, out of nowhere, the most intimate and erotic images presented themselves to her.

Luke sleekly wet and naked... Luke bending over her as one Adonis on the frieze was bending over his lover...

A dizzying surge of sensual heat gripped her body. Fiercely she tried to repel it.

Luke himself, who had previously derided and then ignored the flamboyantly sensual décor of the bathroom, had a sudden and unwanted image of Suzy lying in the ornate tub, her naked body gleaming with pearly iridescence. Would the tangle of curls between her thighs be the same unique shade of gold as her hair? And when he lifted her out of the water and laid her down, so that he could caress the taut peaks of her breasts with his fingers, before he touched her more intimately, would those curls cling lovingly to his fingers as he parted the folded lips of her sex?

Furious with himself, Luke turned away from Suzy to stop her from seeing the effect his thoughts were having on him. His erection was straining against his clothes and throbbing almost painfully. The physical rebelliousness of his body was a hazard he had not accounted for, never having had to deal with it before, and mentally Luke cursed that unexpected kiss Suzy had given him the first time they had met.

Then she had caught him off guard, and somehow superimposed on his body and his arousal mechanism an imprinted response to her which right now he seemed powerless to destroy!

'The shower is over there,' he told Suzy curtly,

breaking off as they both heard a discreet knock on the outside door to the suite. 'That will be your stuff.'

Glad of a reason to escape from the overwhelming sensuality of the bathroom, Suzy hurried back into the suite, Luke at her heels. A young Italian was standing beside the door with Suzy's case. As Suzy thanked him he gave her an intense and admiring look.

'I'll take that,' Luke announced tersely, somehow managing to insert himself between Suzy and the young man as he dismissed him. 'You've got half an hour before dinner,' he told Suzy as he closed the door, shutting her inside the suite, on her own with him. 'I've only used part of the wardrobe, so you'll have plenty of space for your stuff.'

Her stuff? It was just as well that the exclusivity of her hotel meant that she had brought a couple of outfits with her more formal than she would normally have packed for a holiday, Suzy acknowledged.

'You can use the shower first if you like.'

'Yes, thanks—I will,' she told him woodenly, unzipping her case and trying to be discreet as she extracted clean underwear. But it was next to impossible when Luke was standing right next to her.

'If you need anything pressing now's the time to say,' he told her, ignoring her discomfort.

'Well, what kind of thing should I wear? I mean, how formal…?' she began uncertainly. Something told her that Sir Peter Verey was not someone who sat down to dinner wearing a pair of jeans!

'Will these be okay?' she asked reluctantly, removing a pair of linen trousers from her case. She hated to have to ask him for anything, even a small piece of advice, but she knew that she had no choice.

'They won't need pressing,' she told him, and he nodded his head.

Quickly hanging them up, she found her toilet bag and headed for the bathroom. As she did so she thought she heard Luke call something after her, but she refused to turn back to find out what it was. Another criticism of her, no doubt, she decided, and she closed the bathroom door with a satisfying bang.

Fortunately the shower was modern and plain, and no way in danger of inclining her toward wanton thoughts concerning her jailer!

Determinedly Suzy pushed away her dangerous fantasies and turned on the shower, carefully adjusting the heat and letting the water run for a few seconds before testing it to make sure the temperature was right.

Quickly stripping off her clothes, she stepped into it, enjoying the warm cascade of water over her skin. The warmth of the water was just perfect.

'Aaagrh!' Suzy screamed as suddenly icy cold water pelted her unprepared skin. Frozen, she reached for the towel she had hung over the shower door, but felt it slip from her grasp. It only took her seconds to escape from the shower's icy blast, but by the time she had she was shivering with cold and shock.

'I tried to warn you about the water but you didn't bother to listen.'

Soaking wet, shivering and totally naked, she stared in affronted outrage at Luke, who was standing in the doorway, having heard her scream and guessed its cause.

CHAPTER SIX

'HERE.' In two quick strides Luke was beside her, having grabbed hold of a towel.

'No, don't—I can manage.' She began to protest, but the words became a muddled muffle as he wrapped her unceremoniously in the towel and started to rub her dry so fiercely that her skin began to glow.

His actions were spare, rigorous and practical, and there was no reason at all why they should remind her of the loving care of her mother when she was a little girl, but they did. And then she turned her head and stiffened as she saw the way he was looking at her. He had stopped towelling her, and what she could see in his eyes was making her heart turn over and her resistance melt.

Frantically she forced herself to remember who he was and what he had done! Glaring at him, she turned away and headed for the bedroom, only to give a gasp of shock as she tripped on the hem of her towel.

The speed with which Luke moved was very impressive. One minute he was standing beside her, the next he was catching her in his arms and swinging her up off the floor, so that instead of taking a nasty tumble she was held securely against his warm chest.

Initially she struggled to break free, then suddenly the whole world stopped turning and her heartbeat was suspended with it.

'Luke…'

She had barely whispered his name, but he must have heard her because she could feel him registering it. His body tensed, as though there was something in her one little word that he needed every bit of his formidable artillery of weaponry to repel.

'I just don't need this,' Suzy heard him mutter savagely, but then his hand was pushing through her hair, securing her head at just the right angle for his mouth to home in on hers, to take it and make her want to return the passion she could feel in his kiss. It was the same passion that was running through her like liquid fire and honey. Any thought of resisting him or of denying herself the pleasure her body craved was forgotten!

She lifted up her arms and put them round him. This time it was *her* tongue-tip that probed the line of *his* lips, but it was Luke who drew it deep inside the dark, warm sensuality of his mouth, coaxing it, encouraging it, and then fiercely mating with it. Her heart was bouncing around inside her chest like a yo-yo. She could hardly breathe—and not just because of the way Luke was kissing her.

Like a snake sloughing off an unwanted skin, she wriggled her body until the towel dropped off, her action driven by instinct and not any deliberate thought. She was incapable of that! Incapable of anything other than responding to the subtle pressure of Luke's hard hand holding her head, Luke's equally hard mouth on hers.

His hands were on her naked back, splaying out against her skin, sliding downwards to her waist and then her buttocks, cupping their rounded softness and then pulling her fiercely into his own body, his own arousal. Helpless to stop herself, Suzy ground her hips against him.

What he was doing was crazy, Luke warned himself. He must be out of his mind for even thinking about contemplating what he was contemplating. If he had any sense he would back off right now and—

He felt Suzy's body move against his own, heard the soft, hot sound of excitement she made against his skin and his aroused body refused to obey his demands. He lifted his hand to cover her naked breast, feeling the taut nub push eagerly against his palm.

Suddenly Suzy realised what she was doing. With a small moan of anguish she pushed at Luke's chest.

Immediately he set her free. His face was hard with anger and her own face felt tight with shock and misery.

Unsteadily Suzy retrieved her towel, dreading what Luke might be going to say. Had he guessed what he had done to her? How he had made her feel? How he had made her want him?

To her relief he strode towards the bathroom without saying anything, leaving her alone to dress.

In the bathroom Luke fought furiously to sandbag his feelings. How could he have allowed himself to react to her like that—to respond to her like that? He tried to pinpoint the second things had got out of control, and the reason, rerunning the whole thing through his head in order to reexamine it and sort out some kind of damage limitation plan. But to his disbelief he realised that remembering how Suzy had looked standing there naked was already arousing him again.

Turning on the shower, Luke stepped under its icy blast, savagely angry with himself and equally angry with Suzy. Did she really think he had been deceived by the role she was trying to play, or by the white-faced look of despair he had seen in her eyes as she tore herself out of his arms?

As she tore herself out of his arms. The icy jets of water needled onto Luke's skin unnoticed as he stood still.

Suzy had been the one to end their intimacy, not him, and if she had not done so by now she would be lying beneath his body.

Cursing himself Luke tried to ignore the images his mind was relaying to him. He was a man who intended to live his life to a specific moral code; she was a woman who didn't have a moral bone in her body! An impossible coupling! And he intended to ensure that it remained impossible!

'Ready?'

Numbly Suzy nodded her head, not trusting herself to speak.

She was wearing a simple linen top with shoestring straps with her trousers, and Luke frowned as he looked at her, recognising how effective the outfit was at making her appear fragile and somehow vulnerable.

As he opened the suite door for her Suzy snatched a brief look at Luke, helplessly aware that the sight of him, in a pair of immaculate dark-coloured trousers and an equally immaculate soft white shirt, was doing things to her she had no wish whatsoever to acknowledge.

As they descended the impressive staircase together, Suzy was acutely conscious of him at her side. When they reached the hallway he touched her bare arm lightly, and immediately she flinched.

'We're a couple, remember?' Luke warned her in a low, cold voice.

As he reached past her to push open the door Suzy caught the clean male smell of his skin, and immediately a quiver of response ran down her spine. She felt an overwhelming urge to turn round and bury her face in his throat, just breathe in the smell of him until she was drunk on it.

'In here!'

The door opened and Suzy stepped through it, Luke behind her. The two children she had seen earlier were seated on a windowseat, their heads bent over a computer game. Suzy felt an unexpected tug of emotion as she saw that, despite their clean clothes, they somehow had a heart-rending air of neglect about them.

Was it because of her own childhood she was so immediately and instinctively aware that these children lacked a mother's loving input into their lives? Suzy wondered ruefully as she watched them.

Sir Peter was picking up the drink which had just been poured for him by the smartly dressed waiter. As he saw them he put it down.

'There you are! Suzy, my dear, what will you have to drink, Luke, are you going to break your normal abstinence tonight?'

For all that he was their host, Suzy could see that

Sir Peter was actually a little in awe of Luke, and she watched the interaction between the two men curiously as Luke announced that he would simply have a tonic.

'And Suzy?' Sir Peter pressed, giving her another warm smile.

'Tonic for me too,' she echoed.

'I'm afraid we have to let the children have dinner with us,' Sir Peter apologised to Suzy as the young Italian waiter handed her her drink. 'It really is a nuisance having them here, but I'm afraid I wasn't given the opportunity to refuse.'

A heavy sigh accompanied the frowning look Sir Peter gave his children, and Suzy's sympathy for them increased.

'Perhaps I should go and introduce myself to them,' she suggested gently, leaving Luke standing with Sir Peter whilst she made her way over to the windowseat.

As Suzy walked away Luke discovered that his gaze was focused on the gentle sway of her hips and the rounded curves of her bottom.

'Lovely girl,' he heard Peter saying appreciatively at his side. 'I envy you, old chap.'

Luke saw that the other man's gaze was lingering on Suzy's curvy posterior as well.

For no reason he could think of Luke moved to block his view.

'I wish we could hear definitely that our chap is going to come through…' Peter was complaining, and automatically Luke turned his attention to what he was saying.

'Hello, I'm Suzy.' Suzy introduced herself to the children with a smile.

'You're Lucas's girlfriend, aren't you?' the little boy demanded, adding importantly, 'Maria told us. She's one of the maids.'

Luke's girlfriend! Something turned over inside Suzy's chest, and an odd and unwanted feeling of loss and pain ached inside her.

'Charlie, you shouldn't gossip with the servants. Mummy wouldn't like it,' the little girl announced primly, and Suzy could see the mixture of anxiety and protectiveness in her eyes as she looked at her younger brother.

'You can't tell me what to do, Lucy,' He retaliated immediately. 'Does being Luke's girlfriend mean that you are going to get married?' he asked Suzy.

Married! To Luke!

A feeling of fierce intensity shot through her.

'Charlie, it's rude to ask personal questions,' Lucy told him imperiously.

'Our mother and father were married,' Charlie told her, ignoring his sister, 'but they aren't any more. Our mother is married to someone else, and he doesn't like us, does he, Lucy?'

'Charlie, you aren't supposed to say things like that,' Lucy hissed, red-faced.

'Why not? I heard Mummy saying it to Aunt Catherine.'

Poor children, Suzy thought sadly. Charlie was still too young to be aware of what he was saying, but Lucy was old enough to be embarrassed and upset by her younger brother's revelations. Suzy could see that, so she gently distracted them, asking, 'What was that game I saw you playing?'

Her simple ploy had the desired effect. Immediately Charlie began to enthuse about the game and his skill with it.

As she listened to him Suzy turned to look at Lucy. The little girl gave her a hesitant smile. The pristinely laundered dress she was wearing, whilst unmistakably expensive, was too short and too tight, Suzy recognised, and she wondered absently if she had perhaps chosen to wear it because it was an old favourite.

Still listening to Peter complaining about the way the visiting Head of State kept changing the carefully made arrangements, Luke looked towards the window.

The children were now seated either side of Suzy, apparently hanging onto her every word—nestling against her, almost.

For some absurd reason the sight of the three of them together aroused an emotion inside him he wasn't prepared to name, and it was with relief that he heard the sound of the dinner gong.

'Suzy, my dear, you don't know what a pleasure it is for me to have the company of such a very attractive and charming young woman,' Sir Peter announced flatteringly once they were all seated around the magnificent antique table. 'And I'm sure the children agree with me—don't you, children?'

Obediently Charlie and Lucy nodded their heads.

'Luke, you are an extremely fortunate man. I just hope, Suzy, that we will be able to persuade you to spend some time with us as well as with Luke. The children would certainly welcome your company, I know.'

Suzy hid a smile as she realised what Sir Peter was trying to do. He obviously saw in her arrival an opportunity to persuade her into helping out with his children. And to be honest, she acknowledged, she would be perfectly happy to do so. It would give her something to occupy her time during her enforced imprisonment.

With that in mind, she smiled compliantly at her host.

'You must take Suzy for a walk through the gardens after dinner, Luke,' Sir Peter announced amiably, after giving Suzy a warmly approving smile. 'The grounds to the villa are very beautiful. There's a lake—'

'And a grotto,' Charlie broke in eagerly. 'I want to explore it.'

Immediately his father gave him a stern look. 'Charlie, I've already told you that you are not to go near the grotto. It's unsafe and too dangerous, and that's why a metal gate has been placed across it—it's too dangerous for anyone to enter!' Turning to Suzy, he told her, 'There is supposed to be some sort of tunnel and an underground chamber beneath the grotto, which was built originally as a folly.'

Suzy shivered as she listened to him. She had always had a fear of such places, and certainly did not share Charlie's enthusiasm.

'But you must show Suzy the sunken garden, Luke. It's a very romantic walk, Suzy,' he added warmly, 'and if Luke hadn't bagged you first, I can assure you I would have enjoyed showing it to you myself.'

Sir Peter was flirting with her!

Hastily Suzy took a sip of her wine, and then choked a little as she realised how strong it was.

The food was delicious, but she seemed to have lost her usual appetite, Suzy acknowledged as her churning stomach prevented her from eating more than a few mouthfuls of her meal.

Was it because every minute that passed meant that it was getting closer to the time when she would have to go back upstairs with Luke to that suite? Their suite. Their bed.

A tense shudder ripped through her and she reached for her wine again, hoping to distract herself.

The children were looking tired and had started bickering. It was far too late for them to be eating, in Suzy's opinion, and the food was surely too rich for young digestion.

'Charlie, that's enough!'

Peter was giving his son an angry look, but Suzy could see that the little boy's behaviour was caused more by tiredness than wilfulness.

'Finish your dinner,' Sir Peter instructed.

'I don't want it. I don't like it.' Charlie resisted stubbornly.

'Charles!'

'I think the children are tired,' Suzy intervened gently. 'It is rather late. I don't know what time they normally go to bed...'

'Of course. You are quite right! It *is* late!' Sir Peter agreed immediately. 'I'd better send for one of the maids to take them upstairs and put them to bed,' he added, signalling to the hovering waiter.

Within minutes a plump, elderly woman appeared, and their father instructed the children to go with her.

A small frown creased Suzy's forehead as both children followed the maid without receiving a goodnight kiss from their father.

Half an hour later, their own meal over, Suzy was beginning to feel tired herself—and to regret the two glasses of red wine she had drunk!

Coffee was to be served in the same salon where they had had their pre-dinner cocktails, and once they had made their way there Sir Peter settled himself on one of the damask sofas. Patting the space beside himself, he invited, 'Come and sit here, next to me, Suzy, and tell me all about yourself.'

Hesitantly Suzy began to walk towards him, only to come to an unsteady stop as Luke stepped in front of her.

'If you don't mind, Peter, I think I'd like to have her to myself for a while,' he announced smoothly, taking hold of Suzy's arm as he did so.

Just the feel of his fingers on her bare arm was enough to make her quiver from head to foot, Suzy recognised dizzily.

'Of course, of course. Don't blame you, old chap,' Sir Peter responded heartily.

Before she could say or do anything Suzy discovered that she was being almost force-marched in the direction of the salon door. She could almost feel the blast of heat from Luke's anger as he opened the door and propelled her out into the hallway, up the stairs and into their suite.

As soon as he had closed the door behind them he

rounded on her, demanding savagely, 'What the devil do you think you are playing at? Or do I need to ask? It's the same old trick, isn't it? I warned you—'

'I'm not playing at anything!' Suzy denied fiercely.

'Liar! You've seen that Peter is susceptible to you, so you're doing everything you can to encourage him...giving him limpid-eyed looks, pretending to be concerned about his children—'

'I *am* concerned about them!' Suzy stopped him. 'And as for me encouraging him—I was doing no such thing! You're behaving like a jealous lover!' she threw furiously at him. 'Accusing me of things I haven't done, and have no intention of doing!'

A jealous lover! Luke stared at her.

Suzy gasped as she was dragged into Luke's arms. She tried to protest. And she tried to resist. But the wine had obviously weakened her resistance. Of its own accord her hand clutched at the sleeve of his shirt and her body leaned into his. Greedily her senses absorbed the feel of him. Tough, male, strong... She looked at his mouth. She looked into his eyes. And then she looked at his mouth again. She could feel the sound he was making in his throat vibrate through his body in a feral growl of warning male arousal.

He was lowering his head and she wanted to reach up and hold it, so that he couldn't escape, so that his mouth had to cover her own...

And it did! How long had she yearned for this? Suzy wondered dizzily as her lips clung to his. Surrounded by the sensual soft dark of the Italian night, she gave in to her own need. She was in his arms and then in his hands—quite literally, she realised in soaring shocked pleasure as they moved over her, shaping her, learning her...

Into the darkness of their room she moaned her un-inhibited delight. She could feel her breasts swelling into his hands whilst her stomach tightened with ex-pectation. She lifted her arms to wrap them around him, her fingers sliding into the softness of his hair. His mouth tasted erotically of wine and man, and she wanted to feed on it until all her senses were sated with the pleasure of him. The straps of her top had slipped down her arms and were digging into her flesh, and she wanted to beg Luke to remove it from her body, right here and right now.

Helplessly Luke gave in to the need he had felt the first time she had kissed him. Then he had denied it, buried it, but somehow it had survived, tormenting him in his dreams. Luke felt his body shudder as his hunger for her ripped through his defences. Now he was be-yond reason, beyond sanity, beyond anything and ev-erything but wanting her. He was, Luke recognised dis-tantly, completely out of control. And she was the one who had done this to him, who had driven him, aroused him, made him so insane with need for her. That eager female sound she had just made had logged straight into his body and switched on every damn thing, send-ing him completely crazy. He lifted his hand to push Suzy's auburn hair off her creamy neck and shoulder, leaving them exposed to the exploration of his hungry mouth. A tiny pulse jumped and skittered beneath his kiss and he paused to touch it with his tongue.

She was openly trembling with longing, Suzy rec-ognised as her head fell back to allow Luke even more access to the curve of her throat. Behind her she had the hardness of the heavy wooden door, and in front of her she had the hardness that was Luke. A deep shudder tormented her as he started to explore the delicate whorls of her ear, his thumb on the pulse at the base of her throat.

Someone was tugging frantically at the straps of her top trying to remove it. How could Luke be doing that and touching her as well?

It wasn't Luke who was tearing off her clothes and exhaling in a rush of fierce pleasure as they fell to the ground, Suzy realised. It was her.

Luke had felt her clothes slither to the floor as his eyes adjusted to the velvet darkness, and now he could see the pale outline of her body. Her almost naked body.

He had known that she wasn't wearing a bra—had known it and registered Peter's equal awareness of that fact—but that knowledge and the knowledge he had now, of the soft, pure nakedness of her torso, with the outline of her breasts sketched in blurred charcoal light, were a world apart.

Almost as though it was happening in slow motion Suzy watched as Luke turned his head and looked down at her body. His hand came out and slid beneath one breast, gently supporting it.

If she was any more perfect she wouldn't be human, Luke thought as he felt the delicious weight of Suzy's breast on his palm. His thumb searched for her nipple.

She gave a sharp, electrified moan and her whole body stiffened in response to his touch.

She was a conniving, manipulative wanton who had

never had a genuine emotion or reaction in her life, Luke told himself savagely. But his body was beyond listening. His hand was working urgently on her breast, preparing it for the hungry possession of his mouth. Every sweet moan she made was causing the sensation in the pit of his belly to screw down harder. If he didn't have the taste of her in his mouth soon he was going to…

His free hand slid down her body and encountered the lacy edge of her underwear. He hooked one finger under what he thought was elastic and then realised that it was a ribbon bow. A bow he could untie with his fingers, or…Luke had a sudden mental picture of himself laying her on the bed, tugging the bows loose with his teeth. He wanted to eat her like a fresh peach, filling his mouth with her taste until the juice of her ran from his fingers and his lips.

His erection was straining against his clothes, and he could tell from the small urgent sounds Suzy was making that she was equally aroused.

They were partners, after all, he reminded himself with inner black humour. Partners on opposite sides of a very sharp divide, he acknowledged, and reality suddenly kicked in.

Suzy tensed as she felt Luke's hand start to leave her breast. Something had happened. Something had made him draw back from her, and she didn't want that something. She wanted *him*.

Suzy's sexual experience was relatively limited. And yet she discovered that her body knew far more than she had given it credit for. It knew, for instance, that if she reached out and touched Luke the way she was doing, just the merest brush of her fingertips, slowly, oh so slowly against that tight bulge she could feel beneath his clothing, that instead of pushing her away he would draw her to him again.

He shouldn't be doing this. Oh, he should not be doing this, Luke warned himself. But that provocative touch that Suzy was subjecting him to, just the slightest brush of delicate fingertips against his erection, was more than he could stand.

He wanted her right now.

He didn't just want to taste her, he wanted to take her and fill her and spill himself inside her.

Taking hold of her hands, Luke pinned them above her head, his body leaning into hers.

Her eyes had adjusted to the dark now, and Suzy could see his expression quite clearly. A fast, furious surge of shocked excitement raced through her. He had lost control now. She could see it in his eyes, feel it in the way he was grinding his body into hers—and she loved it…

As Luke felt Suzy's hips lift and writhe tormentingly against him he knew that there was no going back.

There was nothing he wanted more than to take her right here, against the damned door, as primitively as though every layer of civilisation had been stripped from them both. He wanted to hook his fingers in those ridiculous bows and leave himself free to give her every pleasure. He wanted to lift her up against him and have her wrap her legs around him whilst he buried himself so deep inside her that no other man would ever pleasure her as much.

Her fingers touched him again, and this time she was tracing his erection, gauging it—measuring it?

Suzy's chest tightened as her uncertain touch revealed to her just how much of a man Luke was! She could feel Luke lifting her up against him. Shocked pleasure surged through her on a riptide. He was going to make love to her here against the door!

She weighed next to nothing, Luke acknowledged as he lifted Suzy off the floor. The lacy thong she was wearing left the rounded contours of her bottom free to his touch. He could see the bright, aroused glitter of her eyes and he could feel the exhalation of her breath. His tongue touched her lips and then pierced her mouth. She tasted soft and sweet, warm and welcoming.

'Open your legs,' he commanded her.

Hot, urgent, immediate sex—that was what he wanted with her.

His hand was on his zip before he recognised that he wanted far more than that.

CHAPTER SEVEN

'WHAT are you doing?' Suzy protested as Luke suddenly swung her up into his arms. Had he changed his mind? Wasn't he going to make love to her after all? 'Why—?'

'Why?' He stopped her as he laid her on the bed. 'Because where we were would have been fine for a quickie,' he told her rawly. 'But right now I need to have much more than just that. Much, much more!' he said thickly, and brushed his lips against her half-parted mouth, then touched them to each nipple in turn before returning to her mouth to kiss her with deep ferocity.

Whilst he stripped off his clothes he told her what he wanted to do with her, how he wanted to touch her and how he wanted her to touch him. By the time he was fully nude Suzy was ready to explode. The heat in her lower body was unbearable, and so was the pressure.

Impulsively she reached down to remove her ribbon-tied thong.

'No!'

His hand was over hers, but instead of unfastening the bow he started to kiss her again. Her mouth, her shoulder, her breast, laving the tight peak until she was thrashing around beneath him. And then the other breast, taking his time whilst she cried out, her hands on his shoulders, her nails digging into his skin.

But that was nothing to what she felt when his mouth moved lower, his lips caressing her stomach and then his tongue rimming her navel, tracing the lacy edge of her thong from one bow to the other and then back again. She could feel his hands sliding beneath her, lifting her, and she writhed in urgent need. She felt his breath against her skin and watched in a sensual daze of arousal as he tugged at the bow with his teeth. When it came free he pressed his lips to her naked skin and his hand to her naked body, discovering, exploring, parting the swollen folds of flesh to expose her sex to his touch and his taste.

Suzy heard the sounds of pleasure flooding the room and knew they must be her own, but she had no awareness of having made them. She had no awareness of anything at all other than the touch of Luke's fingers and the lave of his tongue.

She felt the tightening warning of her body, but it was impossible for her to hold back her orgasm. As she cried out her pleasure she felt Luke's mouth taking it from her into his own keeping.

She was still trembling with its aftershock seconds later, when he moved up the bed to hold her, wrapping her tightly in his arms, his breath warm against the top of her head.

Was it because it had been such a long time since he had done this that her reaction had affected him so much? Luke questioned himself. Had he somehow forgotten just how intense the pleasure of pleasuring a woman was for him? Had he somehow managed to overlook the way it made him feel? Because he was damn sure that no one had given him this feeling before. Exhilarated, Suzy clung to Luke. His naked flesh felt smooth and warm beneath her fingertips. Idly she traced the line of his collarbone, and then pressed a small kiss to it for no other reason than that she wanted to. She ran her finger around the aureole of his nipple, dark and flat, unlike the rosy fullness of her own. The nipple itself was different too. She teased it languidly and then burrowed her face against his chest, relishing the scent and taste of him.

'If you keep doing that…' Luke warned her rawly.

'You'll do what?' Suzy challenged him deliberately.

'This,' he responded promptly, rolling her over and then beneath him.

Eagerly Suzy opened her legs and wrapped them round him, welcoming him into her soft warmth. Desire ran through her with liquid heat, but more than that, as her hips lifted and writhed and her body welcomed him with fierce female longing, Suzy recognised that it wasn't just her body that could feel him, that wanted him. It was her heart and her mind as well! And that meant—

But, no, she did not want to think about what that meant right now. In fact she did not want to think at all. She simply wanted to know. To experience. To feel. To be here in this place at this time with this man, and to hold on to what they were sharing for ever.

A sensation of exquisite urgency was filling her, taking her with him through time and space. Each thrust of his powerful body within her own brought them closer, physically and emotionally.

The increasingly fast movement of his thrusts was

pushing her up the bed, and Suzy had to reach out to grab hold of the bedpost behind her.

In that same moment she heard his harsh cry, and felt again that same rainbow explosion within herself as she reached her climax, and it showered her whole body with quick silver darts of pleasure.

Soul mates. Meant to be together.

The words, the knowledge floated through her like precious stars set in a perfect sky.

As they lay in a damp and relaxed tumble of arms and legs, Suzy's head on his chest, his arms wrapped hard around her, Luke marvelled again at the intensity of his own pleasure. He had been so overwhelmed by his need for her that he hadn't even had time to think about any practicalities.

In his youth, when he had been as keen on exploring sex as any other teenager, he had practised safe sex—primarily because he had had no wish to become a father before he was ready. Over the last few years his career had meant that sex, safe or otherwise, simply wasn't on his personal agenda. But he had taken Suzy to bed without even taking the most rudimentary health precautions. She would be protected against pregnancy, of course, but it was a bit late now to demand a full report on her sexual health and history!

Moonlight streamed in through the window, leaving a silver trail on Luke's naked body. Suzy traced it with one loving finger, frowning as she suddenly found the hard ridge of a scar. Leaning up, she looked down at it, her heart twisting as she saw its raw newness. Overwhelmed by her feelings for him, she bent her head and tenderly placed her lips against the puckered ridge of flesh.

Immediately Luke tensed, wrenching himself away from her.

'What is it?' Suzy asked him in concern. 'Did I hurt you?'

When he shook his head she asked softly. 'How did it happen, Luke?' She couldn't bear to think of him being in danger, being hurt.

Pushing her away, Luke said harshly, 'If you must know it was caused by a woman just like you!'

He could see the shock in her face, but he ignored it.

'She may not have fired the bullet that caused it, but she was still responsible.'

A dark, frightening anger filled his expression, banishing the intimacy they had shared. Bitterly Luke contemplated what he had done. How could he not have controlled himself? Stopped himself? How could she have made him feel like that? How could she have made him want like that, when she was everything he did *not* want in a woman? Anger and self-disgust left a sour taste in his mouth.

'Luke?' Suzy whispered hesitantly.

Why wasn't he saying anything to her? Why was he turning away from her instead of holding her as she longed for him to do?

He had to make it plain to her that what had just happened between them hadn't left him vulnerable or open to any kind of persuasion, Luke told himself. He could still feel the soft warmth of her lips against his scar. Anger burned through him. A gunshot wound was nothing compared with what he could see inside his head. He saw the smouldering rubble of what had once been a home, the body of the pretty young woman who had lived in it lying on the ground like that of a broken doll, murdered, and all because some damn female journalist had ignored his explicit instructions so that she could get her human interest story…

'Don't make the mistake of thinking that the fact that we've had sex changes anything,' he told Suzy brutally. 'It doesn't! After all, we both know that sex is the currency you favour. On this occasion it didn't work!'

A cold feeling of sickness was crawling through her. Shock, anguish, despair—she could feel them all.

Luke was making it humiliatingly plain that he had simply used her for sex. How could she have been so stupid as to allow herself to think— To think what? That because for her sexual intimacy was inextricably linked to emotional intimacy Luke would think the same thing? That because she could not stop herself from feeling the way she did about him he shared those feelings? Was she totally crazy? Hadn't he just made it brutally plain to her that he did not?

Silently Suzy turned away from him, whilst pain raked her with burning claws.

CHAPTER EIGHT

'I'M BORED!'

Charlie's petulant comment was a welcome interruption to Suzy's agonised inner examination of what had happened with Luke last night.

She and the children had breakfasted alone, Lucy informing her with a world-weary sigh that, 'Daddy and Luke are talking business and we aren't allowed to interrupt them.'

Was it business that had been responsible for Luke's absence from both the bed they had shared last night and the suite when she had woken up this morning? Suzy didn't really care! She was glad he seemed to have forgotten his threat to stay with her day and night, and was just relieved that she hadn't had to go through the embarrassment and humiliation of seeing him.

In fact she wished passionately that she might never have to see him again! How could he have used her so cold-bloodedly—and more importantly, how could she have let him?

'It's a beautiful day,' she responded to Charlie's statement of his boredom. 'Why don't you go for a swim?'

She had seen the swimming pool from her vantage point on the hillside above the villa, and had admired the elegance of its tranquil setting.

'We can't go swimming,' Charlie told her crossly.

Suzy frowned, wondering if perhaps their father had put a ban on them swimming without adult supervision. But before she could say anything Lucy told her unhappily, 'We can't swim because Mummy sent us with the wrong clothes. She forgot about packing our swimming things.'

Forgot? Suzy felt a sharp stab of anger against the children's mother as she looked at Lucy's downbent head, and wondered cynically if it *was* just that the children's swimming things had been forgotten or if she had deliberately sent them away with the wrong clothes in order to make life difficult for their father.

'Well, perhaps you could ask Daddy to buy some new things for you?' she suggested practically. The resort had any number of shops selling clothes and, whilst they might be expensive, Sir Peter Verey did not strike her as a man who had to watch his budget!

A maid came in to clear away the breakfast things, and through the open door Suzy could see a powerfully built man standing in the hallway.

One of Luke's men? Although there was no obvious evidence of the villa being heavily guarded, Suzy suspected that if she tried to make any attempt to leave she would find that she wasn't allowed to get very far.

Idly she wondered just what it was that demanded Luke's presence here. Certainly the soldiers she had seen departing must have something to do with it. It must be politically delicate rather than dangerous, she suspected, otherwise the children wouldn't be here. Sir Peter might not be a particularly hands-on father, but surely he wouldn't risk exposing his children to danger?

'It's no use us asking Daddy to take us shopping. He'll just say that he's too busy.' Lucy informed Suzy, her words breaking into her thoughts.

The weary resignation in her voice made Suzy's heart ache for her. It told of a small lifetime of being told that her parents were 'too busy'.

'But Suzy could take us! Lucy, let's go and ask Daddy if she can!' Charlie suggested excitedly, getting off his chair.

'If she can what?'

Suzy spun round as Sir Peter and Luke came into the room.

'Daddy, Mummy forgot to pack our swimsuits and our shorts and things,' Lucy answered her father, a little reluctantly.

She obviously felt that what she was saying was a betrayal of her mother, Suzy recognised.

'Yes, and we want Suzy to take us out and buy some new ones,' Charlie added importantly.

Suzy could feel both Sir Peter and Luke looking at her. The relaxed approval in Sir Peter's eyes certainly wasn't mirrored in Luke's.

Suzy's heart gave a painful jerk. The sight of him was releasing the despair and anguish she had been fighting to ignore. Self-contempt and misery crawled through her veins like poison. And yet, as she dragged her gaze from Luke's face, Suzy acknowledged that it wasn't the anger she should be feeling that was making her tremble inwardly, but a destructive and humiliating ache of longing!

She was distantly aware of Sir Peter exclaiming enthusiastically, 'What an excellent idea! My dear, you are a godsend!'

'Peter, I don't think—' Luke began, an ominous expression in his eyes as he cast Suzy a freezing look of contempt.

'Luke, I know you want her all to yourself, and I can't blame you.' Sir Peter smiled. 'But we mustn't disappoint the children!'

Luke had intended to spend the morning catching up on some paperwork and trying to see if there wasn't some way that President Njambla could be pinned down to a definite date in order that he could wind up the whole exercise with as much speed as possible. He told himself he should have guessed that Suzy would try to pull this kind of trick.

He had already given orders that no one was to be allowed to leave the villa without his permission, and thanks to the high wall that surrounded the property it was impossible to leave other than via one of the discreetly guarded gates.

The staff all lived in, and had been thoroughly vetted, and it should have been an easy task to ensure that Suzy did not have any outside contact with anyone. He had taken possession of her mobile phone and her passport.

Taken possession! Luke wished his brain had not supplied him with those two particular words. Last night he had physically taken possession of Suzy herself, but only because his desire for her had taken possession of him!

'Indeed we mustn't,' Luke answered Sir Peter

grimly. 'I'll organise a car. Are you ready to leave now?' he asked Suzy curtly.

'Well, I need to go upstairs and get my bag,' Suzy responded shakily as she tried to withstand the look he was giving her.

'I'll come with you,' Luke announced, leaving her with no option other than to walk towards the door, uncomfortably aware as she did so that he was following her.

Halfway up the stairs she asked herself bitterly why, after what he had done to her and what he had said to her, the reaction of her body to the knowledge that he was so close behind her now was one of longing and not rejection.

Quickening her step, she headed for their suite. But as she reached for the door handle Luke was there before her. Suzy flinched as she felt the brief brush of hard fingertips against her wrist.

'Quite a clever move,' Luke said conversationally as he closed the door, imprisoning her with him in the room's heavy silence. 'I had forgotten that female reporters are different from the rest of their sex and do not possess any scruples where children are concerned.'

There was a look in his eyes that confused Suzy—a mixture of biting contempt and savage anger laced with pain, as though somehow his words had a personal meaning for him.

'I am not using the children!' Suzy denied heatedly. 'It was their idea to approach their father. And besides, I could hardly manufacture the fact that their mother has been spiteful enough to send them here without proper holiday clothes. The dress Lucy was wearing last night looked so uncomfortable. Poor little scraps— I feel so sorry for them,' Suzy told him emotionally.

Luke could feel himself tensing as he listened to her. Why, when he knew she was acting, was he allowing himself to react to her faked emotions, allowing her to needle her way under his professional skin, letting her touch personal nerve-endings he had no damned business allowing her to touch?

'And as for using them! You're a fine one to talk about that!' she accused him angrily. 'You're keeping me imprisoned here because whatever it is that is going on might potentially be dangerous—and yet you are using the children as camouflage!'

'The children's presence here is directly against my wishes,' Luke told her shortly, looking away from her.

'So you mean that there is actually someone who can't be bullied, threatened and coerced into doing what you want?' Suzy couldn't resist demanding.

Immediately Luke turned round, subjecting her to a narrow-eyed gaze that made her want to shiver, as though her flesh had been touched by a blast of cold air.

'Coerced?' Luke challenged her. 'If by that you are trying to imply that last night I coerced you...you certainly didn't give me the impression that you didn't want what was happening. In fact—'

'I don't want to talk about last night,' Suzy interrupted him wildly. 'I don't.'

Was that because she didn't want to have the pathetic remnants of the fantasies and daydreams she was holding onto wrenched from her? Why not? What was the point in stubbornly clinging to them? They were worthless…meaningless…like the physical act she had shared with Luke!

'Save the emotional histrionics for Peter,' Luke told her contemptuously. 'He's becoming besotted enough with you to believe them!'

His words made Suzy frown. Certainly Peter was enjoying pretending to flirt with her, but a pretence at flirtation was all it was. If Suzy could see that she wondered why Luke, who was surely trained to observe and analyse people's behaviour and reactions, could not.

'The children will be waiting,' she told him stiffly. 'I'll just get my bag.'

Before she could move, Luke said, 'Stay here. I'll get it.'

His unexpected chivalrous gesture caught her off guard, but nowhere near so much as his casual question as he picked up a briefcase and opened it.

'Are you all right for money?'

'Yes. I've got enough of my own.' Suzy stopped him quickly.

His concern for her after his earlier comments was like balm on a painful wound, and she watched silently as he closed his case and then crossed the room to pick up her small handbag. It looked tiny grasped in his large hand as he brought it to her.

'And just remember,' he warned her grimly, 'I'm going to be right beside you. If you were thinking—'

'You mean that you're coming with us?'

Luke's hand was pressing against her wrist and Suzy

could barely think for the effect his touch was having on her body.

'Why not? You're my partner, after all, and according to Peter I can't bear to let you out of my sight,' he told her derisively.

He certainly wasn't exhibiting any concern for her now, Suzy recognised. He was standing so close that she felt as though she could hardly breathe.

Automatically Suzy stepped back. Her mind and body were tearing her apart with the ferocity of the conflicting messages they were sending her. She wanted to go somewhere quiet and dark and stay there until she felt able to cope. Instead she was going to have to go to the resort, with Luke at her side and a smile pinned to her face.

Impulsively she turned to Luke, driven to get him to believe her and to set her free, but the words died unspoken as she saw the look on his face.

Well, if he could feel contemptuous about her then somehow she would learn to feel the same way about him, she told herself fiercely, and walked towards the door.

As he watched her Luke too was prey to conflicting emotions. He had absolutely no doubt that his suspicions concerning her were correct. And, that being the case, it was essential that he prevented her from having any kind of contact with anyone she might pass information on to. In that sense, in the professional sense, she was his enemy.

But his anger and bitterness towards her because of what she was—they were not professionally objective feelings, in any way, shape or form. They were personal. And on that personal level those feelings were unacceptable, Luke told himself grimly. Unacceptable and potentially prejudicial to his ability to do his job.

When fighting men became battle-weary they ceased to be effective. That was one of the reasons why he had left the Army. Because he had begun to feel he had fought too many wars and seen too much death. Was he now experiencing a similar syndrome within his current work? Was Suzy Roberts getting to him because for some reason he was no longer an effective operative? Or was he no longer an effective operative because Suzy Roberts was getting to him?

It wasn't going to be the latter. No way would he allow himself that weakness! To lose it over a woman like her? To want her, ache for her; hunger for her to the point where those feelings dominated every other aspect of his life?

No way!

Her subtle manipulation of the children this morning proved that he was right to be suspicious of her. So why, knowing all of that, when she had looked at him earlier with that faked pain in her eyes, had he been driven to take her in his arms and—?

And what? And nothing, Luke told himself savagely. Absolutely nothing!

'Luke, there's a parking space.' Suzy called as she looked out of the window of the large four-wheel drive vehicle in which Luke had driven them down to the resort.

'I've seen it,' was Luke's clipped response, and he neatly reversed the large vehicle into the small space.

Her eyes shadowed, Suzy turned her face away from him, angry with herself for letting such a small and unimportant rejection of help bring betraying tears to her eyes. She turned to get out of the Jeep.

'Wait there,' Luke told her imperiously, sliding out of his own seat.

Was he afraid that she might jump out and try to run away? Suzy wondered scathingly as she watched him come round to her own door and open it. Immediately she made to scramble out, but as she did so Luke took hold of her, lifting her bodily out of the car and placing her gently on the ground.

Raw pain scalded Suzy's throat, making it impossible for her to speak as she stood stiffly in his hold.

To anyone looking at them his gesture would have seemed one of loving consideration. But he did not love her. He loathed and despised her!

The pain in her throat had reached her chest. She could feel Luke looking at her, but she refused to return his gaze. She did have some pride, and there was no way she was going to let him see the anguish she knew must be in her eyes.

With a small twist of her body she pulled away from him in mute rejection, and then tensed as she felt him tighten his grip on her, constraining her. Now she *did* look at him, resentment emanating from every pore of her body as she resisted his hold.

What the hell was that damned perfume Suzy was wearing? Luke wondered savagely as the air around filled with the scent of her. It conjured up for him mental images his senses had retained: her body, silky smooth beneath his hands, fire and passion beneath his touch as she moved against him, with him...

A thousand brilliant images flooded his senses as the warm morning air wafted her scent around him. It might be morning outside his body, but inside it, inside his head, it was night, with its soft, sensual darkness, its dangerous memories...

Against his will Luke felt his gaze sliding slowly from her eyes to her mouth, to absorb in greedy silence its shape and beauty. His mouth already knew its texture, her texture, but those memories were not enough. Suddenly he wanted to know it again. To trace its tender outline, to stroke its soft warmth, to probe the sweet resistance it offered him and capture its innermost sweetness.

Suzy felt as though she was about to collapse. Luke was looking at her mouth and his look was scorching her, making her want to lift her face to him and plead for his kiss. Frantically she dragged her hot gaze away from his face and looked at the car.

The children! To her shame, she realised that she had actually forgotten about them!

Her small frantic movement brought Luke back to reality. Releasing her, he turned towards the car and went to help the children out.

CHAPTER NINE

'LUKE nearly kissed you then,' Lucy confided innocently to Suzy as she fell into step beside her, whilst
her brother, boy-like, immediately stationed himself at
Luke's side.

Kissed her? What for? Punishment? A gesture of his
contempt? Suzy wondered sadly as the four of them
made their way from the car park to the town's quaintly
narrow and very steep streets.

'I think there's a children's shop not far from here,'
Suzy announced, indicating the small square they were
just entering.

Before they had left Sir Peter had handed her a very
large sum of euros, telling her to get whatever she thought
the children might need. And Suzy intended to do just
that! It appalled her that their mother should be so selfish
as to send them on holiday without the necessary clothes
purely to spite her ex-husband, without giving a thought
to how the children themselves might feel.

However, she was by nature thrifty—she had had to
be, she acknowledged wryly. So she would get the best
she could for the money.

Several cafés fronted onto the ancient cobbled
square, their canvas sun umbrellas adding a bright
splash of colour to the greyness of the weathered stone.

'It's just down here,' Suzy told Luke, indicating the
narrow alleyway in front of them.

The children's clothes shop was three doors down, and Suzy could see Lucy's eyes light up as they walked inside. Within seconds the little girl was standing in silence, absorbed in the racks of clothes. Silent maybe, but her expression said it all, Suzy reflected as she watched the pleasure and excitement illuminating her face.

'Tell me what you think you would like, Lucy,' she suggested. 'And then we can have a look.'

She could feel Luke standing behind her, and in any other circumstances she would have suggested that he take Charlie to the other side of the shop and pick out some clothes for him. But she was too conscious of Luke's biting statement that he was going to remain glued to her side to do so.

Instead she waited patiently whilst Lucy went slowly through the rack, stopping every now and then to look enquiringly at Suzy.

'You need a couple of swimsuits and some shorts, Lucy,' Suzy said gently. 'Some tee shirts, and perhaps a dress?'

A tender smile curled her mouth as she saw that Lucy was hovering over a trendy pre-teen outfit of which wasn't really suitable for holidaywear, but Suzy could see its appeal for her.

Watching the interplay between child and woman, Luke reminded himself angrily that Suzy was a skilled actress.

More than an hour after they had entered the shop both children were kitted out, and Lucy's face was glowing with delight because Suzy had ruefully agreed that she could have the outfit she had set her heart on.

'Can we have an ice cream now?' Charlie asked as soon as they reached the square.

'It's almost lunchtime,' Luke told him, but instead of insisting that they needed to return to the villa to Suzy's surprise he suggested that they find a table at one of the cafés and have an early lunch there.

'Yes!' Charlie exclaimed excitedly.

Five minutes later they were sitting at a table, menus in their hands.

'Suzy, do you think I could wear my new trousers for dinner tonight?' Lucy asked earnestly, after the waiter had taken their order.

Suzy couldn't help it. Over Lucy's head her gaze met Luke's, her eyes brimming with tender amusement.

'I don't see why not—so long as your father doesn't mind,' she agreed.

Completely happy, Lucy leaned her head against Suzy and stroked her bare arm with loving fingers.

Her small, innocent gesture and the message of trust it carried made Luke feel as though a giant clamp was tightening around his heart.

How could one woman be two such very different people?

Different? What the hell was he thinking? She was only one person—a devious, manipulative, despicable person, incapable of any kind of genuine emotion.

The waiter brought their food, and Suzy was just beginning to eat hers when she happened to glance across the square.

Shock froze her into immobility as she saw the man standing only yards away and immediately recognised him. Jerry Needham! He was one of the reporters from the magazine; one of the men who had made her life such a misery when she had worked there.

What was he doing here? Taking a holiday? Or something more sinister—like trying to find out what was going on at the villa? Her heart was jerking around inside her chest as though someone had it on a string. What if he saw her and came over? Introduced himself? Luke would immediately suspect the worst.

Her appetite had completely deserted her, but then she saw Jerry was walking away from them and disappearing into the crowd on the other side of the square. Suzy tried to relax, but her insides were a tight ball of anxiety and apprehension. She had never liked Jerry—he was loud-mouthed, boorish and vulgar, and the sexual innuendo of the comments he had made to her had filled her with nausea. But she knew that he was an exceptionally shrewd reporter.

To her relief she heard Luke asking the children, 'Finished, you two?' He signalled for the waiter and asked Suzy, 'If you're ready to go...?'

Suzy was on her feet before he had finished speaking, but they had no sooner walked back into the crowded square when Charlie suddenly piped up urgently. 'I need the bathroom!'

An innocent enough request, but it was one that caused the two adults who heard it to tense in silent dismay.

One look at Charlie's screwed-up and anxious face

told Suzy that there was no way the little boy could wait.

'There must have been lavatories back at the café,' she told Luke. 'You'll have to take him back there. Lucy and I will wait here.'

Luke looked down at Charlie and inwardly cursed. The square was busy and Charlie was only young— there was no way he could let him go alone. It was obvious that he would have to take him to the lavatory. Which meant that he would have to leave Suzy here unguarded.

'Why don't you take Lucy?' he suggested, as Charlie tugged anxiously on his arm.

'I don't want to go.' Lucy forestalled his attempt to at least keep some check on Suzy.

'We'll wait here for you,' Suzy told him, quickly checking the crowd to make sure there was no sign of the reporter.

Luke hurried Charlie through the crowd. He could not blame the little boy for what had happened, and neither could he accuse Suzy of having engineered the situation.

How much longer were Luke and Charlie going to be? Suzy wondered anxiously, willing them to return so that they could leave.

'Lucy, where are you going?' she protested as Lucy suddenly started to hurry towards one of the stalls.

'It's all right, I just want to look at something,' Lucy called back to her.

Suzy suddenly froze as the crowd parted and a couple of yards behind her she saw Jerry—looking right back at her.

She turned away, hoping to disappear into the throng of sightseers, but he was too quick for her, and she tensed as she felt his hand on her arm.

'Suzy! Suzy Roberts! What a coincidence!'

The oily, speculative look he was giving her made Suzy feel sick as it brought back unwanted memories.

'What are you doing here?' he demanded, still watching her with a look in his eyes which Suzy did not like.

'I'm on holiday with my partner,' Suzy lied uncomfortably, adding quickly, 'I must go. He'll be wondering where I am—we got separated by the crowd.' Turning away from him, she went to where Lucy was standing, looking at a stall selling handmade jewellery.

'Why didn't you stay where I left you?'

Suzy could hear the censorious note in Luke's voice. Had he seen Jerry? She looked round anxiously, but the reporter was nowhere to be seen.

'I wanted to look at one of the stalls,' Lucy answered sunnily. 'Are we going back to the villa now?'

'Yes, we are,' Luke agreed.

Suzy shivered as she saw him looking searchingly at her. Surely if he had seen Jerry with her he would have said something, only too delighted to have his suspicions of her confirmed? But it was not so much her fear that Luke might have seen Jerry with her that was making her feel so anxious, Suzy acknowledged as Luke guided them through the crowd, it was her concern about the reporter's presence here in the resort, so close to the villa.

The owner of the magazine did have excellent sources of sensitive information, although who they were Suzy had never known. It was not entirely beyond the bounds of possibility that Roy Jarvis could have sent Jerry to Italy to check up on what was happening at the villa.

And, that being the case, didn't she, as an honest citizen, have a moral obligation to tell Luke that she had seen him?

From his vantage point several yards away Jerry watched Luke and Suzy making their way through the crowd with the two children.

He had recognised Luke, of course, and unless he was mistaken—and he was sure that he was not—those two kids with them were the Verey kids, who were staying with their father.

Jerry had only arrived at the resort the previous day, sent there to check out a tip-off about Sir Peter Verey's real reason for being in Italy. Now he had the happy feeling that things were very definitely going his way!

Suzy Roberts and Lucas Soames. Well, well, what a piece of luck!

Suzy was still struggling with her moral dilemma when they got back to the villa.

Jerry might just be at the resort on holiday, or even following some other story involving the celebrities who stayed there, she tried to tell herself. But her conscience refused to be convinced.

CHAPTER TEN

'LUKE, can I have a word?'

Luke frowned as the operative he had put in charge of the perimeter security at the villa approached him.

It was twenty-four hours since he had driven Suzy and the children back from the resort—twenty-four hours, far too many of which he had spent fighting against his own emotions instead of concentrating on his professional business, which was why he had this morning finally instructed one of his London operatives to supply him with a full and detailed report on Suzy. He was sure the information in the report would back up his professional distrust of her and help him to banish these unwanted emotions she was causing him! The more information he had about her, the better.

Last night after dinner he had escorted Suzy to their suite and pretended to busy himself with some work whilst she prepared for bed. Only when he had been sure she was soundly asleep had he gone to bed himself, and even then he had not been able to relax.

In her sleep she had turned over to lie facing him, and he had wanted...

Luke did not want to think about what he had wanted to do.

Unable to trust himself not to give in to the temptation she represented, he had got up and spent the rest of the night sleeping uncomfortably in a chair.

He had got up and dressed before she had woken, though, determined not to allow her to suspect how vulnerable he had become to her. He had even caught himself thinking that if things could be different, if they could somehow find a way... To what? he had challenged himself. To forget what she was and what she did? Impossible! Furiously angry with himself, he wished he had never set eyes on her.

She was with the Verey children now, sunbathing beside the pool. The swimsuit she had been wearing when he had walked past earlier had made him remember what it had felt like to hold her naked body.

Hell, but he would be glad when all this was over.

'Yes, Phillips, what is it?' he asked his operative.

'The guards have reported that a chap's been hanging around the gates, asking questions about Ms Roberts.'

Luke's eyes narrowed. 'What chap?' he demanded grimly.

Hugh Phillips was young and keen, and quickly told Luke what he knew.

'He said he was just a friend, and refused to give any name, but according to the guards he was asking rather too many questions—and not just about Ms Roberts.'

Luke felt his stomach churn with anger—and something else! What the hell was he feeling like *that* for? He ought to be feeling vindicated, because he had been right to suspect Suzy, instead of savagely angry.

'Well, if he's so keen to see Ms Roberts, then perhaps he should be allowed to do so, Hugh. Tell the guards to allow him to persuade them to let him in.

Don't make it too easy for him, though. I don't want him getting suspicious. We need to know who he is and what he's up to. Keep him away from the house. You can let Ms Roberts meet him in the surrounds.'

Luke could see that Hugh Phillips was battling not to show any reaction to the mention of Suzy's name. Like everyone else, Hugh believed that Suzy was Luke's own partner.

'Have you got all that?' he checked coolly.

'Yes,' Hugh answered woodenly.

'Good—and remember, the minute he comes back I want to know!'

Once Hugh had gone Luke went to stand in front of the window of the small room he used as his office.

He had received unofficial confirmation this morning that the African President was finally satisfied with the security arrangements and was prepared to set a firm date for the meeting.

With that in view, and his suspicions regarding Suzy confirmed, he should be feeling pleased. Instead of which he felt strangely disappointed. Suzy must somehow have made contact with her 'friend' when he had had to take Charlie to the lavatory, and that was surely a predictable move on her part, so why was he feeling as though what she had done was some kind of personal betrayal? What the hell was happening to him? He was thinking—feeling—more like a betrayed lover than a man with no emotional involvement with her.

And as for the man who had come asking for her! Her 'friend'... Luke's muscles clenched against the pain of the surge of jealousy and male anger that pounded through him. He had to be someone from the magazine—not Roy Jarvis, of course. Another reporter, perhaps.

They would soon know, Luke promised himself, and when Suzy did meet up with him he would need to know what was being said.

He unlocked one of the drawers in his desk and searched through until he had found what he wanted. The minute recording device lying on the palm of his hand was so sophisticated that it was almost impossible to believe that so much technology could be packed into such a small thing. Designed to be slipped underneath a watch, it could record and transmit conversations with remarkable clarity. It could also reveal the location of the wearer to within a metre.

Slipping it on his own watch, Luke locked the drawer and left the room…

'Look, Suzy, watch me dive!' Charlie shouted as he jumped into the swimming pool, sending up a splash of water.

'That isn't a dive,' Lucy told him scornfully when he got out. 'You just jumped in.'

'Yes, it was. It was a dive,' Charlie argued.

'No, it wasn't—was it, Suzy?' Lucy appealed.

'Yes, it was,' Charlie continued to insist.

Ruefully Suzy got up and went over to them. She had a bit of a headache—a legacy from not being able to sleep properly last night, she suspected.

She had gone to bed before Luke, all too relieved to be able to shower and quickly jump into bed whilst he was still in the suite's sitting room. But, much as she had longed to fall asleep before he joined her in the large bed, her guilty conscience had refused to let her.

Eventually she had dropped off, only to wake up to discover that she had turned over and was now lying facing Luke, one hand outstretched, as though she was trying to reach out to him in her sleep. Afraid of waking him up if she moved, she had lain there motionless, worrying about Jerry and what he was doing so close to the villa.

She had still been awake when Luke had suddenly slid out of the bed to pad naked into the suite's sitting room.

The large bed had felt empty and lonely without him, and she had found herself moving over to where he had been lying so that she could breathe in the scent of him from the warm sheets and pillows.

He had been up and dressed when she had woken this morning, and she had been under no illusion as to why he had waited in the sitting room for her whilst she showered and dressed.

In grim silence he had accompanied her downstairs for breakfast, and then later out here, to the swimming pool.

And she still hadn't told him about Jerry! Because there hadn't been any opportunity to do so, she tried to reassure herself.

'Luke's here.'

Lucy's pleased announcement broke into her thoughts and brought a swift surge of colour to her skin.

Hoping that he wouldn't see it, and guess at its cause, Suzy pretended not to have heard Lucy's statement and kept her head down, moving only when Charlie suddenly jumped into the pool and she was showered with water.

'See—that isn't a dive, it's a jump,' Lucy pronounced as Suzy shook the water off her face and stood up. 'Tell him, Luke,' she begged. 'Tell him that he can't dive.'

Smiling at the little girl, Luke surveyed the protected area around the pool. Suzy had left her wrap by her lounger, and when Luke turned his head to look at her an intensely strong physical reaction kicked at her stomach. She could feel her nipples peaking and thrusting provocatively against the fabric of her swimsuit, and she knew from the downward sweep of Luke's eyelashes that he was looking at their wanton flaunting.

She took a deep breath and fought off the desire to wrap her arms tightly around her body.

Luke cursed himself under his breath as he fought to drag his gaze away from Suzy's body. Already the evidence of her swollen nipples was affecting him— arousing him. All it would take was one step forward and then he could tug those thin swimsuit straps down her shoulders and expose the full creaminess of her breasts to his hands and his lips. He could take each of those nipples into his mouth in turn and show them what they were inciting when they tormented his senses until his self-control was at breaking point.

'Luke, Luke—tell her that I can dive.'

Charlie's high-pitched voice broke through the heated pressure of his thoughts, and quickly he turned away from Suzy. Her watch was lying on a small table, along with her sunglasses and some suntan cream. Luke walked towards it.

'Watch this, then!'

There was the sound of a noisy splash, followed almost immediately by an angry scream. Suzy swung round to see Lucy standing beside the pool, dripping wet from Charlie's 'dive'.

His small task completed, Luke strolled over to help calm the commotion.

From now on, until he removed the small device, every sound Suzy made, even down to her heartbeat, would be transmitted to the receiver locked in his desk. There wouldn't be a single word she spoke, a single breath she took whilst she was with her 'friend' that he would not know about!

As she towelled Charlie dry Suzy looked over his head to where Luke was standing. She could tell him now, her conscience prodded her. All she needed to do was open her mouth and just say the words.

But what if he doesn't believe me? What if he thinks that I'm lying, that I'm part of whatever it is that's going on?

What if he did? her conscience demanded sternly. Were her own personal feelings really more important than something that was obviously very serious?

Suzy took a deep breath.

'Luke?'

She stopped speaking when his mobile started to ring, and watched in heavy-hearted disappointment as he answered it and began to walk away.

She could always tell him later, she comforted herself as she reached for her wrap and informed the children it was time to go inside. Perhaps this evening, whilst they were alone and getting ready for dinner.

Her heart did a back somersault that caused just as much devastation inside her chest as Charlie's 'dives' had done around the pool!

'He's back—refuses to give any name, but he's biting on the bait we've floated. He's offered the two guards a fistful of euros to let him in. The guards are making sure he has to work hard to persuade them, and I've told them to say they'll let him in through that side gate in the perimeter wall.'

'The one closest to the lake and the grotto?' Luke questioned sharply.

'Yes, that's the one—is that okay?'

'Yes, that's fine. What's he going to do when he gets in, though? I don't want him wandering freely any-where.'

'That's okay. Nico is going to ask him if he wants a message sent to Ms Roberts, arranging to meet her.'

'Okay, let me know when he's taken the bait, Hugh.'

Suzy had just showered and changed when she heard a knock on the door of the suite.

Going to open it, she was surprised to see a young Italian standing there.

'I have a message for you, miss,' he announced, be-fore Suzy could speak. 'There is a man—a friend of yours. He wishes you to meet him beside the grotto.'

Suzy stared at him, her heart hammering with ap-prehension.

'What man? Who is this man?' she began to demand, but the Italian was already walking quickly away from her.

It was Jerry—it had to be. Although how on earth he had got into the grounds and past Luke's guards Suzy could not imagine.

Anxiously she rushed down the stairs and out into the garden, glancing at her watch as she did so. The lake and the grotto were quite a long walk away from the villa, and she kept looking anxiously around herself as she hurried towards them.

She skirted the lake using the footpath, hurrying past the sign that warned against anyone entering the grotto because it was unsafe. A padlocked iron gate guarded the entrance, and Suzy frowned to see that there was a key in the lock. She must mention it at the villa, just in case the children should stray down this way!

Once she reached the other side of the grotto she paused, looking around uncertainly and then tensing when Jerry suddenly stepped out of the shadow of the trees and shrubs where he had been waiting for her.

'Jerry! What are you doing? How did you get in here?' she demanded apprehensively.

'Never mind that.' He stopped her curtly. 'I want to know what's going on here. Come on, Suzy, spill the beans. What a piece of luck, finding you here. We got a tip-off that there was something important going on.'

'There's nothing going on,' Suzy lied determinedly. Jerry's comments had confirmed her worst fears. She was certainly not going to tell him anything! But perhaps if she found out what Jerry was up to the information might actually be useful to Luke—as well as help to prove her own innocence.

'Oh, come off it! If that's true what's Soames doing here? And how did you get hooked up with him anyway?'

'We're here on holiday, that's all—and as to how Luke and I met, that's not really any of your business,' Suzy told him coolly.

In his office Luke frowned as he listened in on their conversation. Had Suzy somehow realised that they were on to her?

'"Luke and I"?' Jerry mimicked sneeringly. 'Typical that you'd go for someone like Soames—he's as bloody moralistic as you are! Met those kids of his yet, have you?'

Suzy's heart somersaulted. Kids? Luke had children? And children meant a mother, a woman he loved. No, that couldn't be true.

'Just as well he's wealthy. I've heard that their medical bills will run into thousands. Risking his own life to save some refugee brats! I'd have left 'em, myself. Got shot for his pains, didn't he?'

Refugee brats? As she recoiled from Jerry's unpleasantness Suzy felt the tight band of pain around her heart slacken a little. There was no woman Luke loved enough to give her his children. But this was no time to think about her own feelings.

'You've got to leave, Jerry,' she insisted shakily. 'There's nothing happening here of any interest to you or the magazine.'

'You're lying,' Jerry accused her, putting his face so close to Suzy's that she stepped back. 'The boss has had a tip-off. That's why I'm here. Knew I'd got lucky when I saw you with the Verey kids.'

'They're here on holiday with their father.'

'They may be on holiday, but Verey's here for something more than that—and that's why Soames is here as well. They've got guards on the gate, for goodness' sake.'

'The owner of the villa employs the guards,' Suzy fibbed inventively. 'And, as I have just told you, Luke and I are here on holiday. Sir Peter is a friend of Luke's and he invited us to stay.'

'Sleeping with Soames, are you?'

Luke heard the small indrawn breath Suzy took before she told him firmly, 'Yes, of course I am.'

'Well, that's turn-up, isn't it? Little Miss Don't-Touch-Me-I'm-Only-Just-This-Side-of-Being-a-Virgin crawling into bed with Soames. The boss wasn't too pleased with you for leaving like that, you know. He'd got a pretty heavy bet set up that he'd be the one to teach you a thing or two about sex.'

Jerry was leering at her and Suzy had to fight down her furious disgust.

'Good, is he? Soames? I reckon you owe the boss one for depriving him of his pleasure. Come on, Suzy, tell me what's going on—for old times' sake.'

Suzy had had enough.

'For old times' sake?' she snapped, her eyes flashing with fury. 'You and the rest of those disgusting men at the magazine made my life a misery. And if you think for one moment that if there was anything to tell—which there isn't—I would betray national secrets to someone like you… Well, if you want my advice, Jerry, you should leave here right now—before—'

'Before what?' Jerry stopped her, an ugly look on

his face. 'Before you go running to Luke to give the game away?'

A chilly little breeze seemed to have sprung up, and Suzy shivered. Suddenly she felt not just cold but frightened as well.

'Jerry, I don't know what you want,' she began, but Jerry stopped her.

'You know damned well what I want,' he told her viciously. 'I want to know what's going on here, and one way or another I intend to find out.'

As he spoke he reached out and grabbed Suzy's arm, looking past her at the grotto.

'Jerry—what are you doing? Jerry, let me go!' Suzy started to protest, trying to resist as he dragged her towards the grotto and unlocked the iron gate.

'Let's see if you feel a bit more like talking after a few hours in here,' he told Suzy, panting heavily as he released her and gave her a savage push.

Suzy cried out as she lost her balance.

'Jerry, it isn't safe in here,' she protested anxiously as she struggled to get to her feet. But Jerry wasn't listening to her. Instead he was locking her inside the grotto and walking away with the key.

Luke cursed as he got to his feet, rapping out a message to Hugh Phillips to apprehend Jerry. Giving a cursory glance through the office window, he started to hurry out of the villa.

He had been wrong about Suzy! Utterly and completely wrong. And beneath his surprise at the discovery, and his concern for the danger she was in, he could feel a swift, deep tide of joy running through him.

Locked in the grotto, Suzy tried not to give in to her

fear. Someone was bound to come past and rescue her, surely? One of the gardeners, or one of Luke's men.

She tensed as she heard a low, threatening rumble. Stones and debris were falling all around her. Panicking, she ran to the back of the grotto, to avoid being hit by the growing avalanche of boulders, and then gave a terrified scream as the ground suddenly gave way beneath her.

She was falling down some kind of tunnel, Suzy recognised, with twigs and soil raining down all around her in the darkness. And then suddenly her fall came to an end, and the air jolted out of her lungs as she hit the cold dampness of a hard earth floor.

Somewhere in the distance she could still hear rumbling, but as she strained her ears to listen to it abruptly it ceased and there was silence.

Silence and darkness.

Her body hurt, but her fear was much greater than her physical pain. She was trapped somewhere underground beneath the grotto. Dust filled the air above and around her, making her cough and gag. How long would it be before someone found her—if they found her at all?

CHAPTER ELEVEN

LUKE had once run for his school—and, alerted by the sound of falling rocks, he reached the grotto just as it started to collapse in on itself. White-faced he looked at the pile of rubble beneath which Suzy was now buried.

Whilst his mind was coolly and mechanically planning what had to be done his heart was racing, thudding, swelling with emotions he couldn't afford to allow to torment him.

'Get on to the emergency services!' he shouted over his shoulder to Hugh, who had followed him. 'And then get the men down here!'

Suzy! Anguish, guilt, despair—he could feel all of them. Why had he waited so long? Why hadn't he come for her the moment he had realised she had not lied to him? Why had he allowed her to be placed in danger in the first place?

Suzy, Suzy, Suzy. He could feel her name ringing inside his head, inside his heart.

The guards had arrived and quickly he began to instruct them, telling them what to do as he began to move heavy boulders.

As he worked, grimly Luke tried to blot out images of another place and another time. Another pile of debris oozing dust and silence. That one under the heat of the sun, with the taste of smoke and anger in his mouth, the shocked wailing of the bereaved rising from the throats of women as he had looked in bitter fury at the house so unnecessarily destroyed, people killed and maimed by their own. A young woman dead, her children buried beneath the rubble of their home.

'Luke, if they are in there they'll be dead,' one of his comrades had muttered to him, but Luke had ignored him.

They had found the baby first, perfectly still, and then the older child. Luke knew he hadn't been the only one who had wept.

Those images were inside his head now, those images and those desperate feelings. He had hurt then, for those children, but if he had feared for them then that was nothing to what he was feeling right now.

And, what was more, Luke knew that it would not have made one iota of difference to him right now if Suzy *had* been colluding with the magazine, if she *had* been about to betray a hundred security secrets—he loved her, and his love for her was the strongest and most powerful emotion he had ever felt. It was so strong, in fact, that he had been afraid of it—afraid of acknowledging its power over him, afraid of admitting it to himself.

Suzy! He had loved her, he suspected, from the minute he had felt the brush of her soft lips against his own.

'Luke! Take it easy!'

It was only when he felt Hugh's restraining hand on his arm that he realised that he was tearing at the fallen boulders, his throat blocked with the pain of crying her name.

*   *   *

They worked late into the evening, under searchlights which had been rigged up and with the teams of experts Luke had called in.

Several times Luke was told to take a break and allow others to continue with the task that their expertise equipped them for, but he refused to listen. What he wouldn't give for a team of trained sappers here right now, he thought bitterly, as he watched the painfully slow progress, grim-faced.

If Suzy died it would be his fault. He would have killed her, killed the woman he loved, the woman he should have cherished and protected above everyone and anyone else, even above and beyond his duty. That was how he felt about her. How he would always feel about her. Admitting his love for her had been like taking a bung out of a dyke. The pressure of his denied feelings was pouring through him, drowning out everything else.

Why hadn't he listened to his emotions? Why had he persisted in disbelieving her and them?

He knew the answer to that, Luke acknowledged, his gaze never wavering from the harsh beam of light directed on to the fallen rocks. He had been afraid of admitting the truth.

He had decided a long time ago not to marry. He had seen too many Army marriages fall apart under the strain it imposed on them and he had thought he could prevent himself from falling in love, from wanting to spend the rest of his life with that one special person. Until Suzy had come into his life.

Into his life! And out of it?

The harsh lights bleached the colour from his face, leaving it leached of blood, his eyes two dark, burning sockets of pain fixed on the spot beneath which Suzy lay.

For Suzy, trapped inside her small cave, time blurred.

She was a child again, trying to comfort her crying mother, telling her everything would be all right—only her mother wasn't there, and she was the one who was crying.

Images and memories came and went, sweeping over her in waves of semi-consciousness. Curled up in a foetal position, she relived the happiest of her memories and experiences. And thought of Luke, whose name, whose taste would surely be on her lips as she took her last breath…

Luke stood grim-lipped in front of the Italian in charge of the rescue operation.

'I do not care how well trained your men are,' he told him curtly. 'I go in first. And now.'

It was nearly midnight, and the rescue team had managed to tunnel down to where Suzy was trapped— thanks, in the main, to Luke's experience and leadership. The watch Suzy was wearing had registered the fact that she was still breathing, and the bugging device had also helped them pinpoint her location. They had discovered that Suzy had fallen down some kind of tunnel or shaft, and now lay in a small space below it.

'It is still too risky for anyone to go in!' the Italian protested, trying to sound authoritative but failing when confronted by Luke's implacable will and air of command. He tried to persist. 'It will be several more hours before we can send someone in to bring out the young lady.'

'I'm going in now,' Luke told him bluntly.

'The tunnel is not yet secure. It could collapse and bury you both,' he warned, but Luke wasn't listening to him. He had already gathered together everything he might need, including medical equipment, food and water.

As the leader of the rescuers had said, the newly dug tunnel still wasn't safe. Its roof needed strengthening before they could risk bringing Suzy out. But it was strong enough to allow Luke to go to her, and that was exactly what he intended to do. No matter what the risk to himself. He had to be with her!

Moving carefully, Luke crawled slowly through the tunnel. He had never liked tunnelling, it made him feel slightly claustrophobic and all too aware of his own vulnerability, but right now he wouldn't have cared how long the tunnel was just so long as it took him to Suzy.

The brightness of the torch Luke was carrying woke Suzy from the exhausted doze she had fallen into.

Confused, and half in shock, she thought for a moment that she was hallucinating when she saw Luke crawling into the small space illuminated by the torch.

'Luke!' Her voice shook, and so did her body. 'Luke!' she repeated. 'How…? What…?'

Her words were smothered against his chest as he took her in his arms and held her there—held her as though he was never going to let her go, Suzy thought.

She made a sound. Something between a laugh and a whimper, shivering as she clung to the warmth of his body.

'It's so cold in here, and so dark. I thought…' She fell silent, unable to tell him that she had feared she would die here, in this small dark space beneath the ground. 'Are we going to get out now?' she asked him looking towards the tunnel.

'Soon,' Luke answered, giving their surroundings one searching inspection and then switching off the torch—partially to save its light for when they needed it, but also to save Suzy the reality of seeing how dangerous their prison was.

The feel of her in his arms was making his heart thud heavily with emotion. He was with her. He was holding her safe, as he should have held her all along. His hand cupped her face and stroked her hair whilst his other arm held her close to his body.

Half dazed, Suzy decided that she must be imagining the soft brush of Luke's lips against her hair, that it was a fantasy she was allowing herself to drift into.

Even so, she reached out a dusty hand to touch him. Something about the darkness and their intimacy was allowing her to drop the barriers she had put up against him to protect herself.

'I'm so glad you're here. I was afraid I was going to die here.'

Something about the quality of his silence made her tremble.

'We are going to get out of here, aren't we, Luke?' They must be—otherwise he wouldn't be here with her, risking his own life.

There was just the merest pause, the merest missed rhythm in his heartbeat before he told her calmly, 'Yes, of course we are. But we could be here for a while yet.'

'A while?' Suzy's own heart started to thump. 'But if it isn't safe what—? Why—?' Her mouth had gone dry.

'I owe you an apology, Suzy,' Luke told her lightly. 'And now that I've got you to myself, I have got the perfect opportunity to deliver it.'

He was trying to make light of the situation, Suzy recognised, her heart flooding with bittersweet emotion.

There was so much Luke wanted to say to her, but he was fully aware that up above them every sound from their chamber was being monitored via Suzy's watch—hardly an asset when one wanted to whisper words of love and regret.

As he touched her wrist Suzy opened her mouth to ask what he was doing, but Luke silenced her, placing his finger against her lips as he removed the small device and muffled it.

'What—?' Suzy demanded when he'd finished.

'It's what's commonly referred to as a ''bug'',' Luke told her wryly.

'You *bugged* me?'

The pain in her voice tore at his heart.

'I had no choice,' he told her quietly. He gave a small sigh. 'I do owe you an apology, Suzy—we both know that.'

'You were just doing your job.'

Her defence of him made him wonder grimly how

he could ever have thought of doubting her. Her honesty was so patently obvious.

'How long are we going to be down here, Luke?'

'I don't know,' he admitted honestly. 'Are you feeling okay? I've brought some water, and they will be putting an airline through the tunnel.'

'An airline?' Suzy's body trembled. 'You mean in case the tunnel collapses again?'

That was exactly what Luke did mean, and he cursed himself inwardly for adding to her distress.

'It's just a precaution,' he tried to reassure her.

Suzy felt faint and sick. Even with Luke so close to her, holding her, she still felt afraid, her thoughts going round and round.

'We could die in here,' she said in a small panicky voice.

'Don't think about it,' Luke advised her firmly.

'Talk to me, Luke,' Suzy begged him, desperate to have her mind taken off their danger.

'What do you want me to talk to you about?' Luke responded.

'Tell me about the children you rescued,' she replied.

Half of her still didn't dare to believe that he was actually here with her, that she wasn't alone any more. She needed to hear his voice to keep her fears at bay.

Sensing what she was feeling, Luke hesitated and then settled her more comfortably against his body, frowning a little as he realised how cold she was.

The children! Those were the very last memories he wanted to resurrect right now, but how could he deny Suzy anything?

'What do you want to know about them?' he asked quietly.

'Everything,' Suzy answered. 'But first tell me—are they all right now?'

'They're recovering,' Luke told her slowly, 'and with time, and proper medical care, hopefully they will be able to return and live reasonably normal lives. Raschid, the little boy, lost an arm.'

He felt Suzy's tension and cursed himself beneath his breath for having told her.

'Halek, the little girl—the baby—is fine,' he added.

'And their parents—their mother?' Suzy asked tentatively, not really sure why she felt so impelled to ask that particular question.

Was she reading his mind? Luke wondered helplessly.

'Both dead.'

'Tell me what happened,' Suzy whispered.

She could feel the rise and fall of Luke's chest as he breathed in and then exhaled slowly.

'The children's mother was helping us with information. Her husband, their father, had been killed trying to resist the tyranny they were facing. She wanted to avenge his death by helping us to set her people free. It was a dangerous situation for her, and important that we kept her identity hidden, that no one gave away the fact that she was helping us.'

'But someone did,' Suzy hazarded, lifting her head from its resting place against Luke's shoulder to try to peer up into his face.

'Yes,' he agreed heavily. 'Someone did.'

She could feel his remembered anger in the in-

creased thud of his heartbeat, and suddenly out of nowhere she knew!

'Was it—was she a reporter?' she guessed intui-
tively.

She was still looking up at him; he could tell by her
her gentle breaths as they fell on his face.

'Yes, she was,' he confirmed. 'Somehow or other
she'd heard about Maram and decided to she wanted
to interview her for a human interest story. Of course
I informed her that she was going to do no such thing,
and I pointed out to her the danger she would be putting Maram in. She ignored my warning, though, and
managed to find a young rookie soldier foolish enough
to be seduced by her—and I mean literally—into giving her Maram's name. Two days after she interviewed
her Maram was murdered, and that was when I found
out what Sarah had done.'

'Perhaps she didn't realise the danger she was exposing her to,' Suzy suggested huskily.

'Oh, she realised all right,' Luke told Suzy harshly.
'I had told her myself. But she just didn't care. Nothing
mattered more to her than getting her story—not even
another woman's life. She even had the gall to try to
photograph Maram's children as they were being lifted
out of the rubble of their home—the rubble that still
contained their mother's body!'

'Jerry said that you have taken financial responsibility for the children,' Suzy murmured.

'They needed medical attention they couldn't get in
their own country, and they could only be brought to
the UK for treatment if someone agreed to sponsor

them. It was the least I could do, seeing as I was responsible for the death of their mother.'

'No! It wasn't your fault,' Suzy protested immediately.

'I was the Commanding Officer, and I'd had enough experience of the determination of reporters to get their story to realise that this particular reporter wasn't going to put another woman's life before her own career,' Luke responded grimly.

'And is that why you hate women reporters?' Suzy asked him quietly. 'Because of what she did?'

'Well, let's just say that she reinforced everything I'd already experienced and felt about them as a breed,' Luke acknowledged. 'One woman murdered, two children nearly killed, three of my men shot and a gunshot wound myself didn't exactly endear her type to me!'

'You were shot?' Suzy exclaimed anxiously, before putting two and two together and asking softly, 'That scar—is that—?'

'Yes,' Luke told her tersely, anticipating her question, before continuing. 'Fortunately the children are survivors—and once they are medically fit to do so they will be returning to their own country to live with their mother's sister, who will love them as her own. Why are you crying?' he asked Suzy gently.

'I'm not,' Suzy fibbed.

But she was, and her tears were tears of sadness for the children and tears of joy for herself, because she was so proud of the man she loved.

The man she loved! Suddenly Suzy wanted to tell him how she felt, how much she loved him. How she had believed the first time she had seen him that fate had brought them together and that he was her one true love, her soul mate. It didn't matter any more that he didn't share her feelings, or that he didn't love her back. She wasn't going to die without saying the words that were locked up inside her heart.

'Luke,' she began shakily, 'if we don't get out of here I—'

'We *will* get out,' Luke began, and then stopped speaking as a sudden rumbling above them had them both looking upwards. 'Don't worry,' he reassured her. 'It just means that they're closer to getting us out, that's all.'

Suzy stared into the darkness, wishing she could see his face and his eyes so that she might have some clue as to what expression they were holding and if he really believed what he was saying or was merely trying to comfort her.

'Suzy—'

The raw urgency of the way Luke was saying her name had Suzy turning to him.

'This is all my fault,' he told her grimly. 'If I hadn't been so determined not to believe you—'

Suzy felt the pad of his thumb brush against her lips.

'I'm sorry, Suzy,' she heard him whisper. 'Oh, God, I am so sorry. I'd give anything, do anything, to get you out of here safely.'

Suzy could feel the warmth of his breath against her mouth, and suddenly, sweetly, she recognised that he was going to kiss her. She was lifting her face towards him when they both heard the sound of activity in the tunnel.

A shower of debris fell down from the ceiling above

them, and immediately Luke moved to cover Suzy's body with his own.

'Luke, what's happening?' she demanded, terrified.

'It's all right,' Luke reassured her, holding her tightly. 'Everything's going to be all right. We'll soon be out of here.'

Just hearing his voice made her feel better, Suzy acknowledged as she leaned into him, soaking up the comfort of his presence and his warmth whilst his hand shielded her head from the stones rattling down around them.

Suzy was still wrapped in Luke's arms ten minutes later when their rescuers arrived.

'Take Suzy first,' Luke instructed them. But when they came to lift her away from him she could hardly bear to let go!

CHAPTER TWELVE

'LUKE?'

The moment he heard the small, anxious cry Luke was awake, throwing off the duvet he had covered himself with and padding across the suite to where Suzy was lying frozen with terror in the middle of the large bed.

It was three days since they had been rescued from the grotto, and every night Suzy had had the same nightmare. Every night Luke had gone to her to take her in his arms, to comfort her and reassure her that she was safe. And once he had done that he had gone back to his makeshift bed on one of the sofas.

It was Suzy who had been insistent that there was no point in declaring now that they were not partners—not with the African President's visit so imminent.

'You've got enough to worry about without having to explain who I really am,' she had told Luke when he had told her that although he would prefer it if she didn't leave the villa until after the meeting, he would, if she wanted, make it clear to Sir Peter that they were not partners and ensure that she was provided with her own room.

In the event it was perhaps just as well that they were still sharing the suite. Her nightmare had woken her every night, leaving her shivering with cold and fear, only able to go back to sleep once he was holding her safely in his arms.

'They'll stop soon,' Suzy had told him last night, her teeth chattering as she clung to him.

Luke hadn't said anything. Locked away in his desk drawer was the report he had commissioned on her. And the information it contained had increased his guilt and his shame. She was innocent of everything he had accused her of. She had not lied to him. She had told him the truth and he had refused to believe her. He had treated her with contempt and cruelty. Luke knew he would never forgive himself. When he had read about her life as a child, with her mother, Luke had felt the acid burn of tears stinging his eyes, and his anger against himself had trebled. His anger, but not his love. His love, he recognised now, had been born fully formed and complete the moment he had set eyes on her!

His love. Broodingly, Luke went towards the bed, lithe and silent as a panther as he moved through the darkness. His love was a burden he would never lay on Suzy's shoulders. His report had told him what kind of person she was: the kind of person who put others before herself, the kind of person who gave up her own future to look after the mother who had never cared enough to love and protect her as she deserved. One day Suzy would meet someone for whom she felt as he felt about her. Someone she could love as he loved her!

A savage pain tore through him. He had reached the bed and he sat down on it. Because of Suzy's nightmares he had taken to wearing a pair of boxers to bed, but he still had to turn sideways so that she wouldn't see the telltale outline of his erection.

'It's all right Suzy, I'm here,' he told her gently.

'Oh, Luke hold me, please!' Suzy begged him.

Her nightmare terrified her. In it she was trapped underground on her own. She could hear Luke talking to her, but he wasn't there with her, and she was afraid. Afraid that she would die without seeing or touching him again.

Physically she had not suffered any harm from her incarceration in the vault beneath the grotto, but emotionally and mentally it was taking her longer than she had expected to recover.

Reluctantly Luke took hold of her, tensing as she burrowed closer to him. His body registered the fact that she wasn't wearing anything other than a pair of silky briefs.

Here in Luke's arms was the only place she felt safe, Suzy acknowledged as the nightmare receded and the warmth of his body comforted her. Comforted her and then aroused her, she admitted shakily, as the familiar feelings of longing and love filled her.

Unable to stop herself she leaned forward and brushed her lips against his shoulder, and then his throat, her tongue-tip investigating the taut flesh over his Adam's apple.

Luke felt as though he had been speared by a firebolt His erection was no longer a mere outline beneath his boxers, but a hard and obvious straining of flesh, aching to be touched and tasted as she was touching and tasting his throat.

'Luke, please kiss me,' Suzy whispered against his lips.

'Suzy…'

'Please,' she begged.

'Suzy, this isn't—'

'I love you, Luke,' Suzy burst out, unable to keep her feelings to herself any longer. 'I love you and I want you. You saved my life, and in some ancient cultures when a person saves another person's life it means that that person belongs to them for ever. And I want to belong you, Luke—even if it is just for to-night.' She was speaking so quickly her words were falling over one another. She had had it all worked out, what she would say to him, but suddenly, halfway through her planned speech, her courage began to desert her. 'You are my soul mate, Luke,' she whispered.

Everything she was saying was true, but once she would never, ever have said such words—because her pride would not have allowed her to do so! Her brush with death had changed her, Suzy recognised. She was no longer afraid of being laughed at or rejected. She wanted—she needed Luke to know how she felt.

Luke tried to control what he was feeling. She didn't mean it! She might think she meant it, but she didn't. It was the trauma of what she had experienced that was making Suzy feel that she loved him. That and her belief that he had saved her life. After all, she hadn't loved him before, had she? Once she was over her trauma she would realise that she didn't love him at all.

Just because he loved her it didn't mean that he could take advantage of what she was offering right now.

'Luke…'

Her pleading whisper burned into him like fire. Her hand was touching his belly, tracing the curve of his scar. Luke felt as though he was about to explode with need and hunger.

'Luke…'

Her breath whispered past his mouth and Luke knew that he was lost. Hungrily he possessed the softness of her lips, savouring them, parting them, thrusting his tongue with hard demand into the sweetness of her mouth.

Without him knowing how it had happened his hand found her breast and cupped it, moulding it, teasing the peak to rise up into his palm as he stroked and tugged its tautness.

He wanted her.

He loved her!

Abruptly Luke reined in his feelings. He loved her and he had to protect her from her traumatised belief that she loved him.

The small whimper of distress she made as he firmly put her from him tore at his heart as nothing ever would tear at it again.

'Luke…' Suzy protested achingly. 'Please stay with me, Luke. Please…'

But he had already gone, firmly closing the door between the bedroom and the sitting room and leaving her on her own.

Suzy gave a small start, unable to believe she had slept for so long. She had originally come up to the bedroom halfway through the afternoon, intending to catch up on the sleep she had lost the previous night, lying awake and longing for Luke.

Luke! She wasn't sorry that she had told him how she felt about him. She was glad! She was proud of her love, and proud of loving him. Her brush with death had altered her attitude a great deal, she acknowledged, but it did not seem to have altered Luke's attitude towards her.

He might not love her, but he wanted her, Suzy told herself. Last night he had wanted her—even if he *had* left her.

Getting out of the bed, she went into the bathroom. She still hadn't got used to the sensuality of the room, or the open sexuality of its erotic décor. She hadn't used the huge bath as yet—which was more of a sunken pool than a mere bath—but suddenly she was tempted to try it.

Returning to the bedroom, Suzy picked up the ice bucket and the complimentary book of matches from the pretty desk. Back in the bathroom, she pushed the door closed, put down the ice bucket and then carefully lit the candles that surrounded the bath. Even their shadows seemed to cast intimate and erotic dancing images around the room, and a sensual shudder ran through her. This was dangerous. She knew it was dangerous. But still she filled the bath. The water gushing from the dolphin jets glittered against the mosaic tiles.

The circular pool was so deep that she had to walk down into it. Like a Jacuzzi, it had a ledge to sit on, and was easily large enough to accommodate two people. Two people? Her and Luke? Suzy scooped up a handful of blue-green bath crystals from the jar beside her. As she dropped them into the water it turned a deep cloudy aquamarine before slowly clearing to the colour of the purest sea water. Self indulgently she lay back in it, floating in sumptuous, languid pleasure.

Worriedly Luke opened the bedroom door. It had been Lucy who had told him that Suzy had felt tired after lunch and had gone to lie down. A doctor had checked her over after her ordeal, and had pronounced her fine, but what if he was wrong—what if he had missed something?

And where was Suzy now? Not in either the suite's sitting room or the bed. Had she got up and gone back outside to join the children by the swimming pool?

It had been a long day—he had been cooped up in his office all morning, rearranging security for the President Njambla's visit because he had not been happy with it after all. He felt hot and tired and in need of a shower.

Unfastening his shirt, he removed it. In the mirror he could just see the tip of the small, still livid scar that disappeared below the belt of his chinos. The scar Suzy had touched and kissed.

Luke dropped the shirt and rubbed his hand across his forehead and then his eyes. He had to put Suzy first, not himself! But he couldn't stop thinking about how she had touched him last night in bed, how she had told him that she loved him! Irritated with himself, he stripped off the rest of his clothes. Somehow Suzy had got under his skin in a way that no other woman

ever had—under his skin and into his heart. Just thinking about her brought a familiar ache to his body—a
fiercely elemental and dangerous ache!

He opened the bathroom door and strode in. And
stopped. And stared. He cursed under his breath, because his body was way ahead of him, in reacting to
what he could see, and there wasn't a damn thing he
could do about it other than make a grab for a towel.

What the hell was Suzy doing anyway? Just lying
there, so that from where he was standing he could see
quite plainly every silk-skinned inch of her. She hadn't
seen him yet, though. She was facing away from him,
and the steam from the water had made her hair curl
wildly.

The scent of the candles she had lit filled his nostrils.
Heat, need, hunger poured through him in an unstop-
pable torrent, filling every nerve-ending.

The towel slid from his fingers as he advanced towards the tub.

The candlelight seemed to highlight the sexuality of
the wall frieze, and Suzy stared at it, lost in her own
private Luke-filled fantasy. If Luke was with her
now... A liquid ache of longing curled up through her
body. And then she blinked as suddenly she saw that
he was actually standing in front of her.

Pleasure touched her every nerve. She gave him a
blissful, adoring smile and murmured his name on a
happy sigh before asking curiously, 'Is that really physically possible?'

As Luke looked up and saw what she was studying
a hard burn of colour ran up under his skin. That round-
eyed look of innocence she was giving him was de-

stroying him—and his self-control! He looked at the frieze again, and then back at her, where she lay floating in the bath, surrounded by the candles. His gut twisted as he saw the wet tangle of curls between her thighs and the dark peaks of her nipples.

Ignoring her, he headed for the shower.

Suzy could hear its noisy water running and her face burned as she wondered what on earth had possessed her to make such an idiotic remark.

Luke turned off the shower. It had been a wasted exercise, since it had cooled neither his emotions nor his arousal. Padding naked back to the tub, he demanded grimly, 'Do you want me to tell you if it's possible—or do you want me to show you?'

'Luke!' Suzy turned over too quickly and choked on a mouthful of water as Luke stepped down into the tub beside her.

He was crazy for doing this. Luke knew that. And even more crazy about the woman who was staring at him, her huge eyes already darkened with smoky, sensual arousal and excitement.

'Which one do you want to try first?' Suzy heard Luke whisper in her ear as he nibbled deliciously on the lobe and stroked a wet fingertip along her collarbone, and down to the valley between her breasts, and then along the upper curve, seeking out the wet thrust of her nipple where it surged above the water in excited eagerness for his touch.

'Mmm… Well?' Luke was demanding.

She gave a shocked gasp, her thoughts scattering like raindrops as Luke sank beneath the water, only the top of his head visible, his hair seal-dark and wet. His mouth was cool and firm as he took captive the nipple he had previously claimed, and the sensation of her body floating in the water, Luke's head between her breasts, his mouth on her nipple, his hand moving determinedly between her thighs was too much for Suzy's self-control.

The water in the tub might be cooling, but the wetness inside her certainly wasn't. She could feel its heat spreading through her as Luke's fingers found her—found her and touched her, stroked her, opened her...

She was beyond reason, beyond reality—beyond anything but this. The stroke of his hand, the suckle of his mouth, the soft rhythmic sensation of the water...

She could feel the surge of her orgasm beginning to mount, as unstemmable as the tide itself, and, as though Luke could feel it too, he picked her up and carried her towards the steps.

The thud of his own arousal beat through his body and echoed in his ears. This wasn't need, and it wasn't desire. It went way, way above and beyond that, and it had taken him to a place where he was a stranger, a humble acolyte, only just beginning to learn the true meaning of the new world he had entered.

As he carried her up the steps to the floor, Suzy could see their reflections in the mirror. Water ran from their bodies and her nipples, swollen from his caresses, peaked dark and hard in the candlelit room.

'Which position do you want to try first?' he asked again.

Luke had placed her on a pile of soft towels and was leaning over her. Excitement, shock and disbelief ran through her veins like liquid fire. Her body ached heavily with unsatisfied need, and Suzy knew she didn't care how he completed their union just so long as he did. She was in physical pain with her desire to have him inside her, her emotions and her body coiled to breaking point.

'This one?' His voice was a dark, tormenting whisper against the back of her neck as he moved her.

Shudders ran through her body as his hands stroked the skin of her bowed back. In the mirror she could see him leaning over her, his erection straining from the silky mat of hair surrounding its base.

'Is this what you want?' he whispered dangerously.

His hands were on her hips, and as she tilted her head back to look above the mirror and over their reflections she could see the position he was mimicking on the wall above them.

Violent shudders convulsed her.

'Or would you prefer this one?'

Suzy had to grit her teeth to prevent herself from crying out for him to stop tormenting her as he moved her again. Her body seemed to have no means of moving by itself. It had become completely obedient to his touch, whilst deep inside her the tension continued to grow so that she felt as though at any second it would spill from her and flood through her.

Her gaze embraced his erection with a molten look of longing and hunger. She reached out and touched him, hot flesh beneath her shaking fingertips, stretched over him, the foreskin pushed back to expose the rounded tip, dark and rosy. She rimmed her fingertip around it feeling his whole body jerk.

Luke could feel himself starting to shudder as his

control collapsed in on itself. Her touch was destroying everything he had put up against her. He had become a mindless physical instrument, reliant on her touch, dependent on her response.

He could feel the onset of his orgasm. From a distance he could hear her moaning his name, pleading with him to fill her with his body.

They were still lying on the towels together, and Luke was holding her, lifting her, entering her only just in time. On a surging explosion of relief and release his one powerful thrust carried them to completion on fierce, unending surges of pleasure that racked them again and again whilst he spilled hotly into the waiting, wanting heat of her body.

They were only just in time for dinner. Suzy was pale and lost in her own private bliss-filled world. Her mouth was swollen, but nowhere near as swollen as her breasts and nipples, which she had thankfully been able to conceal beneath her clothes. Her eyes looked slumberous, and somehow sensuously knowing.

As they reached the drawing room door she drew back a little unsteadily to look up at Luke, her gaze filled with so much emotion it hurt Luke to look back at her.

It wasn't real, he told himself grimly. She just *thought* she loved him. He had had no right to do what he had just done, and one day she was going hate him for it!

As he already hated himself!

He could feel Suzy quivering at his side. He looked at her again. Her face was pale, her eyes luminous, her mouth... Luke could feel his own pupils dilating in response to the message of those swollen lips. Inside his head he could see, feel, taste the more intimate flesh their swollen softness mimicked.

To his disbelief, Luke realised he had an erection.

'You go in,' he told Suzy curtly. 'I've got something I need to do.'

Oblivious to the real meaning of his words, Suzy tried to calm herself as he walked away from her, leaving her to enter the room alone.

Immediately Lucy and Charlie bounded over to her side. They were lovely children, she acknowledged tenderly, and they deserved to have a woman in their lives who truly loved them.

As he stood in his office and willed his erection to subside Luke knew that he could not allow the situation to continue. For Suzy's sake. If he allowed her to stay on at the villa now he knew he didn't have a hope of keeping out of her bed...their bed.

Right now she believed she loved him, but Luke knew that she did not. He had to send her away!

CHAPTER THIRTEEN

SUZY stared out of the salon window. She felt heavy-eyed from another night of too much thinking. And she had no idea where Luke had spent the night—it certainly hadn't been with her, in the suite!

The salon door opened and she spun round quickly, but it was Lucy.

'Are you waiting for Luke?' she asked Suzy. 'He's with Daddy. I wish you were going to be with us always, Suzy,' Lucy burst out, and then blushed. 'Some of the girls at school have got stepmothers and they say that they don't like them, but I think it would be cool if we had one—especially if she was like you.'

Suzy couldn't stop herself from giving the girl a fierce hug. She was still holding her when the door opened and Luke walked in. He had been avoiding her since they had made love in the bathroom, and Suzy knew it was only Lucy's presence that prevented her from begging him to tell her why.

'I wish that you were my stepmother, Suzy,' Lucy said passionately, hugging her tightly.

Luke frowned when he heard Lucy's outburst. It was no secret to him that Peter Verey was attracted to Suzy—what sane man would not be? He had had to fight off his own jealousy every evening since Suzy had been at the villa as he'd watched the other man flirting with her, but now it was surging almost out of control, forcing him to turn on his heel and stride out of the room.

Suzy watched him go, confusion filling her. What had caused him to suddenly walk away.

'So, it looks as though the President isn't going to show, then?' Sir Peter questioned.

'I'm afraid that it does look very much like that,' Luke agreed grimly as they stood together in his office. 'We've spoken to his people, and reiterated to them just how important this discussion is, but apparently he feels that he would be too exposed if he comes to Europe.' Luke's mouth compressed. 'He's playing with us, of course. We all know that. But there's nothing we can do other than wait. There's a rumour that he needs to be at home at the moment to quell some potential unrest. If that's true it could be several months before he's ready to set up fresh talks.'

'It looks like we've dragged you out here for nothing, Luke,' Sir Peter apologised.

Luke remained silent. After Sir Peter had left, he typed out a report and made several telephone calls. He had e-mails to answer and a variety of other correspondence to deal with…

It was late afternoon before Luke saw Suzy again. She was playing with the children, oblivious to the fact that he was watching her with a hungry lover's gaze. Right now he wanted nothing more than to take her in his arms and take her to bed, make her tell him how much she loved him.

But he wasn't going to it. No he was going to send her away.

Suzy looked up as she saw Luke approaching them Her skin was glazed with perspiration and her hair was sticking in exercise-dampened curls to her neck and face. She had enjoyed herself with the children, but Luke had never been out of her thoughts. Automatically she went towards him, and then stopped as he stepped back from her.

'You shouldn't be out here overdoing things.' His voice was clipped, and Suzy stifled her dangerous need to believe that he was speaking so because he cared.

'I'm fully recovered now,' she told him valiantly.

'Good, I'm glad to hear it.' He paused and looked at her, and something went still and cold inside Suzy's heart. 'Sir Peter's meeting with President Njambla has been cancelled,' Luke went on, in the clipped voice. 'I've booked you on to a flight for London mid-morning tomorrow.'

'What? No—Luke…' Suzy started to protest, but he was already walking away from her, leaving her white faced and desolate as she struggled to contain her pain.

She was still aching with misery a couple of hours later, when she went back to the suite to pack her clothes and have a shower.

For some reason she couldn't explain, even to herself, she did something she had never done the whole time she had been staying at the villa—and that was to turn the key in the outer door to the suite, locking herself inside and Luke outside! Out of temptation's way!

Her packing finished, she went to shower, determinedly refusing to look at the tub as she walked past it on her way back to the bedroom, before tiredly wrapping herself in a towel and crawling onto the bed.

Luke frowned as he turned the handle of the suite and realised the door was locked.

Wryly he wondered if Suzy had the least idea of what his Army training had equipped him for, and several seconds later he opened the door with silent ease.

She was lying on the bed, curled up on her side with her back towards him, quite obviously asleep.

Stripping off, he headed for the shower. He had a busy night ahead of him, sorting out the chaos caused by the African President's machinations, and he had come up to the room to grab a power-nap first.

Half an hour later he was to all intents and purposes still fast asleep on the sofa in the sitting room when he heard it. The smallest of muffled sounds. But he was awake immediately and on his feet in one smooth, predatory move.

Suzy was still asleep—but no longer peacefully. Her hands were clenched and she was moving frantically in panic. She gave a small, shrill whimper of terror. She was having her nightmare again!

Luke reached out and touched her bare shoulder.

Immediately she screamed, and then woke up. She sat up, shivering as she wrapped her arms around her knees, oblivious to her own nudity.

'Luke!' Suzy's eyes rounded, her gaze flickering towards the door to the sitting room. 'How…? What are you doing in here?' she demanded.

'It's our room,' Like reminded her calmly.

'Our room?' Suzy looked bravely at him. 'But you don't want me here.'

She was starting to tremble, and Luke had to grit his teeth to stop himself from reaching out and taking her in his arms.

'Why don't you try and go back to sleep?' he suggested.

It would certainly suit him if she did, and it would suit him even more if she covered herself up. Right now just the knowledge that he had only to turn his head and he would be able to see the silky curve of her naked shoulder, the small hollow at the base of her throat which he had already explored so thoroughly, was driving him crazy.

'No!'

The vehemence of her denial made him freeze.

'No. I can't go back to sleep. I'm afraid that I'll start dreaming again about the grotto,' she whispered.

Like her, Luke must have showered, she recognised, because he was wearing a towel wrapped around his hips so low that she could see the beginnings of his scar. Automatically she reached out and touched it with her fingers, and then with her lips. He stood at the side of the bed as immobile as a statue.

What was she doing? Was she going crazy? Suzy didn't know and she didn't care. She was high on the scent and the taste of Luke, drugged by her own need for him.

Luke tried to resist, to remind himself that it was for her own sake that he was sending her away, but his body overruled him. One minute he was telling himself he wouldn't touch her, the next she was in his arms and he was kissing her as though he was starving for the taste and feel of her!

Kissing her was like tasting a freshly picked peach—each taste made him eager for another, and then another, so that he could posses her unique sweet juiciness for ever...

Suzy pulled away from Luke's kiss to press her lips to his throat, and then his chest, stroking her fingertips through the soft warmth of his body hair as just for this moment she allowed herself to pretend that Luke was really hers, that she had rights of territorial possession over his body—it was hers to do with as she wished, to enjoy as she wanted, to touch, explore and know in a hundred different ways, so that she could store that knowledge for her future enjoyment.

Her tongue-tip rimmed his navel and felt the fierce clench of his muscles. She lifted her head and looked sideways at the purple scar, and she reached out to touch it again, liquid emotion shining in her eyes. A badge of courage and more importantly—to her, at least—a badge of love for his fellow human beings.

She bent her head, her lips poised to breathe a tender kiss against it. But Luke's harsh objection savaged the silence, and suddenly she was rolled underneath him, pinned there by the hard weight of his body whilst he stilled her soft sounds of pleasure with the savage heat of his mouth.

She shouldn't be doing this, Suzy knew. Luke did not love her as she did him. But how could she stop? How could she resist the need that was filling her, overruling reason and pride? She loved him! She wanted him! And right now nothing else mattered other than that he was holding her.

As his hands sculpted Suzy's body Luke told himself that it was for the last time. He cupped her breasts, savouring the malleability of them. He wanted to kiss them, lick them, pleasure them until she arched under him and writhed against him in hungry need. He wanted...

'No!'

Abruptly he released Suzy and stood up, his back to her as he stared out of the window.

Suzy waited, whilst her heart jerked in pain, and then, when he didn't move, she picked up her towel, wrapped it around herself and walked silently into the bathroom so that she could cry her eyes out under cover of the noise of the running shower.

Oh, why hadn't she stopped him before he had rejected her?

Outside in the bedroom Luke touched the scar on his side. She had touched it, kissed it, looked at him with luminous loving eyes.

She *didn't* love him, he reminded himself. She just thought she did. She just believed she did because she thought he had saved her life! If she did love him she would have known it before that time in the grotto, just as he had known he loved her.

But love could grow, Luke told himself fiercely. And if Suzy believed that she loved him then who was to say that she might not in time—?

No, Luke told himself savagely. No. He would not

do that to her. He would not lock her into a relationship that denied her the right to love freely. He could not.

He could not bear to let her go—but he had to for her own sake!

The first thing Suzy saw when she woke up was the small package on the bedside table. Picking it up, she opened it. Inside was her passport and her flight ticket, plus a generous amount of euros.

Tears filled her eyes as she carefully removed the money and put it down on the bedside table.

She had breakfast in her room—though there was no need for her to feel so anxious, she assured herself miserably. Luke wasn't likely to come in and say goodbye, so there was no risk of her flinging herself into his arms and telling him how much she loved him, begging him to give her a chance.

A chance? Did she really think there was one after the way he had rejected her last night—even though his body had wanted her? That could only mean that he didn't love her. She knew that!

There was nothing for her to linger for. She had already said her goodbyes to the children, and to Sir Peter, and given him her thanks for their hospitality.

'Will you come and see us at school?' Lucy had begged Suzy, tears in her eyes as she hugged her fiercely.

'Of course I will,' Suzy had assured her.

Poor little scraps! They had so much in material terms, and yet so very little in all the ways that mattered.

She stayed upstairs until she saw the taxi arriving from her bedroom window, and then she went down, carrying her small case with her.

The children were waiting to wave her off, wearing the clothes they had bought together. Suzy had to blink away tears as she hugged them and promised again to keep in touch.

Unable to stop herself, she looked towards the closed door to Luke's office, willing him to come out. But to what purpose? The only thing she really wanted him to say was, Please don't go! followed by, I love you! And she was not likely to hear him say those words, was she? Forcing a wan smile, Suzy gave the children one last kiss and then walked out to her taxi.

Standing in front of the window of his small office, Luke watched her. He had been deliberately avoiding her—why make problems for himself? Why put himself in a situation he already knew he couldn't fully control? She was opening the taxi door. By the time he took one deep breath and counted to ten she would be gone.

One deep breath...

He flung open the door to his office and raced towards the front door. He had almost reached it when Sir Peter suddenly emerged from his own office and called out urgently to him, 'Luke—quick! I need you. The Prime Minister's on the phone, Njambla's people have been back in touch. The meeting's on again.'

For a second Luke was tempted to ignore him—breaking one of his own unbreakable rules—but he could hear the taxi door closing, and his conscience was telling him that he had to let her go. His face stripped of expression, he turned away from the front door and walked towards Sir Peter.

CHAPTER FOURTEEN

SUZY had read the breaking story about a certain African President's meeting in Italy over her breakfast, not long after her departure from the villa—the same morning, in fact, as the post had brought her another letter advising her that regretfully its senders could not offer her a job with them.

Following her return home, she had written to every library and organisation she could think of, determined to pursue her dream of finding work as a trainee archivist. But it was a narrow field, with very few vacancies.

'You mustn't give up,' Kate had told her firmly.

'I don't want to,' Suzy had admitted. 'But it's not an easy market to break into, and at my age—'

'Your age?' Kate had shaken her head chidingly. 'For heaven's sake, Suzy, you aren't old!'

'I'm not twenty-one, and just down from university,' Suzy had reminded her ruefully. 'Potential employers want to know what I've been doing for the last few years, and why I didn't finish my degree first time round.'

'What? You were nursing your mother,' Kate had defended indignantly.

'And then there's the fact that I left the magazine— and I don't have any references from them.'

'They were subjecting you to sexual harassment,'

Kate had argued, but Suzy had been able to see from her friend's expression that Kate knew that things did not look good for her.

'Still, there is somewhere I can get a job,' Suzy had told Kate cheerfully.

'Yes—with us,' Kate had replied promptly.

Even though she was grateful to her friend, Suzy had shaken her head. 'No, Kate. You know that I won't take charity,' she had told her gently. 'I was referring to the supermarket—I've worked there before.'

'Suzy, you don't need to do that!' Kate had protested. 'You know we'd love to have you working for us.'

'Kate, you told me yourself only last week that you were struggling to find enough work for the part-time girl you've already got,' Suzy reminded her. 'No. The supermarket will be fine!' she had told her, and she had meant it.

She felt very guilty about the fact that she had said nothing to Kate about either Luke or her time at the villa. But somehow she had just not been able to bring herself to do so...

'I hate this job. I've only been working here a week and it feels like for ever. And as for that supervisor— she's more like a prison warden!'

Suzy smiled sympathetically at the pouting teenage girl sitting grumpily at the till next to her own.

'It's okay once you get used to it,' she assured her, whilst privately acknowledging that she could understand her dislike of their supervisor, whom Suzy thought was a bit of a bully.

The supervisor apart, though, Suzy quite enjoyed working on the supermarket checkout— After nearly three months she actually had her own regular customers, who favoured her till—old ladies, in the main, who were lonely and appreciated the fact that Suzy did not rush them and had time to listen to them.

The bullying supervisor didn't approve. She constantly hectored Suzy about the time she spent listening, complaining that Suzy wasn't pulling her weight because she wasn't dealing with as many customers as some of the other girls. She had urged Suzy to discourage them.

'But they're lonely,' Suzy had protested.

'So what? We aren't here to provide them with someone to talk to!' the supervisor had told Suzy angrily. 'And it's not as though they spend very much. Just a few bits and pieces, that's all.'

'They like coming in because they can go to the coffee shop,' Suzy had responded. But her defence of her elderly customers had only infuriated the supervisor all the more.

'Yes, and they'll go in there and sit all day if they can, just drinking one cup of tea!' she had snorted grimly.

Suzy tried not to think about her supervisor. She needed this job because she needed the money. They had had a good summer, so at least she hadn't had to spend money keeping the flat heated. Every penny counted now—she had even thought of applying to the council for an allotment. Fresh air and fresh food would be good for her—

She checked her thoughts and she looked down at

the small bulge of her stomach. To say that it had been a shock to discover that she was pregnant was more than an understatement!

Of course the discovery of her pregnancy had meant that she'd had to come clean to Kate about Luke, and although she had been surprised, her friend was being wonderfully supportive.

Luke's baby!

A soft absorbed look filled Suzy's eyes followed by a flash of fiery maternal protectiveness. Unlike her own mother, she was not going to bring her baby up in an atmosphere of misery and complaint. But if her baby was a girl, Suzy had decided she would warn her against falling for a man like her father!

Her doctor had assured her that everything was fine and normal—single motherhood didn't raise any eyebrows or comments any more—and now that she had got used to the fact that she was pregnant Suzy was thrilled and excited. But not as thrilled and excited as she would have been if she had been sharing things with Luke—a Luke who loved her...

Now she was entering fantasyland, she derided herself. And what was more she was demeaning herself by even thinking about wanting to have him love her.

There was a lot of commotion and noise coming from the supervisor's office, which was behind her and several yards away, and in front of her at the checkout a young mother with a screaming toddler was struggling to unload her trolley.

Suzy smiled sympathetically, unable to stop herself from mentally fast-forwarding to the arrival of her

baby. Money would be very tight, but she was determined that somehow she would manage.

There was still a lot of noise coming from behind
her. She could hear the supervisor's voice raised in
protest, and she could hear a man. A man? That was
Luke's voice—she was sure of it.

Luke had had enough.

The last fourteen weeks had been the longest of his
life. First he had told himself that he was a man of
honour, and that as such he was honour-bound to leave
Suzy to make a life for herself without him. Then he
had told himself that it was only natural that he should
check up on her to make sure she was okay after what
she had been through.

Then he had admitted that if he *did* check up on her
he was going find it damned hard to walk away—especially if she was still under the delusion that she
loved him. And then finally he had admitted that there
was no way he could live without her and that he had
to see her again!

He had finished the contract he'd been working on,
handed over his active role in their shared business to
his partner, and announced that from now on he was
going to be running the small estate he had inherited.

A hiccup in the children's recovery and their return
to their homeland had added to the delay, making it
fourteen weeks instead of the fourteen days he would
have preferred before he was finally free to seek Suzy
out.

When he had called round at her flat the woman who
had the apartment below hers had informed him that

she was at work. It had taken him an hour and a good deal of patience and flattery before she had finally given him the information that Suzy was working in a supermarket.

He had wasted another hour driving through the traffic to find it, and now this shrill-voiced woman was telling him that it was impossible for her to take Suzy off the till she was operating, and that if he wanted to see her he would have to wait until her shift was over.

Luke wasn't prepared to wait a single minute longer—not after having waited nearly four months—and so, ignoring the supervisor, he strode towards Suzy.

'Luke!' Suzy wasn't even aware that she had spoken his name, never mind stood up, to stare in disbelief as Luke strode towards her.

Then he stopped, his gaze going from her face to her body. He couldn't possibly tell, Suzy assured herself frantically. She was barely showing. Her bump was still relatively small. Even so her hand crept protectively towards it as she tried to cover it from him.

Shock and awe! Where had he heard those words before? Luke wondered, dazed. Certainly not in connection with what he was feeling right now. Suzy was pregnant! Suzy was having his baby!

Whilst the young mother watched in fascinated interest, Luke shifted his gaze from Suzy's stomach to her face.

'Go and get your things,' he commanded brusquely.
'My things?' Suzy gulped. 'What? I—'
'We're leaving—and now!' Luke told her fiercely.
Suzy told herself that she should refuse to have any-

thing to do with him, but instead she heard herself protesting shakily, 'Luke, I can't just leave. I'm working. There's no reason—'

'There's every reason,' Luke corrected her savagely.

And before Suzy could stop him he had reached for her and placed his hand where hers had been, flat and hard against her belly, where his child was growing.

'There's this, for starters,' he told her thickly. 'My child. And if that isn't enough...'

Suddenly Suzy was conscious of the silence surrounding them. The curious looks of the customers and the angry face of her supervisor.

'If you leave this till now you will be in breach of your employment terms and your job could be at risk,' the supervisor was intoning.

'She'll be handing in her notice anyway,' Luke answered coldly.

Handing in her notice? Suzy glared at him.

'You can't say that!' she hissed, as Luke put his hand beneath her elbow and almost frogmarched her away from the till. 'I need this job, Luke.'

'What you need and what I need are not my prime concerns right now,' Luke told her flatly. 'Our child's needs are.'

He shouldn't be feeling like this, Luke told himself. He shouldn't be feeling triumphant, exuberant, delighted that the child Suzy was carrying—his child—meant that he had a logical and undeniable reason for forcing his way into her life. But he was!

Our child! Suzy could have wept.

Outside in the car park he bundled her into a large four-wheel drive vehicle and then got in himself. It was nearly four months since she had seen him. And he hadn't even looked at her properly, never mind attempted to touch her...kiss her...

'I've just got back from seeing the children,' Luke said to her. 'They're well enough to receive treatment from a hospital in their own country now, and their aunt has officially taken charge of them.'

'Oh, Luke, that's such good news,' Suzy responded in delight.

'Yes, it is,' he agreed quietly. 'Suzy, why didn't you let me know about the baby?'

'Let you know?' she stared at him. 'I...'

How could she tell him that she hadn't wanted him to feel responsible, that she hadn't wanted him to feel that she had deliberately allowed herself to become pregnant in order to trap him. He already knew how much she loved him, and she imagined that in a man's eyes a woman who became pregnant with his child after he had rejected her had to be doing so in order to force his hand.

She didn't feel she could tell him any of that, so instead, she simply said huskily, 'I...I just didn't think that it was necessary.'

Luke felt the pain of her words explode inside him.

'I heard from Peter the other day. He mentioned that you've kept in touch with the children,' he announced abruptly.

'Yes...yes, I have,' Suzy agreed. 'I feel so sorry for them. They need a woman in their lives who loves them. A stepmother, perhaps.'

As she spoke Suzy was thinking of the young woman Lucy had written to her about—the daughter of some older friends of Peter's who had taken quite an interest in Lucy and Charlie.

'Thinking of applying for the job yourself, are you?' Luke demanded harshly.

Suzy stared at him, his words coming as a shock after her own private thoughts.

'How could I?' She asked. 'I'm pregnant with your child.'

Her answer wasn't the one Luke wanted to hear. What he wanted was to hear her telling him, as she had done before, in that soft, loving voice of hers, that she loved him and only him and that she would always do so!

'Why are you working in that supermarket?' he asked curtly.

'Because it was the only place I could get a job!' Suzy returned tartly. 'Now that I'm going to have a child to support—' She stopped and bit her lip. The last thing she wanted was for him to think she was trying to get money out of him.

'*You* are going to have a child to support?' Luke demanded as he turned the car in the direction of the motorway. 'This child is our child, Suzy, and I consider that I have as much responsibility for supporting him or her as you do—if not more.'

'Luke, where are you taking me?' Suzy asked, as she silently digested his statement.

Things were happening too fast. She was still in a state of shock. In fact she was still expecting to wake up and open her eyes and find that she had been dreaming!

'Home,' Luke replied, further astounding her.

They were heading towards the country, leaving the city behind.

'Home?' Suzy queried uncertainly. 'But...'

'Where else would I be taking you?' Luke asked. 'After all, it's where you and our child now belong!'

'I have my own home,' Suzy protested sharply. 'I have my flat.'

'You can't bring up a child up there,' Luke told her flatly. 'And you certainly will not be bringing up *my* child there.'

Suzy drew in a sharp breath of indignation. 'There is nothing wrong with my flat,' she told him. 'You have no right to do this, Luke.'

'You are carrying my baby,' Luke said harshly. 'How much more right than that do I need?'

'Maybe I am—but that doesn't mean that you can just walk into my life and...take over...or kidnap me!' Suzy wasn't far from tears of emotional reaction.

'No? I beg to differ. You see, the way I look at it, Suzy, you gave me some damn important rights when you gave yourself to me—when I gave you my child.'

Shocked into silence, Suzy leaned back in her seat and closed her eyes. She just could not believe that any of this was happening—that Luke had conducted this swift and effective campaign of repossession which had brought her totally into his power.

As she tried to fight the wave of tiredness that suddenly gripped her Luke turned off the motorway.

'It isn't very far now,' he told her. 'The estate is just the other side of the village. You'll be able to see the church spire first.'

Estate…village…church spire. Suzy's head was thumping with a reactionary headache.

They were right in the heart of the English country-side at its quaint best. Autumn might be just around the corner, but the trees were still in full summer dress—the hedges heavy with leaf, fields of crops waiting to be harvested stretching away from the road.

Suzy saw a sign, Flintock-upon-Adder, and then they were driving through a picturesque village. Its houses clustered around an immaculate green, with weeping willows dipping into the waters of a sedate river and then the road curved past a small Norman church to run alongside a stone wall. Beyond it Suzy could see a small park, and then she caught her breath at the beauty of the Queen Anne house she could just glimpse through the trees.

Luke was turning in to a tree-lined drive and the house lay in front of them.

As he brought the car to a halt outside it Suzy turned and told him determinedly, 'Luke, I want you to take me back to my own flat.'

'Not yet,' Luke refused calmly. 'Not until we've had time to talk. Come on—I'll take you in and introduce you to Mrs Mattock. She's the housekeeper—I inherited her along with the house.'

'You inherited this house?'

'Yes, from my father. It's been in the family ever since it was first built.'

Mrs Mattock was calm and welcoming, apparently not in the least bit fazed that Luke had returned with an unexpected guest.

Although she was both pleasant and discreet, Suzy

suspected that the housekeeper was well aware of her pregnancy as she escorted her upstairs to a pretty guest bedroom. It was decorated in a simple and traditional style, complete with its own bathroom so that Suzy could, as the housekeeper put it, 'freshen up'.

'Mr Luke said that I was to serve tea in the library, miss,' she informed Suzy before turning to leave. 'It's the third door on your left off the hallway. A lovely room it is too. It was the old master's favourite. He would have been right pleased that Mr Luke had taken it over, that he would!'

From the window of the guest room Suzy could see the house's lovely English country garden, and the church just visible through the greenery of ancient trees.

In the bathroom, with its plain white sanitaryware, she found immaculate white guest towels and a tablet of what looked like handmade soap. Against her will she found herself thinking what a wonderful home this house would be for a family.

A wonderful home, maybe, but never *her* home—nor her child's, she reminded herself sharply as she left the room and headed for the stairs, breathing in the soft scent of lavender and beeswax from the well-polished furniture.

Dutifully following Mrs Mattock's instructions, she resisted doing more than just peeping inside the half-open door of what was a lovely sunny south-facing sitting room, and headed instead for the door to the library.

Outside the room she paused, reluctant to go in. But determinedly she took a deep breath, and then reached for the door handle and turned it. As she opened the door and walked in, Suzy acknowledged that the very masculine panelled room, with its impressive partners' desk, suited Luke. She could see that he felt very much at home in this lovely house. But then why shouldn't he?

'Suzy.' As he came towards her she backed away from him. 'Mrs. Mattock is going to bring us some tea,' Luke said.

'Yes. She told me,' Suzy answered curtly, wondering what on earth they were doing, exchanging such stilted small talk when they had far more important matters to discuss—like Luke's high-handed virtual abduction of her!

'Luke, you shouldn't have done this,' she said angrily. 'You have no right to—'

'To what? To be concerned about the welfare of my child and his or her mother?'

Suzy had to blink frantically to banish her threatening tears. Hormonal emotions, she told herself crossly.

'This baby I am having wasn't planned, Luke—we both know that,' she reminded him. 'He or she was…was an accident. I don't consider myself to have any claim on you—and anyway, you don't…'

'I don't what?'' Luke probed, when Suzy fell silent without finishing her sentence.

'Suzy took a deep breath. 'You don't love me!' There—she had said it! 'You don't love me. You don't even like me very much.'

'I don't love you?' Luke gave a harsh laugh.

'And why on earth did you come to the supermarket in the first place?' Suzy persisted, ignoring him.

Luke had had enough! It was hell on earth for him, having her standing there in front of him when what he wanted more than anything else was to have her in his arms—her *and* their child!

'Why did I come to the supermarket? Why do you think I came?'

Suzy's heart was beating crazily now, with a mixture of dangerous emotions.

'I don't know,' she admitted, wetting her lips nervously with the tip of her tongue. She had been so caught up in Luke's reaction to the discovery that she was pregnant that she hadn't been able to think past it and question why he had come looking for her in the first place.

'In Italy you told me that you loved me,' Luke said curtly, half turning away from her as he stood staring out of the library window.

Suzy could really feel her heart thumping now. Yes, she had told Luke that she loved him and he had shown her in no uncertain terms that he did not want that love. She had more than her own feelings to consider now. She had her child's to think of as well! No way was her child going to suffer the same unhappy childhood she had known! For her baby's sake she needed to be strong.

'I did say that, yes,' she acknowledged a little unsteadily. 'But I realise now that I—'

Idiotically she discovered that something inside her just would not let her say the words *I don't love you!*

'That you made a mistake.' Luke finished her sen-

tence for her flatly, causing relief to surge through her
as he inadvertently rescued her.

'I...'

Suzy had to bite on her lip to hold back the pain
seizing her as she tried to deny her love. Something
inside her was telling her that to deny her feelings was
as great a betrayal of her child as humiliating herself
by loving a man who did not want her.

'You didn't have to come to the supermarket to find
that out, Luke,' she said instead. 'Surely the fact that
I haven't made any attempt to contact you must have
reassured you that I—'

'Reassured me!' The violence in Luke's voice as he
swung round to confront her silenced her. 'Reassured
me?' he repeated savagely. 'What the hell are you talking about, Suzy?' He broke off abruptly as there was
a discreet rap on the door and Mrs Mattock came in
wheeling an immaculately set tea trolley, complete
with a heavy silver teapot.

'Will Ms Roberts be staying the night, Mr Luke?'
she asked politely.

'Yes!'

'No!'

Locked in mutual anger, Suzy and Luke glared at
one another as the housekeeper discreetly departed.

'Would you like me to pour the tea?'

As Luke nodded tersely Suzy had to quash a hysterical sound of mingled pain and disbelief. Here they
were, in the middle of a situation so tense and painful
that she felt faint from the stress of it, and she was
pouring tea—like someone out of a Victorian novel!

But automatically she went to pick up the heavy teapot.

'Of course I realised that your belief that you loved me sprang from the trauma you'd undergone,' she could hear Luke saying tightly behind her. 'I may have realised I loved you before that event, but—'

The teapot wobbled in Suzy's hand as shock weakened her muscles. There was tea in the cup, in the saucer, and on the immaculately starched traycloth.

'Suzy!'

Luke grabbed the heavy silver teapot with one hand and put a steadying arm around her.

'What did you just say?' she demanded weakly. She was shaking so much she could hardly stand, and it was heaven to lean into Luke's warm strength. 'Are you trying to say that you fell in love with me before I got trapped in the grotto?' she asked dizzily.

'Yes. Not that I wanted to admit it. I was still labouring under a misapprehension about you then, and whilst a part of me wanted to be proved right about you, a much larger part of me most certainly did not.'

Suzy was having to struggle to assimilate what he was saying. Luke loved her? Luke had loved her even when he had thought he ought to hate her? Joy was beginning to well up inside her, flooding through her veins.

'Are you feeling all right?' Luke was fussing, man-like. 'Why don't you come and sit down?'

'No,' Suzy told him fiercely. 'No. I'm not going anywhere, and most especially not out of your arms, Luke, until you tell me exactly when you knew you loved me!'

'Exactly when?' Luke looked down into her un-guarded face, and what he could see there made his heart start to sing.

'Probably the first time you kissed me,' he admitted ruefully. 'And certainly by the time you ran away from me on that hilltop and I realised that if I didn't do something you were going to hurt yourself.'

A pink blush stained Suzy's face as she remembered how he had held her, her body spread on top of his.

'When I told you I loved you, you rejected me, though,' she pointed out quietly. She could feel his chest rising and then falling with the intensity of his sigh.

'I had to, Suzy. It's well known that the kind of trauma you went through can make a person feel the strongest kind of emotion towards the people they shared it with. I knew I loved you, but I didn't want to trap you into a relationship when I was afraid that your love might not be the real thing.'

'Oh, Luke I fell in love with you the moment I set eyes on you,' Suzy told him softly. 'I looked at you and it was just as though… I looked at you and I knew you were my soul mate,' she told him huskily.

For a moment she thought he wasn't going to make any response, but then he put down the teapot and turned her gently in his arms. Placing one hand on her belly, he whispered softly, 'Sorry baby, but I think you'd better close your eyes whilst I kiss your mother!'

And then he lifted both hands to Suzy's face and, cupping it, began to kiss her with a slow, gentle passion that grew and built until they were so closely entwined that even their heartbeats matched.

'I can't begin to tell you how long these last fourteen weeks have felt,' Luke whispered achingly to her. 'First the meeting with Njambla, and then I had to persuade my partner to take over my active role in the business. Then there were problems with the children, and all the time I kept warning myself that by the time I did get to see you, you would have realised that you didn't love me after all. You don't know how many times I cursed myself for not keeping you with me when I had the chance, for not taking the love you were offering me. And then when I saw you today and I realised you were pregnant...'

She could see the pain in his eyes, as well as the love.

'I didn't want you to feel you owed me anything,' she told him quietly. 'I didn't want anything from you, Luke, that you couldn't give with love.'

'Are you sure you're feeling okay?'

'I'm fine,' Suzy reassured Luke as he led her out of the church and into the late autumn sunshine to the joyful sound of wedding bells ringing.

Her elegant cream silk dress discreetly concealed the curve of her belly, and under the benign gaze of their wedding guests Luke leaned down to kiss her.

'Who would have thought that first kiss you stole from me would lead to this?' he murmured teasingly in her ear.

Suzy laughed in real amusement. 'I may have stolen it,' she reminded him, 'but you returned it—and with interest.'

Luke laughed back, placing his hand on the curve of her belly as he did so.

A hovering photographer snapped the pose, and then the one following it, when Luke drew Suzy firmly into his arms and kissed her tenderly and thoroughly.

EPILOGUE

'LUCY looks very serious and important.' Luke smiled at Suzy as they watched Lucy, Charlie and Sir Peter, along with Anne, the young woman he had asked if he could bring with him to baby Robert's christening, getting out of their car.

'Well, being Robert's godmother is a very serious and important role for her,' Suzy told him with a smile.

Lucy had been thrilled when Suzy had asked her if she would like to be one of Robert's godmothers, along with Kate.

'Oh, Suzy, do you mean it?' she had asked, her face pink with excitement.

Suzy smiled now at the memory, shifting Robert's sturdy six-month weight in her arms as she looked at Luke.

They had had Sir Peter, Lucy and Charlie to stay with them over Christmas, and Suzy had heard a great deal then from Lucy about Anne, the young family friend who was now Sir Peter's fiancée.

'I know Lucy is perhaps a little young, but it means so much to her, Luke. She told me that she is hoping that when her father remarries there will be babies.'

Robert's two godfathers were friends of Luke's from his Army days and, like Sir Peter and his family, they had been regular visitors over the months since Luke and Suzy's marriage.

Knowing the sad story of how Luke had lost his parents, and how lonely he had felt, had increased Suzy's determination to provide their own children with the kind of warm, happy family environment neither she nor Luke had known.

When Luke had taken her hand, white-faced and worried after Robert's birth, anxious for her, having witnessed her labour, Suzy had smiled up at him and warned teasingly, 'You're going to have to get used to this, Luke, because this baby is not going to be lonely, like we were.'

A small smile touched Suzy's mouth as she remembered this and then looked down at Robert.

Some might consider it too soon, but she suspected that she was already pregnant with their second child, and had told Luke so only this morning.

'What? Already?'

'What do you mean, already?' she had teased. 'It only takes one successful attempt, as we both know.'

Luke had smiled, giving her a deeply sensual look that had made her both laugh and colour up a bit. 'Of course, if you would like to be sure…' he had said as he advanced towards her.

'Luke!' Suzy had protested as he had removed the bathrobe she had been wearing and taken her in his arms. 'Luke, we've got guests,' she had reminded him mock primly. 'And they will be waiting for their breakfast.'

'Let them wait,' he had murmured, finding the exact

spot at the side of her neck where the touch of his lips always reduced her to hungry need.

'It's Robert's christening today,' she had added, several seconds later, but without any real urgency in her voice.

'Mmm…so it is,' he had replied.

If any of their guests had found it odd that they should arrive at the breakfast table rather later than planned none of them had been impolite enough to say so, but Suzy thought she had caught Sir Peter Verey's fiancée, Anne, focusing on her thoughtfully.

She liked Anne, and thought she would make Sir Peter a good wife and the children an excellent step-mother. Already she was building rapport with them, and it made Suzy smile to hear how many times Lucy mentioned her name when she was talking to her.

The sun was shining and their guests were now filing into the old church.

Robert woke up and looked around with interest.

He was very much his father's son, Suzy reflected— and not just in the way he looked. He had Luke's some-times imperious and questioning manner, even at six months old.

As they followed their guests into the church Luke took Robert from her, cradling him expertly. And as she watched them Suzy saw father and son exchange a knowing male-to-male look.

Her heart flooded with emotion and instinctively she moved closer to Luke. She was so happy, so blessed, so loved.

Luke was her other half and she his. Deep down

inside herself Suzy knew that they had been fated to meet. Fated to meet one another and fated to love one another.

They were soul mates.

In Luke's arms Robert smiled up at his father, and Suzy touched her stomach gently.

Mistress to Her Husband

PENNY JORDAN

CHAPTER ONE

'KATE you'll never guess what! John told us this morning, whilst you were at the dentist. The business has been taken over. And the new boss is coming in tomorrow to interview everyone!'

Kate Vincent digested her co-worker's excited comments in silence. Dropping enviably thick, dark lashes reflectively over topaz eyes, she considered what she had been told. She had only been with the company for six months, as before that she'd only been able to manage a part-time job whilst she was completing her Master's. With the qualification nicely enhancing her CV she had felt confident enough to apply for this post, which previously she would have considered out of her range.

'So who's taking us over?' Kate questioned Laura, absently flipping the smooth length of her chestnut-brown hair over her shoulder as she did so. It had been hot outside in the street, and the coolness of the office's air-conditioning was very welcome.

'Well, John wouldn't say,' Laura responded, suppressing a small envious sigh as she studied Kate's elegantly slender body, clad in a neat white T-shirt teamed with a chocolate-brown linen skirt.

Laura had been with her when Kate had bought the skirt, an end-of-line sale buy which she herself would have deemed dull. But on Kate it looked not just good, but also somehow discreetly expensive.

'Apparently everything has to be kept hush-hush until tomorrow.' She gave Kate a rueful look.

'I suppose we should have seen it coming. After all, John has been hinting for ages that he'd like to take early retirement—but I never thought he was contemplating selling out. Mind you, he and Sheila don't have any children, do they? So I don't suppose there's much point in hanging on when they could be spending their time in that condo of theirs in Miami.'

Kate listened intently to Laura as she booted up her computer. The business John Loames had set up to supply specialist facilities and equipment to the building trade had been very successful, but Kate had seen for herself since she had started to work for the small private company as its accounts executive that John was growing less and less inclined to seek out new contracts. Which was a pity, because she knew that the business had a great deal of potential, and she was not entirely surprised that someone had bought John out.

'Everyone's worried about what might happen,' Laura confided to her. 'None of us want to lose our jobs.'

'Someone new taking over might not necessarily be a bad thing,' Kate pointed out to her calmly. 'There's ample room for the business to be expanded, and then there would be more than enough work for all of us—provided, of course, the new owner doesn't already own a similar business and just wants to amalgamate John's with his own.'

'Oh, don't say that!' Laura begged worriedly, giving a small shudder. 'Roy and I have only just increased our mortgage so that we can extend the house.' Her face became slightly pink. 'We're trying for a family, and a baby will mean that we definitely need extra space. The last thing I need right now is to lose my job! Which reminds me—John told us that he wants us all here especially early tomorrow. Apparently the new owner has said specifically that he will be here at eight.'

'Eight?' Kate switched her attention from her e-mails to Laura, her forehead crinkling in a worried frown. 'Are you telling me John wants us here at *eight*?'

'Yes.'

Kate's porcelain-clear skin paled slightly. It was impossible for her to make it to the office for eight o'clock in the morning. Pre-school didn't start until eight, and she would have to leave Ollie at seven-thirty at the very latest if she was to make it here for eight. She could feel the tension cramping her stomach.

It was hard enough for any mother to work full time— a constant finely-judged balancing act—but when one added into that delicate balance the fact that the mother in question was a single parent, fighting desperately hard to give as much emotional security as two loving parents would, plus the fact that she had not told her employers that she had child, then that balancing act became dangerously unstable.

Just thinking about Ollie was enough to have her stomach twisting in knots of maternal protective anxiety.

'What's wrong?' Laura asked curiously, sensing her tension.

'Er…nothing.'

Kate hadn't told anyone at work about Ollie. All too sensitive to the attitude of colleagues and employers to the difficulties that came hand in hand with a worker who was a mother—especially a single mother—Kate had made no mention of her son during her interview with John. It had only been after she had started to work for the company that she had learned that John had a somewhat old-fashioned attitude about employing women with very young children. By then she had realised how well suited she was to her job, and it to her, and although it had caused her some sleepless nights and many qualms, she had decided to keep Ollie's existence a secret. Since she was fiercely honest by nature, this decision had pricked her conscience on more than one occasion, but she had told herself that it was a necessary omission if she was to succeed with her career plans.

She was well qualified now, and she was determined to provide her son with at least some of the material benefits he would have enjoyed had his father not abandoned her.

His father! Kate could feel the cold sickness and despair laced with anger spewing up inside her—it was a mixture as dangerous and toxic as arsenic, but she was the one it threatened to poison and destroy, not the man who had broken her heart and deserted her.

Now she considered that she and Oliver were better off without him—even though what she was earning only just covered the mortgage she was paying on the tiny cottage she had bought in a pretty village several miles away from the town and Oliver's out-of-school childcare, leaving just enough for food and other essentials.

Childcare! Her lips, normally soft and sweetly curved, hardened and thinned. *She* was the best person to be providing her son with childcare, but she was not in a financial position to be able to do so.

Her current job was the first rung on the career ladder she was going to have to climb in order to support them both properly. The head of her department was due to retire in two years' time, and Kate had secretly been hoping that if she did her job well enough John might promote her into the vacancy.

Her twenty-fifth birthday wasn't that far away, and

neither was Ollie's fifth. His fifth birthday and her fifth
year of being alone, of being without— Swiftly Kate
buried the potentially damaging thoughts. She didn't
need them, she didn't want them, and she damn well
wasn't going to let them disturb her hard-won peace of
mind.

It was her future she needed to focus on, and not her
past! This takeover could destroy any chance she might
have had of such a promotion, but it might also give her
increased opportunities, she reflected, as she studied
some comparison charts she had set up on her own initiative, to see which customers could be approached to
increase their orders.

As she stood in the open doorway of the small village
nursery and watched her son run towards her, his face
lighting up as he saw her, Kate felt her heart contract
with love. When she bent to scoop him up into her arms,
and buried her face into the warm flesh of his neck to
breathe in his delicious little-boy smell, she knew that
no matter what sacrifices she had to make, or how hard
she had to work, she would do it for Ollie's sake.

A small frown pleated her forehead as she looked
round the classroom, empty now of the other children.
She had chosen to live in the village because she had
wanted to provide Ollie with a sense of belonging and
community, to provide him with the kind of childhood
she herself had been denied. But living here meant she
had to travel to the city to work, which in turn meant
that Ollie had to wait for her long after the others had
been collected.

She had never intended that her child should grow up
like this—an only child with no family other than her.

She had wanted things to be so different for her child, her children, than they had been for her.

Two loving parents, siblings, the sure knowledge of being loved and wanted. *The sure knowledge of being loved and wanted!*

Pain gripped her. It had been five years—surely only a woman with no sense of self-worth or self-respect would allow herself to think about a man who had betrayed her love and rejected her? A man who had sworn love for ever, who had sworn that he shared her dreams and goals, who had taught her to trust and love him, and who had whispered against her lips as he took her virginal body that he wanted to give her his child, that he wanted to surround that child with love and security.

A man who had lied to her and left her broken-hearted, disillusioned, and completely alone.

To be with him she had gone against the wishes of the aunt and uncle who had brought her up, and because of that they had disowned her.

Not that Kate would have wanted her aunt and uncle involved in the life of her precious son. They might have given her a home when she had been orphaned, but they had done so out of duty and not love. And she had craved love so badly, so very badly.

'Ollie was beginning to worry.'

The faint hint of reproach in the nursery teacher's voice made Kate wince inwardly.

'I know I'm a bit late,' she apologised. 'There was an accident on the bypass.'

The nursery teacher was comfortably round and in late middle age. She had grandchildren herself, and her small charges loved and respected her. Kate had lost count of the number of time she had heard Ollie insisting, 'But Mary says…'

Ten minutes later Kate was unlocking the door to their small cottage. It was right in the centre of the village, its front windows overlooking the green, with its duck pond, and at the back of the house a long narrow garden.

Ollie was a sturdily built child, with firm solid muscles and a head of thick black curls. An inheritance from his father, although Ollie himself did not know it.

So far as Kate was concerned the man who had fathered her son no longer existed, and she refused to allow him any place in their lives. Ollie's placid nature meant that until recently he had accepted that he did not have a father, without asking Kate very many questions about him. However, the fact that his new best friend *did* have a father had led to Ollie starting to want to know more.

Kate frowned. So far Ollie had been content with her responses, but it made her heart ache to see the way he watched longingly whilst Tom Lawson played with his son.

Sean unfurled his long body from the seat of his Mercedes and stood still whilst he looked at the building in front of him.

His handmade Savile Row suit sat elegantly on his lean-limbed body, the jacket subtly masking the powerful breadth of his shoulders and the muscles he had built up in the years when he had earned his living hiring himself out to whichever builder would take him on.

His sweat had gone into the making of more than one motorway, as well as several housing estates, but even in those days as an ill-educated teenager he had promised himself that one day things would be different, that one day he would be the man giving the orders and not taking them.

As a young child he'd literally had to fight for his food until, aged five, he'd been abandoned by his hippie mother and been taken into care. In his twenties he had spent his days building extensions, and anything else he would get paid for, and his nights studying for a Business Studies degree. He had celebrated his thirty-first birthday by selling the building company he had built up from nothing for twenty million. Had he wanted to do so, he could have retired. But that was not his way. He had seen the potential of companies such as John's and had seized the opportunities with both hands. He was now thirty-five.

He had big expansion plans for the business he had just acquired, but for his plans to succeed he needed the right kind of workforce. A dedicated, energetic, enthusiastic and ambitious workforce. This morning he was going to meet his new employees, and he was going to assess them in the same way he had assessed those who had worked for him when he had first set up in business—by meeting them face to face. Then—and only then—would he read their personnel files.

He was an arrestingly good-looking man, but the early-morning sunlight picked out the harsh lines that slashed from his nose to his mouth and revealed a man of gritty determination who rarely smiled. He wore his obvious sexuality with open cynicism, and it glittered in the dense Celtic blue of his eyes now, as a young woman stopped walking to give him an appreciative and appraising look.

In the years since he had made his millions he had been pursued by some extraordinarily beautiful women, but Sean knew that they would have turned away in disgust and contempt from the young man he had once been.

Something—part bitterness and part pain—took the warmth from his gaze and dulled its blueness.

He had come a long way from what he had once been. A long way—and yet still not far enough?

Locking his car, he started to stride towards the building.

Kate could feel perspiration beginning to dew her forehead as she willed the traffic lights to change. Her stomach was so tight with nervous anxiety that it hurt.

She had swallowed her normal pride last night and asked Carol, Ollie's best friend's mother, if she could leave Ollie with her at seven-thirty for her to take him on to school with her son George. The pain in her stomach intensified. She hated treating her precious son as though he was a…a bundle of washing!

Why on earth had the new owner insisted on them arriving so early? Was he just unthinking, or uncaring? Whichever it was, it did not bode well for her future with the company, she decided fretfully.

As she reached the traffic lights she saw the broken-down car which had been the cause of the delay. It was already ten past eight, and it would take her at least another ten minutes to get to work.

Half past eight! Kate gritted her teeth as she hurried into the building. She was already walking fast, and she broke into an anxious run as she covered the last few yards. But the hope she had had that she might be able to slide discreetly into John's office whilst the meeting was still in progress was destroyed as the door opened and her colleagues came out into the corridor.

'You're late!' Laura whispered as she saw Kate. 'What happened?'

It was difficult to talk with so many people in the corridor.

'I'll tell you later—' she began, and then froze as two men came through the door.

One of them was John, and the other...the other...

The other was her ex-husband!

'Perhaps you'd like to tell *me*—now?'

How well she remembered that smooth chocolate voice, with its underlying ice.

People were staring at her, Kate realised, and she fought off her sick shock.

John was looking anguished and uncomfortable. 'Sean, I think perhaps... I am sure that...'

Arrogantly ignoring John, Sean demanded, 'In here!' He was holding the door open, waiting for her to walk past him and into John's office.

For a moment their gazes met and clashed, battled, topaz fighting dense blue for supremacy.

Her ex-husband was their new boss!

How could fate have dealt her such a low blow?

When Sean had walked out of her life to be with the woman he was leaving her for she had prayed that she would never, ever have to see him again. She had given him everything she had had to give—defying her aunt and uncle to be with him, helping and encouraging him, loving him—but that had not been enough for him. She had not been enough for him. The success she had helped him to achieve had meant that he no longer considered her good enough for him.

She was holding her breath and badly needed to exhale, but she was terrified that if she did she was going to start shaking—and there was so way she was going to allow Sean to witness that kind of vulnerability.

How well she remembered that challenging hard-edged blue gaze. He had looked at her like that the first time they had met, defying her to ignore him. No one would dare to ignore him now.

'Kate is a very—' She could hear John about to defend her.

'Thank you, John. I shall deal with this myself,' Sean announced curtly as she walked past him into the room, and he closed the door, excluding John from his own office.

'Kate?' he demanded grimly. 'What happened to Kathy?'

Just hearing him say that name resurrected far too many painful memories. She had been Kathy when he had taunted her the first time they had met, for being too posh to dance with a man like him. And she had been Kathy too when he had taken her in his arms and shown her— Fiercely she pushed away the tormenting memories.

Tilting her chin, she said coldly, 'Kathy?' She gave a mirthless laugh. 'She doesn't exist any longer, Sean. You destroyed her when you destroyed our marriage.'

'And your surname is?' Sean wondered whether she could hear or understand the cause of the anger that was making his throat raw and his voice terse as he grappled with his own shock.

'Kate Vincent,' Kate answered him coldly.

'Vincent?' he questioned savagely.

'Yes, Vincent. You didn't think I would want to keep your name, did you? And I certainly didn't want my aunt and uncle's—after all, like you, they didn't want me.'

'So you remarried just to change your name?'

Anger darkened Kate's eyes as she heard the contempt in his voice.

'Why were you late?' Sean demanded abruptly. 'Didn't he want to let you out of his bed?'

Furious colour scorched Kate's face.

'Just because you—' she began, and then stopped, swallowing hard as out of nowhere the memories started to fill her head. Sean waking her up in the morning with the gentlest of kisses…that was until she was fully awake…and then…

She could feel the tension building up inside her body, a tension activated by memories crowding out the reality she was trying desperately hard to cling on to, to use as a bulwark.

A bulwark? Against what? The love she had once felt for Sean had been completely destroyed, and by Sean himself. Cruelly and deliberately. Her body stiffened with pride. She was glad that he thought she had found someone else. Married someone else.

Had he married the woman he had left her for?

Sean's mobile rang, and he answered it, frowning briefly as he told Kate that she could go.

As she turned to leave Kate heard a female voice saying, quite clearly, 'Sean, darling…'

Kate was halfway through clearing out her desk when Laura came in.

'What on earth are you doing?' she demanded.

'Clearing my desk. What does it look like?' Kate responded tersely.

'You're leaving?'

Kate could see how shocked and dismayed Laura was.

'You mean he's sacked you just for being late?'

Kate permitted herself a thin and slightly bitter smile. 'No, he hasn't sacked me, but let's just say I'm leaving ahead of having him do so.'

'Oh, Kate, no!' Laura protested, obviously upset. 'I can see that things have got off to bad start for you—!' She stopped, biting her lip and looking uncomfortable.

Laura would never make a politician, Kate reflected wryly, witnessing her colleague's discomfort.

'Laura?' she prodded firmly.

'Well, I'm sure he didn't mean anything—to be critical...or unkind. But I did hear Sean asking John where you were,' Laura admitted reluctantly, adding quickly, 'I'm sure he'll be understanding, Kate. He seems such a sweetie, and so gorgeous.'

A sweetie! Sean! Kate suppressed a bitter laugh.

Sean might be many things, but he had never been a sweetie—not even when she had first known him.

A tough, streetwise, untamed rogue male, who could make a girl go weak at the knees and hot in places she hadn't previously known existed with just one taunting look, that was what he had been. And she...

Her face started to burn as she recognised where her unwanted thoughts were leading. She switched on her computer and started to type.

'Oh, thank goodness you've changed your mind,' Laura began, with relief, but Kate shook her head.

'No, I haven't. I'm just typing out my notice,' Kate informed her crisply.

'Your notice! Oh, Kate.' Laura looked aghast, and immediately tried to dissuade her, but Kate refused to let herself be swayed.

Finishing her typing, she checked and then printed off her letter, placing it neatly in an envelope, which she put in the internal post tray.

Her task completed, she headed for the door.

'Where are you going?' Laura demanded anxiously.

'I'm leaving,' Kate answered patiently. 'I've written my resignation letter. As of now, I no longer work here!'

'But, Kate, you can't leave just like that—without telling anyone!' Laura protested.

'Watch me!' Kate answered succinctly, walking calmly towards the door.

But inwardly she was feeling far from calm. Frantically she clamped down on her treacherous thoughts.

Kathy was working here! Sean paced the floor of his office, having terminated the call from the wife of his financial adviser. She had called to invite him to a dinner party she was planning, but Sean did not do dinner parties. His mouth twisted bitterly. Until he had met Kathy he hadn't even known the correct cutlery to use. She had been the one who had gently taught him. Gently rubbed off his rough edges. And he...

He strode angrily over to the office window and stared out of it. He had deliberately not kept track of Kathy after their divorce. There hadn't been any point. The marriage had been over and he had made her a generous financial settlement, even if she had returned it to his solicitor intact. Who had she married? When had she married him?

He went back to the desk and picked up the personnel files he had not yet read.

CHAPTER TWO

As SHE climbed out of her car Kate acknowledged that really there was no way she should have been driving. She was shaking from head to foot, and she had no real idea of how she had driven home. The entire journey had been a pain-fuelled blur of fighting back unwanted memories whilst surge after surge of panic and anger had washed through her.

'Kate!'

Kate tried to looked relaxed and smile as Carol, her friend and neighbour, came hurrying towards her.

'What are you doing back so early?' Carol asked, adding teasingly, 'Did the interview go so well that the new boss gave you the rest of the day off?'

Kate opened her mouth to make a suitably light-hearted response, but to her chagrin she could feel her lips starting to tremble as emotions overwhelmed her.

'I've handed in my notice,' she told Carol shakily. 'I… I had to… My…the new boss is my ex-husband!' Tears filled her eyes. She was shaking so violently she could have been in shock, Kate recognised distantly.

'Come on, let's get you inside,' she heard Carol announcing in a motherly voice. 'And then you can tell me all about it.'

Ten minutes later, after she had made them both a cup of coffee and chatted calmly about their sons, Carol turned to Kate and said gently, 'I'm not going to pry, Kate, but if you want to get it off your chest I'm a good

19

listener, and I promise it won't go any further.' When Kate made no response, but simply continued to sit huddled in her chair, her hands gripping her coffee mug, Carol added quietly, 'Not even to Tom, if that's what you want.'

Kate turned her head to look at her, her gaze blank and withdrawn, then forced herself to focus on her friend.

Taking a deep breath, she began to speak, slowly and painfully. 'I met Sean when I was eighteen. He was building an extension for my aunt and uncle's neighbours. We'd had a very hot summer, and he worked bare-chested in a pair of old tight-fitting jeans—'

'Mmm, sexy. I can picture the scene.' Carol smiled encouragingly, relieved to see just the merest twitch of humour lifting Kate's mouth.

'I used to walk the long way round just so that I could see him,' Kate admitted. 'I hadn't thought he'd notice me, but then one night at a local club he was there and he asked me to dance. Fantasising over him when I walked past the building site was one thing. Being confronted with him there in front of me in the flesh was another! I felt intimidated by him.' Kate gave small shrug and looked at Carol.

'I was a naïve eighteen-year-old virgin, and all that fierce, potent hot male sexuality was a bit overwhelming. Unfortunately he thought I was rejecting him, and...' She shook her head. 'I didn't know it then, but like me he'd had a very unhappy and lonely childhood, which had left him with a bit of a chip on his shoulder and a determination to succeed. I can see now that I was a bit of a challenge to him, because I was a girl from a different background. A trophy girlfriend, I suppose the press would call it nowadays, and for a while I was good enough for him as just that. Good enough to marry, in fact. But once he'd become very successful I think he began to realise that I wasn't much of a trophy after all, and that with his money he could afford a much, much better one than me.'

Carol could hear the pain in Kate's voice. 'You obviously loved him,' she said softly.

'Loved him?' Kate looked at her starkly, her emotions darkening her eyes. 'Yes, I loved him—totally and completely, blindly and foolishly I realise now. Because I believed then that he felt the same way about me!'

'Oh, Kate!' Carol sympathised, her own eyes prickling with emotion as she covered Kate's cold folded hands with her own.

Kate swallowed and then continued. 'My aunt and uncle were furious when it came out that I was seeing him—especially my aunt. There was a dreadful row, and it came out that she had never liked my mother, had been appalled when she had married her brother. She told me that if I didn't agree to stop seeing Sean they would wash their hands of me and disown me. But I couldn't give Sean up. I loved him too much. He had become my whole world! And when I told him what my aunt had said he told me that he wasn't going to let me go back to them, to be hurt and bullied, that from now on he would look after me.'

Kate exhaled in a deep sigh.

'We were married six weeks later. Sean had finished the extension by then, and was ready to move on to his next job.'

Carol could see the events of the day were beginning to catch up with Kate and, surveying her friend's exhausted hollow-cheeked face, she stood up and told her firmly, 'Look, you're all in. Why don't you have a rest?

I'll collect Oliver from nursery, if you like, and give him his tea.'

Kate was tempted to refuse. But while a part of her was longing desperately to have the warm, solid feel of Oliver's sturdy body in her arms, so that she could hold him and take comfort from his presence, another part of her said that this was not fair to her son and that she must not get into the habit of leaning on him emotionally. And anyway, she had things to do, she reminded herself grimly. Like finding a new job for a start!

'You're very kind,' she told Carol wanly.

'Nonsense. I know you'd do the same for me.'

She would, of course, but it was hardly likely that she would ever be asked to do so, Kate acknowledged wearily after Carol had gone. Carol had a loving husband, and George had two sets of adoring grandparents only too willing to spend as much time as they could with their grandson.

And Oliver only had her. No grandparents. Just her. Just her? What about Sean? He was Oliver's father, after all, Kate reminded herself angrily.

Sean!

Her whole body felt heavy with misery and despair. She had struggled so hard, and it seemed so unfair that she should have her precious financial security snatched from her because her ex-husband had taken over the company.

For the first time since Sean had announced that their marriage was over Kate felt angry with herself for not accepting the generous pay-off he had offered her. Two million pounds and she had turned it down! She had turned it down not knowing that she was already pregnant with Oliver. And then, when she had realised... Well, she had sworn that she would never ask for anything from the man who had cold-bloodedly told her that he had changed his mind about wanting to be a father and that he had no desire to tie himself to a wife he no longer loved.

The pain was just as sharp as she remembered it being, and she stiffened against it. It should not exist any more. It should have been destroyed, just like Sean had destroyed their marriage.

All those things he had said to her and she had believed in; like how he, too, longed for children. All those promises he had made her—that those children, their children, would have the parental love neither of them had ever known. They had all been lies.

Against her will Kate could feel herself being drawn back into the past and its painful memories.

There had been no warning of what was to come, or of how vulnerable her happiness was. In fact only the previous month Sean had taken her away on an idyllic and very romantic break to an exclusive country house hotel—to make up, he had told her lovingly, for the fact that the negotiations he had been involved in to secure a very valuable contract had gone on so long that they had not been able to have a summer holiday.

They had arrived late in the afternoon and had enjoyed a leisurely and very romantic walk through the grounds. And then they had gone back to their room and Sean had undressed her and made love to her.

They had been late for dinner, she remembered—very late. And during it Sean had handed her a large brown envelope, telling her to open it. When she had done so she had found inside the sale details of a pretty Georgian rectory she and Sean had driven past early in the year.

'You said it was the kind of place you had always

wanted to live in,' he had reminded her simply. 'It's coming up for sale.'

She'd spent the rest of the evening in a daze, already excitedly planning how she would decorate the house, and insisting that Sean listen to her as she went through the house room by room.

They had made love again that night, and in the morning. And afterwards she had lain in Sean's arms, her eyes closed, whilst she luxuriated in breathing in the sexually replete scent of him and wondered what on earth she had done to merit such happiness.

Less than a month later she had been wondering what on earth she had done to merit such intense pain.

One minute—or so she had thought—Sean had been negotiating for the purchase of the rectory; the next he had been telling her that he no longer loved her and that he intended to divorce her.

Kate closed her eyes and lay back in her chair. She felt both physically and emotionally exhausted. What she should be doing right now, she told herself grimly, was worrying about how she was going to get another job, instead of wallowing in self-pity about the past.

She would have to enrol with an employment agency, and then probably take on as much work as she could get until she found a permanent position. She had some savings—her rainy day money—but that would not last for very long.

Why, why, *why* had Sean had to come back into her life like this? Hadn't he hurt her enough?

Tiredly Kate stopped trying to fight her exhaustion and allowed herself to drift off to sleep.

The dream was one she had had before. She tried to pull herself awake and out of it, as she had taught herself to do, but it was too late. It was rushing down on her, swamping her, and she was already lost in it.

She was with Sean, in the sitting room of their house. It was mid-afternoon and he had come home early from work. She ran to greet him, but he pushed her away, his expression not that of the husband she knew but that of the angry, aggressive man he had been when she had first met him.

'Sean, what's wrong?' she asked him, reaching out a hand to him and flinching as he ignored her loving gesture. He turned away from her and walked over to the window, blocking out its light. Uncomprehendingly she watched him, and the first tendrils of fear began to curl around her heart.

'I want a divorce.'

'A divorce! No… What…? Sean, what are you saying?' she demanded, panic, shock and disbelief gripping hold of her throat and giving her voice a hoarse, choked sound that seemed to echo round the room.

'I'm saying that our marriage is over and I want a divorce.'

'No! No! You don't mean that. You can't mean that!' Was that piteous little voice really her own? 'You love me.'

'I thought I did,' Sean agreed coldly. 'But I've realised that I don't. You and I want different things out of life, Kathy. You want children. I'm sick of having to listen to you boring on about it. I don't want children!'

'That's not true. How can you say that, Sean?' She stared at him in disbelief, unable to understand what he was saying. 'You've always said how much you want children,' she reminded him shakily. 'We said we wanted a big family because our own childhoods—'

If he heard the pain in her voice and was affected by it he certainly didn't show it.

'For God's sake,' he ground out. 'Grow up, will you, Kathy? When I said that I'd have said anything to get into your knickers.'

The contemptuous biting words flayed her sensitive emotions.

'Look, I don't intend to argue about this. Our marriage is over and that's that. I've already spoken to my solicitor. You'll be okay financially…'

'Is there someone else?'

Silently they looked at one another whilst Kathy prayed that he would say no, but instead he taunted her. 'What do you think?'

Her whole body was shaking, and even though she didn't want to she started to cry, sobbing out Sean's name in frantic pleading disbelief…

Why the hell was he doing this? Sean's hands clenched on the wheel as he drove. What was the point in risking resurrecting the past? She was easily replaceable. But Sean knew that he was being unfair. She was, according to John and from what he had been able to recognise himself, an extremely intelligent and diligent employee—the kind of employee, in fact, that he wanted. No way was he going to allow her to walk out of her job without working her statutory notice period.

She was his ex-wife, damn it, Sean reminded himself grimly. But this was nothing to do with her being his ex-wife, and nothing to do either with the fact that he had discovered from her records, contrary to his assumptions, she was not married.

He was in the village now, and his mouth hardened slightly. Oh, yes, this was exactly the kind of environment she liked. Small, cosy, homely—everything that her life with her appalling aunt and uncle had not been.

He swung the car into a parking space he had spotted, stopped the engine and got out.

He hadn't told anyone as yet about the fact that she had handed in her notice. Officially she was still in the company's employ...in his employ.

He skirted the duck pond, his eyes bleak as he headed for Kate's front door.

He was just about to knock when an elderly woman who had been watching him from her own front gate called out to him.

'You'll have to go round the back, young man.'

Young man! Sean grimaced. He didn't think he had ever been young—he had never been *allowed* to be young! And as for being a man... Something dark and dangerous hardened his whole face as he obeyed the elderly woman's instructions.

It took him several minutes to find the path which ran behind the back gardens of the cottages. The gate to Kate's wouldn't open at first, and then he realised that it was bolted on the inside and he had to reach over to unbolt it. Hardly a good anti-thief device, he reflected, giving it a frowning and derisory look as he unfastened it and walked up the path.

He frowned even more when he realised that the back door was slightly open. If Kate had had his upbringing she would have been a damn sight more safety conscious!

His hand was on the door when he heard her cry out his name.

He reacted immediately, thrusting open the door and striding into the kitchen, then coming to an abrupt halt when he saw her lying in the chair asleep. He felt as though all the air had been knocked out of his lungs, his chest tightening whilst he tried to draw in a ragged breath of air.

He had always loved watching her as she slept, absorbing the sight of her with a greedy secret pleasure— her long dark lashes, lying silkily against her delicate skin, her lips slightly parted, her face turned to one side so that the whole of one pretty ear was visible. The very fact that she was asleep made her so vulnerable, showed how much she trusted him, showed how much she was in need of his protection...

Without thinking Sean stepped forward, his hand lifting to push the heavy swathe of hair off her face, and then abruptly he realised that this was the present, not the past, and he stopped.

But it was too late. Somehow, as though she had sensed he was there, Kate cried out his name in great distress. For a second he hesitated, and then, taking a deep breath, he put his hand on her shoulder and gave her a small squeeze.

Immediately Kate woke up, and as she opened her eyes he demanded brusquely, 'Sean, what?'

Kate stared up at him. Her dream was still fogging her brain, and it took her several valuable seconds to wake up fully, incomprehension clouding her eyes.

'You were crying out my name,' Sean prompted softly.

Kate felt a prickle of awareness run over her. And then the reality of what she had been dreaming hit her. Her face started to burn. All at once there was a dangerous tension in the small room.

'I was dreaming, that's all,' she defended herself sharply.

'Do you often dream about me?'

The danger was increasing by the heartbeat.

She could feel her skin tightening in reaction to his taunt. 'It was more of a nightmare,' she retaliated quickly.

'You haven't remarried.' He said it flatly, like an accusation, in an abrupt change of tack.

Clumsily Kate got to her feet. Even standing up she was still a long way short of his height. She cursed the fact that she was not wearing her heels, and felt the old bitterness mobilising inside her

'Remarry? Do you really think I would want to risk marrying again after what you did to me?' she demanded hotly. 'No, I haven't remarried, and I never will.'

And there was also a very good reason why she wouldn't, but she had no intention of telling him so. It was her son. Her precious Ollie was not going to be given a stepfather who might not love him. Kate had firsthand knowledge of what that felt like, and she was not going to subject her son to the same misery she had known whilst she was growing up.

'Why did you change your name?'

So he still had that same skill at slipping in those dangerous questions like a knife between the ribs. She wanted to shiver, but she folded her arms instead, not wanting him to see her body's betrayal of her anxiety.

'Why shouldn't I? I certainly didn't want your name, and I didn't want my aunt and uncle's either, so I changed my name by deed poll to my mother's maiden name. What are you doing here anyway?' she demanded angrily. 'You have no right—'

'I've come round here because of this,' Sean said curtly, stopping her protests as he removed her letter of resignation from his jacket pocket, and with it another fat white envelope.

'This is your contract of employment,' he announced. 'It binds you to working a statutory notice period of four weeks. You can't just walk out on your job, Kate.'

Kate's mouth had gone dry, and she knew that her eyes were betraying her shock and her chagrin.

'You…you can't hold me to that,' she began valiantly. 'You—'

'Oh, yes, I can.' Sean stopped her swiftly. 'And I fully intend to do so.'

'But why?' Kate demanded wildly, stiffening as she heard in her own voice how close she was to the edge of her self-control. 'I should have thought you'd want me gone as much as I want to go, given the speed with which you ended our marriage! You can't want me working for you. Your ex-wife, the woman you rejected? The woman you—'

'Rules are rules—you are legally obliged to work your notice and I want you back at your desk so that you can hand over your responsibilities to your replacement.'

'You can't make me!' Kate protested. Her voice might sound strong and determined, but inside she was panicking, she recognised. She did, after all, have a legal obligation to work her notice period, and if she didn't it could cause other employers to think twice about taking her on. With Oliver to bring up she just could not afford to be out of work.

'Yes, I can,' Sean corrected her. 'You may have walked out on our marriage, but no way are you walking out of your job!'

Kate's shock deepened with every word he threw at her.

'I left because you were having an affair—you know that. You were the one who ended our marriage, Sean.'

'I'm not interested in discussing the past, only the present.'

His response left her floundering and vulnerable. It had been a mistake to refer to their marriage, and even more of a mistake to mention his affair. The last thing she wanted was to have him taunt her with still suffering because of it.

'I like value for my money, Kate. Surely you can remember that?'

His comment gave her a much needed opportunity to hit back at him, and she took it.

'I don't allow myself to remember anything about you.' The angry, contemptuous words were out before she could stop herself from saying them. She could feel the tightening of the tension between them, and with it came dangerous memories of a very different kind of tension they had once shared.

'Anything?' Sean challenged her rawly, as though he had somehow read her thoughts. 'Not even this?'

The feel of his hands on her arms, dragging her against his body, the heat of his flesh, the feel of his body itself against her own, was so shockingly and immediately familiar and welcome that she couldn't move.

Somehow, of its own volition, her body angled itself into Sean's. Somehow her hands were sliding beneath his jacket and up over his back. Somehow her head was tilting back and her eyes were opening wide, so that she could look into the familiar hot, passionate blue of his.

Shockingly, it was as though a part of her had been waiting for this, for him, and not just waiting but wanting, longing, needing.

The steady tick of the kitchen clock was drowned out by the sound of their mingled breathing: Sean's harsh and heavy; her own much lighter, shallow and unsteady.

The touch of his hand on the nape of her neck as his thumb slowly caressed her skin sent a signal to her body which it immediately answered.

Now she had to close her eyes, in case Sean could read in them what she could feel—the small, telling lift of her breasts as they surged in longing for his touch, the tight ache of her nipples as they hungered for his mouth, the swift clench of her belly and, lower than that, the softening swelling moistness of her sex.

She felt the hard warmth of his mouth and her own clung to it, her lips obediently parting to the fierce thrust of his tongue—a feeling she remembered so well.

Her fingers clenched into his shoulders beneath his suit jacket as the familiar possessive pressure of his kiss silenced the moan of pleasure bubbling in her throat.

When his hands dropped to her hips, and his fingers curled round the slenderness of her bones, Kate went weak with longing. Soon he would be touching her breasts, tugging fiercely at her clothes in his hunger to touch her intimately. And she wanted him to. She wanted him to so much.

Fine shudders of eager longing were already surging rhythmically through her. If she slid her hand down from his back she could touch the hard readiness of him, stroke her fingers along it, tormenting him, tormenting them both until he picked her up and—

'Mummy…?'

The sound of Oliver's voice from the other side of the back door jolted her back to reality.

Immediately Kate pulled back from Sean, and equally immediately he released her, so that when the door opened and Oliver came in, followed by Carol, they were standing three feet apart, ignoring one another.

'Ollie wanted to come home, so—' Carol came to a halt as she saw Sean, and looked uncertainly at Kate.

'Thanks, Carol.' Kate bent down to receive the full weight of Oliver's compact sturdy little-boy body as he ran towards her, only too glad of an excuse to conceal her face. Picking up Oliver, she avoided looking at both her neighbour and Sean.

'Er…I'll be off, then,' she heard Carol saying hurriedly as she backed out of the door.

Sean stared at the child in Kate's arms in shocked disbelief. She had a child—it was her child; he knew that. She had a child, which meant… Which meant that some other man must have…

Oliver was wriggling in her arms and demanding to be put down. Reluctantly Kate gave in and did so. The moment his feet touched the floor he turned to look at Sean, and Kate felt as though her heart was being clenched in a hard, hurting fist when he demanded, 'Who are you?'

'Ollie, it's bedtime,' she told him firmly, and without looking at Sean she added, 'I would like you to leave.'

'I meant what I said about working for me, Kathy,' Sean responded grimly.

'Don't call me Kathy!'

Too late Kate realised that Oliver was reacting to the anger in her voice. His eyes rounded and he put his hand in hers and stared at Sean. But her distress at upsetting him was nothing compared to the rage she felt when Sean told her curtly, 'You're upsetting the boy!'

To her shock, and before she could voice her fury, Sean bent down and picked Ollie up in his arms.

Kate waited for her son to struggle, as he always did when anyone unfamiliar touched him, but to her chagrin, instead of pulling away from Sean he leaned into him, looking at him gravely in silence before heaving a huge sigh and then saying determinedly, 'Story, please, man!'

Kate felt as though her heart was going to break. Her ex-husband was holding their son, and Oliver was looking at his father as though he were all of his heroes rolled into one. The pain knifing into her was unbearable. She wanted to snatch Oliver out of Sean's arms and hold him protectively in her own. Her poor baby didn't know that his father had rejected the very idea of him even before he was born!

'Oliver's friend's father reads him a story when he comes home from work,' she told Sean in a stilted voice, in explanation of her son's demand.

Oliver! She had even called the child by the name he had... And yet as he looked into the little boy's solemn eyes Sean found it impossible to resent or hate him.

'Story?' he enquired, smiling at him and ignoring Kate.

Oliver nodded his head enthusiastically. 'Mummy—book,' he commanded imperiously, turning his head to look at Kate.

'Please use proper sentences, Oliver,' Kate reminded him automatically.

'Mummy, give me book for man to read, please.' Oliver smiled winningly and Kate could feel her whole body melting with love.

'Sean has to go,' she informed Oliver, automatically using Sean's name without thinking. 'I will read you a story later.'

'No. Sean read Oliver story!'

The frowning pout he was giving reinforced Kate's awareness that her son was overtired, and all too likely to have one of his rare tantrums if he was thwarted— the very last thing she wanted him to do in front of Sean, who would no doubt enjoy seeing her in such an embarrassing situation.

'Why don't you just give me the book?'

The quiet voice and its soft tone made Kate turn her head and stare at Sean in surprise. Oliver was already lying against Sean's shoulder.

'It isn't really his bedtime yet,' she said.

'Is there a law which says he can only have a story at bedtime?'

Mutely Kate shook her head, too caught up in the heart-wrenching sight of her son in his father's arms to protest any further as she went to get Oliver's favourite story book.

Half an hour later Sean nestled Oliver deeper into his arms and told Kate, 'By the looks of him he needs to be in bed.'

'Yes. I'll take him up.'

Automatically she moved to take Oliver from him, but Sean shook his head.

'I'll take him up. Just tell me which room.'

Weakly, she did so.

As he laid Oliver down on his small bed Sean felt the ache of an old and powerful emotion he had thought safely destroyed. Kathy's child. He could feel his eyes starting to blur and he blinked fiercely.

As he left the room he hesitated outside the other bedroom door, and then quickly opened it.

'Where are you going? That's my bedroom!'

He hadn't heard Kate come up the stairs, and they confronted one another on the small landing.

'And you sleep there alone?' He couldn't stop himself from asking the question he knew he had no right to ask.

'No. I don't!' Kate turned her head, not wanting him

to see the expression in her eyes and therefore missing the one in his. 'Sometimes Oliver comes in and gets into bed with me,' she continued.

He had no valid reason to feel the way he did right now, Sean acknowledged, and no valid right either!

'How do you manage on your own? I know you work full-time.' He was frowning, looking as though he was genuinely concerned, and Kate turned away from him quickly and hurried towards the stairs. She wasn't going to make that mistake again—thinking that Sean had real feelings.

'I manage because I have to, for Oliver's sake. I'm all he's got—'

'You mean his father abandoned you?' His voice was harsh and almost condemning. 'He left you?'

Kate could hardly believe the censure she could hear in his voice. 'Yes, he did,' she agreed as calmly as she could, once they were both back downstairs. 'But personally I think that Ollie and I are better off without him.'

She walked purposefully to the front door and unlocked it, pulling it open and making it clear that she wanted Sean to leave.

'I want you back at your desk tomorrow morning,' Sean warned her curtly.

'Well, I'm afraid I'm not going to be there,' Kate responded, equally curtly.

'I warned you, Kate—' Sean began.

'Tomorrow is Saturday, Sean,' she reminded him dryly. 'We don't work weekends.'

There was a small, telling pause, during which Kate wondered what the woman who now shared his life thought about the fact that he obviously worked seven days a week, and then he said, 'Very well. Monday morning, then, Kate. Be there, or face the consequences.' He walked past her and out of the door.

CHAPTER THREE

'No!' ANGRILY Kate sat up in bed. It was three o'clock on Monday morning and she needed to be asleep, not lying there thinking about Sean, remembering how it had felt when he—

'No!' she protested again, groaning in anguish as she rolled over and buried her face in her pillow. But it was no use; neither her memories nor her feelings were going to be ignored.

Well, if she couldn't ignore them then at least she could use them to remind herself of how Sean had hurt her. To inoculate herself against him doing so again, because on Friday, when he had kissed her, she had nearly forgiven him...

She could feel the sharp quiver of sensation aching through her body. So her body remembered that Sean had been its lover, she acknowledged angrily—well, her heart had an equally good memory, if not an even better one, and what it remembered was the pain he had caused it.

But the love between them had been so...so wonderful. Sean had been a passionate and exciting lover who had taught her things about her own body, as well as his, and their mutual capacity for pleasure had been something she had never even dreamed could exist.

Why was she torturing herself like this? And if she was doing it then why didn't she do it properly and remember just what it had felt like that first time he had made love to her?

38

After she had left her aunt and uncle's house—she had never thought of it as home—she had moved into Sean's small flat, but he had told her that he was not going to make love to her properly until they were married. Through the weeks and months when he had courted her he had steadfastly refused to take their passionately intense love-play to the conclusion she ached for, warning her thrillingly—for her—that he was afraid that if he did so she would become pregnant.

'There's no way my baby is going to be born a bastard like I was,' he had said grimly.

He had been reluctant to talk to her about his childhood at first, but she had slowly coaxed the painful truth out of him, and they had shared with one another their dream of creating for their own children the idyllic, love-filled childhood neither of them had known.

'But we could use some contraception,' she had suggested, pink-cheeked.

'We could, but we aren't going to,' Sean had replied with that dangerously exciting hunger in his voice. 'Because when we make love, when you give yourself to me, Kathy, I want it to be skin to skin, not with a damn piece of rubber between us,' he had told her earthily.

They had married in the small country town where her own long-dead mother had originally come from—a wonderfully romantic gesture on Sean's part, so far as Kate had been concerned. And in order to marry there they had had to live in the town for three weeks prior to the wedding. The completion of some work project had given Sean enough money to rent a small house for them.

Three weeks was an eternity when you were as passionately in love and as hungry for one other as they had been then, Kate acknowledged. But Sean had made sure that they did wait. He had had that kind of discipline and determination even then.

They had spent their wedding night completely alone in the small rented house. And it had been so perfect that even thinking about it now she could feel her eyes filling with tears of emotion.

'Mummy.'

The voice interrupted her wayward thoughts. Immediately Kate got out of her bed and hurried into Oliver's room.

'What is it, darling?' she asked him lovingly.

'My tummy hurts,' he complained.

Kate tried not to sigh. Oliver was prone to upset tummies. Having checked that he was okay, she sat with him and soothed him, tensing when unexpectedly he asked her, 'Mummy, when's Sean going to come and see us again?'

This was the first time Oliver had mentioned Sean, and she had managed to convince herself that her son had completely forgotten about him.

'I don't know, Oliver.' That was all she could find to say. She felt unable to tell Oliver that he would probably never see Sean again, even though she knew she ought to do so. She had always tried to answer his questions honestly, but this time she could not, and the reason for that was the look of shining anticipation in her little boy's eyes.

By the time Oliver had gone back to sleep she was wide awake herself, her heart jumping uncomfortably inside her chest.

It couldn't be possible for Oliver to somehow sense that Sean was his father, could it? Her little boy couldn't have taken so uncharacteristically well to Sean because he felt some kind of special bond between them?

'It's a wise child that knows its own father,' Kate muttered grimly to herself, clinging to the old saying to protect her from her own wild imaginings.

Apprehensively, Kate parked her car and walked across the car park. The last person she wanted to see was Sean. Why had fate been so unkind as to bring him back into her life? She hated knowing that she was going to be working for him, but, as Carol had pointed out to her when she had told her what had happened, she could not afford to risk him carrying out his threat of pursuing her through the courts.

She nibbled anxiously on her bottom lip as she hurried into her office. Oliver had assured her that his tummy was better when he had woken up this morning, but she had still warned the nursery school teacher that he hadn't felt well during the night when she had dropped him off that morning.

'Kate!' Laura gave her a beaming smile as she came into the office and saw her. 'You've changed your mind and you're going to stay after all!'

'You could say that! Our new boss made me an offer I couldn't refuse,' Kate answered lightly, and then realised what she had done when she saw the curiosity in Laura's eyes.

'He did?' Laura sighed enviously. 'Don't you think he's just the most gorgeously, dangerously sexy-looking man you have ever seen?' she added dreamily.

'No, I do not!' Kate responded, fighting to ignore the sudden backflip performed by her heart.

'Well, if that's true you are the only female working here who doesn't,' Laura told her forthrightly. 'And when you think that he's single and unattached...'

Now her heart was turning somersaults. 'Says who?' she challenged her friend and colleague.

'John,' Laura informed her smugly. 'Apparently Sean told him himself.

Kate wondered what Laura would say if she were to tell her that, contrary to what Sean had told John, he had one very substantial attachment in the form of her son!

Sean was frowning as he ended his telephone conversation with his accountant. But it wasn't his business affairs that were causing him problems. He felt as though he was on an emotional see-saw—something more appropriate for a callow youth than a man of his own age. Moreover, a man who considered himself totally fireproof as far as his emotions and his control over them were concerned.

When he had ended his marriage to Kate he had closed himself off completely from everything that concerned or involved her. He had deliberately and clinically expunged everything about her from his life. From his life, maybe, but what about from his heart?

Nothing had changed, he reminded himself angrily. The same reasons why he had divorced her still existed today, and would continue to exist for ever. Sean knew that he could never alter them. Nor forget them!

Pushing back his chair with an unusually uncoordinated movement, he got up and strode to the office window.

Was that really true? And if it was then what the hell had he been doing this weekend? He did not normally spend his weekends in toy stores, did he? And he certainly did not spend them doing idiotic things like buying ridiculously expensive train sets.

Sean closed his eyes and pushed his hands into his pockets, balling his fists in angry tension.

Okay, so he hadn't deliberately set out to buy the train set. And he had had every excuse to be in the large department store as he had gone there in order to replace some household items. It had been mere coincidence that the toy department was on the same floor as the television set he had been looking at. He didn't really need to put himself through rigorous self-analysis just because he had bought a train set, did he? After all, he had only bought the damn thing because he had felt embarrassed not to do so when the sales assistant had mistakenly thought he was interested in it!

And then he had got rid of it at the first opportunity.

A gleam of reluctant amusement lit his eyes as he recalled the expression on the face of the young boy he had given his embarrassing purchase to. His tired-looking mother had protested at first, but Sean had insisted. He just hoped she didn't think he had had any kind of ulterior motive for doing what he had done. Not that she wouldn't have been right to be suspicious of his motives—they certainly would not withstand too much scrutiny! Dwelling on the past and buying toys just because... Just because what? Just because the warm weight of Kate's son in his arms had reactivated memories from a time in his life that...

A time in his life that was over, Sean tried to remind himself. But the stark truth was already confronting him, even if he did not want to recognise or acknowledge it.

'Fancy going to the pub for lunch?'

Kate shook her head without lifting her gaze from her computer screen. 'Can't, I'm afraid, Laura,' she responded. 'I want to get this finished, and anyway I've brought sandwiches.'

Lunch at the pub with her co-workers would have been fun and relaxing, but as a single parent Kate was always conscious of having to watch her budget.

After Laura had gone, Kate got up and collected her sandwiches. The company provided a small restroom, equipped with tea- and coffee-making facilities and a microwave, for the workforce to use during their lunch and tea breaks. She had just reached the end of the corridor and had started to descend the narrow flight of stairs when suddenly Sean came out of one of the lower level offices and started to hurry up the stairs towards her.

To Kate's dismay her reaction was immediate and intense, and unfortunately a relic from the days when they had been a couple. So much so, in fact, that she had taken the first of the few steps that would put her right in his path before she could stop herself.

Immediately she realised what she was doing and froze in pink-cheeked humiliation as a visual memory came vividly alive inside her head. A memory of Sean rushing up the stairs of their small house to grab her in his arms and swing her round in excitement before sliding her down the length of his body and beginning to kiss her with fierce sexual hunger.

Later they had gone on to celebrate the news he had brought her—that he had secured a new and lucrative contract—in bed, with the champagne he had brought home…

Red-faced, she pulled her thoughts back under control,

'Kathy!' Sean demanded grimly as he saw her shocked expression. 'What the hell's…? What's wrong?'

Alarmed, Kate tried to move away, but Sean stopped her, curling his fingers round her bare arm.

'It's not Kathy any more,' she reminded him sharply. 'It's Kate! And as for what's wrong—do you really need to ask me that?'

She might be Kate now, but Kathy was still there inside her, Kate was forced to acknowledge. Because in direct contradiction of her angry words her body responded to Sean's touch. Was it because no one had touched her since he had ended their marriage that her caress-starved flesh was quivering with such intense and voluptuous pleasure? Was it because it was Sean who was touching her? Or was it simply that when he had kissed her he had unleashed memories her body could not ignore? Kate wondered frantically.

Was it a past need her flesh was responding to, or was it a present one? She knew what she wanted the answer to be! But somehow she couldn't stop herself from stepping closer to him, exhaling on an unsteady sigh of pleasure. Sean was looking at her and she was looking back at him, with the mesmeric intensity of his blue gaze dizzying her.

She could feel his thumb caressing the inner curve of her elbow, just where he knew how vulnerable and responsive her flesh was to his touch—so vulnerable and responsive that when he had used to kiss her there her whole body had melted with wanton longing.

It would be so easy, so natural, to walk into his arms now and feel them close protectively around her. To look into his eyes and wait for the familiar look of hot eagerness darken them, whilst his mouth curled into that special smile he had...

A door opened noisily, bringing her back to reality. Abruptly she stepped back from Sean, her face burning.

Maybe years ago she had not needed to hide her feelings from him—her lover, her husband, her best friend—nor her longing and sexual excitement when he looked at her and touched her. But things were different now, Kate reminded herself as she pulled away from him.

'What's that?' she heard him demanding as he released her and frowned at the box she was carrying.

'My lunch.'

'Lunch? In that?' he derided grimly as he looked at the small plastic container. 'I should have thought for your son's sake you would want to make sure you ate properly.'

As she listened to his ill-informed and critical words, her passionate response to him a few minutes earlier was swamped by outrage and anger.

'For your information—not that you have any right to question anything I choose to do any more, Sean—it just so happens that it is for Ollie's sake that this is my lunch,' she told him, waving the plastic container defiantly. 'It costs money to bring up a child—not that you'd know or care anything about that, since you chose not to burden yourself with children,' she added sarcastically. 'And a packed lunch is a lot less expensive than going out to the pub. What's wrong, Sean?' she demanded when she saw his fixed expression. 'Or can I guess? You might come across to everyone else here as a caring, sharing employer, but I know different. And I also know, before you remind me, that you are rich enough to eat in the world's most expensive restaurants these days. But there was a time when even a sandwich was a luxury for you.'

As she saw his face tighten with anger Kate wondered if she had gone too far, but she wasn't going to back down, and she hoped that the determined tilt of her chin told him so.

'I imagine that your child has a father,' Sean said coldly. 'Why isn't he providing for his upbringing?'

Kate looked at him in silence for a few seconds, bitterly aware of how much he was hurting her and how little he cared, and then told him evenly, 'Oliver's father isn't providing for him financially—or in any other way—because he didn't want him.'

Unable to risk saying anything more without her fragile control being destroyed, Kate stepped past him and hurried down the stairs.

Sean watched her go. Packed lunches, a too-thin body, tension and worry that showed in her eyes. Even if she thought she had it well hidden, her life now was a world away from the luxuries he could have surrounded her with.

Had she thought of him at all when she was with the man who had fathered her son?

Grimly Sean shut down his thoughts, all too aware of not just how inappropriate they were but also how extremely dangerous.

All through her lunch hour, and the two hours following it, Kate couldn't concentrate on anything other than Sean. Her heart was racing at twice its normal rate and she was so on edge that her muscles were aching with the tension she was imposing on them. And the situation could only get worse. She knew that.

Only the knowledge that she had had to protect the life of the baby growing inside her had given her the strength to get through the pain-filled months after Sean had ended their marriage. What was more, she'd had to make the best of it for Oliver's sake. Her love was going to be the only parental love he was going to have.

She had discovered she was pregnant two months after Sean had announced that he wanted a divorce and walked out on her. She had fainted in a store, exhausted by the brutality of her grief.

Until then she hadn't cared if she lived or died. No, that was not true. Given the choice, she would have preferred death. She hadn't been able to imagine how she could go on living without Sean, whose callous words—'You'll soon get over me and meet someone else and start producing those bloody babies you want so much.'—had cut her to the heart. The only man whose babies she had wanted was his. But he no longer loved her. The house they had shared was empty and she'd been living—existing—in rented accommodation, fiercely refusing to take any money from Sean. She had had no idea where he was living. And then she had found out that she was having his child. The child he had told her he did not want!

It was in that knowledge that she had made her decision not to let Sean know she was pregnant. He had rejected her and the pain had almost destroyed her. She wasn't going to inflict that kind of pain on her baby.

She had promised herself that she would find a way to stop loving Sean, and when Oliver had been born she had thought that she had. Until now.

She had to get away from Sean. She had believed that she had stopped loving him, but now she was desperately afraid that she had been wrong. A pain that was not all pure pain, but part helpless longing was unfurling slowly inside her. No matter what Sean might threaten to do she had to leave here, and she was going to tell him so…right now!

Agitatedly she got up and hurried to her office door, dragging it open and hurrying towards the office which had once been John's and which Sean was now using whilst he familiarised himself with the day-to-day running of the business.

There was no one in the outer office, and, too wrought-up for formalities, Kate rushed into the inner office, only to stare around it in dismay when she saw that it was empty.

Or at least she had thought it was empty. The door to a small private room which contained a changing room and shower facilities was half open, and she could hear someone moving about inside it. Someone? It could only be Sean.

Taking a deep breath, Kate walked purposefully towards it and then hesitated, her hand on the door handle. A part of her wasn't ready for another confrontation, but another part of her just wanted to get the whole thing over and done with.

Clearing her throat nervously, she took a deep breath and called out, 'Sean—are you in there? Only, there's something I need to speak to you about...'

In the empty silence that followed Kate began to lose her courage. Perhaps she had been wrong. Perhaps Sean wasn't even here...

She started to turn away, stiffening with shock when the door was wrenched back and Sean was standing there naked, apart from the water running over his skin and the towel he was still wrapping around his hips.

For half a dozen seconds she couldn't move, couldn't speak, couldn't do anything other than stare at him whilst her eyes widened and her face burned.

'Oh. You were having a shower!' Was that really her voice—that soft, breathy, almost awed thread of sound?

'I *was*,' Sean agreed dryly, emphasising the past tense of his statement.

As she fought down the aching feeling that was spreading through her body Kate seized on anger as her main weapon of defence, telling herself fiercely that Sean should have done more to cover his nudity than simply drape—well, not even drape, really, simply hold, Kate decided, before hurriedly dragging her traitorous gaze away—the smallest of towels around his hips.

It was whilst she was doing battle with her suddenly rebellious sense of sight—and coming close to losing—that she heard Sean saying laconically, 'You'd better come in—and close the door.'

What?

She was just about to object, and in very strong terms, when he added dulcetly, 'That is unless you want to risk someone else coming into the office and finding you here with me like this.'

Kate knew there must be a hundred objections she could raise to what he was saying, but as she fought to find one of them Sean reached behind her and quietly closed the door. Closed it and locked it.

'Why…why have you locked the door?' Kate demanded, ashamed to hear the betraying quaver of anxiety in her voice.

'Because I don't want anyone else wandering in here,' he told her dryly. 'Why did you think I'd locked it? Or were you remembering…?'

'I wasn't remembering anything.' Kate stopped him in panic. 'I just wanted—'

He had moved slightly away from her and inadvertently she glanced at him, her gaze held in helpless thrall by the sight of his virtually naked body.

He had already been a fully adult male when they had

met, and she had been thrilled at her first sight of his
naked body, her gaze openly eager and hungry to see
every single bit of him. She had thought then that it
would be impossible for him to be more physically perfect—from the silken strength of his throat and neck to
the powerful width of his shoulders, to the arms which
had held her so close, the hands that had taken her to
places of unimaginable pleasure, the chest so magnifi-
cently broad, tapering down to his belly, flat and tautly
muscled, with its fascinatingly sensual line of male hair
that her fingers had ached to explore.

But she had been wrong! Or had time just done her
the favour of allowing her to forget the sexually erotic
and perfect maleness of him, her own awareness of it
and of him, to save her pain?

An ache at once both familiar and bewildering started
to spread out from the pit of her stomach, overpowering
her attempt to tense her body against it. A longing that
tore at her emotions and her self-control grew with it.

Just above where the towel was knotted she could see
the small white scar she remembered so well. The scar
was the result of an accident he had had when he had
first started working as a labourer, as a boy of fifteen
who should have been at school. When he had told her
how he had suffered with the pain of his wound, rather
than risk being ridiculed by the other men on the gang
and also lose a day's pay, she had wept and pressed her
lips to the scar whilst Sean had buried his hands in her
hair.

And then he had…

As she recognised the erotic path her thoughts were
taking, and that it was not so much a memory from the
past that was arousing her but a shocking need to ex-

perience it in the present, Kate started to panic. She had to get out of here, and now!

Quickly she turned towards the door.

'Kate!'

Caught off-guard by her sudden agitated movement, Sean reached out to stop her. The wrist within his grip felt far more fragile than he remembered. It angered him that she should have so little care for her own wellbeing, and it angered him even more that the man whose child she had conceived had hurt her and left her. The thought of anyone hurting her made him want to hold her and protect her.

Before he could stop himself Sean pulled her into his arms, ignoring her demands to be set free as he burrowed his hand into her hair, unwittingly bringing to life at least a part of Kate's own sensual memory.

'I'm glad you haven't cut your hair.'

The thick, raw words shocked Kate into stillness. She could feel the heat of Sean's hand against the back of her head. And against the front of her body she could feel the heat of…him.

Overwhelmed by her own feelings, she made a sound somewhere between a sigh and a moan, and as though it was the signal he had been waiting for suddenly Sean was kissing her, possessing her mouth with a fierce, driving need and a hunger that her own body instinctively recognised.

There was no past, no pain, only the here and now—and Sean.

His free hand was cupping her face, his fingers caressing her skin, sliding down her throat and then tracing her collarbone.

Hungrily Kate pressed herself closer to him, her fingers automatically seeking the unwanted barrier between them and tugging away the towel. Her actions were those of the woman she had been and not the woman she now was. That woman had had every right to lay claim to the intimacy of Sean's body, to touch it and caress it however and wherever she wished, just as Sean had had every right to do the same with hers. Those rights had been bestowed on one another with love and strengthened by marriage vows.

And though Kate tried to remind herself that they no longer shared those rights, her senses were refusing to listen. They were too drugged by pleasure.

Sean groaned as he felt Kate's eager touch against his naked flesh. It had been so long! Too long for his damned self-control, he acknowledged, as his mouth found the tender hollow at the base of her throat and he buried the sound of his need there, registering the pulse that had begun to beat frantically in response.

Unable to stop himself, Sean allowed his hands to dispose of the layers of clothing denying him access to Kate's body.

Was it Sean who was shaking with pleasure as his hands cupped her naked breasts or was it her? Kate wondered achingly. She could feel the urgent peaking of her nipples and she knew that Sean must be able to feel it as well. When he rolled the tight, aching flesh between his thumb and finger the ferocity of the pleasure that shuddered through her made Kate press herself pleadingly into Sean and grind her hips against him.

'You know what happens when you do that, don't you?' Sean groaned thickly.

In response, Kate took hold of his hand and guided it down her body.

'Two can play at that game,' Sean warned her, but

Kate didn't resist when he placed her hand against the hard, hot flesh of his erection.

She hadn't touched a man in all the years they had been apart. She hadn't so much as wanted to touch a man, never mind even think about it, and yet immediately and instinctively her fingers stroked lovingly over him in silent female acknowledgement of his potency before slowly caressing him.

'Kate…Kate.'

The anguished, tormented sound of her name only added to her arousal, and she stroked him again, moving her fingertips swiftly around the swollen head and down the underside of the thick shaft. The ache deep inside her mirrored the rhythmic movement of her fingers over him.

This was heaven—and it was hell. It was everything he had ever wanted and everything he could never have, Sean recognised as he submitted helplessly to Kate's power over him. But he was too much of an alpha male to allow Kate to take the lead for very long. Hungrily he pulled her into his arms and started to kiss her with fierce, possessive passion.

She wanted him so much, so very much. Eagerly, Kate clung to Sean, waiting…wanting… And then abruptly they both tensed as a phone rang shrilly in the outer room.

Mortified by what she had done, Kate straightened her clothes and fled, ignoring Sean's command to her to stay where she was.

CHAPTER FOUR

'AND now there's this wretched virus going round...'

Kate pressed a hand to her temple, trying to ease the pounding of her headache and concentrate on what Carol was saying to her.

'It's a really nasty one!' Carol was continuing. 'I've been wondering whether or not I should keep George away from nursery for the time being.'

Through the pounding of her headache Kate tried not to feel envious of her friend for having the luxury of being able to make such a decision. Without childcare she could not work, and if she didn't work how were she and Oliver to live?

After Carol had gone, Kate looked a little worriedly at Oliver. Although he had been playing happily enough with George, he was somehow more subdued than usual.

'Have you still got that pain in your tummy, darling?' Kate asked him anxiously, but Oliver shocked her into silence.

'Will Sean come again?' he asked her.

There was a huge hard lump in Kate's throat, and a pain in her heart like none she had ever known. She wanted to take hold of her son and hold him tightly in her arms, so that no one and nothing could ever, ever hurt him. But there was no point in trying to hide the truth from herself any longer. This afternoon in Sean's arms she had known that she still loved him.

And it was that knowledge that had made her run away from him. He didn't love her any more. He had told her that five years ago. And once it had died love could never be resurrected, surely?

'No, Oliver. He won't be coming again,' she told him gently, her chest locking tightly as Oliver pouted.

'But I want him to,' he said truculently.

Kate could feel her self-control being ripped to pieces by her pain. As she stroked his hair Oliver looked back accusingly at her, and then to Kate's horror asked her the question she had dreaded.

'Why haven't I got a daddy, like George?'

Anguish and despair washed icily through her. How could she tell him that he did have, but that his father hadn't wanted him? He was too young to understand the truth, but she couldn't bring herself to lie to him.

'Not all daddies and mummies live together like George's mummy and daddy do,' she explained gently, watching as he silently digested her words.

'So where does my daddy live, then?'

It was the pounding in her head that was making her feel so sick, Kate tried to reassure herself. But the knowledge that one day Oliver would not be so easily sidetracked felt like a heavy weight dragging down her heart. 'It's bedtime, Oliver. What story would you like me to read tonight?'

For a moment she thought he was going to refuse to be sidetracked and then repeat his question, but to her relief he didn't.

Sean stared bleakly out of the window of the luxurious penthouse apartment he was renting whilst he assessed the future of his new acquisition. On the rare occasions when he had allowed himself to think about Kate ever since their divorce, he had visualised her living in contented rural bliss, with a doting husband and the houseful of children he had known she wanted to have. The reality of her life had shocked him. Yes, she had fulfilled her longing for motherhood—but where was the man who should be there with her, loving her and supporting her?

Sean hadn't forgotten the life he had had before he had become wealthy—how could he?—and he knew her current life must be a hard financial struggle for Kate.

Why the hell hadn't she made at least some kind of financial claim on the bastard who had deserted them both? In Sean's opinion any man who fathered a child should contribute financially to its upbringing. Sean thought of his own childhood—he knew how hard a child's life could be when growing up in poverty. Not that Oliver was growing up in poverty, but it was obvious that his mother was having to struggle to support him.

Angrily Sean pushed his hand into his hair. When he had met Kate—Kathy, as she had been then—he had been an uneducated, anti-social young man with a very large chip on his shoulder. Kathy hadn't only given him her love, she had given him a lot more as well. She had helped and encouraged him in every way she could, and it was because of her faith in him, her love for him, that he was the man he was today.

If only he could acknowledge that debt to her.

He turned away from the window. The penthouse looked like something out of an expensive magazine, and it was definitely not child-friendly. Not like the rectory he had once promised Kate he would buy for her.

Sean closed his eyes and took a deep breath. Had she loved the man who had fathered Oliver? And who the hell was he anyway?

His car keys were on the immaculate kitchen worktop.

It would take him less than half an hour to drive to Kate's cottage.

Sean had made up his mind what he was going to do. He was going to insist that she give him the name of Oliver's father and then he was going to make sure that the man was made aware of his responsibilities to both his son and his son's mother, and that he fulfilled them.

Oliver was in bed and asleep, and her headache had finally dulled. The washing she had hung out to dry this morning before leaving for work was dry and ready to iron, filling the kitchen with its clean fresh-air smell.

Kate liked to do as many of her chores as possible in the evenings, when Oliver was asleep, so that she could keep her weekends free to be with him. The village possessed a small shop, and it was part of their weekend ritual to walk there every weekend to collect the papers and chat with their fellow villagers.

Kate was determined to do everything she could to provide Oliver with a sense of community and belonging, even if she wasn't able provide him with his father.

A shadow darkened the kitchen window, causing her look up from her ironing. She froze when she realised that the shadow belonged to Sean.

A tiny shudder ran through her, the hairs lifting on her skin as she fought against an illogical fear that somehow her own thoughts were responsible for his presence.

Her thoughts or Oliver's need?

She must not think like that, she told herself firmly as she unplugged the iron and then hurried to open the door before he could knock. She didn't want him waking Oliver.

What had he come for? To tell her that he had changed his mind and that he didn't want her working for him after all? Irrationally, instead of bringing her pleasure, that thought only brought her more pain. Pain and a fear that her response to him earlier might have caused him to recognise, as she had, that she still loved him.

Whatever else he was, Sean was certainly not the kind of man whose vanity was so great that he would enjoy knowing a woman loved him when he could not and did not love her back. Judging from his determination to remove her from his life, he would be equally as brutal now as he'd been when he had divorced her.

As Sean strode into the kitchen she just about had time to reflect on how ironic it was that now she was fearing him sacking her when it wasn't long since she'd been determined to hand in her resignation from the company.

'Sean. What are you doing here? What do you want?' Kate demanded, but as she spoke she was achingly aware that what she wanted was for him to take her in his arms and then...

Already a familiar and dangerous weakness was slipping through her veins. He was standing far too close to her—close enough for her to see that he had shaved, and that there was the smallest of nicks on his throat.

Out of the past she could see herself standing opposite him on the sunny street where he had been working. He had been teasing her and she had tried to tease him back, commenting naïvely on his unshaven face. He had looked at her and then he had responded with deliberate sensuality to her comment, telling her that he preferred to shave before he went to bed. 'So I won't scratch your skin,' he had added, watching the bright colour burn her face as the meaning of his words sank in.

A sense of desolation and loss rolled over her.

'Who is Oliver's father, Kate?'

The way Sean was looking at her made Kate's heart turn over inside her chest.

What?

Weakly Kate clung to the edge of her kitchen table as she battled with her shock, wondering wildly how on earth—and, more importantly, *what* on earth she could answer. And then suddenly she knew there was only one way, and that was to tell him the truth.

Before she could lose her courage and change her mind, she took a deep breath and answered him quietly, 'You are, Sean.'

In the silence his face lost its entire colour, and then it burned with a dark tide that swept slowly over his skin until his cheekbones glowed with its heat.

'No.' He denied her words explosively.

His denial ricocheted around the room, burst apart and then bounded back off the walls at her like a deadly missile. Kate's hopes died under its onslaught.

'No!' Sean was repeating savagely, shaking his head. 'No! You're lying to me, Kate. I know I hurt you when I ended our marriage, and I can easily understand why you would have turned to someone else, but no way do I accept that I am Oliver's father.'

Someone else? Kate could taste the acid bitterness of her own anger as she listened to Sean rejecting his son. Beneath her anger, though, lay the bleakness of her own pain. What had she been expecting? Or could she answer her own question more easily if she asked herself what she had been hoping for?

She'd wanted Sean to take her in his arms and tell her that he had made a mistake, that he still loved her. That in fact he loved her all the more because she had given him a son.

'Yes, you did hurt me then, Sean,' she agreed evenly. 'But believe me that cruelty was nothing compared with what you've just done. You can hurt me as much as you like, but I will never, ever let you hurt Oliver.'

As she forced herself to look into his eyes, her own emotion, her own pain was pushed to one side by the strength of her maternal need to protect her child. For Oliver she would sacrifice anything and everything, and if necessary even herself. She could not ignore or deny the fact that her love for Sean had never really died, but for Oliver's sake she would control and banish that love. And somehow she would learn to live with the pain of having to do so.

Everything about Sean's reaction to her information that he was Oliver's father confirmed the wisdom of her decision not to tell him originally that she had conceived his child. But at the same time everything about it tore at her heart until she could scarcely endure the pain.

But it was her anger and contempt on behalf of her son that was glittering in her eyes now, motivating the scathing tone of her voice as she told him, 'That's right, Sean. Reject Oliver just like you rejected me. But that won't alter the fact that he is your son.'

It gave her a sense of almost anguished satisfaction, along with a feeling as if someone was turning a knife over inside her heart, to see the effect his efforts to rein in his temper were having on him. His face once more leached of colour, leaving it looking bone-white.

'He can't be mine,' he insisted harshly.

'Can't be? Why not? Because you were sleeping with the woman you left me for when he was conceived? What happened to her, by the way, Sean? Did you get

bored with her, just like you did with me?' Too wrought
up to wait for his reply, she threw at him furiously, 'You
can deny it all you like, but it won't alter the truth. He
is your child.'

Kate shook her head angrily. 'Don't you think I wish
that he wasn't?' she demanded passionately when he
didn't respond. 'Don't you think I wish that he had been
fathered in love, with love, by a man who loved me? By
a man who loved him? A man who wanted to share our
lives and be there for both of us? You'll never know
how much I wanted those things, Sean—for Oliver and
for myself. But unlike you I've faced up to the truth.'

She was shaking from head to foot, Kate recognised,
and she was humiliatingly close to tears.

For a minute Sean was too shocked by Kate's angry
and contemptuous outburst to make any response. And
then for a minute more he discovered that he actually
wanted to be able to believe her. She was certainly doing
a good job of believing herself, he recognised cynically.
But all the cynicism in the world could not wipe away
the strength of his immediate response to her emotional
outburst. Pain, anger and unbelievably longing tore at
him in equal proportions.

What had happened to the self-control he had been so
proud of? And what had happened to the honesty that
had been such a strong part of Kate's personality?
Obviously it was something else for him to mourn, along
with his other losses. It took him far too long to suppress
his instinctive urge to go to her and take hold of her,
but eventually he managed to do so, instead telling her
brutally, 'You're wasting your breath. There's no point
in any of this. Oliver is not my child.' He hesitated,
deliberately turning away from Kate so that she would

not see his expression. 'And nothing you can say will ever make me acknowledge him as such.'

Kate stared at him, angry colour burning her skin, her mouth compressing, but before she could say anything, Sean demanded harshly, 'For God's sake, Kate, don't make it even worse than it has to be. I can just accept that you gave yourself to someone else after our marriage was over. I can even accept that if you gave yourself to someone else as an act of retribution against me, and that I deserved such an action, but I damn well can't accept that you slept with someone else whilst we were still together.'

'You mean like you did?' Kate shot at him bitingly. 'What happened to her, Sean?'

'She isn't in my life any more. It was just a short-lived fling.'

He sounded more irritated than concerned, and his response added further fuel to Kate's anger.

'Clever her! She must have realised that ultimately you'd probably betray her, just like you did me.'

Sean gave her a bitter look. 'When it comes to betrayal, you outclass me, Kate. You've committed the worst betrayal of all in trying to pretend that another man's child is mine!'

Kate's face burned with anger. 'I would never stoop to that kind of deceit,' she stormed furiously. 'I can't bear to think of what you've done—not just to me but more importantly to Oliver! You've denied your child the right to know his father and—'

Angrily Sean reached out and took hold of her wrist. 'Oliver is not my child!'

The harsh words echoed round the small kitchen, causing Kate to try and pull away. 'I hate you, Sean,' she told him passionately. 'You don't know how much

I wish I'd never met you, how much I hate myself for letting you—'

'Letting me what?' Sean stopped her.

Kate could feel the hard bite of his fingers in the soft flesh of her upper arms as he dragged her body against the hard tense length of him.

'Letting me make you feel like this?'

His mouth possessed hers, its pressure bending her head back and making her arch her spine. Anger and pride mingled turbulently inside her as longing streaked scarlet trails of danger through her veins. She could feel the fierce judder of reaction galvanise Sean's body, and somehow, shockingly, immediately and against all logic, she was swept back to another time and another kiss.

A time when they had virtually only just met, and a kiss had been taken fiercely from her in the concealing darkness when Sean had walked her home from their first real date.

Then her body had thrilled with shocked and excited pleasure at its recognition of his predatory male passion. She had been young; naïve, but oh, so very, very passionately in love with Sean, and so very eager and aroused.

Now she was...

But where did then end and now begin? Kate wondered with dizzy fatality as the years rolled back and her body, her senses, her emotions were those of that young girl again.

Kate heard the small whimper escaping her lips. Instantly the hot, hard pressure of Sean's mouth caught and answered it. His hands moved from her arms to her back, no longer constraining her but caressing her, as though something in that sound she had made had been a plea and not a protest.

She trembled as his hands cinched her waist, his

thumbs caressing its narrow curve, before sliding lower to cup the rounded flesh of her behind and then urge her even more closely against his own body, holding her tight and hard against the obvious thrust of his erection. Automatically and instinctively Kate tilted her hips hungrily against him and moaned his name.

As she sobbed her arousal and need against his lips Kate felt his hand move to her breast.

She was lost to time and place, to everything but Sean and her need for him. A sound, a high, hot, female-hungry-for-her-mate sound of raw sexual hunger slit the thickness of air, which was filled with the raggedness of breath exhaled in mutual passion.

And Sean responded to it as though a door had swung open, admitting him to a lost and long-sought magic kingdom.

Kate trembled as the hand he had raised to her breast began to stroke and then massage it with familiar intimacy, arousing an equally familiar sensation which spread from his touch through her stomach to the soft warmth within her. A soft warmth that was rapidly turning into a tight, wet, aching heat.

Unable to stop herself from answering the clamouring need, Kate arched her whole body against his touch, moaning into his mouth as his hand cupped her breast and his thumb and finger started to pluck sensually at the hard peak of her nipple.

In a heartbeat of brief lucidity Kate was shockingly aware that just the feel of his erection straining against her was as erotically arousing as if she had still been a virginal teenager. But then Sean groaned, tugging fiercely at her top, and she watched him tense as the pale, soft nakedness of her breast, with the ripe swollen peak of her nipple, was revealed to his sight and his touch. Her lucidity became a thing of the past, to be overwhelmed, overturned by the flash-flood of her own response.

Would Sean remember how much she had liked to feel him stroke the hard flesh of her aroused nipples with his fingertip? How it had made her call out to him in shocked, excited arousal? Would he remember the way he had driven her beyond the boundaries of her self-control with the slow touch of his mouth?

She quivered as she felt his hand on her naked breast—waiting, yearning, needing.

'Kathy...'

The raw sound of her name seemed to have been dredged up from somewhere deep and hidden inside Sean, and Kate tensed immediately in response to it.

Kathy! But she wasn't Kathy any more. She was Kate. She was Kate—and Sean wasn't the man who loved her, he was the man who had betrayed her! The man who refused to accept that he had fathered her child. Sickness rolled through her. How could she feel the way she had, behave the way she had, when she knew...?

She froze as the kitchen door was pushed open and she saw Oliver standing staring at them.

CHAPTER FIVE

SEAN'S reaction had been quicker than hers, and to her shock Kate realised that she was looking at her son from behind Sean's sheltering body. Hot-faced with shock and guilt, she straightened her clothes and moved to go to Oliver, but he was oblivious to her, instead heading straight for Sean.

Frantically Kate tried to stop him, unable to bear the rejection her little boy was going to suffer, but to her disbelief Sean stepped past her, scooping Oliver up as her son held out his arms to him.

Holding Kate's child in his arms, Sean felt a pain like none other he had ever experienced—not even when his mother had left him, not even when he had heard that he could not father a child himself, not even when he had locked Kate out of his life, he acknowledged as he fought down his own anguish and torment.

The small head tilted back and solemn eyes looked into his. Sean felt as though someone had slid a knife into his ribs poisoned with longing, jealousy and despair. Longing for Oliver to be his; jealousy because Kate had given herself to another man; despair because of the situation he was now in.

Abruptly he thrust Oliver into Kate's waiting arms and turned towards the back door.

As he reached it he stopped and turned round, shadows cloaking the pain in his eyes as he demanded, 'When was he born?'

Kate tightened her arms around Oliver, who had already fallen back to sleep, in the way that small children could in just a few seconds, and she told him the date.

After the smallest of pauses, Sean grated, 'So he was conceived two weeks after we separated, then?'

The air in the kitchen felt so heavy and sour with the weight of their combined emotions that Kate felt as though it might choke her.

'He was two weeks overdue.' She answered Sean's unspoken accusation despairingly. Shaking her head, she added huskily, 'They wanted to induce me but I asked them to wait. I...I wanted him to be born naturally.'

Kate closed her eyes and turned away, not wanting to be reminded that she had held out until the last possible minute, clinging desperately and stubbornly to her hope that there would be a miracle and that somehow Sean would be there with her to witness the birth of their child.

But he hadn't been, and in the end there had been no one other than the hospital staff to share her awed and exhausted delight at the birth of her son.

She came out of her reverie to hear the back door closing. Sean had left. But he had already left her life and Oliver's a long time ago, she reminded herself.

Somehow that reminder wasn't as comforting as it should have been. Her pain was too sharp and strong to be so easily soothed.

She could, of course, have challenged Sean to let her prove that Oliver was his son by demanding a DNA test. Kate dropped her cheek onto Oliver's soft springy curls. But proving that Sean was Oliver's father would mean nothing if Sean refused to be that father. No way was she going to expose Oliver to that kind of pain—not even to prove to Sean that she had not, as he had accused, shared her body with another man as he had shared his with another woman!

The pain hadn't changed at all. It was still as strong as it had always been. Where was her pride? Why wasn't it rescuing her from her own vulnerability by reminding her of what Sean had done? How dared he make accusations regarding her when he had told her openly that he had taken another woman to bed?

Oliver was still asleep in her arms, which meant that she did not have to hold back any longer the slow, painful tears burning the back of her eyes. It hadn't just been her that Sean had betrayed, he had betrayed Oliver as well!

Sean grimaced as he accidentally nicked his skin, and put down his razor. 'It's your own damned fault,' he muttered to his reflection as he stanched the small wound. But it wasn't the cut he was talking about, and it wasn't his own face he could see in the mirror—it was Oliver's.

Cursing, he tried to banish his thoughts—but it was too late.

He had seen in Kate's eyes just how she felt about his refusal to accept that Oliver was his child. But no matter how much she had managed to persuade herself that Oliver was his, Sean knew that he could not be.

And he knew for a very good reason.

He closed his eyes and swallowed against the sick taste of his own self-loathing and humiliation.

That reason was that it was medically impossible for him to father a child.

He hadn't known that when he had married Kate, of course. If he had done then he would never have married her, knowing how important having children was to her.

He thought back to the medical appointment which had been responsible for the destruction of his marriage and his life.

'There is one thing I do have to mention,' the doctor had begun. 'One of the tests we ran was a sperm count. I'm afraid I have to tell you that it's highly unlikely you will be able to father a child.'

Even now he still had bad dreams about those words and that meeting with his doctor at which the announcement had been made.

He hadn't been able to take it in at first. How could it not be possible for him to father a child? He was a fit, healthy man in the prime of life. He had protested that the doctor must be wrong, that there must be some mistake, and all the time he had been aware of the humiliating pity in the other man's eyes as he shook his head. The doctor might be twenty years his senior, small, balding, and with a paunch, but suddenly he had become the one who was the virile potent male whilst Sean had been reduced to a mere pathetic apology for a man, at least in his own eyes.

Real men, in the culture of the rough, fight-to-survive world in which Sean had grown up, were not unable to father children.

Inside his head Sean had heard a brief snatch of stored conversation, between his mother and one her friends. They had been talking about a man they both knew, and Sean could remember the mockery in his mother's laughter as she had told her friend, 'He's a poor thing, by all accounts. Hasn't fathered a child yet, nor likely to, and in my book that means he isn't a man at all.'

Not a man at all—just like him.

Another memory surfaced.

'Oh, Sean, I just can't wait for us to have children.'

Now it was Kate's voice haunting him, and he swore savagely beneath his breath.

'I'd hate to have the kind of marriage that didn't include a family, like my aunt and uncle's.'

He could still see the way she had shuddered, as though in revulsion.

'Don't worry, I'll give you as many as you want,' he had boasted, already aroused at the thought of how he would give her the children they both wanted so much.

And each and every time he had made love with her that feeling had been there, that surge of atavistic male pride in the knowledge that he had the power to create a new life within her.

Only he had not had that power. Not according to what his doctor had told him.

It hadn't been just his present and his future the doctor's words had destroyed; it had been his own belief and pride in himself as well. Suddenly he was not the man he had always thought himself to be. Suddenly he was not, in his own opinion, very much of a man at all.

Holding Oliver had brought back with savage intensity all that he could never have, and yet he couldn't hate the little boy—far from it, in fact. Instead of wanting to reject the child another man had given the woman he loved, he had actually felt drawn towards him.

If only Kate knew just how much he wished that Oliver *was* his child! And Kate herself still his wife?

After she had betrayed him by sleeping with another man? A bitter smile twisted Sean's lips.

Kate might have thought that hurling his infidelity at him was a powerful weapon, but instead it was just his own lie to her. His supposed affair had been a lie, made up to expedite the speedy ending of their marriage so that he could set Kate free.

And since the reason he'd been so grimly determined to set her free had been so that she could find another man to father the children he knew were so important to her, it was illogical for him to feel the way he did about the fact that she had done so.

Whoever the man was, he was a fool as well as a scoundrel for abandoning Kate and his son—and for throwing away Kate's love.

The savagery and immediacy of his own pain felt like a hammer-blow against his heart.

'Everyone's surprised that our new boss is spending so much time here,' Laura confided chattily to Kate on Thursday, as she came into her office shortly after lunch. 'I mean, he has two other companies. Do you suppose it means that we can all stop worrying about being made redundant?' she asked hopefully. 'I mean, if he wasn't planning on keeping this place going he wouldn't be spending so much time here, would he? Kate?' she prompted when Kate didn't make any response. 'Other things on your mind?' Laura guessed.

'Sorry—I didn't get much sleep last night,' Kate answered. It was the truth after all.

'You do look a bit peaky,' Laura acknowledged as she studied her.

Peaky! Kate grimaced to herself. She felt as though her emotions had been ripped apart and devoured by a pack of scavengers, and that now all that was left of them was the dead bones.

It was the dry grittiness of her eyes that made her want to blink, not something stupid like crying, she assured herself fiercely. After all, she had done enough of that during the night, hadn't she? With her face buried in her pillow so that she wouldn't wake Oliver.

She was still in shock, Kate admitted to herself, and the cause of that shock was her discovery of just how vulnerable she still was to Sean!

'Oh, no! Look at the time! I'd better go.' Kate hurried past Laura as she made her exit.

Behind her shock and pain lay a huge, deep dam of pent-up anger. How dared Sean refuse to believe that Oliver was his child? How dared he be such a hypocrite as to accuse her of sleeping with someone else?

Thinking of her son made her turn anxiously to her silent mobile. Oliver had complained that his tummy hurt again at breakfast time, but to her relief when she had taken his temperature it had been normal and so she had taken him to school.

Sean drummed his fingers irritably on his desk. Pushing back his chair, he stood up, raking his hair with one hand, and paced the floor as he mentally practised what he intended to say to Kate.

Halfway through the carefully chosen words he stopped abruptly and asked himself angrily what the hell was wrong with him. All he had to say to Kate was that he wanted her to have the money she had refused to accept when they had divorced. Hell, if need be he could tell her that his accountants were insisting it was handed over otherwise he would invoke some kind of tax penalty. His decision had nothing whatsoever to do with Oliver, other than the fact that he hated seeing Kate have to struggle—especially when she had a small child to support.

A small child who wasn't his.

Opening his office door, he instructed his secretary to tell Kate he wanted to see her.

'Jenny rang down to say that you wanted to see me?'

'Yes, I do,' Sean confirmed, turning away to look out of his office window. 'You must have found it hard to make time to study for your Master's?'

'Yes, in some ways I did,' Kate agreed warily, wondering why he had sent for her and what this was leading up to.

'I imagine that it would have been difficult with Oliver,' Sean pressed her.

'Yes, it was,' Kate confirmed.

'Why didn't you ask his father for financial support?'

When she didn't answer, Sean swung round. The light streaming in through the large window highlighted the tension in his face, and for a moment Kate almost weakened. He had been everything to her after all. As she was now everything to Oliver, she reminded herself immediately, before taking a deep breath and asking sharply, 'What are you trying to do? Trap me? You're wasting your time, Sean. *You* are Oliver's father. Nothing and no one—not even you—can alter that fact.'

Her stomach churned as she saw Sean's expression hardening with rejection.

'You are the one who is wasting your time, Kate. Oliver is not my son. He can't be—' Sean tensed and stopped speaking, taking a deep breath before he continued tersely, 'He can't be foisted off on me!'

His heart was hammering against his ribs. It was a sign of the effect Kate was having on him that he had come so close to blurting out the truth! Fortunately he had just managed to stop himself in time!

Kate clenched her hands as she caught the underlying

and suppressed violence in Sean's voice, her dismay giving way to shock as she heard him adding grimly, 'What I wanted to talk to you about was—' He stopped speaking as the abrupt shrill of Kate's mobile cut across his words. Red-faced, she fished it out of her bag, her embarrassment forgotten as she saw that the call was from Oliver's nursery.

'He's been sick and he's asking for me?' Kate couldn't keep the anxiety out of her voice as she repeated what the other woman was telling her. 'He wasn't very well this morning,' she admitted. 'But he didn't have a temperature then...'

Even though Kate tried to turn away from Sean she knew that he could hear the conversation she was having with the nursery school teacher.

'I...I'll try to—' she began, only to find that Sean was spinning her round to face him.

His expression was grim as he took the mobile from her and said tersely into it, 'She's on her way.'

'You have no right—' Kate said angrily, but Sean had ended the call and his hand was on her arm, urging her towards the door.

'We'll go in my car,' he told her. 'For one thing we'll get there faster, and for another you'll be worrying too much to drive safely.'

Kate opened her mouth to protest, but they were already in the car park and heading for Sean's car. He held the passenger door open for her and reluctantly she got in.

'Did the nursery say exactly what's wrong with him? Have they called a doctor?' Sean asked as he slid into the driver's seat and started the engine.

Kate wanted to refuse to tell him anything—after all, he had just rejected Oliver—but her maternal anxiety

overruled her pride, and apprehensively she began to repeat what she had been told. 'He's been sick, apparently.
There's a bug going round. He said this morning that
his tummy was hurting him.'

'You sent him to nursery, knowing that he wasn't
well?'

Kate could hear the criticism and disbelief in Sean's
voice.

'Why didn't you stay at home with him?'

Angrily Kate defended herself. 'I have to work, remember? Anyway, I can't just take time off like that.'

'Of course you can,' Sean contradicted her flatly.
'You're a mother. People would understand.'

'No one at work knows about Oliver,' Kate admitted
abruptly, deliberately turning her head to face the window so that he couldn't see her expression.

'Ashamed of him?'

'No!' Kate denied furiously, and immediately turned
to look at him. She realised too late that Sean had deliberately provoked her, knowing what her reaction
would be.

'Then why?'

'For goodness' sake, Sean, surely I don't have to tell
you the business facts of life?' Kate answered wryly.
'Not all firms will take on women who are mothers,
especially if they are single mothers. I needed this job.
I didn't mention Oliver at my first interview, and then
after I had been offered the job I discovered that John
had an unwritten rule about not employing mothers of
young children.'

'A rule it would be unlawful for him to try to enforce,'
Sean pointed out. 'And Oliver needs you! Hell, Kate,
both you and I know what it's like to grow up without
a mother.'

'Oliver has a mother.'

'But not a mother who can be there for him when he needs her.'

Kate couldn't maintain her barriers against the pain that swamped her. It invaded every nerve-ending and tore at her heart.

'Since you refuse to accept that Oliver is your child, you hardly have the right to tell me how to bring him up, do you?' she challenged him bitterly, only realising as she managed to blink away her angry tears that they had reached the village.

The moment Sean pulled up outside the nursery Kate was reaching for the car's door handle, throwing a stiff, 'Thank you for the lift,' to him over her shoulder.

But to her consternation Sean was already out of the car and opening her door, announcing curtly, 'I'm coming in with you.'

'I don't want you to,' Kate protested.

'Oliver might need to see a doctor,' Sean told her flatly. 'I can run you there.'

A doctor? Anxiously Kate hurried towards the nursery, her concern for her son far more important right now than arguing with Sean.

The moment Kate pushed open the door Oliver's nursery teacher came hurrying towards her.

'Where's Oliver? How is he?' Kate demanded frantically as she scanned the room anxiously, unable to see her son amongst the throng of children in the room.

'He's fine, but he's asleep.'

'Asleep? But—' Kate began, only to be interrupted.

'Has he seen a doctor?' Sean demanded sharply.

It irritated Kate a little to see the immediacy with which the older woman responded to Sean's calm authority.

'I'm a trained nurse,' she informed him, almost defensively. 'I don't think there's anything seriously wrong. Oliver felt poorly before lunch, and then he was sick afterwards, but he seems fine now—if rather tired.'

Turning to look at Kate, she added, slightly reprovingly, 'He seems upset about something, and I do rather think that might be the cause of the problem. Young children often react with physical symptoms to emotional stress.'

Kate flushed sensitively, sure that she could hear a note of criticism in the other woman's voice.

'I'll go through and get Ollie and take him home,' Kate told her quietly, unaware of the way Sean was watching her reaction to the older woman's remarks.

Oliver was asleep in one of the beds in a room off the playroom, and Kate felt the familiar pull on her emotions as she leaned over him. In so many ways he was Sean's son, even if Sean himself refused to accept Ollie as his child. Tiredly she bent to pick him up.

'I'll take him.'

Kate turned round. She hadn't realised that Sean had followed her into the small shadowy room.

'There's no need,' she told him in a small clipped voice, focusing her gaze not on Sean's face but on one dark-suited shoulder. A big mistake, she recognised achingly, when she had to suppress a longing to lean her head against its comforting strength and feel Sean's arms come round her, hear Sean's voice telling her that he believed her and that he loved her, that right now this very minute he was going to take both her and Oliver home with him.

As she stood there, staring fixatedly at his shoulder, Kate was suddenly overwhelmed by the searing knowledge of how alone and afraid she sometimes felt. Her throat ached and so did her head, shocked nausea was churning her stomach, and just the sight of Sean lifting his sleeping son into his arms was enough to make her feel as though her heart was breaking.

Get a grip, Kate advised herself sharply. This kind of emotion was a luxury she simply could not afford.

Once they were outside the nursery Kate stood in front of Sean and demanded, 'Give him to me now. I can carry him home from here.'

'You carry him? You look as though you can barely carry yourself,' Sean told her bluntly.

'I'll carry him!'

They had just reached the cottage when Oliver woke up, stirring sleepily in Sean's arms.

Opening the door, Kate stood just inside it and held out her arms for her son. But to her chagrin Oliver turned away from her, burrowing his head against Sean's chest and going back to sleep.

A huge splinter of ice was piercing her heart. This was the first time Oliver had rejected her in favour of someone else—and not just anyone else, but Sean, his father.

'You'd better give him to me,' she told Sean sharply. 'I'm sure the last thing you'll want is him being sick on your suit.'

As he handed Oliver to her and she put him down gently on the shabby sofa that took up one wall of the kitchen she heard him say quietly, 'No, actually the last thing I want is knowing that you went to another man's bed so quickly after leaving mine!'

Immediately Kate stiffened. 'You have no right to say that.'

'Do you think I don't know that?' Sean retaliated savagely. 'Don't you think I know that I have thrown away all my rights where you are concerned!'

'All your rights?' Horrified, Kate wondered what reckless surge of self-destruction had prompted such dangerous words, and spoken in such a soft, sexually challenging voice. And, as though that was not folly enough, she discovered that she had a sudden compulsion to let her gaze slide helplessly to Sean's mouth and then linger wantonly there, whilst her body reminded her hungrily of the pleasure he had once given it, how long it had been since...

'Kate, for God's sake, will you please stop looking at me like that?' Sean warned her harshly.

Mortified, she defended herself immediately, fibbing, 'I don't know what you mean!'

Instantly Sean took a step towards her, a look smouldering in the depths of his eyes that made a fierce thrill of dangerous excitement race through her.

'Liar! You know perfectly well what I mean.' Sean checked her thickly. 'You were looking at my mouth as though you couldn't wait to feel it against your own.'

What the hell was he doing? Sean challenged himself inwardly. His sole reason for having anything at all to do with Kate was to give her some much needed financial help, and that was all. Nothing else. Absolutely nothing else.

And yet within seconds of telling himself that, Sean could hear himself asking softly, 'Is that what you want, Kate? Because if it is...'

Just the sound of his voice was having a disturbingly erotic effect on her body—and on her senses. Defensively she closed her eyes, and then realised she had made a bad move as immediately she was swamped with mental images from the past.

Sean leaning over her in their bed, the morning sun on his bronzed skin, his eyes gleaming with sensual intent and knowledge between his narrowed eyelids. How quickly that cool look had grown hot and urgent when she had reached out to touch him, tugging teasingly on the fine hair covering his chest, before giving in to the erotic pleasure of sliding her fingers down the silky pathway which led over the hard flat plane of his belly to where the soft hair thickened.

Before she even realised what she was doing, never mind being able to stop herself, Kate felt her fingers stretching and curling, as though they could actually feel the strong, hard pulse of Sean's erection within their grip.

As soon as she realised what she was doing—and what she was feeling—Kate thrust her hands behind her back, guilty heat scorching her skin.

Angry both with herself for feeling the way she had and with Sean for being responsible for that feeling, she told him fiercely, 'No, it isn't.' She lied. 'Why should I want someone who did what you did? Someone who broke his marriage vows and took someone else to his bed? How could I want you, Sean?'

'Snap—that's exactly how I feel about you!' Sean stopped her passionately. 'You do realise, don't you, that I can throw the same accusations at you? How do you think it feels to discover that you didn't even wait a full month before jumping into bed with someone else? Why did you do that, Kate? Was it loneliness, or just spite?'

'I didn't do any such thing,' Kate denied shakily. His words had touched a wound in her heart that she had thought completely healed. But, as she had recently discovered, the scar tissue over it had been vulnerably fragile, and now the pain was agonisingly raw again.

Kate's face went white, but before she could say anything Sean had turned on his heel and was heading for the door.

'Don't come in to work tomorrow, and if Oliver isn't better by Monday let me know. And that's an order,' Sean instructed her grimly. 'I'll make arrangements to have your car brought here for you.'

CHAPTER SIX

'WELL, Oliver might have escaped going down with the dreaded bug, but it doesn't look as though you've been quite so lucky,' Carol commented forthrightly as she studied Kate's wan face.

'I've had a bad night,' Kate admitted reluctantly.

Kate had met her friend as she walked Oliver to school, and now the two boys were walking together, leaving Kate to fall into step with Carol.

'My daddy can do anything,' Kate heard George boasting.

'Boys!' Carol laughed, shaking her head and exchanging a rueful look with Kate.

'Well, Sean can do everything in the whole world!'

Kate bit her lip as Oliver's voice rang out, miserably aware of the comprehensive and sympathetic look Carol was giving her.

'Sounds as though Sean is a big hit with Oliver,' she commented lightly, but Kate could guess what she was thinking. The griping pain in her stomach bit harder and she winced, causing Carol to exclaim with concern, 'You really aren't well, Kate, are you? You should be in bed! Look, why don't you go home and go back to bed? I'll take Oliver to school and collect him for you.'

'I can't. I've got to go to work,' Kate told her. 'I didn't go in on Friday because of Oliver. I can't take more time off.'

'Kate, you can't possibly go to work. You look dreadful,' Carol protested, adding worriedly, 'Look at you!

You're shivering, and it's nearly eighty degrees. This bug is really nasty if it gets a grip.'

'Thanks!' Kate said dryly, adding determinedly, 'Anyway, I'm fine.'

But she could see from her friend's face that Carol knew she was lying, and the truth was that she felt anything but fine.

Unlike Oliver, who had recovered from his upset tummy within a matter of hours, ever since she'd been sick the morning before she had steadily become more and more unwell. Her head felt as though it was being pounded with a sledgehammer, she had been sick on and off all night, and every bone in her body ached. She felt as if she was having flu and food poisoning all in one go.

Now the pain in her head increased, and when she closed her eyes against it a wave of nauseating dizziness hit her.

'No way are you going to work!' Carol's firm voice broke into her misery. 'How on earth are you planning to get there? You can't possibly drive. Go home, and as soon as I've dropped the boys off I'll call in and make sure you're okay.'

Another surge of nausea reinforced the truth of what Carol was saying, and, handing Oliver over to her, Kate hurriedly made her way back home. She was unable to tell which felt worse—the agonising pain in her head, which made her want to crawl into a dark place and with any luck die there, or the knowledge that unless she got home soon she was all too likely to be sick in public.

Half an hour later Carol returned from dropping the boys off. Kate was barely aware of her knocking and then entering through the back door.

'Thank goodness you've seen sense,' her friend exclaimed in relief, finding Kate safely tucked up in bed and adding with concern, 'I'd stay with you, but I promised I'd take my mother to hospital for her check-up today.'

'I'll be fine,' Kate assured her wanly. 'I just need to sleep off this headache, that's all.'

'Well, if you're sure...'

'I'm sure,' Kate insisted, only realising when Carol had gone that she ought to have asked her to telephone the office for her and explain what had happened.

Somehow just the thought of making the call herself was exhausting—and besides she needed to be sick again...

Sean frowned as his gaze flicked round Kate's empty office. Why hadn't she rung in? Was Oliver more seriously ill than anyone had realised?

It was the human resources department's responsibility to check up on why Kate hadn't reported in, not his, Sean reminded himself grimly. He was simply her employer now, and that was all.

A muscle twitched betrayingly in his jaw. Who the hell did he think he was deceiving?

He was supposed to be leaving here today, to return to headquarters for an important meeting, and he had not planned to come back until the following week.

If the woman in human resources was surprised that he should ask for Kate's home telephone number she was professional enough not to show it, Sean acknowledged.

In the privacy of his office Sean dialled the number, his frown deepening as it rang out unanswered.

* * *

Slipping in and out of a feverish half-sleep, Kate was vaguely aware of the telephone ringing, but she felt far too ill to get up and answer it.

Sean waited until he heard Kate's answering machine cut in before hanging up. Where on earth was she? Unwanted thoughts tormented his imagination. Kate sitting in a hospital waiting room whilst medical staff sped away with Oliver's vulnerable little-boy body... His feeling of anguish and anxiety, combined with a need to be there, surged through him and caught him off guard.

He would feel the same concern for any young child, Sean assured himself grittily. Just as he had been himself, Oliver was a fatherless child. He knew all too well how that felt. How it hurt.

A brief telephone call to Head Office was enough to cancel his meeting. How could he chair a meeting when Oliver might be ill?

He stuck it out for as long as he could, punctuating his anxiety with several more unsuccessful telephone calls, but midway through the afternoon he threw down the papers he was supposed to be studying and reached for his jacket.

When Sean reached Kate's house the open back door and the relief on two of the three anxious faces that turned towards him told its own story—or at least some of it.

'Sean!'

'Oh, thank goodness!'

As Oliver raced towards him Sean bent automatically to pick him up.

'My mummy is very sick,' Oliver said, causing Sean to grip Oliver tightly.

'Kate isn't at all well,' Carol explained quickly. 'In

fact when I came round with Oliver after school I was
so worried I sent for the doctor.'

Sean looked at the tired-looking middle-aged man
who was the third member of the trio.

'Kate appears to have contracted a particularly viru-
lent strain of this current virus,' he explained wearily.
'She's dehydrated and very weak, and in no way able to
look after herself at the moment—never mind her child.
She needs someone here to make sure she drinks plenty
of fluids and generally look after her.'

He was looking meaningfully at Carol, who bit her
lip and told him uncomfortably, 'Normally I would have
been only too happy to have Oliver to stay, but—'

'That won't be necessary,' Sean announced firmly,
breaking into the conversation. 'I'll stay with Kate and
look after her and Oliver. I'm her ex-husband,' he explained tersely, when he saw the doctor beginning to
frown.

'I should warn you that she's only semi-conscious,'
the doctor told him sharply, after Carol had left to go
back to her own family. 'And slightly delirious and confused in fact,' he added. 'But that will pass. She's got a
high fever, combined with stomach cramps. I have given
her some medication which should start to make her feel
better within the next twelve hours, although it will be
considerably longer than that before she starts to recover
properly and—'

'Why the hell aren't you admitting her to hospital?'
Sean demanded angrily.

'For several reasons,' the doctor answered. 'One, I
doubt very much that I could get her a bed. Two, she
has a child, who will no doubt be distressed by such an
action. And three, whilst she's very unwell, her condition isn't acute. I appreciate that looking after her isn't

going to be easy. If you're having second thoughts then perhaps you could let me know now, because I shall have to organise some kind of temporary foster care for the child and a district nurse to call round when she can to check on my patient.'

'Foster care! Oliver doesn't need foster care and Kate doesn't need the district nurse—they've got me,' Sean announced protectively.

The doctor tried not to show his relief. This virus was stretching local medical resources beyond their limits.

'Very well. Now, this is what you will have to do...'

Sean listened grimly as the doctor gave him his instructions.

Oliver was still nestled sleepily in his arms, and after the doctor had gone Oliver looked up into Sean's face and demanded anxiously, 'When is my mummy going to get better?'

'Soon,' Sean assured him calmly, but inwardly he was feeling very far from calm.

Ten minutes later, as he stood beside the bed looking down into Kate's pale face whilst she lay frighteningly still, he felt even less so. Her left hand lay limply on top of the duvet, her fingers ringless and her nails free of polish. She had beautiful hands and fragile, delicate wrists, he reflected sombrely. They had been one the first things about her he had noticed. Now, if anything, her wrist looked even narrower than he remembered.

Suddenly she made a restless movement and turned her hand over. He could see the blueness of her veins through the fine skin. Beads of sweat burst out on her forehead and she moaned suddenly, shivering violently, her eyes opening and then widening in confusion and bewilderment as she saw him.

'It's all right, Kate,' Sean reassured her as she looked vaguely up at him. But even as he was trying to reassure her Sean knew that he could not reassure himself. He could feel the heavy, agonised thud of his heartbeat.

'My head hurts,' Kate told him plaintively.

'Why don't you sit up and drink some of this water, take these tablets the doctor has left for you?' Sean suggested gently. 'They should bring your temperature down and help you to feel better.'

Obediently she tried to do as he suggested, but Sean could see that even the small effort of trying to sit up was too much for her.

Without giving her the chance to protest, he sat down on the bed and put his arm round her, supporting her as he plumped up the pillows.

She was wearing some kind of cotton nightshirt, which was soaked with sweat and damp, and as he supported her she started to shiver so violently that her teeth chattered together.

It made Sean's own throat hurt to see the difficulty she had swallowing even a few sips of water.

'My throat hurts so much,' she whispered to him as she pushed the glass away. 'Everything hurts.'

Automatically Sean placed his hand against her forehead.

'That feels good,' she told him quietly. 'Cool.'

Sean had to swallow back the feelings both her words and the burning hot feel of her skin had aroused.

'I feel so hot,' she complained fretfully.

'You've got a bad virus,' Sean told her.

'I don't want to keep you away from work, Sean. Not with the Anderson contract to get finished.'

Her eyes were closing as he lowered her back against the pillows, and Sean watched her with a frown. The

Anderson contract she had referred to was one he had worked on in the early days of their marriage.

'Slightly delirious.' The doctor had warned him. And she was wringing wet, burning up and shivering at the same time.

She had been his wife, his lover, and her body held no secrets from him. How could it when she had given herself so freely to him, when he had been the one to help her to explore and discover the power of its female sexuality? Even so he could feel his muscles clenching as he worked to remove her fever-sodden nightshirt, blessing the fact that it fastened down the front with buttons. Or was it a blessing? Instead of removing it quickly he was having to fight against the savage stab of arousal he felt when he exposed the pale curves of her breasts, to force himself to ignore the sensuality of her naked body and to focus on her illness instead.

Reluctant to search through her drawers for a clean nightshirt, after he had sponged down her fever-soaked body he wrapped her in a towel instead, answering the disjointed questions she asked when she woke up briefly.

By the time he was satisfied that she was both dry and warm, and was finally able to cover her with the duvet, his hands were shaking.

'Sean?'

He froze as he realised she had woken up again. 'Yes?' he replied.

'I love you so much,' she told him simply, smiling sweetly at him before she closed her eyes and drifted back to sleep.

There was, Sean discovered, a dangerous pain inside his chest, and the backs of his eyes were burning, as though they had been soaked with limewash.

*   *   *

It was two o'clock in the morning and Sean was exhausted. Kate's temperature seemed to have dropped a little, much to his relief. And Oliver was fast asleep in his own bed, unaware of the sharp pangs of emotion Sean had felt when Oliver had solemnly explained to him his bedtime routine.

Suppressing a yawn, Sean pushed his hand through his hair. Kate was asleep but he was reluctant to leave her.

He went into the bathroom and had a shower. It had been a long day. His eyes felt gritty and tired. He looked at the empty half of the bed. It wasn't going to hurt anyone if he just lay down and snatched a few minutes' sleep, was it?

Kate could feel the pain of her anguished despair. A bleak, searing sense of loss engulfed her, lacerated by panic and agonising disbelief. In her jumbled fever-induced dream she ran on leaden legs from room to room of a shadowed empty house, frantically searching for Sean whilst the icy-cold tentacles of her fear took hold of her heart.

Sean had left her and she couldn't bear the pain of losing him. She couldn't endure the thought of living without him. She felt bereft, abandoned, and totally alone.

The pain of her dream was unbearable, and she fought to escape from it, dragging herself frantically through the layers of sleep, crying out Sean's name as she did so.

The moment he heard Kate cry out, Sean was awake.

'Sean?'

He could hear the panic in her voice as she repeated

his name, and even in the semi-darkness he could see how her body was shaking.

'Kate, it's all right,' he tried to reassure her, and he placed his hand on her arm and leaned over her.

Kate could feel herself shaking with the intensity of the emotions flooding through her, piercing her muddled confusion. When she managed to force her eyes open she exhaled in relief. She could see Sean's familiar outline in the bed! Sean was here. He had not left her! She had just been having a bad dream!

But, despite her relief, somewhere on the edge of her consciousness something was niggling at her—something she did not want to recognise. Defensively she pushed it away, escaping instead into the comforting security of Sean's presence. But she needed more than just his presence to banish the dark shadows of the dream, she recognised.

Instinctively she moved towards him, wanting, needing to be closer to him. Although her brain felt muddled, and somehow not fully functioning, her senses were sharply acute and her whole body shuddered as she breathed in his warm, musky scent. She could feel the familiar arousal taking over her body.

She wanted Sean to hold her.

'Hold me close, Sean,' she begged huskily, shivering as she told him in a low, unsteady voice, 'I was dreaming that you weren't here... And everything seems so muddled. I can't seem to think straight...'

'You've had a bad virus and a high fever,' Sean told her quietly, deliberately using the past tense so that he didn't frighten her.

'I think I must have been suffering from delusions.' Kate tried to laugh, but her smile disappeared as her whole body shuddered violently. 'It was so frightening,

Sean,' she whispered. 'I dreamt that I was in a house looking for you but you weren't there.'

Emotional tears filled her eyes and Sean listened helplessly. Fever burned in her face and glazed her eyes. She made a small movement towards him and Sean began to draw back. But it was too late. Kate was already nestling trustingly into him.

Sombrely Sean looked down at her. His throat felt tight and he was acutely conscious that this should not be happening. Right now his role was that of nurse and guardian—but how could he explain that to her in her present confused and feverish condition? Would she even understand what he was trying to say? Somehow Sean doubted it. And, as though to confirm his thoughts, he felt her move, saw that his slight hesitation had made her focus on him, her anxious gaze searching his face.

'Sean?' she questioned as she reached out and curled her fingers onto the polished skin of his shoulder.

And then, before he could stop her, she moved closer to him and pressed her face against his chest.

Eagerly Kate snuggled closer to the security of Sean's body. Just breathing in the familiar scent of him was immediately reassuring and calming. Calming? When had anything to do with being close to Sean had a calming effect on her? Kate smiled inwardly at herself. Calm was certainly not the way she was feeling right now, with her heart hammering and her body feeling so ridiculously weak. Weak, maybe, but also acutely and erotically aware of Sean. And her physical longing was heightened by the intensity of her aching, emotional need to be close to him.

It was as though her dream had left her with a vulnerability that only Sean's intimate closeness could repair, Kate acknowledged vaguely. Dismissing her thoughts, she nuzzled into the warmth of his chest, tasting it with absorbed delight. And then, whilst Sean was still grappling with his own shock, she moved her head and placed her lips against his flesh, openly luxuriating in the pleasure of slowly and languorously caressing him.

Sean could feel the shallow, rapid race of his heartbeat as he tensed his body against its immediate reaction to her. He had never for one minute imagined, and certainly not intended anything like this should happen.

But now that it had...

Now that it had he was having to battle against the reality of the situation, against the achingly sensual pleasure of Kate half lying over him. There was no way he could allow himself to even acknowledge what it did to him, having the softness of her lips delicately brushing his skin.

If he didn't put an end to what was happening, and soon, he would be in danger of racing out of control and down a road he had no right to travel. A road which Kate in full health would refuse to allow him to travel.

Determinedly Sean reached out and closed his hands around her upper arms, intending to lift her away from his body and place her back on her own half of the bed. But the minute he tried to move her she moaned and clung to him.

It was more than his self-control could bear.

Sean swallowed hard. He had to put a stop to this.

'Kate—'

'Mmm...' Kate exhaled on an ecstatic sigh as she pressed a small kiss to the corner of Sean's mouth. Helplessly he returned it—with interest—whilst inside him a savagely bitter voice reminded him condemningly that Kate was sick, that she did not really know what was happening, and that just because she was kissing him back, and trying to touch him, it did not mean that he should let her.

It took all the strength he had to lift his mouth from the sweetness of her, and when he did she looked up at him in confused bewilderment.

He had to put a stop to this, and he had to do it now, Sean told himself fiercely.

But the look in Kate's eyes made him want to take her in his arms and hold her there until it disappeared.

The duvet had slipped away to reveal the curves of her breasts, palely silvered by the moonlight streaming in through the window, in contrast to the sensually darkened areolae from which her nipples rose in stiffly erect peaks.

Dizzily Kate watched with open sensual pleasure as she saw Sean's gaze fasten helplessly on her exposed breasts. But she knew that she wanted to feel more than his hot gaze touching her. A fierce shudder gripped her, making her gasp and exhale.

And as he watched her, and recognised what she was feeling, somehow, without him knowing how it had happened, Sean started to lower his mouth towards her lips.

Eagerly Kate offered herself up for Sean's possession, her hands reaching out with surprising strength to draw him to her waiting body. A wild shudder contorted her as she parted her lips for the driving pressure of his tongue, her own mating with it.

Beneath his hands Sean could feel the familiarity of her—the longed-for and long-loved familiarity of her—and it was more than his self-control could stand. He hadn't meant for his hand to touch her breast, to slowly caress its fullness as it swelled sweetly into his hand, and he certainly hadn't intended to allow his fingers to stroke softly against her thigh as she trembled beneath his touch. Dear heaven, he should not be permitting this, Sean admitted helplessly. He should be putting in place the barriers between them that Kate could not. He should be stopping what was happening, not feeling that he would die if he did not hold her and love her.

His need was overruling his conscience and his self-control. The tight, swollen feel of the nipple pressing into his hand, the feel of Kate's mouth against his skin, the knowledge that he had only to move his hand and place it between her open thighs to feel the familiar pleasure of her sweet, wet warmth, was obliterating everything but his overpowering need for her.

He moved her body and cupped her face, kissing her until she was moaning longingly beneath his mouth, her hands seeking his hard arousal as hungrily as his were seeking the swollen wetness of hers.

He kissed her breasts, slowly and then far more fiercely, making her shudder with desire as she felt the rough sensual lapping of his tongue against the sensitivity of her nipples, then cry out in primitive female pleasure when his mouth closed over one swollen peak.

Her own hand pressed over the hand he had placed between her thighs, holding it there as his fingers caressed her receptive flesh.

Sean felt that his actions were not premeditated so much as preordained. What was happening between them just seemed so natural, so right—and so very, very much what their bodies wanted. So much so, in fact, that for a few seconds he allowed himself to suspend reality and give in to his love.

Almost as soon as he touched her intimately Sean heard Kate cry out as her body quickened to his touch. Her hands clamped around his arm as though seeking and needing reassurance—and the small, almost startled cry ended as the contractions of her orgasm began.

'Sean,' Kate whispered dreamily, with appreciative pleasure, lifting her hand to touch his face, but she was asleep before she could finish doing so.

Numbly Sean waited until he was sure that Kate was deeply asleep before moving away from her. He could not comprehend how he had allowed things to get so out of hand, why he had not somehow stopped. Not so much Kate, but more importantly himself. Why and how had he allowed his feelings to become so out of control that he had given in to them? A stab of revulsion against himself hit him like a sledgehammer-blow to his heart.

Deep down inside Sean, despite the trauma of his childhood, was a core of pure old-fashioned male protectiveness that was an essential part of how he regarded himself. As a man who would protect the woman he loved—from everything and everyone, even including himself, if and when necessary. Wasn't that, after all, why he had divorced Kate in the first place? So that she should be free to have with another man the children he knew he could not give her.

That element of his personality was of vital importance to him; it underpinned his sense of who he was and his pride in himself. But how could he be proud of himself now? As his anger against himself grew Sean paced the floor of Kate's room, refusing to allow himself to escape from his own contempt.

A sound from the bed—a whimper and then a small burst of unintelligible words—caused him to freeze, and then go to Kate's side.

It was obvious that the fever was mounting again, and when he woke her to give her the medication the doctor had left, and to make sure she drank some water, the blank, unseeing look she gave him made Sean suspect that she didn't even realise who he was...

She would hate knowing that she had clung to him and begged him to love her, he recognised grimly. Although he doubted that in her feverish state she would remember what had happened. She would certainly not *want* to remember it; he knew that.

But when he laid her down again, and sponged her hot skin, Sean acknowledged that he would remember it, that he would store the memory deep inside himself, where he had already stored so many memories of her.

Bleakly he looked away from her. The pain inside him that never went away was tearing at his gut. Just being here in this small house intensified it almost beyond bearing. Within this house were the woman he loved, always would love, and the child he would give his life to have been able to give her. Kate had no idea what she did to him when she tried to insist that Oliver was his son.

Kate could feel the warmth of sunlight on her closed eyelids. Weakly she struggled to understand the feeling of panic that the warmth engendered, her body stiffening as the knowledge hit her that the sunlight only shone through her bedroom window early in the afternoon.

As she opened her eyes she tried to sit up in her bed, only to collapse against her pillows as her virus-weakened body refused to support her. Shock and panic spiked through her, multiplied by fear as she realised how quiet the house was.

Where was Oliver, and why was she here in bed? She had to get up and find her son. Shakily she pushed back the bedclothes, frowning in alarmed bewilderment as she looked down at the unfamiliar sea-green fine cotton nightgown she was wearing, its hem and bodice lavishly trimmed with expensive lace.

Instinctively she touched the fabric. Once, long ago, she had owned such things—not that she had ever worn them very much. Her expression changed. Sean had always preferred them to sleep skin to skin, and so had she. A tiny shudder gripped her body as a vague, unsettling memory—confusing misty images of Sean and her as lovers—stirred inside her head like ripples on water. And just as elusive to grasp. But she had an urgent and anxious feeling that she had to grasp it.

Her heart was hammering against her ribs; she felt oddly disorientated—light-headed, almost. She put her feet on the floor and stood up, shocked to discover that her legs could barely support her and that she had to cling to the side of the bed.

Whilst she was struggling to keep her balance the bedroom door opened, but her initial relief was quickly swamped by angry panic when she saw Sean coming towards her. Immediately she backed up towards the bed. Sean stood still.

Shockingly surreal and unwanted mental flashbacks were tormenting her. Disjointed but frighteningly potent memories of Sean and herself as lovers, of herself begging Sean to make love to her.

Nausea and pain tore at her in equal measures. She could hardly bring herself to look at him. Her head was pounding, and with every second that passed she felt weaker.

'Where's Oliver?' she demanded anxiously. 'And what are you doing here?'

'Oliver's at nursery, and I'm here because both you and he needed someone here to look after you.'

'To look after me? You've been looking after me?'

Try as she might, Kate couldn't keep the near hysterical anguish out of her voice. 'Why you?'

'Why not me? I was here, and I am your ex-husband.' He gave a small dismissive shrug.

'My ex-husband?'

'There was no one else, Kate.' Sean stopped her almost gently. 'Your friend Carol wanted to help, but she has a husband and a child of her own. I did wonder at one stage if perhaps hospital...'

'Hospital?' Kate could feel the terrifyingly heavy thud of her heart.

'The virus you've had hit you very hard,' Sean told her patiently, adding, 'Look, why don't you get back into bed—?' As he spoke he came towards her.

'No! Don't touch me,' Kate protested in panic when he looked as if he were about to pick her up.

The way he was looking at her made her flush painfully, her skin burning. Just having him stand so close to her was activating all kinds of disturbing memories. It wasn't just some feverish act of her imagination that was responsible, Kate acknowledged miserably. The memories were there because it had happened. She had said and done all those things she was being forced to remember.

Helplessly she waited for Sean to mock and taunt her with the words she could hear ringing so clearly inside her own head, to remind her that she had already begged him to do far more than merely touch her. Instead he said nothing, simply bent down to pick her up and placed her firmly back in the bed.

'You're still very weak—' he told her, and then broke off as the doorbell rang. 'That will be the doctor. I'll go down and let him in.'

As soon as he had gone Kate lifted her hand to her

forehead and pressed her skin tightly as she tried to force herself to remember exactly what had happened. Humiliatingly, all her body could and would remember was the pleasure Sean had given it, whilst inside her head she could hear the ringing echo of her own passionate pleas for his possession.

The bedroom door reopened and Sean ushered in the doctor, whose face was full of concern.

'So, Kate, you are back with us. Good! Your husband has obviously done an excellent job of looking after you.'

Her husband! Kate wanted to remind the doctor that Sean was her ex-husband, but somehow it was too much of an effort. The frightening realisation of just how physically weak she felt was just beginning to hit her.

'You are over the worst now, but that does not mean you are better. You are very far from better,' the doctor told her emphatically.

'So when will I be better?' Kate demanded, with a show of energy she was far from feeling. A little uncomfortably she saw that the doctor was looking at her as though he knew perfectly well how she was really feeling.

'Well, if you do as you are told, and don't try to rush things, I would say that you will be fully back to normal in three weeks or so.'

'Three weeks!' Kate struggled to sit up as she stared at him in shock. 'But, no! That's impossible!' she started to tell him frantically. 'I need to find a new job! I have to go back to work. I've just had a bit of a virus, that's all—it can't possibly take three weeks for me to get better!'

'You've had a very serious strain of the virus, and without wanting to frighten you…' the doctor paused.

'It is fortunate that you have such a naturally strong constitution,' he told her 'And as for you going back to work...' He shook his head. 'No, you cannot do that.'

'Nor will she be doing that, Doctor.' Sean joined the conversation grimly, giving Kate a warning look as he added smoothly, 'I know that no employer would allow her to work anyway, until she has been given a clean bill of health.'

Kate felt distraught, but she had to satisfy herself with giving Sean a seethingly furious look as he escorted the doctor to the door.

When he came back, she told him determinedly, 'I can't not work for three weeks! I would have found a new job by now if I hadn't been ill,' she added fretfully.

When Sean remained silent she reminded him angrily, 'I have to work. I have a child to support and a mortgage to pay.'

'We'll talk about this later,' Sean said in a clipped voice. 'It's time for me to go and collect Oliver from nursery.'

Kate wanted to argue, but her head was pounding and all she could do was watch him leave with helpless fury.

It just wasn't possible that it would take three weeks before she was back to normal! She was sure the doctor was exaggerating her weakness—no doubt prompted and aided by Sean, she decided, scowling. And she was going to prove it!

The moment she heard Sean leave she thrust back the bedcovers, refusing to acknowledge that even that action left her arms aching. She was in her twenties, for heaven's sake, not in her nineties, she reminded herself determinedly, and she ignored her dizziness.

Placing her feet firmly on the floor, she stood up, and immediately had to make a wild grab for the bed as her legs refused to support her properly. Okay, she was feeling a little bit weak—but that was because she hadn't been doing anything, because she had been lying in bed and not using her muscles.

Kate could feel her face starting to burn as she was forced to remember just what she had done in bed. And as she clung unsteadily to the bed other vague images wove themselves in and out of her memory: strong arms lifting and holding her, supporting her whilst she drank, careful hands soothing her hot and hurting skin, the presence of a shadowy but oh-so-comforting figure doing for her everything that needed to be done, even anticipating her every need.

Shakily Kate wondered for just how long the fever had consumed her. She touched her hair; it felt clean and soft. She had an immediate and shocking image of being held beneath the shower, whilst blissfully cleansing water cascaded over her sticky and uncomfortable body.

Sean had done all those things for her. Sean had cared for her as though…as though… As though they were still a couple—a pair bonded together by mutual love and commitment. As though he still loved her!

But he had abandoned her for someone else, she reminded herself fiercely as she forced her weak aching legs to move. He had given the love she had thought exclusively hers to another woman. No matter what her deepest and most secret feelings, she must not allow herself to forget that betrayal.

Her deepest and most secret feelings? A recognition she did not want to acknowledge tightened its hurting grasp around her heart. Gritting her teeth, she took three steps, and then gasped out loud with shock as her legs refused to support her any longer and she sank awkwardly to the floor.

Ten minutes later she was safely back in bed—her bones, never mind her flesh, feeling as though they had been pummelled and bruised, every bit of her filled with an aching, nagging pain she couldn't ignore.

Kate had never really been physically ill, and the only real physical pain she had had to endure was when she had given birth to Oliver—and anyway, that had been different.

This unfamiliar aching weakness was alien to her, and very frightening. She loathed the thought of being dependent on anyone, no matter who it might be, and that it should be Sean brought a whole raft of emotional complications she just did not feel able to cope with. But she was going to have to cope with them. Because, as she had just proved to herself, the doctor had been quite correct—she was far too weak to even look after herself, never mind care properly for Oliver, or find a new job!

Angry tears burned the backs of her eyes, followed by a feeling of panicky fear. How was she going to manage? How would she support them both? It seemed so unfair that after all the hard work she had done this should happen—now when she had finally begun to allow herself to hope that her plans for their financial security would be successful. Hastily she blinked the tears away as she heard the door open, followed by the sound of Oliver's excited voice.

The sight of him bursting into her room and running towards her, followed by Sean, immediately lifted her spirits—although she frowned a little to see that he was wearing obviously new clothes she didn't recognise.

As though he could guess what she was thinking, Sean

explained carelessly, 'I couldn't get the washing dry because of the rain, so I bought some new stuff.'

Oliver had reached the bed and was scrambling onto
it. As she reached down to help him Kate saw the labels
on the new clothes and her mouth compressed, her panic
returning. Expensive designer labels! How on earth was
she going to repay Sean for them? She had only ever
been able to afford to buy Oliver good second-hand
clothes, and sometimes new things from chain stores.

'Mummy, you're properly awake at last!' Oliver
beamed as he kissed her enthusiastically. 'Look what I
painted for you!' he said, triumphantly showing her the
brightly painted paper he was holding.

'It's me and you and Sean, and Sean's house where
we're all going to live.' Immediately Kate went still,
keeping her arm around her son whilst she looked accusingly at Sean. Her heart was pounding so heavily that
it hurt.

'What—?' she began fiercely, but Sean was already
lifting Oliver off the bed.

'Come on,' he was saying to Oliver. 'Let's go down-
stairs and make Mummy some tea. We'll talk later,' he
added quietly to Kate.

'Yes, and then I'll read you a story, Mummy,' Oliver
told her happily. 'We've read you a story every night—
haven't we, Sean? But you weren't properly awake.
Having lots of sleep made you get better, though,' he
informed Kate importantly. With a graveness that tore
at her heart, Oliver continued, 'You have to have lots of
water to drink, doesn't she, Sean?'

'Lots of water, and now some proper food,' Sean
agreed calmly.

Kate could feel her eyes smarting with emotional tears
as Sean disappeared with Oliver.

She had been miserably worried about her illness affecting Oliver emotionally, but now it was plain to her that she had worried unnecessarily. Because Oliver had had Sean. Because Oliver had had his father.

A huge groundswell of emotional pain began deep down inside her. How could Sean behave as he was doing with Oliver and yet at the same time so completely reject the fact that Oliver was his son? And as for Oliver's innocent remark about them going to live with Sean!

Tiredness began to swamp her, overwhelming her angry attempts to fight it off and remain awake.

When Sean walked into the bedroom five minutes later she was fast asleep. Putting down the tray holding the pot of tea he had brewed for her, and the light omelette he had just made, Sean went over to look at her, frowning deeply as he did so. The previous day the doctor had told him that he believed she was over the worst, and today, with her return to full consciousness, Sean had seen that for himself.

He was reluctant to wake her up, but he knew that she needed to start eating again in order to build up her strength.

Going over to her, he reached out to touch her, and then hesitated. The strap of the nightdress he had bought her when he had been forced to go out and buy food and extra clothes for Oliver had slipped down over her exposed shoulder.

Without thinking, his actions still on the automatic pilot of having looked after her, he curled his fingers around the strap and started to tug it back up.

Kate woke up immediately, her whole body tensing as she saw Sean leaning over her.

The sight of the afternoon sunshine falling against his

skin made her stifle a small sound deep in her throat. She had never admitted it to him, but she could still remember how all those years ago, when they had first met, she had deliberately walked past the building site where he was working, unable to stop her avid gaze feeding hungrily on the sight of his naked torso, pin-pricks of dangerous excitement prickling all over her body. Just as they were doing now, Kate realised, as the emotions she was fighting to hold in check swept through her.

She must not allow herself to react to him like this, she told herself fiercely. She must not weaken and let him touch her emotions. She must not forget now much he had hurt her and, much more importantly, how much he could still hurt Oliver.

Thinking of her son gave her the strength to drag her gaze from Sean's and look pointedly at where his hand still rested on her shoulder.

'You must let me know how much you have spent on mine and Oliver's behalf,' she told him stiffly. She knew just from the feel of the fabric against her skin that the nightdress would have cost far more than she would ever have paid—and far more than she could possibly afford. But no way was she going to be beholden to him, even though she felt sick at the thought of having to waste her small precious savings on such unnecessary luxuries.

'There are several things we need to discuss,' Sean told her equably. 'But first you must have something to eat.'

Rebelliously Kate looked at him, the words 'I'm not hungry' dying on her lips as he added gently, 'Doctor's orders, Kate, and if necessary I can assure you I am perfectly willing to feed you myself.'

'That won't be necessary.'

'Good.'

Unable to contain herself any longer, she burst out, 'I can't be off work for three weeks.'

'You can't *not* be,' he corrected her curtly. 'And personally I don't think that your doctor is going to change his mind and allow you to return to work sooner. I take it that you haven't found another job as yet?'

Kate's mouth compressed whilst she contemplated lying to him, but then she was forced to admit that she was unlikely to get away with doing so. 'No,' she answered tersely. 'But I intend to spend the time I have to have off work looking for one.'

'On the contrary,' Sean told her firmly. 'What you are going to be spending the next three weeks doing is recuperating, as I am sure your doctor will inform you. But if you don't believe me you can check with him yourself. He'll be coming back to see you tomorrow, to make sure you're well enough to travel to…' He paused, and then continued coolly, 'To my home.'

'What?' Kate went hot and then cold with shock and disbelief. 'Oh, no. No way!' Kate shook her head violently. 'No way am I ever, *ever* going to live with you again, Sean…'

'Oliver is already looking forward to it,' he said blandly.

Kate felt as though she had been kicked in the stomach. 'You had no right to say anything to Oliver. Nor to use him to—'

'To what?' Sean challenged her. 'Right now you need someone to look after you—someone to look after you both. Physically and financially,' he emphasised unkindly.

'You don't know anything about my financial situation,' Kate denied hotly. 'And you have no right—'

'I know that on the salary you are being paid, given the outgoings you must have, you will have to budget carefully.' He gave a small shrug to conceal from her what he was really feeling. 'Logically it seems unlikely that you have a financial cushion to fall back on if, for instance, you are unable to work. As is the case now!'

Kate could feel a dangerous prickle in her throat as her emotions reacted to his extremely accurate assessment of her situation.

'I may not have your wealth, Sean, but I don't need your charity, or—' she began, only to be cut short as Sean interrupted her.

'Not for yourself, maybe, Kate. But you do need it for Oliver's sake—and don't bother trying to deny it!' He gave another dismissive shrug and turned slightly away from her so that she couldn't read his expression.

Helplessly Kate acknowledged that what Sean had said to her was true. For Oliver's sake she had no option other than to give in and agree to what Sean was suggesting.

Besides, wasn't there somewhere deep inside her still a foolish little shoot of hope that, given time and the opportunity to be with Oliver, Sean would somehow recognise and accept that Ollie was his child? And a part of her wanted that desperately—not for her own sake, but for their son's.

'The only person you have is me!' Sean told her abruptly. 'Unless, of course, you want to get in touch with Oliver's father,' he added harshly, shattering her fragile fantasy.

Kate felt sick with rage and pain. She wanted to scream at him that she did not need anyone, and that if she did need someone she would die before she let that someone be him.

'Carol will help me,' she began sharply, but Sean immediately shook his head.

'She has her own family to look after; you know that! And besides—'

'Besides what?' she demanded angrily.

'Besides, I don't think it would be in Oliver's best interests.'

For a few seconds Kate was rendered speechless with disbelief. When she did find her voice she could hear it trembling with the intensity of her rage.

'You don't think—! Since when have you concerned yourself with Oliver's best interests? Or don't you think it would be in Oliver's "best interests",' she mimicked, 'to be acknowledged and loved by his father?'

'Oh, for God's sake.'

Kate flinched as she heard the savagery in his voice.

'Regardless of who Oliver's father is, you are his mother and Oliver should be near you. If Carol were to look after you both that would necessitate her having Oliver spending a great deal of time at her house, away from you. I'm not denying that she would do her best for both of you, but...'

Kate closed her eyes. She knew exactly what Sean was saying, and what he was not saying—and, even worse, she knew that he was right.

'So who are you proposing will look after us?' she asked defeatedly.

'Me.'

Kate lifted her head and stared at him. 'You? No... That's not possible!'

'On the contrary, as I think I have proved these last few days, it is perfectly possible.'

'But you have to work. You've got your business to run,' Kate reminded him wildly.

'I can run my business from home,' Sean answered laconically. 'And it seems to me that I can look after you and Oliver and work much more easily in a house with more than two bedrooms. At least that way I'll have my own bed to sleep in.'

His own bed!

Kate could feel her anger giving way to panic. This was definitely not a line of conversation she wanted to pursue.

'So where is this house with more than two bedrooms?' she forced herself to demand. 'Oliver is very happy at nursery, and I don't want him upset.'

'Oliver won't be upset. It's only for a short while, and he needs to get used to change as he'll soon be leaving nursery anyway, to start school.' He started to frown. 'Your nearest infant school is nearly ten miles away...'

'I know that,' Kate snapped at him. Of course she knew it! Hadn't she been worrying herself sick for the last year about the fact that the village was too small to have its own school?

'Oliver has got used to having me around,' Sean said abruptly as he walked away from the bed and stood with his back to her, looking out of the window. 'It seems unfair and definitely not in his best interests to subject him to further changes. He's naturally been very upset by your illness, but he's looking forward to the three of us being together.'

The three of us!

A fierce pang of sharp pain stabbed at Kate's heart. How could she deny her son the opportunity to be with his father?

CHAPTER SEVEN

'Now, don't worry about the cottage. I'll keep an eye on it whilst you're away, and it will be here waiting for you when you come back,' Carol assured Kate comfortingly as she bustled around Kate's bedroom, packing her clothes in the suitcases Sean had provided. 'That is if you are coming back,' she added slyly, giving Kate a questioning look. 'Sean's made no bones about telling everyone that the two of you were married.'

Carol's teasing expression changed to one of anxious concern as she saw the tears filling Kate's eyes. 'Oh, Kate, I'm so sorry,' she apologised.

'It's all right,' Kate assured her. 'I suppose feeling emotionally weak is just another manifestation of this wretched virus. Why has this had to happen to me? All I want is for the next three weeks to be over and for me to be back on my feet,' she told her friend fiercely.

'Mmm. Well, Oliver is certainly enjoying having Sean in his life,' Carol said with gentle warning. 'On the way to school this morning I overheard him trying to convince Sean that a puppy was an essential addition to his life.'

Kate groaned. 'He's been on about having a dog ever since he saw the puppies at the farm last year. I'd love to get him one, but it's just not possible with me working.'

'Heavens, I think Sean's bought you and Oliver enough clothes to last twelve months, never mind three weeks.' Carol laughed, ruefully. 'He'll be back soon, and

112

I know he wants to get off as soon as he can. Where is this house you're going to be staying, by the way?' she asked Kate conversationally, and she ruthlessly squashed the last of the new clothes Sean had insisted on buying for Kate and Oliver into the new cases, whilst Kate looked on unhappily.

'I don't know,' she admitted, for the moment more concerned about her irritation with Sean for bringing yet more new clothes that morning than the location of his home.

'Oliver and I aren't charity cases, you know,' she had thrown bitingly at him when he had arrived back from his shopping spree. 'We don't need you to buy clothes for us, Sean.'

'Oliver is outgrowing virtually everything he has,' Sean had replied quietly. 'And, so far as I can tell, your own clothes—'

'Are my own concern,' Kate had snapped viciously.

Sean hadn't made any further response, but Kate had seen the warning grimness of his mouth as he listened to her churlish outburst.

'Okay, that's the car packed.'

Kate forced a smile for Carol and her husband, Tom, who had come round to see them off. Her smile turned to an anxious frown as Oliver and George came rushing towards them, and Oliver missed a step and fell.

Tom was standing closest to him and automatically bent down to pick him up, smiling reassuringly at him as Oliver's bottom lip thrust out and began to wobble.

'I'll take him!'

Kate's head swivelled round in Sean's direction when she heard the curtness in his voice, and she saw the immediate and determined way in which he went to take

Oliver from the other man. When he held Oliver there was a look in his eyes that made Kate's heart turn over. Sean had resented the fact that Tom had gone to Oliver's rescue!

The scuffed knee and bruised pride attended to, Sean put Oliver down whilst he helped Kate to the car. She could walk a few yards now, but she had to admit that it was easier to lean on Sean than to insist on walking by herself. There was surely no real need, though, for Sean to fasten her seat belt for her?

In the enclosed space of the car she was acutely conscious of the scent of his skin, and of the way the dark bristles of his beard were already roughening his jaw. If she leaned forward only just a little she would be able to press her lips to his skin. Her heart turned over and she gazed at him whilst he was absorbed in his task of making her comfortable. The dark thick fans of his eyelashes cast shadows over his skin, making him look unfairly vulnerable. His concentration on his task reminded her poignantly of Oliver whenever he was engrossed in something.

A small sound bubbled in her throat and Sean turned to look at her. At her and into her. His gaze fastened on her eyes and then dropped with merciless swiftness to her mouth. Kate felt her lips parting as though he had willed them to do so. A small, fine shudder ran through her, and she knew exactly why Sean was no longer looking at her or through her, but at her breasts. She could feel the tight betraying stiffness of her nipples as they responded to her sudden arousal.

'When are we going?'

Oliver's impatient demand brought Kate swiftly back to reality.

'We are going right now,' Sean answered him, standing up and closing the passenger door.

Not even the comfort of Sean's luxurious saloon could completely prevent her body from aching, and by the time they had been travelling for three hours all Kate wanted to do was to be able to lie down and go to sleep, but when Sean asked her if she was all right she nodded, refusing to admit how very uncomfortable and exhausted she felt.

'I'm fine,' she insisted doggedly, refusing to look at him even though she knew he had turned his head to look at her.

'There's bound to be a hotel somewhere round here,' was Sean's undeceived and clipped response. 'We can stop there and you can rest.'

'No,' Kate protested. Hotels, like the new clothes Sean had bought for them, cost money—and she was determined that somehow she was going to repay him every penny he had spent on them.

She hadn't realised that Sean's house was going to be so far away, but her pride would not allow her to ask him exactly where it was or how long it would take them to get there.

Oliver, though, had no such inhibitions, and demanded, 'Are we nearly there yet?'

'Almost,' Sean assured him, without turning his head, and Kate knew that he was smiling because she could hear the smile in his voice.

A wave of tiredness swamped her and she started to slip in her seat, unaware of the anxious look Sean was giving her.

'Not much further now,' she heard him saying quietly.

'Just another couple of junctions on the motorway and then we'll be turning off. We can stop then, and—'

'I've already told you that I don't want to stop,' Kate burst out irritably. 'I never even wanted to go to this wretched house of yours in the first place!' she reminded him bitterly.

As she struggled to make herself comfortable she intercepted the wholly male look her son and his father were exchanging. Anger and anguish tore at her in equal measures—because these two males who shared one another's blood had bonded against her. Her anguish grew to fear that she might not be able to prevent her son from ultimately being hurt by his father.

She should never have agreed to allowing Sean to do this, she berated herself inwardly, as she tried to keep awake and failed.

'Mummy's sleeping.'

Sean gave Oliver a reassuring glance as he pulled off the motorway. 'She's still not properly well.' Inside, he was more anxious than he wanted Oliver to know—and not only because of his concern that the journey might have been too much for Kate.

Perhaps it was just as well that she was asleep, he acknowledged as he drove down the familiar lanes, slowing for the small villages they passed through until finally they came to the one that was their destination.

The slowing movement of the car woke Kate, and she stared out of the passenger window, blinking away her tiredness and then freezing as she recognised her surroundings.

Accusingly she turned towards Sean, but he was concentrating on his driving as they went through the pretty little village she had sighed so ecstatically over the first time they had come here. Nothing had changed, she acknowledged numbly. Everything was still the same, right down to the small river and the main street of huddled soft stone houses with their mullioned windows.

They had reached the end of the village now, and Sean had turned, as she knew he would, up past the ancient church and along a narrow lane. A high stone wall guarded the house from her sight, but already she could see it in her memory. She felt sick, shocked, betrayed as Sean turned in through the familiar gates and the car crunched over the gravel drive.

This was the house he had promised he would buy for her; the house she had fallen so deeply in love with; the house she had talked so excitedly to him about as being the home where they would bring up their children. The house she had never lived in because he had told her that their marriage was over before she had had the opportunity to do so.

The savagery of her pain gnawed at her stomach and anger boiled up inside her. If Oliver hadn't been with them Kate knew that, however unwell she felt, she would have insisted that Sean turn the car round and take her back to her own home.

Instead she had to content herself with an acid whisper. 'I can't believe you would do something like this.'

Without replying Sean opened the car door and got out. The early-evening sun was already warming the soft cream stone of the house, and the scent of the lavender and roses filled Kate's nostrils the moment Sean opened the passenger door for her.

'I've told Mrs Hargreaves to prepare rooms for you and Oliver,' he informed Kate distantly, as he moved to help her out of her seat.

'Don't touch me,' Kate almost spat at him, hurt eyes glowing with the heat of her rage.

How could he do this to her? How could he bring her here, to the home she had thought they would be sharing? She had to swallow against the nausea in her throat.

Oliver got out of the car and danced up and down on the gravel, announcing excitedly, 'Sean, I think a puppy would like it very much here.'

'I'm sure it would,' Sean agreed gravely, but Kate could see that he was grinning, and a wave of fury swept her, making her tremble from head to foot.

'Don't you dare—' she began again, and then had to stop as the door to the house opened and a pin-neat middle-aged woman came hurrying towards them.

'I've done everything you asked me to do, Sean,' Annie Hargreaves told her employer, glancing discreetly at Kate and Oliver as she did so.

'Thanks, Annie,' Sean responded easily. 'We won't keep you any longer. I know that Bill will be waiting for his supper.'

'I'll get off, then, shall I?' she answered, turning and starting to walk away from the house.

'Annie and Bill Hargreaves look after the place for me,' Sean told Kate quietly. 'They don't live in, though—they prefer the staff quarters above the garage. I'll take you up to your room and get you settled, and then Oliver and I will bring everything in—right, Oliver?' Sean asked the little boy.

'Right!' Oliver agreed, with a worshipping smile.

Numbly Kate let Sean take her arm and start to guide her towards the house. She wanted to cry very badly but she was not going to allow herself to do so. Not now. Not ever whilst Sean was around.

The large double doors opened up onto the pretty oval

hallway she remembered, with its fairy-tale return stair-
way, but Kate almost faltered and missed a step as she
stared around the room. She remembered it as being
painted a depressing muddy beige. Now the walls
glowed softly in warm butter-yellow—the same yellow
she had excitedly told Sean she wanted to have it
painted.

The linoleum floor had been replaced with black and
white tiles, and an oval pedestal table stood in the middle
of the room. As she looked round the hallway Kate
started to tremble. Everything in it was just as she had
told Sean she wanted to decorate it, but instead of giving
her pleasure the realisation that he had opted for her
choice of decor made her feel acutely sick.

As Sean studied Kate's colourless face and blank
eyes, she started to sway. Cursing under his breath, he
swept her up into his arms. She had always been delicate
and slender, but now she felt frightening frail, he acknowledged as he ignored her husky rejection of his help
and carried her up the stairs, taking them two at a time.

The rooms he had asked Annie to prepare for her and
Oliver connected with one another. Kate herself had told
him laughingly when they had first viewed the house
that the larger of the two would make an ideal master
bedroom, with the smaller one perfect for a nursery.

'The nurseries are upstairs,' Sean had told her, tongue
in cheek.

Immediately she had turned her face up towards his,
and, laughing, told him, 'You can't fool me, Sean.
You're going to want to have our babies close to us.'

'Our babies,' he had murmured huskily. 'You know,
just hearing you say that makes me want to start making
them right here and now...'

'We haven't bought the house yet—and anyway there isn't a bed,' Kate had reproved him, mock primly.

'Since when have we needed a bed?' Sean had asked.

Even so she had refused to make love in the house, saying firmly that it wasn't proper since it didn't belong to them.

'I suppose that's another of those ''good manners'' rules, is it?' he had teased her. But in reality he had been very grateful for the tactful and loving way she had helped him acquire some necessary social polish.

When they had got home, though, it had been a different story. He had wrapped his arms around her the moment they were inside their front door, and the only sound she had made had been one of eager approval...

'Put me down—I can walk!'

Kate's fiercely independent demand told Sean that she was certainly not sharing the bitter sweetness of his sensual memories.

'Maybe you can walk,' he countered grimly. 'But on the evidence of what just happened I doubt that you could have made it all the way up these stairs unaided.'

Kate wanted to argue with him, but she was too conscious of the frantic beat of her heart. She could still remember how she had teased Sean when they had first started dating about the way he loved picking her up, accusing him of wanting to show off his superior male muscle power. But secretly inside a part of her had been thrilled by such evidence of his strength.

Now, though, it was resentment that was responsible for the rapid flip-flopping of her heartbeat, she told herself firmly, determinedly ignoring the small, conscientious inner voice that cautioned her that her resentment was desperately self-defensive.

Why should she need to feel self-defensive, after all?

she asked herself in silent bitterness. There might be a very small rebellious and unheeding part of her that was still physically responsive to Sean, but that was all. How could she, a loving and responsible mother, ever forget Sean's refusal to accept that Oliver was his son?

It was just the realisation that he had brought her here to this house—the house she had fallen in love with, had believed she would bring their family up in—that was making her feel so vulnerable, making her long to pillow her head against his shoulder and let her body relax into the comfort and security of his.

'Here we are.'

Sean used his foot to nudge open the heavy door and Kate swivelled her head to look into the room beyond it.

Sunlight warmed the soft cream walls, and wonderfully heavy curtains made of terracotta and cream toile de Jouy fabric hung from the windows, draped the antique half-tester bed. A cream carpet covered the floor, and the whole colour scheme set off the pretty late-Georgian mahogany furniture.

When Sean placed her on the bed Kate had to struggle not to give way to her emotions. The room was exactly as she had excitedly planned to decorate it, right down to the elegant cream blind at the window.

'I've had a bed put in the nursery for Oliver,' Sean was telling her practically, clearly oblivious to the emotional impact the room had on her. Had Sean converted the room next to the nursery into a bathroom, as she had wanted?

She didn't feel she could trust herself to ask, and was glad that she hadn't when Oliver came rushing in, his face alight with excitement.

'Annie says that I can go and see her dog if you say yes, Mummy,' he announced importantly.

'Annie?' Kate checked him swiftly. Sean might refer to his housekeeper and her husband by their Christian names, but Kate wasn't going to have Oliver copy his father unless he had been given permission to do so.

'Annie prefers to be addressed by her first name.' Sean stepped in immediately, reading her mind so easily and so quickly that for a moment Kate couldn't reply. 'And Oliver will be perfectly safe with her dog,' Sean continued. 'I'll take him down to meet her myself.'

Ignoring Kate, Oliver threw his arms around Sean's legs and hugged him tightly, looking up at him with an expression of beatific adoration.

Looking on, Kate could feel her heart turning over slowly and painfully inside her chest, its cavity tight with pain and love and fear.

'Can we go now?' Oliver was pleading, but Sean shook his head.

'No, not now. We'll go tomorrow morning.'

Kate held her breath warily, half anticipating that Oliver might refuse to accept what Sean had told him. Certainly he scowled, and looked as though he was about to object, but, as if he had prepared himself for Oliver's reaction, Sean simply ignored his behaviour.

'Come and have a look at your bedroom, Ollie,' Sean said instead. 'It's right here, next to Mummy's.'

Sean's use of that familiar sweet 'Ollie' made Kate clench her hands into small fists—as did the automatic way in which Sean put his hand down so that Oliver could put his much smaller one into it. Hand in hand, father and son went to inspect the room, leaving her to stare anxiously after their departing backs.

From inside the room she heard Oliver saying,

'There's plenty of room on the floor in here for your sleeping bag, Sean. You'll be able to sleep in my room, and not Mummy's.'

'Well, I'd like to do that, Oliver,' Kate could hear Sean responding seriously. 'But, you see, I have my own bedroom here—like you do at your house.'

'But I want you to sleep here with me and my mummy,' Oliver was insisting, and somehow, without knowing how she knew, Kate sensed that Sean had bent down and picked Oliver up.

'Well, when we were at your house your mummy wasn't very well, was she? And I had to be there in case she needed me. But she's much better now.'

'Well, you could sleep in the same bed, like George's mummy and daddy do,' Oliver offered, with almost-five-year-old logic that made Kate's eyes burn with dry pain.

In the room where a small child's bed had been set up for Oliver, Sean turned towards the window, the boy still in his arms. He could still feel the gut-wrenching kick of longing that Oliver's innocent suggestion had prompted.

Kate—the Kate who was no longer his gentle, loving Kathy—would never willingly welcome him into her bed. Sean knew that. Yes, on one fever-racked night when she had not known the difference between their past and their present she might have been his Kathy once again, but not in reality.

It was growing dusk and Oliver was leaning heavily against him. Reluctantly Sean remembered the emotions that had struck him when he had seen Tom go to Oliver's rescue, when he had felt irrationally that the other man was usurping his rightful role. His arms tightened around Oliver. Was the emotional bond he was beginning to develop with Oliver caused by the fact that

Oliver was Kate's child? Or was it because somehow he had begun to love Oliver for himself, to feel a fatherly love towards him?

'Why don't I put a video on for you, Ollie?' he suggested gently now. 'And then you can sit and watch it for a while before bed.'

'And then will we read Mummy a story?'

Sean ruffled the thick hair ruefully. Determined not to be accused by Kate of using the television as a baby-minder for her son, Sean had instituted a bedtime ritual, aided by Oliver, of them reading a story together. Quite why he had decided that this should be done in Kate's bedroom he had no real idea, other than that he'd known how important it would be to her that she shared in her son's life in every way she could.

A small sound by the door made him turn round, and the tightening of his mouth concealed his anguished concern as he saw Kate standing there, holding onto the door itself for support.

'You're supposed to be resting,' he said curtly.

'Only when I need to, and right now I don't need to,' Kate answered evenly, refusing to look at him and holding out her arms to Oliver instead.

'Why don't I read you a story tonight, Ollie?' she suggested. 'I'm sure that Sean has lots to do.'

To Kate's shock, instead of wriggling to be set free by Sean, Oliver leaned even further into him as Sean set him on his feet.

Kate looked out through the french windows of the pretty sitting room to where Oliver was playing excitedly on the lawn with the Hargreaveses' good-natured collie dog. Child and dog were indulging in what was obviously a mutually blissful game of chase, and when

Oliver stumbled and fell on the lawn the dog was immediately all canine concern, standing anxiously over him as the little boy got to his feet undamaged.

They had been living in Sean's house for just over two weeks, and Kate was convinced that she was now fully recovered. Which meant…which meant that it was time for her and Oliver to return to their own home and their own lives.

Kate couldn't deceive herself that Oliver would want to leave. He adored Sean. Kate tensed as she saw Sean strolling across the lawn towards their son. He had left the house shortly after breakfast to attend a business meeting. The moment Oliver saw him he ran towards him, laughing happily when Sean picked him up and swung him round.

As she watched them, inside her head Kate could see another picture. In this one she was standing at Sean's side as Oliver ran towards them both, and Sean's arm was holding her close to his side whilst her head rested on his shoulder.

Her legs felt weak and her whole body was trembling—but not because she had been ill. No, she had to face up to the truth that was responsible for her physical malaise.

It seemed that nothing, not even his rejection of his son, could totally destroy her love for Sean. It was too deeply embedded within her.

Panic, anger and fear fought frantically inside her. She had to tell Sean that she wanted to leave and she had to tell him now!

Taking a deep breath, Kate went out to join them.

As he saw her approaching Sean put Oliver down.

'I'm going to take Nell home for her tea now,' Oliver

announced importantly to Kate, manfully taking a firm hold of the obliging dog's collar.

At any other time Kate knew she would have been tenderly amused, ruefully suspecting that it was the dog who was in charge of her son rather than the other away around as the two of them headed to where the house-keeper was waiting for them. But as she watched them Kate was acutely conscious of Sean coming to stand by her side. Immediately she moved slightly away from him. Letting him get too close to her was dangerous!

Bending his head, he told her quietly, 'I've been thinking there's no real reason why Oliver shouldn't have a dog of his own. In fact I called in to see a litter of Labrador pups on my way back this afternoon. They aren't quite old enough to leave their mother yet, but if you feel up to it we could drive over there tomorrow and Ollie could choose his own—'

'No! Oliver is not having a dog!' Kate stopped him sharply and Sean started to frown.

'Kate, he's desperate for one.'

'Do you think I don't know that?' Kate challenged. 'You might have been "thinking", Sean, but you obviously haven't thought enough,' she told him passionately. 'Surely you must realise how impossible it would be for him to have a dog at home? You know that I have to work.' Angrily she turned away from him.

'Kate—' Sean protested, putting his hand on her arm.

Immediately Kate tried to snatch her arm away, demanding furiously, 'Let go of me. I hate you touching me.'

'What?'

When she saw the expression darkening Sean's eyes Kate knew that she had gone too far. But it was too late to retract her reckless words, because he was pulling her into his hold, his arms pinioning her to his body as he looked down into her face.

'No!' Kate protested, but her denial was already being crushed beneath the pressure of Sean's angry kiss. His lips ground down on hers and his fingers tightened into the soft flesh of her arms.

Anger boiled through her veins, making her return the savage intensity of Sean's kiss. But it was an anger bred from longing and need, Kate recognised helplessly, as her own body turned traitor against her and she heard herself moaning softly with liquid pleasure beneath the demanding pressure of Sean's mouth.

Somehow the past and his betrayal of her slipped away. Without her realising it, her hands had lifted to hold Sean's face, and her heart leapt with shatteringly intense emotion. Just the slightly rough feel of his morning-shaved skin was enough to take her arousal levels dangerously higher.

Whilst her hands held Sean's face, his were moulding her body with familiar caresses, kneading her shoulders, then stroking down her spine, spanning the back of her waist and then moving lower. Kate could feel herself starting to tremble as his hands slid past her hips. His thumbs grazed her hipbones themselves, and were then withdrawn as he pulled her fiercely against his own body.

It should have been impossible for her to feel the same shockingly intense thrill of sensual arousal now, as she felt the hard fullness of Sean's erection, as she had done that very first time he had held her like this—but she did. If anything her awareness and the reaction of her body now, as a woman and not as a girl, was far more immediate and fiercely erotic than it had been then.

Perhaps it was because then she'd had no experience

by which to measure the pleasure his arousal could lead to, whereas now she most certainly did. Already her imagination had broken free of her control and was filling her head with wanton images, bombarding her senses with messages and promises that totally destroyed her defences.

Within the space of a few seconds her own body was as eager for his as it had been when she was eighteen.

The movement of his hand from her bottom to her breast evoked a low sound of delirious pleasure from her throat and she angled her body so that her breast filled his hand.

'No, Sean. No… Mmm, like that…' Kate could hear herself whispering incoherent urgent words of praise and pleasure between the frantic hungry kisses with which she was caressing his mouth. She no longer cared about what she might be revealing, only what she was feeling! 'Sean.' As she moaned his name she covered the hand he had placed over her breast with her own and whispered achingly, 'Touch me properly, Sean.'

'Properly?'

She could hear the thick male arousal roughening his voice and her skin prickled in female response to it.

'You know what I mean,' she urged him hotly. 'You know what I like.'

'You mean this?'

He was caressing the tender flesh surrounding the tormented nub of her nipple and Kate trembled violently in reaction.

'Mmm, yes. That,' Kate agreed huskily. 'And more, Sean—but without my clothes. No clothes. Just you,' she continued. 'Just you and me.'

'No clothes? Not even like this?' Pushing down her

bra, Sean used his thumb and finger to delicately rub the silk fabric of her top against the stiff thrust of her nipple.

Immediately Kate cried out in agonised pleasure.

'Good...? That was good?' Sean's voice was so thick and low Kate could barely hear it, but she didn't care. He had pushed her clothes completely aside now, and she could see the creamy swell of her breast filling the darkness of his hand as he slowly caressed her eager nipple.

Standing silently in his hold, she gave in to the violent shudders of pleasure ripping through her.

'And with your mouth...' she begged him. The words were jerked from her lips as her body suddenly convulsed against him.

'Kate! Kate!'

Just the way he was saying her name touched every one of her senses. He took hold of her hand and dragged it against his own body. Her fingers curled eagerly around the erection straining against his clothes, making a feverish exploration of their remembered territory. But she wanted to feel him without anything in the way.

She was stretching her hand towards his zip when his mobile rang shrilly, the sound jerking Kate back into reality.

What was she doing? Pulling away from Sean, she started to run towards the house, wanting to escape not just from him but also from her own self-imposed humiliation.

'Kate!'

Sean cursed under his breath when she refused to listen. The mobile was still ringing. Impatiently he switched it off, then started to follow her.

*　　*　　*

As soon as she reached her room Kate opened the wardrobe and pulled out the suitcases Sean had bought for them. Opening one of them, she started to drag clothes off the rail and throw them into it.

'What are you doing?'

The sound of Sean's voice made her swing round. 'What does it look like?' she snapped. 'I'm packing. Oliver and I are leaving! We should never have come here in the first place. I knew—'

'You knew what?' Sean stopped her.

He was looking at her with a glint in his eyes that made her heart thump and apprehension feather chillingly down her spine, but angrily Kate refused to bend.

'I know that I just don't want to be here with you, Sean,' Kate answered angrily. 'Look, I don't want to talk about it,' she threw at him when he didn't answer her.

'Less than five minutes ago you were in my arms and—'

'I've just told you I don't want to talk about it!' Kate stormed 'That...what just happened...meant nothing. It was just...'

'Just what?' Sean challenged her with a softness that was far more dangerous than anger would have been.

He was trying to make her look at him, Kate recognised, but if she did she knew he would see in her eyes how vulnerable she was. Keeping her face averted from him, she insisted stubbornly, 'Nothing!'

Something in his voice had warned her of what was to come. Panicking, Kate dropped the clothes she was holding and started to run, only realising when it was too late that—idiotically—she had run towards the bed instead of the door. Now she was backed up against it, with Sean standing in front her and no option but to turn round and try to scramble over it.

'Nice move,' she heard him say with soft amusement from behind her, and his fingers curled round her ankle as he kneeled on the bed looking down at her.

'I always did think that you've got the sexiest backside I've ever seen: nicely curved and temptingly peachy. And I can remember…'

Kate did not want to hear what he could remember, and for a very good reason. She feared that listening to what Sean could remember might make her feel even more dangerously vulnerable.

Surely there was no good reason why she should feel almost the exact same mix of nervousness and excitement lying here on a bed now, with Sean leaning over her, as she had done that very first time they had been together like this? They had been lovers; they had been married and they had been divorced—his body was almost as familiar to her as her own.

But she did feel the same, and she did feel… Stubbornly Kate tried to deny her feelings, to ignore as well the sensual caress of the bracelet of Sean's fingers round her ankle. She stiffened her body against it, just as she refused to look away from Sean when he turned his head to smile into her eyes.

'Now, about this ''nothing'',' he murmured, almost affably. 'Let's go through it all again, shall we? Starting right here…'

Somehow he was down on the bed beside her, the upper half of his body pinning hers to the bed, and shamingly Kate knew that a part of her was already greedily soaking up the pleasure of having him so close.

One look at his eyes told her what was going to happen. He was looking directly and deliberately at her mouth, and somehow that look was making her part her lips and wet their nervousness with the tip of her tongue.

'Nothing?' His fingertip traced the curve of her jaw and then the shape of her lips, slowly and heart-stoppingly, whilst he continued to look down at her.

'You know that I'm going to kiss you now don't you?' he whispered.

She tried to say no. She tried to mean no. But Sean was using unfair weapons against her. He knew how very vulnerable she had always been to that slow, sensual, oh-so-seductively-sweet way he had of kissing her, that made her insides melt and her lips cling to him, and the reason he knew was because she herself had told him so, over and over again, in their shared past. And maybe more recently in the heat of that fevered night? Right now all she seemed capable of doing was focusing on his mouth, whilst her heart-rate accelerated.

It had been a bad mistake to close her eyes, Kate acknowledged helplessly, a flurry of heartbeats later, because closing her eyes had somehow transformed her back into the girl she had been the first time Sean had kissed her like this.

Now, as then, her lips parted willingly and eagerly, her senses tensely aroused by the passionate intimacy of his tongue against her own, primed by the kisses they had already shared. Shockingly Kate recognised that her body was rebelliously impatient of any gentle preliminaries, that she was being consumed by a fierce, hungry surging need.

She lifted her hands to Sean's shoulders and held onto them, needing the security of their strength as her own longing smashed down on her, carrying her bodily in its fast-paced flow.

Beneath Sean's, her mouth clung and hungered, and her hands left his shoulders to press his body down harder into her own. She felt Sean tense and lift his mouth from hers to look down into her face.

Surely the hand lifted to his face, the fingers dragged sensuously against his jaw and then raised to trace the shape of his lips and run over and over his mouth could not be hers? Surely that liquid aching heat spreading through her body could be controlled if she really tried?

Surely this wasn't her, lifting her head off the bed and cupping Sean's face so that she could press impassioned kisses into his skin whilst she moaned her need softly into his mouth?

'Touch me, Sean.' *Love me,* Kate whispered silently inside herself as she stroked a trembling finger over the mouth she had just kissed. 'Make it like it used to be for us...'

Had she really said that?

'Like it used to be?' she heard Sean repeat softly. 'You mean when we were so hungry for one another that not being together was a physical pain? Is that what you mean, Kate? That you want me like that? Like this?'

As he spoke his hands were shaping her body, and Kate could feel the small flames of desire inside her, feeding on his words and growing stronger. Soon there would be a conflagration which would threaten to destroy her, and yet somehow she no longer cared about her danger—all she cared about was this, and now, and Sean's hands on her flesh, Sean's mouth on her mouth, Sean's body covering her body. The wild, untrammelled flood-force of her own dammed-up love and need crashed through the barricade, taking every single last bit of her resistance with it.

Willingly, eagerly and passionately she savoured the hot, urgent strength of Sean's kiss, meeting it and matching it just as she had done when their love was new and her faith and trust in him whole and unbroken. With her eyes closed she could even almost smell the scent of their shared past—the hot dusty air in the small suburban street mingling erotically with the fresh male heat of Sean's skin and her own excited arousal.

But the hand she lifted to curl round Sean's neck, to hold him whilst she prolonged their kiss, was the hand of the woman she was today—and today she wanted Sean as the woman she was, Kate recognised emotionally. And how she wanted him! So much, so very, very much. Her body hungered for him like parched earth crying out in silent agony for the caress of rain.

Only her need wasn't silent any more. It poured from her lips in a soft litany of longing, word on word, plea on plea, as she begged him, 'Sean—my clothes… I don't want them. I want you—your hands, your skin. You.' Kate could feel herself shuddering with the intensity of her own feelings as she twined her arms around him and her body moved restlessly against his. 'I want you, Sean,' she told him. 'The whole essence of you…all of you…'

It had always amazed her that those big, strong hands could be so delicately gentle and assured when removing her clothes, but now their unexpected impatience as Sean pulled and tugged at fabric and fastenings sent a fierce thrill of pleasure through her.

'Kate. Kate. Oh, God, how I've missed you—and this—us…'

The words tumbled thickly from Sean's tongue and were breathed against her skin as he kissed the flesh he was revealing. The sensual drift of his hands had become an urgent, compelling possession that demanded her body give itself over to him completely. The hard need of his mouth on hers spoke of a hunger so long denied that it might easily devour them both. But Kate only gloried in the realisation. How could she not when it so exactly mirrored her own feelings? The fierce thrust of Sean's tongue against her own; the heavy weight of his hand cupping the curve of her hip so possessively; the grinding heat of his body against her own—she welcomed them all.

'Take off your own clothes, Sean,' she begged him huskily. 'I need to feel you against me.' As she spoke she shuddered slightly, remembering how it had felt to have the hot satin of his skin next to her own.

'You do it,' Sean answered.

When she hesitated, he took her hand and lifted it to his body.

'Did I ever tell you how much it turned me on when you undressed me?'

When Kate just looked at him, in passion-soaked silence, he added thickly, 'Do you want me to tell you how much you are turning me on now? Do you want me to show you how much you are turning me on now, Kate?'

She was trembling so violently that she couldn't even unfasten the buttons on his shirt.

'You do it like this,' Sean said huskily, covering her hand with his own. 'And then you do this—' He guided her hand to push his shirt off his body. 'And I do this...'

Kate's whole body arched as he cupped her breast with his hand and then bent his head to cover her tight nipple with his mouth. Kate heard her own raw moan of fierce arousal as his tongue stroked the hard nub of flesh, teasing it, tormenting it. Sean seemed to know exactly when she reached the point where she couldn't bear the torment any longer, because suddenly he took the hard, wanton ache of her nipple into his mouth and drew rhythmically on it, until Kate felt as though that same rhythm was pulsing throughout her whole body, gathering deep inside her, making her want to open her legs and wrap them tightly around him.

Fiercely she tugged at his clothes and Sean helped her.

'Kate!'

The explosive denial Sean made as he virtually pushed her away made Kate stare uncomprehendingly at him.

'If I let you touch me like that I'll come too soon,' he told her rawly. 'And I don't want to do that until I've given you more pleasure than you've ever known. Until I've given you that pleasure and watched you take it from me. Until I'm inside you, where I've ached to be every single night since I've been without you. Until I've done this…'

Long, long before the leisurely journey his hands and his mouth were making over her body had reached the small swell of her belly, Kate was trembling visibly with desire.

As she felt the brush of his mouth against the soft skin of her inner thigh she closed her eyes in aching mute anticipation. His hand covered her sex, making the demanding, hungry pulse deep inside her beat faster. When his fingers parted the arousal-swollen lips of her sex she cried out loud eagerly, almost unable to bear the searing pleasure of his touch.

Her body ached and pulsed, and just the touch of his fingers against her wetness made her rake her fingers against his skin. But the eager sensual movement of her body stilled when Sean exposed the swollen, secret nub of pleasure those lips had concealed to the hungry caress of his tongue.

Kate was helpless to stop the feeling that ran through,

over her, filling her and taking her over, making her cry out and lift her body to Sean's mouth as he brought her to that place she had not known for so very long.

And then, when Sean moved and positioned himself in between her legs, taking her in his arms, Kate welcomed him with fierce pleasure. This was what she ached for—this total possession of him and by him, this hard, purposeful thrusting of him within her, that fulfilled and completed her. This climbing together towards that shimmering, shining place where for a brief heartbeat of time they were almost immortal.

Kate reached it first, crying out, her body tensing round Sean to take him with her. And as she felt the familiar pulse of his satisfaction within her Kate's eyes filled with tears.

That this act, so very, very intense and erotically a pleasure beyond all pleasures for those who loved one another, could also be the creation of life, had always given it an extra special intensity for her.

Once she had believed that Sean shared that feeling with her—he had even said that to her the first time she had shyly confided to him her deep, almost spiritual feelings about making love.

And yet now he was denying his own child!

Bitter self-loathing filled her. Where was her pride and her self-respect?

She could feel Sean withdrawing from her, not just physically but emotionally as well, and suddenly a black wave of misery and exhaustion swamped over her.

Sean looked down at the bed where Kate lay fast asleep. He had left her to go to the bathroom, and when he had come back she had been asleep. Anguish shadowed his eyes and hollowed his face as he watched her.

Whilst making love with her he had forgotten there had been another man in her life—someone man enough to give her a child. Bitterness carved his mouth into hard anger.

In his arms she had responded to him as though no other man had ever touched her, as though she had never wanted any other man to touch her... And God alone knew how much he ached and needed to believe that she hadn't. The sweet taste of her still clung to his lips, and the scent of her filled the air around him.

He couldn't endure to live without her any longer, Sean recognised bleakly. Even knowing all that he knew about her!

CHAPTER EIGHT

KATE woke up slowly and languorously, her mouth curling into a smile of remembered bliss. Still half asleep, she stretched her body. Its telltale ache made her smile deepen. There was nothing like waking up in the morning filled with feel-good hormones, she acknowledged happily, reaching out her hand to Sean.

Sean! The speed with which she was catapulted from her warm security to stark reality physically hurt.

She sat up in the bed, her mind an agitated jumble of anxious, angry thoughts. The clothes she had been intending to pack had gone, and so too had the suitcases! The realisation that it was nine o'clock in the morning increased her agitation. It had been late afternoon when she had come up here, and...

Frantically she reined in her speeding thoughts. She couldn't believe she had slept so long and so deeply—although Sean had always teased her about it, claiming that he took it as a compliment that his lovemaking fulfilled her to such an extent.

The very words 'Sean' and 'lovemaking' linked together were making her heart thud erratically—with fury, she told herself crossly, not because of any other reason.

The sudden opening of her bedroom door brought an abrupt halt to her thoughts.

'Mummy!'

Kate's heart turned over as she looked at her son. He was wearing some of the new clothes Sean had insisted on buying for him: a pair of workman-like denim dungarees that made him look heartbreakingly grown up and yet endearingly little-boyish at the same time.

'We've brought you your breakfast,' he said excitedly.

Kate's heart plummeted at his 'we', and she prayed it was the housekeeper he was referring to, not Sean. But the tension in her stomach told her that it was Sean even before he followed Oliver into her room, carrying a heavily laden tray.

'You've been asleep for a very long time,' Oliver reproached her, and then beamed from ear to ear. 'Mummy, I made your toast—and my daddy helped me...'

All three of them froze, and above and beyond her own anguish Kate was seared by the look in Oliver's eyes, his face scarlet as he ran to her and clambered onto the bed, burying his hot, embarrassed face against her body. Automatically she wrapped her arms protectively around him. Unlike Kate, he was too young to recognise why he had called Sean his daddy, but he was not too young to know that he should not have done.

Over Oliver's downbent head Sean looked at Kate, and he put down the tray in silence before turning to leave.

It couldn't be put off any longer, Kate told herself fiercely. Her heart had bled drops of pure concentrated emotion for her son, his betrayal of his feelings and his need, but Oliver's innocent indication of the role he longed to have Sean play in his life had hardened her resolve to leave.

It filled her with a pain like no other she had ever known to recognise her son's vulnerability. How much unintentional damage had she already done by letting him know Sean?

She was well aware of the old cynical saying that it was a wise child that knew its own father. But what if somehow, somewhere, unknown to modern scientists, there was a primitive, instinctive bond between father and child that had been activated by Sean's appearance in Oliver's life?

The feelings she had experienced at Oliver's realisation of his *faux pas* in calling Sean his 'daddy' went way beyond tears. Of course she had pretended not to be aware of the cause of Oliver's crimson face and discomfort, had coaxed him to share her toast and to tell her about the previous afternoon's activities, when the housekeeper had let him play with the dog and then given him his tea.

But even that had been a mistake, Kate reflected unhappily. Because Oliver had gone on to tell her that Sean had collected him from the housekeeper's quarters, brought him back, given him his bath and read his story to him.

'D— Sean said that you were very tired and needed to sleep.' Oliver's innocent comment had torn at her heart as Kate had acknowledged just why she had 'needed to sleep'.

But even worse than that had been the longingly hopeful look in Oliver's eyes when he had looked up at her and told her, 'I want to stay here for ever, with Nell... and with Sean...'

Kate's heart had sunk when he had suddenly avoided looking at her.

'Well, it has been very nice here,' she had agreed, trying to sound calm. 'But what about George? He's your friend and—'

Oliver had stopped her stubbornly. 'Sean is my friend, and so is Nell. A dog can be a friend, and Nell is mine!' And had completely defeated her when he had added, 'I wish that Sean was my daddy.'

Now, from the sitting room window, she could see Oliver industriously helping the gardener to 'weed'. Helplessly she closed her eyes against her own pain.

When she opened them again she could see Sean's reflection in the glass beside her own. Immediately she turned round.

'We need to talk,' Sean told her flatly.

'There's nothing to talk about.' Kate stopped him bitterly. 'I've almost finished packing, and—' Unable to stop herself, she said quickly, 'I know you must think that I primed Oliver to...to say what he said. But I didn't. He sees George with Tom and... He...he's had this bee in his bonnet for a while, about not having a father...'

Sean recognised that the new name she had chosen for herself suited her. She was Kate now, a woman. Not Kathy, a girl. And he knew that there was something about Kate that he responded to as a man. Kathy the girl had gone, and it grieved him to know that this maturing process had taken place without him being there to share in it. And if that grieved him how the hell was he going to feel if she spent the rest of her life apart from him?

'I've got a proposition to put to you,' he said curtly. 'Or perhaps I should more properly say a proposal,' he amended heavily into the silence that followed his initial words.

'A proposal?' Kate tasted the word cautiously, her stomach churning. What was he going to do? Offer her money to take Oliver away and deny that he was his father? 'What kind of proposal?' she challenged him suspiciously. The look he was giving her was decidedly ironic.

'I thought you knew, Kate, that in my world there is only one kind of proposal a man makes to a woman the morning after they have spent the night together. Anything else *would* be a proposition.' When she went rigid and simply stared at him, he elucidated tiredly, 'I am asking you to marry me, Kate.'

The shock ran through her like lightning, a vivid flash of disbelief followed by an unbelievably intense and coruscating pain, out of which she could only demand sharply, 'Why?'

'Why? Because I want you back as my wife, and—' Sean turned his head and looked out across the lawn, his face averted so that Kate could not see his expression as he added emotionlessly, 'And because I want Oliver as my son.'

It was, Kate decided, almost as though she was hearing Sean speak from very far away, through an impenetrable glass wall.

The angry and rejecting words, *But Oliver* is *your son* rolled like thunder through her heart, but somehow she managed to hold them back. And she held them back because inside her head she had a painfully clear image of a small boy who desperately wanted a father. If she knew anything about Sean she knew that he was a man who committed himself totally and completely to everything he decided to do—almost single-mindedly so at times.

She had seen for herself the rapport he was developing with Oliver, and she knew that to pretend such a bond was simply not in Sean's nature. But she could not and would not take risks with her son's emotional future!

'Your son?' she questioned coldly 'But, Sean, you

have already refused to accept that Oliver is your son. You have told me that you believe another man fathered him, and, believing that—'

'That isn't a road I'm prepared to go down.' Sean stopped her sharply. When he saw her face he demanded savagely, 'Don't you realise how it feels for me to know that there's been another man in your life? In your bed? Didn't last night tell you anything about how much I still want you? The only way I can deal with this is to draw a line under it, Kate, to box it up and bury it somewhere so deep that it can never be disinterred.'

'Do you think it's any different for me? You were unfaithful to me, Sean.'

'You can forget all about her, Kate. She never really—'

'Meant anything to you?' Kate stopped him bitingly.

Sean looked away from her. He had almost fallen into the trap of saying that the other woman had never really existed!

What would Kate think if she knew the pitiful, pathetic truth about him? How would she react? Would she pity him? Reject him? Would knowing the truth enable her to understand how deeply and completely he loved Oliver and wanted to be a father to him?

A part of him yearned to share his knowledge and his pain with her, but his pride held him back.

'Oliver needs a father,' he said heavily instead. 'And I—'

'You want to take pity on us?' Kate suggested angrily, reluctant to admit even to herself just how strongly his impassioned words had touched her emotions.

'No,' Sean denied, the glimmer of ironic self-mockery glinting in his eyes, concealing his pain. 'I want you and Oliver to take pity on me.'

It was as close as he could bring himself to telling her the truth.

When she didn't answer he told her bleakly, 'Both of us know how it feels to grow up without the love of a parent. Oliver wants a father.'

Kate couldn't stand any more. The words *Oliver has a father* burned on her lips, but in the garden she could see her son, and already she knew how much it would mean to him if she agreed to what Sean was suggesting. 'I—I...' As she tried to squeeze out her denial all she could hear was Oliver calling Sean his daddy.

She might be able to resist all the emotional pressure that Sean could possibly put on her, but no way could she resist that special sound she had heard in her son's voice.

She took a deep breath. 'Very well. I accept. But if you ever, *ever* do anything to hurt Oliver I shall leave you there and then,' she warned him passionately.

She had already turned away from him when she heard him coming after her. As she stopped moving he took hold of her, imprisoning her in his arms whilst he kissed her with fierce passion.

Helplessly Kate felt her mouth softening beneath his, and her traitorous body, still flooded with sensual memories of his lovemaking, simply softened into his until she was moulded against him so closely that she might have been a part of him. He might have started the kiss, but she was the one who prolonged it, Kate recognised hazily as her mouth clung to his, and she gave in to her need to trace the shape of his mouth with her tongue-tip and to slide her fingers into the thick darkness of his hair.

Against her body she could feel the hard pulse of his erection. Mindlessly she pressed closer to it, waiting for

Sean to cup her breast with his hand and discover the hard eagerness of her nipple. But instead he pushed her way from him, breaking the kiss.

Humiliated, she was about to walk away from him when she heard him saying in quiet explanation and warning, 'Oliver!'

It shocked her to realise that Sean had been more aware of their son's approach than her, but her hope that Oliver had not witnessed their intimacy foundered as he stepped through the open french window and immediately demanded, 'Why were you kissing Sean, Mummy?'

Before Kate could think of anything to say, Sean answered for her, telling him calmly, 'We were kissing because we are going to get married, and that's what married people do.'

As he finished speaking Sean kneeled down and held out his arms to Oliver. 'I've asked your mummy to marry me, Oliver. And now there's something I want to ask you.' Kate couldn't help it; emotion welled up inside her. But it was nothing to what she felt when Sean continued, 'Will you let me be your daddy, Oliver?'

The look on Oliver's face as it lit up with delight was all the answer he needed to give—that and the fact that he threw himself bodily into Sean's arms!

As Sean stood up, hoisting Oliver onto his shoulder, the little boy was chanting, 'Daddy—Daddy. I can call you Daddy now, can't I, Sean?'

As Sean nodded his head Kate was sure she could see the glint of moisture in his eyes.

CHAPTER NINE

SEAN had insisted on a church ceremony, much to Kate's surprise, and even more surprising was just how very much like a new bride she actually felt, standing in the doorway of the small church ready to walk down the aisle to where Sean was waiting for her.

The graceful dress she was wearing was cream, the heavy satin fabric rustling expensively as she turned to look down at Oliver. 'Ready, Ollie?' she asked him tenderly.

He had been so excited about today, but now that it was here he looked round-eyed and slightly over-awed.

John was going to give her away, but it was Oliver who was going to walk down the aisle with her. That had been her decision, and one that Sean had listened to in shuttered-eyed silence.

Inside the church, with the heat of the sun shut away, the timelessness of this place where people had worshipped century upon century cast its own special grace over them as Oliver reached up and slipped his hand into hers.

Together, as the sound of the organ music surged and swelled, mother and son walked towards the man waiting for them, and into whose care they were giving themselves.

They had almost reached him when Oliver tugged on Kate's hand and announced in a loud stage whisper, 'Mummy, I'm really glad that Sean is going to marry us.'

Kate completed the last few steps in a blur of tears, totally overwhelmed by her emotions.

The artfully simple bouquet of lilies and greenery she carried were removed from her by Carol, but when her friend went to take Oliver's hand, to lead him away, Sean shook his head and took it himself.

Then, with Oliver standing between them and both of them holding one of his hands, the vicar began the service that would reunite them, bind them not just as husband and wife, but this time as parents as well.

'Okay?'

As the bells pealed in celebration of their marriage and the sun shone down Kate nodded mutely. Surely she wasn't still brooding on the perfunctory kiss with which Sean had acknowledged his new commitment to her, was she?

She had remarried him because he was Oliver's father, and not for any other reason, she told herself fiercely.

Their wedding breakfast was being held in a private dining room at a very exclusive local hotel, and from there they were flying to Italy for a few days. Initially she had tried to protest, but Sean had overruled her, announcing that the three of them needed time together alone, away from their normal environment, to start establishing their new roles in one another's lives.

Of the three of them, Oliver had certainly had no difficulties whatsoever in adapting. The word 'daddy' seemed to leave his lips with increasing regularity. In fact she could hear him saying it now, as he beamed up at Sean and told him importantly that he was now his little boy.

A small shadow touched Kate's face.

'I want to adopt Oliver legally,' Sean had told her abruptly the previous week.

Kate had refused to respond. How could he adopt his own son?

Kate opened her eyes reluctantly, unwilling to abandon the dream she had just been having in which she had been lying in Sean's arms, their naked bodies entwined. The huge bed in their hotel suite was empty of her husband, though. Last night, following their arrival, when she had seen the suite, she had unwisely exclaimed, 'Are we all in the same room?'

'I thought you'd prefer it that way,' Sean had responded.

'Yes. I do,' Kate had agreed, but she knew that a tiny part of her couldn't help comparing the circumstances of this, their second honeymoon, to the first one they had shared. Their surroundings might not have been anything like as luxurious, but even the air in the small room had been so drenched with the scent of their love and hunger for one another that it had been an aphrodisiac all on its own.

That had been then, though, and this was now!

And where was Oliver? The small bed Sean had insisted on having set up in their room was also empty.

Anxiously she pushed back the bedclothes and reached for her robe. They'd arrived so late in the evening that she had done no more than nod in acceptance of Sean's description of their suite and its facilities, but now, as she pushed opened the door onto their private patio, she caught her breath in delight.

The hotel had originally been a small palace, and their suite was at ground level for Oliver's benefit. From the patio Kate could see the still blue water of the hotel's breathtakingly effective infinity pool. The sound of splashing water to the side of her caught her attention, and she froze as she realised that it was Oliver who was causing it, and Sean stood at his side in what was obviously a children's swimming area, encouraging him to swim.

Encouraging him to swim! But Ollie couldn't swim. She had done everything she could to get him to swim, right from him being a baby, but he had steadfastly clung on to his terror of the water. Until now… Until Sean…

Out of nowhere a feeling she just did not want to analyse struck her. She felt excluded, unwanted. She felt jealous, Kate recognised, angry with herself for having such feelings.

Sean had told her that he wanted to remarry her because of Oliver, but suddenly it was striking her exactly what that meant.

Sean had always wanted a son, and now, as a very successful businessman, no doubt he wanted one even more. Given his own childhood, Kate could see that creating his own dynasty would appeal to Sean. But that did not mean that he loved Oliver—and it certainly didn't mean that he loved her.

Had she done the right thing in marrying Sean? Or had she given in to her emotions? Hadn't there been somewhere deeply buried inside her a small, desperate hope that somehow Sean would come to recognise that Oliver was his son and that in doing so he would…?

He would what?

She could hear Oliver and Sean making their way back. Quickly she pushed her anxiety to one side.

The moment they walked onto the patio Oliver ran

towards her, shouting excitedly, 'Mummy—Mummy, I was swimming.'

As he launched himself at her Kate caught him up in her arms, closing her eyes as she savoured the echoes of his babyhood in the smell of his skin and its softness.

'I can't believe you haven't taught him to swim,' she heard Sean commenting grimly, and he reached out and took Oliver from her arms with the automatic action of a man who knew it was his right to hold his child.

Kate held her breath, telling herself fiercely that it wasn't disappointment that filled her when Oliver went happily to Sean.

'I tried.' She answered Sean's criticism defensively. 'But right from being a baby Ollie has been frightened of water...'

'Well, he isn't frightened now,' Sean announced. 'Shower now, Ollie, and then breakfast,' Kate heard him saying firmly as he put Ollie down.

Once he was out of earshot Sean said, 'Perhaps he could sense that you were afraid for him? Children need to feel that they are safe.'

'Thanks for the child guidance lecture,' Kate snapped furiously. 'But I'd just like to remind you, Sean, that I've been Oliver's mother from the moment he was conceived.'

'And I am now his father,' Sean replied fiercely.

They were words which were constantly inside her thoughts and her heart over the following few days of their brief 'honeymoon', as Sean and Oliver formed a close male bond from which she felt totally excluded.

And now, with their holiday over, Kate couldn't help observing as they walked towards Sean's parked car that Oliver was even beginning to talk like his father.

Mrs Hargreaves was waiting to welcome them when they arrived home, and although Kate was vaguely aware of the conspiratorial look the housekeeper exchanged with Sean, she didn't pay very much regard to it, or to the few private words she hurried to have with Sean.

Upstairs, she was turning to head for her bedroom when Sean stopped her.

'I've asked Mrs Hargreaves to move your things into the master bedroom.'

Kate's stomach muscles quivered. Angry with herself for the fierce stab of pleasure the thought of sleeping with Sean again caused her, she forced herself to object. 'But that's your bedroom.'

'It was my bedroom,' Sean agreed coolly. 'But it's now our bedroom.'

Their bedroom. The unwanted feeling intensified and spread. Kate knew that she was perilously close to giving in to her renewed love for Sean. He might want her sexually, but he had told her himself that he had remarried her for Oliver's sake.

She wasn't going to humiliate herself by offering him a love he didn't want!

How long, though, would she be able to keep her feelings to herself if she was sleeping with him every night and all night?

'I don't—' she began.

'Not in front of Oliver,' Sean checked her firmly, leaving her to wait to resume their conversation once Oliver had been introduced to and safely established in his own new bedroom.

'That was ridiculously extravagant, Sean, buying him a computer games console,' Kate protested when Sean had finished showing Oliver how to operate his new toy and they were back on the landing outside his room.

'It will be good for his spatial dexterity,' Sean told her without a glimmer of contrition. 'Come and see how the master bedroom looks,' he added, guiding her to the door.

The first thing Kate saw when he opened it was the huge new bed. And her concentration remained stuck on it.

'It's a double bed!' she pronounced foolishly.

'King-size, actually,' Sean corrected her dryly.

Panic filled her. Double or king-size, it didn't really matter. What mattered was that she would be sharing it with Sean and she knew, just knew, it would be impossible for her to stop herself from snuggling up to him and allowing herself the luxury of behaving as though they still were the loving couple they had once been.

Blindly she swung round, and then found that her exit from the room was blocked by Sean's arm, Sean's hand holding the door—a door which he promptly closed and leaned against, folding his arms as he watched her furious agitation.

'I can't sleep in that bed with you!' Kate burst out.

'Why not? We shared a room when we were away!'

'That was different!' Kate insisted, wishing he wouldn't give her that look of slow, deliberate scrutiny that made her feel he could see right into her head.

'We are married, after all,' Sean reminded her. 'And besides, the bed's plenty big enough for us to keep our distance from one another, if that's what you want!'

'Of course that's what I want,' Kate lied quickly. He couldn't have guessed how much it affected her to think of sleeping in the same bed with him, could he?

'We've got to think of Oliver,' Sean told her firmly.

'What kind of impression is it going to give him if we have separate rooms?'

She had been outmanoeuvred, Kate recognised, unable to do anything other than retaliate furiously, 'I saw the look Mrs Hargreaves gave you when we arrived, and now I realise why,' she accused him wildly.

To her surprise her comment seemed to have a more powerful effect on Sean than she had anticipated, because he suddenly started to frown, and a look she couldn't translate shadowed his eyes.

'I've told Mrs Hargreaves that from tomorrow we'll both have a light tea with Oliver at five o'clock, and then our own dinner later on, when he's in bed. I think it's important that we share his mealtimes with him. And I thought I'd take him over to the farm tomorrow—the pups are almost ready to leave their mother, and Mrs Hargreaves has told them we're going to have one. Ollie can choose his own.'

It was nine o'clock at night. Oliver was already tucked up and fast asleep in his new bed, and she and Sean were eating the delicious meal Mrs Hargreaves had left ready for them before going home. Suddenly the last thing Kate felt like was eating.

'Since when did you and Mrs Hargreaves make arrangements concerning Oliver without me being informed?' Kate demanded ominously. As she spoke she stood up, throwing down her linen napkin and gripping the table in her fury.

'He's desperate to have a dog of his own,' Sean told her. 'You know that!'

'I also know that I said I didn't want him to have a puppy yet.'

'Because he would be at nursery and you would be

working. That doesn't apply any longer,' Sean pointed out firmly.

Kate was shaking with a mixture of anger and misery without really knowing why—other than that it had something to do with that large master bedroom and its huge bed, in which she and Sean were going to sleep— with most the bed between them...

'I'm not listening to any more of this,' she told Sean angrily, pushing back her chair and almost running out of the room, ignoring his pleas to return.

'Kate! Come back!'

Idiotically, it was the master bedroom she headed to for refuge, swinging round white-faced as Sean followed her into it, shutting the door.

'What's got into you?' he demanded.

'I've managed to spend five years bringing Oliver up without your assistance and without your interference, Sean. I am his mother...and I—'

'And you what?' Sean challenged her savagely. 'And you shared another man's bed in order to conceive him?'

The raw emotion in his voice shocked through her. She had never seen him so out of control, and the intensity of his unexpected outburst paralysed her.

'Do you think I don't think about that every single day, every damned hour? Hell, Kate, do you think that because I can't father a child, because I'm not man enough to father a child, I'm not man enough to think about you and him and this?' Silently they stared at one another.

Kate drew a ragged breath and demanded shakily, 'What do you mean, you can't father a child?'

Her mouth had gone dry and her heart was thudding in heavy, erratic hammer-blows. Even through her own shock she was aware of the look of sick, anguished despair in Sean's eyes, and she could feel the intensity of his pent-up emotions.

When he started to turn away from her she reached out and took hold of his arm.

'You are Oliver's father, Sean,' she said quietly.

'No, I'm not. I can't be,' Sean denied bitterly. 'I can't father a child. It isn't medically possible.'

'I don't understand,' Kate said in a dry whisper as she struggled to take in what he was telling her.

It was too late for him to backtrack now; Sean knew that. Behind the shock he could see in Kate's eyes he could also see a growing determination. He knew she would insist on being told the truth—and what point was there in hiding it now, after what he had just said?

He took a deep breath.

'At a routine annual check-up for my private medical insurance the doctor suggested that I might as well have the full works.' He gave a small bitter shrug. 'It was just a formality, or so I thought—just a means of putting on paper what I believed I already knew. That I was a healthy, fully functioning man. When the results came back there was a problem...'

He paused and Kate waited, aching with compassion for him, but with the sure knowledge that, no matter what he had been told, the experts had got it wrong. He had fathered Oliver.

'It seemed—he said... He told me that my sperm count was so low it would be impossible for me to father children,' he said bleakly. 'I refused to believe him at first. In fact I was so convinced he must be wrong that I demanded that they run the tests again. They weren't wrong!' He closed his eyes. 'Shall I try to explain to you, Kate, how savagely humiliating I found it to have to stand there and listen to the doctor telling me that I wasn't capable of giving you a child? How I wished I hadn't heaped fresh humiliation on myself by demanding they re-run the tests?'

'Why didn't you tell me...say something?' Kate demanded in a dry whisper.

'I couldn't,' Sean said bleakly. 'I couldn't bear to see your face when I told you that I couldn't give you the children I knew you wanted so much.'

So much, Kate wanted to tell him. *But never, ever more than I wanted you, Sean.* She knew what he was like, though. She knew how deeply such news would have cut into him, into everything he'd believed about himself.

'I had a right to know, Sean,' she told him quietly.

'And I had a right to protect you from knowing,' he countered.

'To protect *me*?'

Sean's mouth compressed. 'I knew if I told you you would insist on...on accepting that there could never be any children for us and...and sacrificing your own chance to be a mother because of that. I decided there and then that I wasn't going to let you do that, and that I...I had to set you free to find another man to...to give you what I could not.'

'To set me free?' Now that she was over her initial shock Kate was beginning to get angry. 'You were unfaithful to me, Sean, and—'

'No!'

'No?'

'There wasn't anyone else. I...I just made it up because...because I knew how you would feel and how you would react. I didn't want to keep you trapped in our marriage, sacrificing yourself to it for my sake, pitying me and eventually hating me for what you were being denied. I must say, though, that I didn't expect you to find someone else quite so quickly. Was that why it didn't last?'

A lump had lodged in her throat and she could only shake her head in helpless denial. She didn't know what was hurting her the most—her pain for Sean or her pain for herself.

'Sean, I don't care what the medical reports said. Oliver is your child,' she told him passionately. 'Sometimes such things are possible and—'

'No!' His harsh, haunted cry made her flinch.

'Don't offer me that kind of temptation, Kate. You are worthy of so much more than deception, and so is Oliver.'

Kate went white, but before she could defend herself he was continuing rawly.

'Can't you understand how I feel? How much I wish that Oliver could be mine? How much it hurts me that he isn't? I only have to look at him, never mind hold him, to feel my lo—something here inside me that... Having children with you, giving you our children, was so deeply rooted in me, so instinctive, that I thought I could never endure knowing that another man had given you what I couldn't. I thought it would drive me quite literally mad to see you with another man's child. But—'

'Oliver *is* your child,' Kate protested emotionally. 'He is yours, Sean—ours...'

'Don't do this to me, please, Kate. I can't bear it! What do I have to do to stop you lying to me? This?'

Kate couldn't move when he took hold of her, the fierce pressure of his mouth on hers bending her head backwards against the hard strength of his arm. The heat of their emotions, anger on anger, welded them together, and sent a shaft of pure molten reaction speeding through Kate.

How could it be that such a fierce primeval desire could be born out of anger? Her whole body shook in recognition of her vulnerable naïveté. She hadn't recognised her danger and tried to evade it. It was too late now.

She was held in thrall, emotionally and sexually, as much to the intensity of her own surging need as she was physically to Sean's iron-armed imprisonment of her.

When he broke the kiss, lifting his mouth from hers, his chest rising and falling quickly, Kate tried to pull away from him. But Sean refused to let her go.

'Perhaps the only way I can stop thinking about it is to put my own sexual imprint on you, for ever.'

'You were the one who divorced me, Sean,' Kate reminded him, trying to free her senses from the effect his hot, turbulent gaze was having on them, and at the same time fighting frantically to stem the excited surge of liquid sexual longing that was pulsing through her.

'I may have divorced you but I didn't replace you in my bed, Kate,' he answered her bitterly. 'How much did you want him?' he demanded rawly.

'Sean! No!' Kate protested, torn between shock and pain—shock that he could actually believe she had given herself to someone else when he knew how much she had loved him, and pain for him, for herself, because he did.

'No? You didn't say no to him, did you?' he challenged her thickly. 'I'm going to make you forget that you ever knew him, Kate. I'm going to make you want me so much that you'll forget he ever existed.'

Sean was already caressing the side of her neck with

his lips, deliberately seeking the special place where, she had once confessed shyly to him, feeling his mouth made her melt with longing for him.

'Did he do this?'

The words muffled against her skin made her throat ache with agonised suppressed tears, her only response a mute shake of her head.

'You didn't tell him how much it turns you on?'

There was an ugly note in Sean's voice that spiked her heart with angry pain. To her own shock, despite her anger, she ached to be able to reassure him, to convince him that no man ever had or ever could take his place in her life. In either her life, her heart, or her body. But the words wouldn't come, despite Sean's angry assault on her senses.

'Did he touch you like this, Kate? And like this?'

The angry, destructive words hammered into her like blows, numbing her body and freezing her emotions. A cold emptiness was spreading inside her, squeezing the life out of her love with icy binding tentacles of rage that stiffened her body into furious rejection.

'Oh, God, Kate.'

The groaned, anguished words were expelled with so much force that she could feel their pressure against her skin.

Releasing her, Sean went over to the bed and sat down on it, his elbows on his knees as he dropped his head into his hands.

'What the hell am I doing?'

The suffocating anguish of his pain filled the space between them.

With his head bent over his hands, she could see how exactly like Oliver's his hair grew, Kate noticed. For some reason that knowledge made her take a tentative step towards him.

'What the hell's happening to me? I know I've always been a jealous bastard where you're concerned, but—'

The muffled words bled shocked despair.

Kate lifted her hand and placed it on his head.

Immediately his whole body froze.

'For God's sake, Kate, don't touch me. How can you touch me?' he demanded savagely.

As his hand moved Kate saw the telltale moisture on his face and her heart turned over with love and compassion. An extraordinary feeling of strength and understanding filled her. Reaching out, she placed her hand over his.

Immediately Sean pushed her hand away and stood up, in rejection of her touch.

'I'll sleep in one of the other rooms tonight,' he said stiffly.

As he started to walk away from her Kate saw the way the light falling against his thigh revealed the swell of his arousal, and something inside her, something elemental and untamed, reacted to it.

Quickly she stepped in front of him, looked up into his face.

'No more, Kate,' Sean told her wearily. 'I don't want—'

'This?' She stopped him, placing her lips against his and caressing them slowly and sweetly, letting her senses and her heart revel in self-indulgent pleasure as she did so. She felt the involuntary movement of his body as he tensed it against her, but she wasn't going to give in.

'Or this?' she whispered against his mouth, sealing it

with her own as she let her hand drop to his body so that her fingers could stroke possessively against him.

He didn't respond for so long that she was almost on the point of giving up, and then suddenly and explosively the power was taken from her and he was returning her kiss—not angrily, but passionately, hungrily, as though he was starving for her.

Just as she was starving for him?

Somehow, some way, somewhere, the anger between them had taken another direction, had pushed through the barrier of her self-protection and found that place deep within herself where she was still the girl who loved Sean and responded to his lovemaking with eager, open passion.

She could feel that passion flooding through her now, taking her to a place she had thought lost to her for ever.

Clothes tugged and pulled by impatient fingers left a trail to the bed, where they stood body to naked body. Kate's arms wrapped around Sean's neck as she continued to kiss him with fierce female hunger.

'Kate!'

She felt his hands on her breasts, holding and shaping them, and she shuddered, racked by fierce tremors of pleasure at his open appreciation of their soft weight in his hands. A wild wantonness had entered her blood and taken her over. As she was now taking him over! It manifested itself in the hot sensuality of the way she kissed him, touched him, the way she subtly and deliberately encouraged and invited him, winding her arms around him, pressing her naked body against him, driven by a force she could neither control nor deny.

A force she didn't want to control or deny, Kate recognised with feverish arousal, and she slid her hands down Sean's torso and through the soft thickness of his body hair, stroking over the hardness of his erection and then curling her fingers around the hot swollen shaft, caressing it slowly and then more urgently whilst the tension seated deep inside her own body tightened and ached until she knew it could not be contained any longer.

Sean! As she held out her arms to him Kate let the top half of her body drop onto the bed.

The last of the light was fading across the bedroom, but there was still enough left for her to see Sean's expression, to watch the way his glittering gaze was drawn to her body, over the firm swell of her breasts, over her nipples, dark rosy peaks of open arousal. The last glow warmed her belly and highlighted the soft little curls decorating the swollen mound that signposted her sex.

Deliberately she opened her legs, and watched the shudder that racked Sean's body.

Briefly she gave in to the temptation to stroke the wetness of her own sex, watching the way Sean's gaze followed her small erotic movement, and then blazed with heat. A fierce spiral of female excitement ran through her.

'You do it,' she told him boldly.

And, as though he knew what she was feeling, Sean groaned and reached for her.

Possessively Kate wrapped her legs around him, moaning her pleasure as he touched her just as she had wanted him to do, replacing his fingers with his body when he realised how close she was to her orgasm.

Within seconds it was over, her climax so immediate and so intense that her womb actually ached with its aftermath.

Her womb!

Bright tears glittered in her eyes and she turned her

head away so that Sean couldn't see them. Once she would have taken that fierce clenching of its muscles as a sign that it was claiming the seed of life Sean had planted there, but Sean refused to believe that he could give her a child.

CHAPTER TEN

'READY, then?' Sean asked curtly, not looking directly at Kate herself as he strode into the sitting room, but crouching down instead to hold out his arms to Oliver, who immediately ran into them.

He had been like this with her—cold, distant and rejecting—ever since the night they had made love. If he had written them out in ten-feet-high letters he could not have made his feelings plainer, Kate admitted unhappily.

He might share the large bed in the master bedroom with her, but he slept with his back to her, and the cold space between them might as well have been impassable snow-capped mountains. His whole body language told her he didn't want her anywhere near him.

And why should he? In his eyes he had got what he wanted out of their marriage, after all, Kate acknowledged bleakly, as she looked down at her son and her husband.

'You don't have to take us to the hospital, Sean,' Kate told him now. 'This check-up is only a formality. The doctor said that himself, and I already know that I'm fully recovered.'

'I thought you said you wanted to check on your house?'

'Yes, I do,' Kate admitted. 'I know that the letting agent says he's found someone who wants to rent it right away—'

'You'd be better off selling it,' Sean interrupted her grimly.

Now it was Kate's turn to look away from him. How could she explain to a man in Sean's enviable financial position how she felt about the small home she had worked so hard to buy? And how could she tell him there was a part of her that was afraid that somehow history might repeat itself, that she might find herself on her own and in need of the security her little cottage could provide?

'I prefer to keep it,' she answered him.

'I spoke to my solicitor yesterday,' Sean announced, standing up. 'About the adoption.'

Oliver was running towards the door, but even so Kate gave Sean a warning look—which he obviously misinterpreted. As Oliver hurried out to the car Sean's face hardened.

'In your eyes I might be Oliver's father, Kate, but in my own eyes I am not—so I want to make sure that I am in the eyes of the law, for Oliver's sake as much as my own.'

Too heartsore to make any response, Kate followed him out to the car.

They had stopped off on their way to have some lunch, and now Sean was parking his car outside the doctor's surgery.

'There's no need for you and Oliver to come in with me, Sean,' Kate said as she opened the car door, but she might as well have saved her breath.

Not only did Sean insist on waiting with her to see the doctor, he also insisted on going into the room with her.

'I can understand your husband's concern,' the doctor further infuriated her by saying placatingly. 'You were very poorly.' He shook his head. 'Yours was certainly the worst case of this virus I have seen.'

'Perhaps she should have a full medical—with heart and lung checks?' Sean suggested.

'Sean, there is nothing wrong with me,' Kate told him angrily.

'Mummy was sick after breakfast!'

In the silence that followed Oliver's innocent but revealing piece of information all three adults turned to look at him.

'I...it was the red wine I had with dinner,' Kate explained uncomfortably.

Immediately the doctor's expression relaxed, although he did tell Kate warningly, 'Red wine can sometimes prove too strong for a delicate stomach.'

'You barely touched your wine last night,' Sean pointed out as they left the surgery.

'Because I wasn't enjoying it,' Kate returned quickly.

To her relief he didn't pursue the matter. Instead he said, 'We might as well leave the car here and walk to your house. It isn't very far.'

Automatically Kate fell into step beside him, with Oliver in between them.

Perhaps the walk was too familiar to her, or perhaps her mind was on other things—Kate didn't know which, but obviously her concentration wasn't what it should have been, because when Oliver pulled his hand free from hers and shouted out the name of his friend she didn't react as quickly as she could have done. Oliver had run into the road before she had realised what was happening.

She did see the huge lorry bearing down on him, though, and she did hear her own voice screaming out his name in anguished terror as she started to run towards him, even though she knew she would be too late.

There was a blur of movement at her side as Sean ran past her and into the road, grabbing hold of his son in a rugby tackle movement, covering Oliver's body with his own.

Kate heard Oliver's screams and the hiss of air brakes. She could smell the odour of burning rubber, taste her own fear in her mouth. The lorry had slewed to a stop and people were running into the road to stand over the still, crumpled figure lying there.

But Kate got there first.

Sean lay motionless on the tarmac, blood oozing from a cut on his head, one of his legs splayed out at a sickeningly unnatural angle. And, lying safely next to Sean's unconscious body, Kate could see Oliver, his eyes wide with shock as he whimpered, 'Daddy…'

There were people everywhere—the doctor…sirens… an ambulance…

Hugging Oliver tightly to her, Kate got in it—after the paramedics had carefully lifted Sean onto a stretcher and placed him inside.

His face was drained of colour and Kate had to fight back the sickly sensation of wanting to faint as one of the paramedics expertly set up a drip and started to check his vital signs.

'His body's in shock, love,' one of them said, trying to comfort Kate as she stared at him in anguish. Unable to stop herself she took hold of one of his hands. It felt icy cold—as though…

Her heart lurched against her ribcage, her gaze going fearfully to the heart monitor.

'Hospital's coming up now. And we've got one of the best A&E departments in the country here,' the friendly medic told her proudly. 'Good timing, too. We've still got over half the golden hour left.'

'The golden hour?' Kate questioned numbly.

'That's what we call the window we get after an accident—leave it too long and—' As he saw Kate shudder he checked himself and looked uncomfortable, realising he had said too much.

In Accident and Emergency a nurse took Oliver from Kate's numb arms whilst Sean was rushed past them on a trolley.

'I want to go with him—' Kate began, but the nurse stopped her firmly.

'We've got to get him ready for the duty surgeon to see him. You wouldn't want to watch us cutting off those good clothes he's wearing, would you? Now, let's have a little look at this young man, shall we?'

Distractedly, Kate tried to focus on what she was saying.

Miraculously Oliver had sustained little more than some grazes and bruises—no, not miraculously, Kate recognised. Because Sean had risked his life to save him.

A huge lump rose in her throat. Sean was right. It did take more than fathering a child to be a father, and he had proved that today. And he had proved, too, just how much he loved Oliver.

The medical staff were kind, but nothing could really alleviate the anguish and fear Kate experienced as she waited to hear how Sean was.

To her horror, a neurologist had to be called in to examine Sean and check for brain damage.

An hour passed, and then another. Oliver fell asleep in her arms and Kate's eyes prickled dryly with the weight of her unshed tears. After what felt like a lifetime, a consultant strode into the waiting area and came across to her.

Numbly Kate focused on the spotted bow tie he was wearing. 'My husband?' she begged anxiously.

'He's sustained a broken leg, and some cuts and bruises, and for a while we were concerned that the bump on his head might turn out to be rather nasty.' When he saw Kate's expression he gave her a kind look. 'Fortunately it's nothing more than a bad bump, but we had to make sure. I'm sorry that you've had to wait so long, but you'll understand that we had to be certain...'

Tears of overwrought emotional relief were pouring down Kate's face.

'We've had to mess him around rather a lot, and we've had to operate on his leg. We've still got a few samples to take, but he's fully conscious now. He won't accept that his son—Oliver, is it?—is all right until he has seen him. Susie will take you through,' he told Kate kindly, waving a hand towards a nurse waiting next to him.

But Kate didn't move. She couldn't. An idea...a hope...was burning on her tongue.

'The samples you have to take,' she began in a fierce rush. 'Would you—could you...?' Taking a deep breath, she told him helplessly, 'Sean won't believe that Oliver is his son, but he is. If you could do a DNA test—'

The consultant was frowning. 'That would be most irregular.'

'Sean already loves Oliver,' Kate told him desperately. 'He risked his own life to save him.'

'How sure are you that the child is his?' the consultant asked bluntly.

'Totally sure,' Kate answered him.

'I'm afraid that I can't do as you ask without the pa-

tient's permission,' the consultant told her, adding quietly as her face fell, 'However, I believe it is possible to
have such tests conducted via certain Internet Web sites,
should a person deem it necessary to do so.'

'But how—?' Kate began helplessly.

'All that is required is a small sample—a snippet of
hair, for instance.'

Kate swallowed hard. 'You think I should…?'

'What I think is that anyone doing such a thing should
be guided by their own conscience,' the consultant told
her seriously.

Biting her lip, Kate turned to follow the nurse down
the corridor.

Sean was in a small private room, surrounded by a
heart-stoppingly serious-looking battery of medical
equipment, and when Kate saw the 'bump' on his head
the consultant had referred to she almost cried out loud.

It looked as though the side of his head had been
dragged along the road—which it most probably had,
she acknowledged shakily.

'Look, Sean, we've brought Oliver to see you, like we
promised,' said the nurse.

As Sean turned his head Kate had to fight the compulsion to hand Oliver to the nurse and run to his side,
to take Sean in her arms.

How could such a big man look so frail? Her heart
turned over as she whispered his name—but Sean wasn't
looking at her. His whole attention was concentrated on
Oliver.

'Daddy!' Oliver exclaimed, suddenly waking up and
holding out his arms to him.

'Give him to me,' Sean demanded in a hoarse croak.

Uncertainly Kate looked at the nurse, who nodded her
head briefly. Gently Kate carried Oliver over to the bed,

but instead of handing him to Sean she sat down on the bed next to Sean, keeping hold of Oliver, afraid that her son might inadvertently hurt his father.

'He's all right?' Sean asked Kate as he lifted his hand and touched his son.

'He's perfectly all right—thanks to you,' Kate replied, her voice trembling.

It wasn't Oliver she wanted to hold and protect right now, she recognised achingly, it was Sean himself. But she knew that he wanted neither her comfort nor her love.

'Gently, Oliver,' she protested automatically as Oliver leaned forward to give his father a big smacking kiss.

'There's no need for you to keep visiting me twice a day like this, Kate,' Sean announced curtly as Kate opened the door to his private room.

Suppressing her hurt, Kate forced herself to smile. 'Mr Meadows says that you'll be coming home tomorrow.'

Sean frowned.

'Oliver can't wait,' Kate told him.

Immediately the frown disappeared.

'He's been pining for you, Sean.'

Ruefully Kate decided that she wasn't going to tell him what she had done to try to alleviate her son's longing for his father—he would discover the new addition to their household for himself soon enough. Kate had to admit that she had been pleasantly surprised at how quickly Rusty, as Oliver had decided to call his new puppy, had become housetrained.

'Did you get the neurologist to check that absolutely no damage had been done when he…?'

Every time she visited him Sean demanded to know how Oliver was, and even though she kept telling him that he was fine he still persisted in worrying. Kate suspected that he wouldn't be reassured until he was home and could observe Oliver's excellent and boisterous good health for himself.

'I spoke to my solicitor this morning,' he announced abruptly. 'He says you're refusing to sign the adoption papers.'

Kate poured herself a glass of water from the jug at Sean's bedside in an attempt to quell the feeling of nausea the hospital smell was giving her.

'I'm not refusing, Sean, I...' Crossing her fingers behind her back, she said quickly, 'Your adoption of Oliver is such an important and...and special thing, I didn't want it to be purely businesslike and clinical. I thought if we waited until you came home we could have a little celebration.'

'So it isn't because you're having second thoughts, then?' Sean cut across her hesitant excuse.

The temptation to tell him emotionally that the only time she could have had second thoughts about his role as Oliver's father had been nine months before Oliver's birth was something she had to stifle before she could give it voice.

Deep down inside she still felt guilty about that little snippet of hair she had cut from his head whilst he had been sleeping. As the consultant had hinted, she had found a Web site offering the kind of service she had needed and Sean's hair, together with a lock of Oliver's, had been sent to it. She had no doubts, of course, as to the result she would receive back.

Automatically her hand dropped to her stomach and rested there.

So far as Sean's accident was concerned, the consultant had told her cheerfully that she was worrying for nothing, that Sean was a fit, healthy man with a skull thick enough to protect him from its contact with the road and a broken leg that was healing extremely well. But Kate knew that as long as Sean was here in this hospital she would continue to feel that he was vulnerable and needed to be treated with care.

Dry-eyed, Sean watched Kate leave. He had had time and more to spare during these last few days to think. And he'd had plenty to think about. The past and the future.

The present situation was a warning to him of how the people who mattered most to him were precious and yet so vulnerable. *All* that mattered to him, Sean acknowledged fiercely, was Oliver, the child he had come to love with a true father's love, and Kate, the girl he had loved, the woman he still loved, beyond and above anything and everything that had happened or might happen.

Oliver and Kate. He couldn't bear the thought of losing either of them. Even in that half-second as he'd recognised Oliver's danger he had known that it didn't really matter that he hadn't fathered him, or even that there had been another man for Kate. That was the past. He had their present, and he wanted their future.

'So, no playing football with that leg, and come back for your check-up in six weeks,' the consultant told Sean breezily as he gave him his final examination before discharging him. 'You'll be looking forward to getting home to your wife and son,' he added easily, but he was watching Sean as he spoke.

Following Kate's request, he had sent for and checked all Sean's medical records. One of them recorded a specialist's opinion that it would be a miracle if Sean ever managed to father a child.

'You were damn lucky not to be much more seriously injured, you know,' he commented. 'But then, as we in the medical profession are often forced to accept, miracles do happen!'

Sean closed his eyes. He wasn't going to dispute what the consultant was saying; after all, he had his own private, secret miracle to rejoice in.

Five years ago, if someone had told him that there would come a day when he would not only accept another man's child as his son but he would love that child more deeply than he had ever imagined he could or would love anyone, apart from Kate, he would have denied it fiercely and immediately. But that was how he felt about Oliver.

When he had seen the little boy standing in the path of the lorry he had known that he loved Oliver as fiercely and protectively, as deeply and instinctively as though he were his biological father. Oliver was his son, and he loved him as his son. But legally Oliver was *not* his son, and if for any reason she chose to do so Kate could simply take Oliver and walk out of Sean's life with him.

Any reason? Sean's mouth compressed. Kate had a very good reason to want to leave him, and he had given her that reason that night they'd made love...

It made no difference to Sean's contempt and disgust for himself that ultimately mutual passion had flared between them. His only excuse was that his pent-up jealousy had overwhelmed him, and that was no real excuse at all. He loathed himself for what he had done, and he knew that Kate must loathe him as well—for all that she was concealing it.

The door to his room was opening. A smiling nurse came in, and behind her were Kate and Oliver.

When Oliver broke free of Kate's hold and ran towards him Sean bent his head over Oliver's to conceal his emotions.

'He refused to wait at home for you,' Kate explained as Sean picked up the crutches he would need to use.

Immediately Kate was at his side, but Sean refused to let her help, turning away from her.

White-faced, Kate watched as the nurse went to Sean's aid…Sean's side…taking the role which should have been hers. Sean might have remarried her, but he didn't want her as his wife, Kate acknowledged bleakly.

'I've asked Mrs Hargreaves to move my things into one of the other bedrooms.'

Kate was glad she had her back to Sean, so that he couldn't see her reaction to his words, although she couldn't stop herself from demanding, 'But what about Oliver? You said—'

'I've told him that it's because of my leg,' Sean answered her curtly.

But of course that was just an excuse, and Kate knew it! He didn't want to share a room with her, a bed with her, any longer—because he didn't want her!

They were standing in the hallway, Sean leaning on his crutches whilst Oliver chased his puppy around the room, trying to catch him so that he could show him to his father.

'I see you changed your mind,' Sean commented sardonically as he looked at her.

'I'm a woman. I'm entitled to,' Kate replied as lightly as she could. There was, though, another reason she had

decided that this was the optimum time to allow Oliver
to have his puppy.

Had Sean recognised the pup as being the one he himself had picked for Oliver? she wondered. If he had he
didn't make any mention of it, and ridiculously, after
everything else that told her how he felt about her, she
felt absurdly disappointed and hurt.

'I'll help you upstairs,' she offered, going to his side.
But immediately Sean stepped back from her in such an
obvious gesture of repudiation that Kate froze, then
turned round so that Sean wouldn't see the humiliating
tears burning her eyes.

CHAPTER ELEVEN

NAUSEOUSLY Kate put her head back on the pillow and closed her eyes. Perhaps it was just as well that Sean was not sharing the room with her.

Sean!

It was Sean's birthday today. She reached for the packet of dry biscuits she had bought herself earlier in the week, when she had bought his birthday card.

She took her time getting up, waiting for the nausea to subside before going in to Oliver.

He was as excited as though it was his own birthday, Kate acknowledged ruefully as he collected the present they had wrapped together so carefully the previous day.

Sean was already sitting in the breakfast room when they went in, and immediately Oliver ran over to his father and scrambled onto his knee, shouting, 'Happy birthday, Daddy!'

Bending her head to hide her own emotion, Kate picked up the card Oliver had dropped in his excitement, reflecting that it was just as well she had carried the present for him.

'Happy birthday, Sean,' Kate echoed more sedately, adding, 'And it's a double celebration now that your plaster cast is off!'

He had had the plaster cast removed the previous day, and the consultant had expressed himself totally satisfied with the way the leg had healed.

'I've got you a card and a present!' Oliver exclaimed importantly, still sitting on Sean's lap.

Obediently Kate handed over the card and the present.

'You've got to open this one first—it's my card,' Oliver instructed. 'Mummy has a card for you, too, and so does Rusty. He's put his own paw mark on it,' Oliver told him excitedly. 'Mummy made some special mud, and we put his paw in it, and then we put it on the card!'

'Some special mud? That sounds clever!'

Was that really a gleam of amusement she could see in Sean's eyes as he looked at her? Kate's heart somersaulted inside her chest.

'That explains the odd marks on Mummy's jeans yesterday, then, does it?' he added dulcetly.

'We did have a couple of aborted attempts.' Kate laughed, but when she looked at him Sean wasn't sharing her laughter. Instead he was looking at Oliver's card. And he continued to look at it for a several seconds, before lifting his head and looking at Kate.

'Do you like it, Daddy?' Oliver demanded, tugging on his arm.

'I love it, Ollie!' Sean assured him gruffly. 'But I love you even more.'

As he hugged him he put the card down and Kate reached for it, standing it up on the table. Oliver's writing wasn't very good as yet, but his message to his father was: 'I love you lots, Daddy.'

'And you've got to open my present now,' Oliver insisted.

Kate watched as Sean unwrapped the photograph she had taken of the two of them and had framed. As Sean studied it she held her breath. Could he see, as she had, the likeness between them?

If he could he obviously wasn't going to say so.

The rest of the cards were opened, including the one from Rusty. Then Sean assured Oliver gravely that he was indeed looking forward to his birthday tea, and eating the cake Oliver and Kate had made for him.

Kate said nothing.

'Mummy, you haven't got a present for Daddy,' Oliver piped up suddenly.

'Yes, she has, Ollie,' Sean told him, before Kate could say anything. 'Your mummy has given me a very, very special present—the best present in the world.'

'Where is it?' Oliver asked him, bewildered.

Over his head, Sean looked at Kate. 'You are it,' he answered. 'Your mummy has given me you.'

Kate knew that she should have been thrilled to hear Sean's words of love for Oliver, and of course she was, but a part of her ached with pain because she knew that they confirmed what she didn't want to hear: that Sean only wanted her because he wanted Oliver.

That was not the kind of relationship she wanted with the man she loved, the man who—

Abruptly, she got up.

She had left her gift for Sean in the room he used as an office. When he found it he would realise that in order to have Oliver he did not need to have her as well.

'Kate, where are you going? You haven't eaten any breakfast.'

She didn't turn round.

'I'm not hungry,' she answered, and instinctively her hand went to her stomach.

Not hungry? Sean wondered bitterly as she walked away. Or not able to endure his company?

As soon as they had finished their breakfast, Sean took Oliver out into the garden, along with the puppy. Did Kate even realise she had picked the same pup he had chosen?

As they walked side by side Oliver chattered happily

to him, and when he looked down at him Sean felt a
stab of pain for the years of his life he had missed, for
not being there at his birth. His large hand tightened
around Oliver's smaller one. Oliver was his son, but he
had not been entirely truthful when he had said that
Oliver was the most precious gift he could have been
given.

He was precious, very precious, but Kate's love was
just as precious. There hadn't been a night since it had
happened when he had not lain awake, hating himself
for the way he had treated Kate. No wonder she couldn't
bear to be in the same room as him.

It was lunchtime before he went into his office and saw
the large white envelope lying on his desk.

Frowning, he picked it up, recognising Kate's hand-
writing on it,

'For you,' she had written, 'and for Oliver.'

Still frowning, Sean opened it. Removing the contents, he read them, and then read them again. And then
again, trying to focus through the blur of his own
shocked emotions.

He had fathered Oliver. It was here in black and white.
The incontrovertible proof in their DNA records.

He read them again, and then again, over and over,
until finally it sank in that there was no mistake.

Miracles do happen, the consultant had told him, and
now Sean knew that it was true! But his miracle had
come at a dreadful price, he recognised as the reality of
what the results meant sank in.

He had refused to believe that Kate had not slept with
another man. He had done so much more than refuse to
believe her...

He heard the office door open.

Kate walked in and closed the door. She looked at the desk, and then at him.

'So you've opened it?'

'Yes. But I wish to hell that I hadn't!'

Kate felt sick. What was he trying to say? 'But it proves that Oliver is your son!' she protested.

'Oliver was already my son!' Sean told her harshly. 'Here in my heart was all the proof that I needed or wanted—even if it took a near tragedy to make me realise that. Kate! This—' he told her, furiously picking up the results, 'means nothing!'

Kate was too shocked to speak.

'I want Oliver to grow up knowing that my love for him comes from here,' he told her, as he touched his own heart, 'and not from this!' Angrily he threw down the piece of paper. 'I had a lot of time on my hands to think whilst I was in hospital, Kate, and what I thought, what I learned, and what I finally accepted was that love—real love—should and can transcend all our weaker human emotions. Jealousy, doubt, fear. I love you as I have always loved you,' he continued thickly. 'As the only woman for me. My other half, who I need to complete me...my soul mate. Nothing can change that. Nothing and no one. And I love Oliver as the child of my heart.

'This...' he gestured towards the test results '...underlines the fact that I haven't just abused you and your trust once, but twice. That I have created yet another barrier between us with my own selfishness and stupidity.'

Dizzily Kate looked at him. 'You love me?'

Sean frowned, caught off guard not just by her question but by the exultant pleasure that lightened her voice.

'You want me to?' he demanded.

'Oh, Sean!' Tears blurred her vision as she took a step towards him, and then another, until she was close enough to wrap her arms around him. 'Always and for ever. You and your love.' Emotion choked her voice and she shook her head. 'If you love me, why have you been rejecting me? Why have you—?'

A tide of colour began to creep up under Sean's tan.

'I thought—I felt... That night when we made love... God, Kate, do I have to spell it out for you? I lost control and I—'

Gently Kate placed her fingers against his lips to silence him.

'We both lost control, Sean, and as a result of that...' She paused. 'Do you really mean this, Sean? Do you really love me?'

'How could you even ask?' Sean groaned as he pulled her closer and kissed her downbent head.

'Well, it isn't just for myself that I have to ask,' Kate answered slowly, trying to pick her words as carefully as she could.

It was obvious to her when he put his hand under her chin and tilted her face up towards his own so that he could look into her eyes that he hadn't grasped what she was trying to say.

'You mean because of Oliver?' he asked her, puzzled. 'You know I love him.'

'No, not because of Oliver,' she told him. 'But you're on the right track.'

Encouragingly she looked at him, until he made a smothered sound and bent his head to take the softness of the half-parted lips she was offering to him.

Their kiss lasted a long time and said a great deal, promising love and commitment and sharing sadness and regret, but eventually it ended, and Sean demanded rawly, 'You can't mean that you're pregnant?'

Kate gave him a quizzical look. 'Who says I can't?' she teased flippantly, before giving a small shrug that didn't quite manage to conceal her excitement.

'Apparently modern research has shown that a woman's body has the capability to fight hard to receive and cherish the sperm of the man she loves—and after all, Sean, it only takes one!'

Tenderly Sean drew his fingertip down the curve of her cheek. 'Well, this is certainly not a birthday I'm going to forget.'

'Mmm, and it isn't over yet,' Kate reminded him softly, adding naughtily, 'You know how women get cravings for things when they're pregnant...?'

Dutifully, Sean nodded his head.

'Well, my craving is for you, Sean,' she told him gently. 'And besides, you don't want your baby to think you don't love her mother, do you?'

'*Her* mother?' Sean questioned softly, several hours later, as he propped his head on his hand and looked down into Kate's face.

Her mouth was curved in a smile of warm, sensual satisfaction whilst her eyes glowed with love and happiness.

'Well, I think she's a girl,' she answered him lovingly, before adding, 'It's because of the pregnancy that I got Ollie his puppy now. One baby at a time is enough for any household!'

'Oh, God, when I think of what I could have lost. What I did lose in those hellish years without you,' Sean said, drawing her back into his arms and nestling her against his body. 'Thank you for forgiving me for what

I did, for making it possible to have you and Oliver in my life.'

'Once I understood why you had done what you did, it changed everything—especially when I saw the way you were bonding with Ollie. Of course I hated the fact that you were refusing to accept that Oliver was your child, but from a logical point of view I understood why you'd refused to believe it. And I never stopped loving you, even if I didn't like admitting it!'

'Well, from now you aren't going to be allowed to stop loving me,' Sean told her softly. 'And I am certainly never going to stop loving you.'

EPILOGUE

'I THOUGHT you said that one baby at a time was enough?'

Kate gave Sean a rueful look and they both looked at the two perfect and identical babies sharing the same hospital cot.

Their daughters had been born within ten minutes of one another earlier in the day, and after bringing Oliver to see his new sisters Sean had taken him home and put him in the care of Mrs Hargreaves before returning to the hospital to be with Kate.

'I thought you said it was impossible for this to happen!' Kate responded, and then felt her eyes moisten with ridiculous emotional tears as she saw the male pride in Sean's eyes battling with the awareness that Kate had done the hard work of carrying and giving birth to them.

From the moment they had known Kate's pregnancy was twins Sean had worried anxiously over her, but now...

Gently Sean reached for her hand and carried it to his lips. 'Without you this wouldn't have been possible,' he told her emotionally. 'You could have fallen in love and had your children with another man, Kate. But somehow I know that my problem would have made it impossible for me to father children with anyone but you.'

Of course she ought to tell him that he was being silly, but she wasn't going to, Kate decided. No, what she was going to do was to cherish this moment for the rest of her life.

'I see Rusty has managed to send one of his unique paw-print cards,' she murmured teasingly. 'Three paw-prints, too, and two of them pink!'

Sean laughed. 'I've got a confession to make,' he warned her. 'The creation of that card involved the destruction of several items of clothing and Annie Hargreaves threatening to leave! But Oliver was insistent! Fortunately the lure of the twins was enough to make her change her mind!'

The babies were waking up and would soon be demanding a feed, Kate knew. But there was still time for her to lean forward and show their father how much she loved him, and she placed her lips to his.

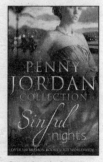